WHAT FOLLOWS

DYLAN H. JONES

Copyright © 2022 Dylan H. Jones

The right of Dylan H. Jones to be identified as the Author of the Work has been asserted by him in accordance with the Copyright, Designs and Patents Act 1988.

First published in 2022 by Bloodhound Books

Apart from any use permitted under UK copyright law, this publication may only be reproduced, stored, or transmitted, in any form, or by any means, with prior permission in writing of the publisher or, in the case of reprographic production, in accordance with the terms of licences issued by the Copyright Licensing Agency.

All characters in this publication are fictitious and any resemblance to real persons, living or dead, is purely coincidental.

www.bloodhoundbooks.com

Print ISBN 978-1-5040-6805-5

ALSO BY DYLAN H. JONES

THE DI MANX CASES

Anglesey Blue

Doll Face

Shadow Soul

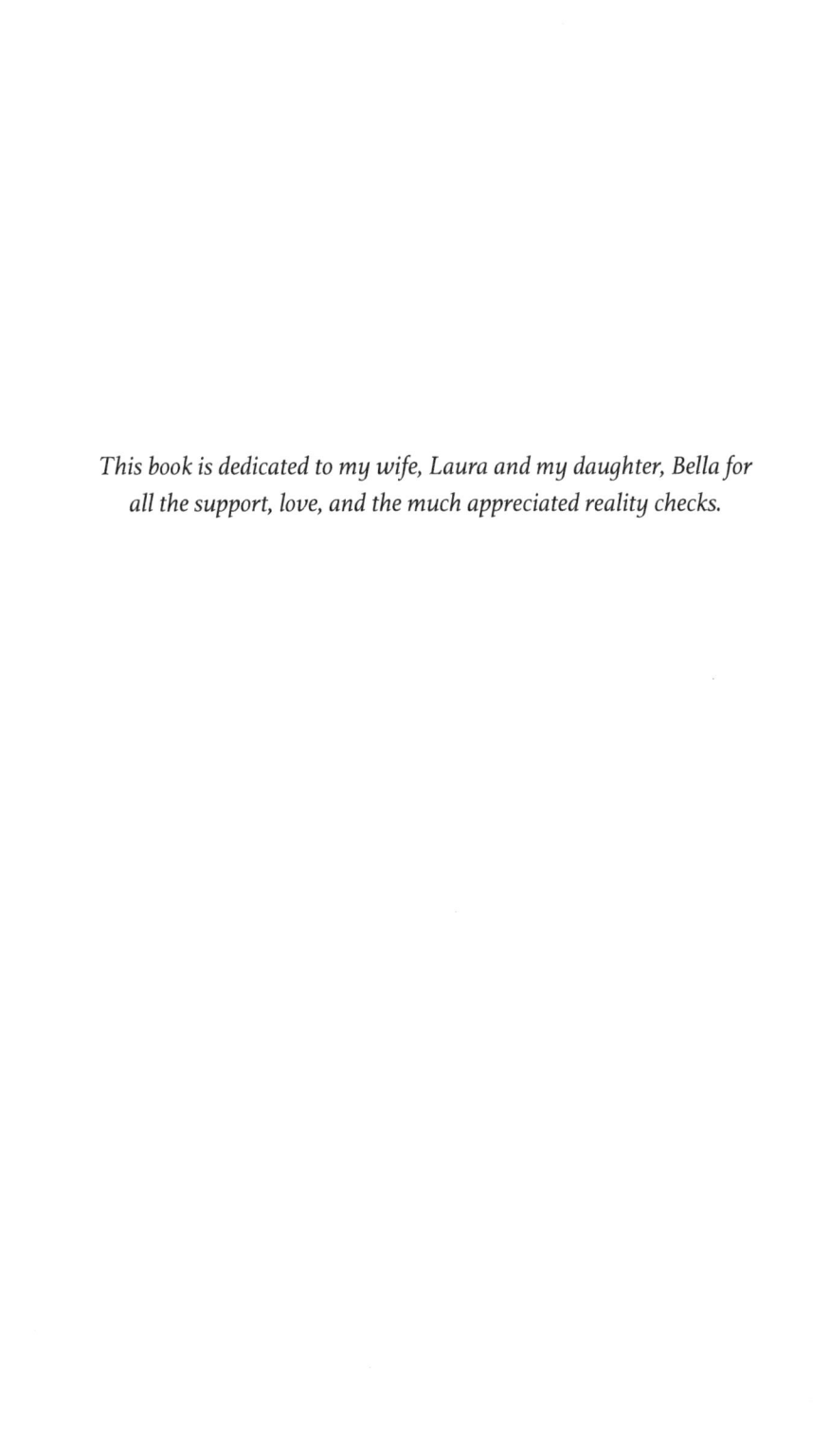

This book is dedicated to my wife, Laura and my daughter, Bella for all the support, love, and the much appreciated reality checks.

PART I

FAULT LINES

1

A girl runs across the sand.

Above, the stars appear more luminous than usual as if tweaked a notch above their regular brightness.

For a moment she imagines they're shining only for her, guiding her some place beyond here; someplace better.

The thought unsettles her.

What if she wants to stay? Enjoy for a while longer the warm sand between her toes, the gentle breeze on her lips; the bounce of her hair across her bare shoulders.

Behind her, someone follows. His voice is distant, as if calling to her from below the lake water. Or maybe he's directly behind her, whispering wicked things into her ear.

Her chest hurts from the running. But it's more powerful than pain, more possessive. It's the sensation of fingers reaching deep inside, squeezing until her head swims. For a moment, all around her is liquid and formless.

The girl buckles and falls, knee-bound, into the molten sand.

She glances up at the moonlight and takes a breath.

Her last.

Someplace else, sometime later, a boy casts his eyes skyward.

He glimpses the girl's face carved out in the shape of the stars, her hand reaching to him as she passes to a place he can't follow, taking her secrets with her.

2

Lake Temescal, located off Highway 13 in the Oakland Hills, is six hundred feet long and sixteen feet at its widest point. Few people are aware the lake was formed by a long-forgotten earthquake as it buckled the earth under the Northern California coast. Much of the topography around the San Francisco Bay Area had been formed in this way; nature at its most violent and destructive.

On the morning of July 2nd, the parkland surrounding the lake was festooned in red, white, and blue in anticipation of the July 4th weekend. Tight grids of miniature American flags stood like toothpicks in the soft grass, while the picnic tables and barbeque grills were draped in star-spangled burlap ribbons that fluttered in the breeze. The lake water was mirror-still, cracked only by the splash of curious catfish breaking the surface. Above the lake a stubborn morning mist drifted, phantom-like, obscuring the tips of the oaks, willows, and thimbleberries.

Detective Roscoe Tanner set his jacket across his forearm as he picked his way through the parched undergrowth towards the CSI blackout tent on the narrow stretch of sand. Every few steps he lifted the sleeve to wipe another layer of glistening perspiration from his brow. The ghost of handsomeness past lingered around Tanner, as if he may have been considered a good catch at some point but had been blissfully unaware of that slim window of opportunity to take advantage of it. His eyes were deep hazel and prone to holding on to sorrow longer than they needed to. If there was one aspect of his appearance he'd never questioned, it was his hair; still as thick as it was when he was in his prime, with dark, wood-shaving curls lightly peppered with grey where his widow's peak met his brow. When he smiled, the gesture always seemed vague, as if he'd heard the joke but was still trying to figure out the punchline.

Tanner stopped at the CSI truck, chatted briefly with one of the technicians, slipped on his oversuit, and headed across the sand to speak with Madeline Ambrose, Crime Scene Leader. Under the canvas, Ambrose was kneeling at the body of a young girl, gently removing evidence from what remained of her clothing, and slipping it into clear plastic bags.

"Darned peachy start to the holiday weekend, Ambrose," Tanner said. "What you got?"

"Female," she said, wiping the back of a hand across her brow, which this time of year always erupted in a riot of freckles. "No surprises there. As I'd expect, negligible bodily decomposition due to tepid water temperature. No indication of bodily trauma, however, the victim sustained several bite marks on the upper thigh region, probably breakfast of champions for the local scavengers."

Tanner stepped closer. After thirty-five years of police work, the cruel damage long periods submerged in water could inflict on the human body still made his gut roil. The body had bloated to twice its normal size, the limbs marbled into putrefied shades of blue and green. The girl's skirt was drawn past her hips, underwear torn and caked in mud. Her top, no more than a belt-sized scrap of red Lycra had ridden over her chest to reveal the distended globe of her abdomen. From her belly button, the dark-grey tissue of her intestines seeped out in fleshy globules. More disturbing were the girl's lips, cracked and dry like old bone and slacked open as if she were inhaling her final breath before it was snatched from her.

"Any theories?" Tanner asked, feeling the undeniable stiffness of his sixty-two-year-old knee joints as he squatted next to the body.

"Theories? Way too early, Tanner."

"Facts then?"

"Facts, we got. Human bodies float on the ventral surface, that is, they float belly-side down. They also decompose at an accelerated rate in freshwater rather than on land or saltwater. We can provide a more detailed estimate after we've tested the ambient water temperature, but don't hold your breath, establishing time of death with a body at this stage of decomposition is like throwing a dart at a moving target."

She ran her index finger in the air above the girl's belly. "If you look closely at the surface of the exposed intestines, you'll notice a number of dead maggot pupae. The pupae are heat averse, so they typically perish before they have time to hatch, which leads me to believe we're looking at a classic Goldilocks Phenomenon."

"Goldilocks? Like a papa bear kind of thing?" Tanner asked, confused.

"No, Tanner, the porridge. The water temperature was neither too hot nor too cold, which slowed the soft tissue breakdown, but we'll need more tests to determine the decomposition rate before we even get close to a time of death."

"Right you are. What about any environmental forensics?"

Ambrose stood. "No tire tracks leading to the beach, and no CCTV footage in the parking lot. There's been no attempt to hide the body, but I did notice one of the rowboats at the dock is facing the opposite way to the rest of them."

"Significance?"

"The recent heatwave exaggerated the cyanobacteria levels in the water—that's blue-green algae to you, Tanner. The toxin numbers are way above state advisory thresholds, which means the East Bay Regional Park District closed the lake to any water activities; swimming, fishing—"

"Boating?" Tanner interrupted.

"Glad you've caught up. I'll get some of the techs onto it. If that boat was taken out, I'm betting there's DNA from our victim all over it."

"Killed elsewhere, driven here, thrown in the lake?"

Ambrose snapped off a protective glove and rolled on a fresh one. "That's a lot of assumption, Tanner, we haven't established COD yet."

"But you think it's our girl?"

"Unless you've got another missing teenager with a similar birthmark on her neck, then I'd say it's her," Ambrose confirmed, tracing her fingers above the birthmark which was shaped liked an apple; the one distinguishing mark the next-of-kin had provided.

Tanner stood, felt his knee joints pop, and tugged his pants over the soft, muffin-top of his belly. His doctor had cautioned him some months ago to cut back on the beer and junk food or face the consequences somewhere down the line. It was sound advice, but between working police shifts and living alone, Tanner figured a change of diet was a "nice to have" rather than a directive. "Mother Francis," he said. "Two days before the Fourth of July. We're going to have to shutter the whole dang place."

"Fun times," Ambrose said. "Now, if you don't mind…"

Tanner took the hint and stepped out into the daylight.

The morning mist was slowly clearing. In the woodland, a chorus of birdcalls echoed through the trees as if it were just another day. *Sugar on a stick*, Tanner thought. There'll be a near riot when they close the park, not to mention securing overtime for a homicide investigation over the Fourth of July weekend. He was certain his chief, Martin Dugdale, would approve the additional officers. This would be Dugdale's first homicide since taking his new office; he'd be eager to throw a bunch of resources at the case for a fast close and a solid conviction.

Oakland's Mayor had appointed Dugdale to the position two months ago after a long recruitment campaign to lure him from the San Jose Police Department. She'd been impressed with Dugdale's track record in reversing a rising homicide rate with more community-style policing, and recruiting more Latino officers. Tanner remained unconvinced. Dugdale was the aggressive, ambitious type, and didn't seem to care who knew. Tanner had already heard rumblings of layoffs, lateral career moves, and forced early retirement, though nobody provided any specifics to confirm the rumors. Dugdale, only forty-eight years old himself, favored younger, more dynamic officers whom he'd lured to Oakland PD Homicide Division with the promise of promotions, better pay, and guaranteed overtime. To date, five officers had taken Dugdale up on his offer. Tanner imagined this was the tip of a very deep iceberg which Tanner himself would have to navigate carefully around or find his own career shipwrecked five years before his retirement.

As he watched the techs carefully haul the girl's body into the mortuary ambulance, a familiar weariness, like the weight of a freight train, bore down on him. As the responding officer, he'd have to break the awful news to her parents, a gentle Hispanic couple who lived in an apartment above a supermercado on International Boulevard. He drew a hand across the back of his neck; it felt swampy, like he could wade through it.

"You should probably take a look at these," Madeline Ambrose said, as she walked towards him, pulling off her protective cap and smoothing down her strawberry-blonde hair, which was pulled back in a style reminiscent of a ballet instructor.

"Shoes?" Tanner asked, glancing at the evidence bag.

"Expensive," she said, reaching for her SPF 50 sunscreen. "Hardly your Discount Shoe Warehouse bargain."

Tanner took the bag and peered at the brightly colored shoes. "Meaning?"

Ambrose slathered a palmful of the lotion across her face. "Meaning, Tanner, these are Jimmy Choos, this season's, which makes me wonder how a teenage girl working a few hours a week can afford to buy twelve-hundred-dollar footwear."

"Maybe they were a gift."

Ambrose took back the evidence bag. "And if they were a gift, what the hell does a seventeen-year-old girl need to do to deserve a gift like that?"

Tanner sighed, looked out over the lake. The water was deceptively peaceful: a smooth shimmer of glass, that for now, was holding on tight to its secrets.

"The calm before the shitstorm?" Ambrose said.

"Something like that," Tanner confirmed.

Three miles away, in the streets of East Oakland, the snap and sputter of firecrackers and bottle rockets exploding like machine-gun fire carried towards the lake on the morning air. Over the horizon, plumes of smoke spiraled skyward like vapor trails, then evaporated into the blue. Tanner stuffed his hands deep into his pants pockets and shook his head. *"Dinkleberg,"* he muttered. One of his more unreserved cuss words, which he only uttered on occasions like this.

3

"Get your skinny ass off my porch. I ain't talking to you 'bout nothin'."

Jessica Swift took a tentative step towards the doorway, offered her best sympathetic smile.

"Nu-huh. You ain't comin' no closer," Lachelle Welch said, her palm held out in the "stop in the name of love" fashion.

According to Jessica's records, Lachelle Welch was forty-three years old. Her face told a different story. The sunken shafts of her cheekbones and the cracked flesh of her lips gave the impression of a woman at least a decade older, as did her eyes, which were buried deep in their sockets as if in hiding.

"I was hoping to speak to your son, Nelson––"

"He ain't here. Now get the fuck off my property already." Lachelle scratched a talon of glitter-crusted fingernails across the long history of needle tracks pitting her forearm.

As Jessica checked her notes, a boy, no more than ten years old, emerged from behind his mother's hips. "Hi, what's your name?" Jessica asked. Another smile, this one less forced.

"Tyler. But ain't none of your bidness."

Jessica kept her smile fixed.

"Yeah," the woman confirmed, kicking the door shut with the heel of her boot. "What the kid said." The rotten floorboards on the porch shook as the door slammed hard into its frame.

"I'll leave the leaflet then," Jessica called out, slipping the document under the door. "And thanks for the compliment, been a long minute since anyone's called me skinny."

Jessica flopped into the driver's seat of her Toyota Camry; a 2005 model, with 163,000 miles on the clock. The seller had insisted the car's color was teak. Jessica's daughter, Sabine, had nailed it more correctly as "shit brown" and typically referred to the car as the *"shitmobile"*. Sabine had a habit of calling things as she saw them, but the vehicle transported Jessica from one appointment to the next, and besides, a salary of $52,000 a year barely covered the rent on a two-bedroom apartment in Lower Rosemont, let alone a new car. The cost of a rental unit that swallowed sixty percent of her take-home pay was a calculated sacrifice Jessica had made ten years ago. Rosemont High School was the top performing public school in Alameda County, and one of the top ten public schools in California. Sabine was bright, almost too bright, Jessica had often thought. Heading into junior year Sabine's grades were fast-tracking her to a generous college scholarship from one of the better UC schools. Jessica hoped the *"shitmobile"* survived the next half decade, or at least until her daughter graduated and started earning a living.

Studying her clipboard, she scratched Nelson Welch's name off the list. Seventeen more to go. She pushed on the windshield washer stalk to erase the hazy layer of dust ground into the glass. As the wipers hand-danced haltingly across the grime, a burgundy Lexus, its oversized rims glinting, stopped at the corner. The two African American men scouted the block for any police activity before confirming the coast was clear. A hurried transaction through the driver's window and the car headed north in a spin of rubber and a shimmer of sparkling chrome.

Another day in paradise, Jessica thought, reaching for her lunch; leftover pasta with shredded Monterey Jack cheese. After three hours stagnating, it had taken the form of warm plastic. She picked aimlessly at the yellow mush and looked out over the neighborhood.

She'd heard rumors of gentrification, though there was little evidence of it here in East Oakland. The small, craftsman-style houses, typical of the neighborhood, stood like decaying teeth in their foundations and Jessica doubted many would remain standing when the next "big one" struck. The dealers' houses, which she'd learnt to spot two weeks into her job, were marginally better maintained, but with iron bars drilled into the window frames, barbed wire running through the six-foot-high fences, and the always famished crossbreeds chained to the front porch, panting in the heat and desperate, like all dogs, for a kind word from their masters.

It seemed to Jessica the city's urban regeneration strategy favored the already well-off, concerned with lowering rents on commercial buildings and handing out generous tax breaks to tech start-ups moving into the newly refurbished downtown warehouses and multi-purpose lofts; a trickle-down economic policy where the trickling had run dry before it reached the communities most in need of its relief. Recently, she'd noticed a raft of new office spaces available for short-term lets around the Uptown and Grand Lake districts. They advertised themselves with fancy names like CoLabNation and HiveSpace, where you paid by the hour to rent a desk or an office. What she wouldn't give for a job where she could rent a desk for a goddamn day and turn up and leave whenever the hell she liked.

She checked the next name on her list. The address was several blocks away. She checked her Facebook notifications and lost herself for a few minutes in the carefully curated lives of her friends before clicking on an episode of *Carpool Karaoke*, which she watched until the sound of gunfire ricocheting through the neighborhood sent her pulse racing.

Another volley of shots, louder and closer, startled her enough to make her duck down into the passenger seat. She waited, let out the breath she'd been holding as she noticed a trace of smoke cascade skywards and explode in a powdery burst of green and red. Of course, the Fourth of July was only a couple of days away. The streets were always thick with the spit and crackle of illegal fireworks this time of year.

She sat back up and typed the next location into her phone. As she tipped the rearview mirror to check her makeup a shadow fell across the window. Jessica's chest tightened as the tip of a gun barrel rapped hard on the glass.

4

The young man urged Jessica from her car, his handgun at the small of her back, and marched her towards the temporary tent encampment in the shadow of the 580 Freeway overpass. The stench of sun-dried urine and stale feces caught in her throat as they walked. From inside one of the ragged shelters she heard the carnal groans of hurried, desperate sex, while outside, a man, his pants pulled to his ankles, was leering through a tear in the canvas. *It didn't get any lower than this*, she thought. It was a place ravaged of all human dignity. In a few weeks, when the Oakland Police Department got their shit together, the camp would be torn down and moved elsewhere. That was the nature of homelessness in the city; there was no permanent solution, just a shifting of the problem further down the road.

At a graffiti-tagged pillar, the man spun Jessica around and shoved her against the structure. Above, the early afternoon commuter traffic rolled past like the rumble of thunder.

"Me and you, we don't ever met. You read me?"

The young man was in his early twenties, Jessica guessed, with a handsomeness he was still growing into. A grey pallor circled his eyes and the mottled veins along the back of his hands were raw from scratching. He pressed the nub of his pistol to her temple.

"You alone?"

"Just me and the baby seat," she said, gesturing at the Camry. It was a trick one of her fellow investigators had taught her; secure a baby seat in the back of the car along with some toys and a blanket, it made you look less suspicious, less of a threat.

"So, what do I call you?" she asked. It wasn't the first time she'd been held at gunpoint, that sort of risk came with the job, but each situation called for a different response. She waited for an answer before deciding.

"Ain't none of your motherfuckin' business what my name is or isn't, bitch." He stepped back, dropping the gun to his side.

Jessica made her decision. "You kiss your mom goodnight with that mouth?"

The man reached inside his NorCal hoodie, took out a crumpled leaflet and threw it at her feet; the same leaflet she'd slipped under Lachelle Welch's doorway less than an hour ago. "You been talkin' to my mom 'bout this?" The man tugged at the saddle of his jeans, which were pulled down low over the thin blades of his hips.

"It'll only get worse if you ignore it, Nelson. Come in for treatment and you'll be clear in a few weeks, no one need know."

He looked Jessica over, chewing on the inside of his cheek as he considered her words.

"But we do require a list of your sexual partners over the past twelve months. Names and addresses."

He laughed; bright white teeth dazzling against the dark luster of his skin. "Gonna be a long list. How long you got?"

"Oh, I get it, you're a player," Jessica said. "Handsome stud like you, probably no shortage of ass, right?"

She hated reverting to that kind of language, but it helped level the playing field; it was a role she played to get what she needed. Her dark skin also helped, especially in this neighborhood. Her mother was African American, originally from New Orleans, her father from stout Irish stock. Jessica had inherited enough of her mother's looks to give the impression that, if circumstances were different, she could have belonged here. *"There but for the grace of God,"* she'd uttered to herself more than once.

She'd learned early in the job not to pretend to be anything other than who she was; someone who was just trying to help. People around here may be poor, but they weren't stupid. There was an expected level of appearance that helped get her foot in the door, especially when most of the gatekeepers were women. An extra layer of foundation, her eyeshadow a tone too bright, long red acrylic fingernails, a snug-fitting blouse opened a button too low, and high-heel-wedge shoes she could run in. It was her uniform, one that gave the impression of a friend you could gossip with on the street corner; someone who could keep secrets, however dark, not because she looked like she completely belonged but because she looked a single notch better than the women whose doors she knocked on. A better version of themselves that with a degree less makeup, a visit to the nail salon, and a few lucky finds at TJ Maxx, was achievable. If you were willing to put in the effort.

Jessica looked the man directly in the eyes. "So, you tweaking right now? Barbs? Apple Jacks? Buzz Bombs?"

Nelson averted his gaze, stared down at the dirt.

"Fine, play the silent type, but let me educate you on what's going on, Nelson. You probably have genital lesions, which is why you keep grabbing yourself, am I right?"

A flicker passed over his left eye. She had his attention.

"There's a rash on your hands that you can't stop scratching.

Your eyes water and feel like they're burning a hole in your skull, but believe me, that's a cakewalk compared to what's to come. Over the next few weeks it'll get worse; welts, dizziness, blindness and eventually paralysis. How's that sound?"

He stepped back, waving the gun aimlessly. "You lying, bitch."

Jessica stood her ground. "You think I'm coming into this neighborhood for my own well-being?" She reached into her pocket and handed him a business card.

"Come in and see me tomorrow, Nelson. And put that gun away, I'm not your goddam enemy."

Back in the safety of her car, Jessica's heart pounded so hard it seemed her entire body throbbed to the beat. She'd had a gun pulled on her precisely three times since starting the job, it didn't get any easier, but the young man's attitude seemed forced. Someone older, with more serious steel in his eyes, and she'd have backed off. A young man like Nelson needed to come in for treatment. But it wasn't the men that bore the worst of it; it never was. It was the young girls who traded their bodies for a hit of whatever drug they were addicted to that month: prescription opioids, crystal meth, crack cocaine; heroin. Youth and prettiness were the girls' currency, which they used with impunity, as if it would always be theirs to trade, that it would never fade or lose its inherent value. That was a lie. Syphilis was an equal opportunity disease, one that didn't care how young or pretty you were.

As Jessica fired up the engine, a shape crossing the horizon caught her attention. A young boy on a BMX-style bike rode towards her, almost in slow motion. He stopped some twenty feet away, and settled his feet on the ground. It took a second for her to recognize the boy: Nelson's brother, Tyler. The boy lifted his right arm, extended his index finger and thumb into the symbol of a handgun and directed it at Jessica with a half-wink of his eye, as if he were taking aim. In that moment he looked older, dangerous beyond his years. Tyler smiled and rode off, leaving a trail of dust in his wake.

5

The oar snapped into the water with a vicious bite, breaking Alexus's rhythm. She pulled a hard left, realigning the single scull back to her preferred line and focused on her breathing: *one, two, three... exhale. One, two...*

She made fast progress past the horseshoe-shaped flatlands north of Lake Merritt and swept past the glass-fronted Catholic church that dominated the lake's border. At the turn, she crabbed her sweep for a second time, almost twisting the oar free from the oarlock.

It was her body telling her to *"slow the hell down."*

She drifted to a slow stop and lifted the oars clean from the water. Her heart thumped: 158bpm, according to her heart rate monitor. Taking a deep inhale, she looked over the shimmering patina of the lake which spanned three miles between Lakeshore and downtown Oakland. Alexus loved it here, especially this time of day when the late morning sun reflected off the roofs of the houses perched high on the Oakland hills as if anointing them with some kind of divine blessing.

She took a minute to catch her breath before rowing back to

the dock. As she pulled up against the old timber moorings, a man's hand reached out to her.

"Out breaking records, again, Alexus?" Ben Strauss said.

Alexus took his hand. "Go big or go home, right?" she said, securing her footing on the deck.

Ben lived three blocks from Alexus. She'd run against him in Rosemont's last mayoral election four years ago. He'd won, but only by a slim margin, as she liked to remind people if they brought it up in conversation.

Ben stuffed his horn-rimmed shades into his shirt pocket and helped her haul the scull from the water. "You should sign up for Merritt Strokes, we'd be lucky to have you."

"I'm not big on team events."

"If you change your mind, we have an opening."

"I won't," she said, and looked over at a group of six teenagers loitering at the boathouse entrance. "What's with all the kids? Running a summer camp now?"

"If the path to hell is paved with good deeds..." Ben said, shrugging. "As a board member of a local non-profit I'm obligated to supervise three field trips a year. Today's lesson's all about teamwork; everyone pulling in the same direction to reach the same goal. Great training for these kids if they ever find themselves climbing the corporate ladder."

"I wouldn't know, it's been way too long," Alexus said, recalling she and Ben had once shared an office in the same San Francisco practice fresh out of law school.

Ben passed a hand over what remained of his hair, which was on the turn from blond to white, and squinted. "I remember you were on the partner track at one time, or am I wrong?"

"Oh, that race is done."

The moment she uttered them, Alexus regretted the words. The statement sounded so final, so undisputable—what someone with nothing left to contribute to the world might say.

Christ! She was only forty-seven: *"Her race was done?"* Ben must have thought her a complete idiot. "Actually, I am still California bar registered," she added, hoping to salvage some dignity. "I'm just out of practice, let's say."

"Or you're in need of a practice?" Ben said, with a snorty exhale.

Alexus smiled. Ben had always struck her as distant, as if he were always looking past her for the next opportunity coming his way. He'd been divorced for seven years, had never remarried, and was oddly forthcoming about why his wife left him: too forthcoming, Alexus had often thought. Ben's struggle with alcohol had been a recurring theme at every campaign speech he gave, adding a unique twist each time and laced with a self-deprecating remark or two depending on the audience.

Alexus had nothing as dramatic to offer in response, only her not-so-unusual story of a middle-aged black woman from a successful family of lawyers. There was no *"poverty, raised by a single mom in the ghetto"* narrative to exploit. She had wanted to win on her own terms; a candidate with a fresh vision for the city. But maybe Rosemont, despite its nod to diversity and inclusion, wasn't as liberal or accepting as it imagined it was, and *"more of the same"* was preferable over a *"fresh vision."*

From the boathouse, a young African American boy shuffled over, hiking up the waist of his jeans. "Mister Strauss, I ain't feeling so good," he said, rubbing a hand over his stomach. "Must have eaten some messed up burger last night. Might be Ebola or some such shit."

"Ebola?" Ben said, beckoning the kid to come closer. He put the back of his hand on his brow. "Doesn't feel like an Ebola level fever to me, Shawn."

"Yeah, I dunno. Had the shits all morning."

"You have a note from your mom, or a doctor?"

Shawn shoegazed and shrugged.

"Then you're sitting your ass in that boat. Go back and tell your friends the same."

Alexus bent down to retrieve her oars from the scull and stood them to attention on the deck. "Got your hands full there," she said.

"Oh, that's nothing. They'll bitch and complain until they get on the water, then they'll brag about it to their friends when they get back. Par for the course."

"We'll see you at the parade on the Fourth?"

"As the mayor, I guess I'm obliged."

"Yes, yes you are," Alexus said. "I'd best be off, got a ton of prep work still to do."

"No rest for the wicked, right?"

Alexus peeled off her rowing gloves. "No rest for me, that's for sure."

Ben looked over the water. "The election's coming up in a few months," he said, leaving the statement hanging for a few seconds.

"And you want to know if I'll be running again?"

"I figured not, since you haven't filed the necessary paperwork."

That much was true, Alexus thought. She'd completed the forms weeks ago, but was still debating sending them into Rosemont City Council and making a formal declaration. "Worried about the competition if I do?" she asked.

Alexus noticed the tight flicker of a twitch on Ben's cheek—as if he'd just been stung by a bee. "It's a democracy, Alexus, all voices welcome."

"Thanks for the civics lesson, Ben," Alexus said, zipping up her vest.

"Here, I'll help you carry these back," Ben said, grabbing one of the oars and heading down the dock.

At the boathouse, he stacked the oars against the wooden

building and gestured to the poster pasted onto the window. "Poor girl, I hope they find her soon."

Alexus looked at the photo of Catalina Gomez staring out from the poster.

"Do you know her?"

"Catalina Gomez. She volunteers at that non-profit I mentioned. We're all very worried."

"God, how awful. I want to hope for the best, but... " Alexus's words drifted off on the breeze.

"Isn't she friends with your son, Jonas?"

"Em, not that I know of. He's never mentioned her. Why?"

"Oh, Catalina may have mentioned him once or twice. Maybe I got it wrong. Teenagers these days, God knows who they're making friends with online, parents would be the last to know—"

The loud crackle of firecrackers spurting across the dock startled them both.

Ben turned. "Hey, Shawn, cut that out!"

Shawn smiled, lobbed a final firecracker into the lake and ran to join his friends.

Ben turned his attention back to Alexus. "Before you go, Alexus, a quick observation. I noticed you twist your scull on the surface as you sweep. I was always taught to just break the surface with a short, clean stroke. Calm and collected on the surface, with all the action and effort focused under the water. What do they call it, the swing?"

Alexus was familiar with the term. The "swing": that near-perfect synchronization of motion where she felt at one with the trinity of scull, oar and water. Lately that kind of fluidity and ease had eluded her.

As Ben headed off to tend to the kids, Alexus called after him. "What if I do decide to run, Ben?"

He turned slowly, stuffed his hands in his pockets. "I've made great strides in the last four years, Rosemont's not ready for a change of leadership."

As he walked back towards her, Alexus noticed a flicker of something in Ben's eyes; a steeliness she hadn't noticed before, or maybe he'd just been good at disguising it.

"Politics is an ugly business. What you've got to ask yourself is, what are you willing to sacrifice to get what you want? Stay safe, Alexus."

6

Francisco studied the flimsy leaflet in his hand and ran a finger tenderly over the photograph of the young girl.

Catalina Gomez, Missing since June 27th.
Have you seen her? Call the Oakland Police Department Hotline at
510 - MISSING.

"Missing"––the word was an understatement. The Spanish word had more power––*desaparecido.* It sounded like he felt; desperate, lost, afraid.

"Francisco! You were meant to be here yesterday," Alexus said, walking towards him. "You know we're expecting five hundred people at least this year." She scrubbed her heel along her parched, rust-colored lawn and sighed. "How much is the damned fine again?"

Francisco shrugged. "I think three hundred dollars, miss."

Alexus frowned and glanced over to her neighbor's yard where the grass was peak verdant, moist from the early morning watering. "He's such an asshole. The old fool doesn't listen, six fines and he still doesn't give a shit. Why don't people listen, Francisco?"

Francisco shrugged and continued working. Questions of those magnitude were too hard to contemplate today.

Alexus's house was on Lansing Avenue, the major thoroughfare cutting through the small city of Rosemont. At two square miles, compared to the seventy-eight square miles of its closest neighbor, Oakland, Rosemont was often said to be a city within a city where the price of single-family homes started at well over two million dollars and the public schools were amongst the best-performing in the state. Rosemont was the kind of city where homes weren't "sold" but "spoken for" (according to the signs hammered into the front lawns) and bedroom windows were as likely to have "Make America Great Again" placards placed in them as they were "Black Lives Matter" posters. The gated mansions, backyard pools, and private tennis courts had the lingering whiff of old money, though the local coffee shop was filled most days with young, stay-at-home moms wearing Lululemon athletic wear destined never be worked out in. They gathered after school drop-off at the Rosemont Roastery to set the world to rights; or at least the two square miles they claimed dominion over.

By Rosemont standards, Alexus's home was considered modest: three-thousand square feet, fronted by four imposing, Doric-style pillars and a front lawn shaped into multiple terraces hedged with geraniums, ponytail palms, spindly yucca plants and perfectly pruned rosebushes. The balcony off the master bedroom afforded a view across San Francisco and the Bay Bridge. Across the road stood the Rosemont recreation center and pool, and beyond that two acres of perfectly manicured greenery that during the summer weekends would host "Movies in the Park". Both of Alexus's children were now well past the age of sitting on their mother's lap watching the latest Disney release, but lately the procession of younger parents walking to the park with toddlers at their side had filled Alexus with a wash of sadness that had no depth or dimension to it, just a shapeless melancholy that seemed to swallow her whole.

It was the natural order of things—children grew up, parents became increasingly irrelevant—but just the same, it cut her to the core. Children would never comprehend the compulsion to protect them and keep them close, at least not until they had children of their own. Alexus imagined she would have done anything to stop Jonas and Sydney from growing up. She understood it was irrational, but recently there was a deep emptiness forming inside her she was certain every mother felt when their children were preparing to leave the nest. If she wasn't a mother, running her kids to soccer practice, band rehearsals or chaperoning school field trips and volunteering on the board of the high school PTA, then who the hell was she?

She shook away the thought and focused on the flags fluttering along the length of Lansing Avenue. As was customary for the Fourth of July, the sidewalks along the avenue were stacked with a long line of lawn chairs. The chairs had been placed there at least two weeks ago by residents eager to secure a front row seat for the parade. It was one of those neighborhood traditions that had sneaked in sooner every year. Not that Alexus minded; the Fourth of July was her favorite holiday, with none of the expectations and stresses of Thanksgiving or Christmas. As this year's Rosemont Parade Chairperson, it was Alexus's responsibility to ensure the day's festivities were flawless, and despite the terminal state of her garden and her husband, Christen's, predictable indifference, she was determined to enjoy the day until she collapsed on the couch, a well-deserved glass of wine in hand.

She turned to Francisco, and gestured to the front lawn

where palliative care seemed the most compassionate option. "Just do the best you can."

Francisco carefully folded the leaflet and slipped it into his toolbox. "My nephew, Jesus, help me, he's very fast, good with his hands."

Alexus squinted at the young boy, his arms sticking out like twigs from his sleeveless vest. "Okay, just make sure he's supervised, I don't––"

Alexus's cell phone buzzed. She pressed accept. "Lori, let me put you on hold."

She waved yesterday's French-nail manicure in Francisco's direction. "I'm here all day, so I'll be checking up on progress. *Comprendes?*"

Francisco nodded and got to work and mumbled something in Spanish to Jesus. Whatever it was, Alexus guessed it probably wasn't complimentary.

Alexus walked into her kitchen—custom-finished with Italian marble counters and Miele appliances—and arranged the vases crammed with trumpet lilies set on the kitchen island. She took a vase and walked it to the living room. Where the hell was Christen? He'd agreed to help her: another half-assed promise. A knot of anger etched in her brow as she glanced at the tangle of lights strewn over the sofa. *Francisco and the thin boy could help her*, she thought. She'd throw them each a twenty for the extra work; more than generous.

As she bundled the lights across her arms, Luna, the family yellow Lab, barked excitedly at the window. An Oakland Police patrol car had pulled up to the driveway. A male detective in a badly fitting suit exited, followed by a uniformed officer, and headed towards the gardener. Francisco nodded nervously as the detective spoke, then shot out his hand to steady himself against the trunk of a Shumard oak tree.

The dog barked again as Alexus's phone rang. "Luna, zip it." She checked the caller ID. "Yes, the fire department's taking care of the pancake breakfast, Lori, just like every year," she said, watching the developing situation as Luna pawed anxiously at the window. "I already emailed you the order of the procession, so there should be no confusion as to who's next to who and what's considered a safe driving speed. I've got to go, something's going on."

Alexus hung up and watched the detective guide Francisco gently from the lawn and into the back of the patrol car. She ran out, Luna barking at her heels. The car pulled away just as she reached the sidewalk.

"What the hell's going on?" she asked, dumping six pounds of string lights into the thin boy's hands.

Jesus reached down to retrieve the leaflet from Francisco's tool bag and passed it gingerly to Alexus.

"Oh God," she said, bringing a hand to her mouth. "I had no idea."

7

Chief Martin Dugdale wedged a toothpick under the nail of his index finger and carved out a stubborn deposit of dirt lodged in there since his yard cleaning last weekend. He turned to Detective Tanner sitting across from him. "Let me get straight to the point, Tanner," he said, bringing his fingertips to his lips as he spoke. "I think you're a square peg in a round hole."

Dugdale was lean, straight-backed with taut, angular features leading to a prominent chin. *He maybe had some Italian heritage*, Tanner thought; thick dark hair and coffee-colored eyes that seemed primed, like bullets in a magazine, for confrontation.

"Not sure I'm following in your tailwind there, Chief."

"Sure you are," Dugdale said, springing up with the litheness of a startled cat.

Tanner caught a whiff of cologne; some notes of leather and citrus, probably expensive.

"Square pegs in round holes get stuck. The more they try to squeeze themselves in there, the harder they are to extricate."

"Still not following, Chief."

"Jesus, do I have to spell it out?"

"Sure might help."

Dugdale leant on his window ledge. "This case is going to be a media circus. Are you the right man for it? That's my question."

Tanner shuffled awkwardly. "It's not my first high profile. I worked the Laci Peterson investigation back in the day. The circus came to town every dang day until we charged her husband with her murder. The crazy wingnut still hasn't confessed, despite being on death row for fifteen years."

"Riveting," Dugdale said. "Look, I've worked with plenty of officers of your persuasion, Tanner, old school oddballs who don't fit in the new order of things."

"Oddball? I wouldn't say that—"

"The guys at the station tell me they've never heard you swear. Not one cuss word in thirty-five years, that can't be right."

"Sure is," Tanner said, pulling the hem of his jacket. "Darned proud of it too."

"That aside, I have my reservations, but as you've been on the case since the girl was reported missing, let's call it status quo, for now."

"Right you are," Tanner said, relieved.

"But I'm assigning you a partner, Detective Shaughnessy."

Tanner leant forward to protest. "I already have a partner."

"Kowlaski's been reassigned. Shaughnessy begins this afternoon, make sure she's up to speed on every minutia of this case."

Tanner considered pushing back, but the "don't mess with me" look in Dugdale's eyes warned him otherwise. "Whatever you say, Chief."

"And?" Dugdale said, opening his palms as if expecting a gift to be dropped into them.

"Oh, shoot," Tanner said, checking his notes. "The parents

identified their daughter's body this morning. We'll inform the press later today."

Dugdale leaned back. "Do you know the leading cause of accidental death in the US last year, Tanner?"

"I could guess. Firearms?"

"Wrong, narcotics. Opioid overdoses mostly, which naturally leads to the question, do you consider the victim to have overdosed?"

"Too early to tell."

"What's your gut tell you?"

"Popular girl, straight-A student, no history of drug use. I'm having a hard time believing she did this to herself."

Dugdale nodded. "Tragic as it is, I'd welcome accidental death over homicide."

"Neither's a good option, Chief."

Dugdale walked over to his office window. He looked over to the harbor at Jack London Square and the rigid architecture of cranes defining the Port of Oakland skyline. "You're aware how fast this city is changing, right?"

"Every darned day."

"One of the reasons I was recruited was to help steer that change. This is an election year and Oakland's mayor has ambitions that stretch beyond her first term. She's counting on me to help facilitate those ambitions. I can't do that without the support and loyalty of the officers under my command."

"Square pegs in square holes, Chief?"

Dugdale turned and smiled. "Glad we're on the same page, Tanner."

8

Christen Hansen peered through his office blinds and looked over FiltrD's open workspace occupied by fifty-three of his employees, most of whom were newly graduated journalism majors. Working at FiltrD was considered a "résumé filler"––a position they hoped would eventually lead to a better paying job on a more prestigious news site.

Christen had founded the company two decades ago as a platform for curating news articles from all corners of the internet, then spitting them out in abbreviated soundbites for an attention-deficient generation. He'd moved the headquarters from Copenhagen to the Bay Area when lured by a healthy cash injection from a Silicon Valley incubator. He had two goals back then; make a shitload of money and retire before he was forty. He'd achieved his first goal but was still at least ten years behind on achieving his second.

Six feet three with the easy gait and build of an Olympic swimmer, Christen liked to imagine himself as the poster boy for Scandinavian healthy living; close-cropped hair, clear, azure eyes and an easy-going manner that his employees often mistook for nonchalance, but was in fact a carefully constructed

What Follows

image Christen projected to the world. His accent carried a lilt of formality found in well-educated Europeans who had learned English as a second language. Beyond this image he had engineered for himself, Christen Hansen harbored desires and addictions that he confessed to few people, including his wife. Especially not his wife.

He flipped his blinds closed, poked his computer mouse, and made himself comfortable as the live video feed he'd been anxiously waiting for got underway. He felt a tremor of excitement as a young, naked woman walked into a semi-darkened room. Inside the room, twenty-five men stood around a velvet-clothed table, waiting.

The woman's eyes scanned nervously across the men. Each of them had paid $200 for the thrill of watching a rat crawl over her naked body and had laid bets on how long she could tolerate the rodent crawling across her skin; the longer she endured, the greater her payout.

A man helped the young woman onto the table and placed a transparent box on her stomach. The cold glass against her skin made her flinch. Another man carefully slid open the box door. She stiffened as the rodent tentatively made its way across her belly. A man to her left started the stopwatch on his phone and held it aloft. The rat nibbled cautiously around the girl's belly button then, with a tweak of its nostrils, padded cautiously towards the thin salve of peanut butter smeared across the young woman's lips.

Few women could withstand those final moments. As the rat crawled over their faces, inching its mouth against theirs, the young women would reach their breaking point, scream, run for the nearest exit.

Christen felt the predictable sensation of disappointment. Despite the determination etched into the woman's face, it was clear she'd fold in the same rush of panic and terror as the women before her. It was to be expected; few people could face their greatest fears staring them directly in the eyes.

He cut off the video feed before the inevitable conclusion.

As he reached for a notebook and jotted some semi-inspirational notes for his next investor meeting, his personal assistant, Mallory Atkins, poked her head from behind his office door. "Your nutritionist's here," she said, with a faint smile.

Mallory was tall, dark-skinned, with eyes that held some promise Christen could never quite put his finger on. She reminded him of a younger version of his wife, Alexus. Maybe that was why he'd hired her. And maybe why, eventually, he'd have to fire her. Still, it amused the hell out of him, referring to Hector as his "nutritionist."

"Send him in," Christen said, clearing a space on his desk.

Hector Figuerello sauntered across the floor, checking out Mallory as she left the office. "That's gotta brighten up the workday, an ass like that in and out your office."

Christen gestured for him to sit.

"Straight down to business, eh?" Hector said, flopping into the nearest chair. "A man like you, no time to fuck around, right?"

Christen watched Hector opening his briefcase. Hector was wiry, with a pencil-thin moustache and eyes that settled nowhere for more than a few moments. He was wearing a suit that Hector imagined lent him an air of respectability; it didn't. The material was cheap and sat across his shoulders as if tailored for a man twice his width. Hector also had the perpetual stench of grease about him; probably from working at his taco truck, which Christen had always assumed he used as a front for laundering money he made from his other nefarious activities.

"Our prime selection," Hector said, turning the case and running his finger along several clear bags of lush cannabis flowers. "We got Hybrid Mango Cookies, Crossroad Chem Eight and 24k Stevia. All this is A-grade shit, amigo, nothing under twenty THC."

"Good, good," Christen said, eagerly scanning the contents.

"If you're into edibles, we got baked goods, olive oil, mango gummies. We got juices too: pomegranate and hibiscus; no added sugar, if you're into that whole healthy living shit."

Christen picked up one of the pre-rolled joints, wrapped in gold-and-black paper with a man's face printed on the cover.

"Ah," Hector said, wagging his finger. "You're a purist." He extracted his Zippo lighter from his pocket and flipped open the lid. "Free toke for you, amigo. Big Mikes Hells Bells. Twenty-point-eight THC."

Christen contemplated the offer. "No smoking zone," he said, gesturing at the sprinklers housed in the ceiling.

"Try before you buy?" Hector insisted, cracking the flint of the lighter. "Strongest I got. Maybe it's too much for you though?"

Christen accepted the challenge. "Fuck it, just a toke," he said, inhaling a lungful of smoke. Immediately, it felt like his whole insides were burning.

"I warn you, amigo," Hector said, gesturing for Christen to hand back the joint which he did without complaint. Hector stubbed out the tip of the joint with his fingertips. "Don't want to set off no smoke alarms," he added, slipping the joint into a small box.

Christen cleared his throat. "I will take twenty of the usual and three of the topicals, Sour Diesel."

"No flowers?"

"Sure. Two, 24k Stevia," Christen said, wiping the back of his hand across his lips.

Hector slid the produce across the desk.

"See Mallory on your way out, she handles the petty cash."

Hector flipped his case and sat back, in no hurry to leave. "The family all good?"

Christen considered the question. "Why the sudden interest in my family?"

Hector smiled. "Just making conversation. Haven't seen you at the Casa lately, you don't come no more?"

"Yeah, I come. You must have missed me."

Hector chuckled, wagged his index finger. "No, no. I remember if I see you. Always remember you."

Christen forced a tight smile. "I'm busy, anything else?"

Hector grabbed his case and stood. "Always a pleasure doing business with you. Hope you'll visit us at the Casa soon. The girls are always asking for you, you're a big tipper, right? The girls always like the big tippers. Adios, Mr. Hansen."

9

The opening kick drum thuds and the raucous guitar riff of "I Love Rock 'n' Roll," thundered through the Jack of Diamonds, a dive-bar with low-lighting and red faux-leather booths. The greasy stench of deep-fried food hung around the bar with the stubborn intent of a belligerent drunk, though the Jack of Diamonds hadn't served food since the late nineties.

Roscoe Tanner looked down the narrow length of the bar from his favorite booth, and watched a crowd of young people huddled around the fuzzy neon glow of the Seeburg jukebox talking loudly as if they imagined the world was hanging on their every word.

"Come here often?" Detective Moira Shaughnessy asked, with a slim smile that was a millimeter short of a smirk.

Tanner shook his glass of bourbon in the crowd's direction. "That, Detective Shaughnessy, is the new Oakland."

"Some people probably like it."

"You like it?"

"It's not my kind of place."

"I guessed as much." Tanner watched her take a tentative sip of her Sauvignon Blanc. "How's the wine?"

"Warm," she said, wiping the back of a hand across her mouth.

Tanner twisted his glass around the table. "A few years back, it was just me and a collection of unsavory locals, now it's full of beards wearing flannel shirts and drinking Pabst Blue Ribbon like it's some new-fangled drink."

"New-fangled?" Shaughnessy shook her head. "They're hipsters, probably think it's ironic."

"Hipsters?" Tanner asked, as the crowd raised their bottles and shouted *"I Love Rock 'n' Roll"* as if it were the first time they'd heard the chorus and were giddy with its raw, anthemic simplicity.

"Thick beards, ironic vintage T-shirts, ride fixed-gear bikes, brew their own beer?"

"Sounds like a lot of work, this hipster thing."

Shaughnessy rolled up the sleeves of her blouse and slumped back in her seat. "So, why am I here? Something about the case you can't discuss back at the station?"

Tanner took a moment to study the detective. She was in her early thirties, her hair a color he might describe as dirty blond, though there seemed nothing "dirty" about her. Shaughnessy had an efficient, clean-cut look, not innocent, but still untouched by the heavy, world-weariness fixed into the faces of most of the detectives in the OPD. Her complexion was pale with flushes of red around the cheekbones; with the name Moira Shaughnessy, she likely had some Irish ancestry branching somewhere off the family tree. He figured her height to be around five-ten, her build muscular judging by the prominent bulge of blue veins running down her forearms and the wire-like tautness of the skin around her neck. Her eye color somewhere between heavy gray and blue; her general demeanor, impatient, like she had some place better to be.

"Thought we should get to know each other, if we're going to be partners."

"What, like a first date kind of thing?"

"Is this a problem for you?"

Shaughnessy sighed. "Sure, what the fuck," she said, shrugging. "Graduated top of my class at the Academy. Made detective before the age of thirty, which had always been my ambition. I worked under Marty, Chief Dugdale, at San Jose, followed him to Oakland. Now, you're all caught up."

"Feels like I've known you all my life, Shaughnessy," he said, raising his glass.

Shaughnessy leaned across the table. "Listen, just because I'm a woman it doesn't make me the touchy-feely type. Marty figured you were in need of a partner due to the high profile nature of the case. If that's a problem for you I'd take it up with him. Here's the thing, I don't need to be familiar with every minutia of your life to be a good partner. I got your back, you've got mine. I'm not new to this."

"Jeez, I'm not looking for a relationship, Shaughnessy, just some dang conversation."

"I thought you'd asked me here to discuss our case."

"You're not curious? Nothing you want to know about me?"

Shaughnessy sat back, folded her arms. "You've been a detective for thirty-five years, always at OPD, which tells me you lack ambition. You probably drink bourbon because your doctor said you were pre-diabetic, and you think it's better for you than beer. By the way you dress and the dog hairs on your jacket sleeve, there's a good chance you live alone. You still wear your wedding ring, even though your wife died a year ago; sorry for your loss, by the way. You prefer shithole bars like this because they don't make you feel your age. You don't like change, fancy espresso drinks, or the fact your kids never call. You listen to

NPR most days, except in the evenings when you like to relax with old jazz records. How am I doing so far?"

Tanner took the glass from his lips. "Jazz? I hate jazz," he said, sensing his life had just been put on a spin cycle and dumped on the table.

Shaughnessy pushed her wine glass away. "If you're done with the chitchat, I've got work to do," she said. "I'm logging the victim's social media accounts and cross-referencing any of them who live in the East Bay."

"We've already interviewed all her close friends—"

"I'm looking broader," she interrupted. "Social media contacts. The victim couldn't be close friends with seven thousand Instagram followers."

"Catalina," Tanner said. "The victim's name was Catalina."

"Sure, I saw what you did just there," she said. "You think by humanizing the victim I'll be more motivated to solve the case. Personally, I've found clinical detachment yields more effective results." Shaughnessy folded her jacket stiffly across her arm. "Enjoy the rest of your evening."

Jeez, that went well," Tanner muttered to himself as Shaughnessy shoved her way through the crowd. Maybe the woman was right about one thing; he should find himself another watering hole where the young bucks weren't quite so young. Change? Yeah, it was a dang son-of-a-biscuit, all right.

10

"New mugshots arrived, get 'em while they're hot!" Alyssa Bennett, office receptionist, handed Jessica a lanyard with her official Alameda County Department of Health ID. Jessica looked dismissively at the laminated rectangle: *Jessica Swift, Senior Public Health Investigator, Alameda County.*

No surprises there. But the photo, surely that wasn't her? The photograph of the former *"most likely to kick-ass"* high-school graduate bore little resemblance to the fifty-seven-year-old single mother Jessica Swift did battle with every morning at her vanity mirror. The gem-blue eyes were as prominent as ever, as were the lightly freckled cheekbones that had withstood the onslaught of gravity while all else around her seemed to have surrendered. Her hair looked passable; she'd had it straightened and semi-highlighted the day before for what the HR department had insisted on calling "Selfie Thursday", having completely failed to grasp the concept. Everything else; the dark blotches on her forehead, the shadow above her top lip, the crow's feet sprawling like parched riverbeds from the corner of her eyes, she put down to poor lighting. The photo reminded her of a software program designed to illustrate what a missing person might look like ten years from the day they disappeared. Jessica sighed and held the badge next to her face, smiling at the receptionist with a shrug of her shoulders.

"Don't blame me, honey, I just hand them suckers out," Alyssa said, raising her hands in the "don't shoot the messenger" manner.

"Definitely not one for the dating sites."

"Hell no. You're still a hottie."

"Is that right?"

"Telling it like it is, that's all, honey," Alyssa said, sitting back as if she'd just delivered the solution to the world's problems.

"After the day I've had, I'll take the compliment."

"Yeah, you will. Now get your ass in there, he's called a meeting."

"This late in the day?"

"Got to admire the man's dedication."

Jackson Cain, Senior Director of Public Health––two hundred and fifty pounds, bald, and prone to intermittent flare-ups of gout––limped to the front of the conference room and sat on the edge of the desk, his right foot slightly raised. He cleared his throat. "I'll make this brief, as I'm sure you all want to haul ass out of here for the long holiday weekend."

The three Public Health Investigators nodded in agreement. The other two, Trinity Greene and Matthew *"call me Matty"* Barton, had hoped to skip out after lunch, but were forced to wait for Jessica's return. She felt their eyes burning deep into her shoulder blades.

"Matty," Jackson said, consulting his papers. "Friendly's Chicken Shack. What's the deal?"

"Yeah, man," Matty said, shuffling impatiently. "Cockroach

infestation. It's like a freakin' John Carpenter movie back there. Served them with a cease and desist until they clean up their shit."

"Trinity?"

"Oakland Children's hospital. Three recent cases of newborns with Hepatitis B. I'm counseling the mothers next week."

Jackson shook his head. "Wish they'd damned well come in for counseling before it reaches critical mass. Prevention, not just the cure."

"Good luck with that," Jessica said. "We don't exactly spread joy and happiness in people's lives."

"You got anyone coming in for treatment, Swift?"

"No, sir. Do we have any antivirus yet?"

"Monday. Guaranteed."

"They said that last week. What's the point of me busting my ass if there's no vaccine? These people wouldn't pee on me if I was on fire, Jackson. Hell, they'd probably warm their hands and sing campfire songs."

"It's a sensitive subject, gonna take some time."

"Yeah, how many more get infected between now and then?"

Trinity and Matty sighed in unison and rolled their eyes.

Jessica reached for her files. "Oklahoma, Detroit, Seattle, all report outbreaks of early stage syphilis. It's a damned epidemic and we're waiting on a drug company that doesn't give a shit because they won't make money selling to sex workers and addicts. Where's the damned accountability, Jackson?"

"Not factually correct, Swift," he explained. "Like most of the world, we all thought syphilis was eradicated. The CDC hasn't seen a case for twenty years and Remedium is the only big pharma with the facilities to scale to mass production."

"We're dealing with a seventeen percent cut in the Federal

Prevention budget. Can we even afford to treat these people?" Jessica asked.

"We'll cross that bridge in due time, but my guess is that they're producing the vaccine as fast as they can."

"Yeah, I'm sure you believe that." Jessica stuffed the papers back into her bag.

Jackson rubbed his hands together, addressed the room. "Right, Fourth of July's coming up. I'm headed home to watch the city of Oakland blow shit up and eat my body weight in meat and baked goods."

"What's your gout got to say about that?" Jessica asked, gesturing at Jackson's foot which he was swiping left and right as if divining for water.

Jackson smiled. "It says mind your own damned business, Swift."

"And all those people waiting for treatment? What do I tell them? You do know this is only going to get worse, people are going to die, Jackson."

"You do your job, Swift, reassure them we're doing the best we can. Meeting over, y'all have a happy Fourth."

11

Christen observed that Alexus had a welcome lightness in her step as she dropped a thick box file onto the kitchen island. She was humming a pop tune he recognized from the radio; one of those songs that on first hearing would earworm itself into his head and not relent its grip for the rest of the day.

Alexus had always seemed happiest when busying herself with some project or other. Over the past few weeks, Christen sensed there was something on her mind; something she wasn't willing or ready to share with him. After twenty years, he should probably have been better at picking up on the clues. Then again, a strategy of blissful ignorance had worked well for him in the past. Whatever was bugging Alexus he was sure it would pass soon enough without the need for endless discussion and analysis.

"Dollar for them," Alexus said, turning to face her husband.

"Just work, nothing worth paying for," he said, raising his glass. "Join me?"

Alexus ran a hand through her hair. "Probably not a good idea."

Christen rattled the ice cubes. "Are you sure?" he said,

setting out a fresh glass and pouring a long shot of Absolut vodka with a short measure of tonic.

Alexus reached for the glass. "Sure, I guess one won't hurt."

As she sipped, Christen noticed how softly the light from the overheads fell across the dark curl of her hair and onto those deep brown eyes that had captivated him so completely twenty years ago. Where the hell did the time go? Or more importantly, he thought, where did the love go? He hadn't fallen out of love with Alexus; it was more like, as it was in many marriages he imagined, they'd just fallen into a routine. He stood behind Alexus, reached his arms around her, lifted her hair in his palm and kissed the soft skin of her nape.

"Really, tonight?" she said, shrugging him off.

He drew her closer. "Sydney won't be back until later and Jonas is sleeping over."

Alexus sighed. "Do you have any idea how much work I have to do before tomorrow's parade? I don't have the time and neither do you. You promised to help me with the lights."

"I thought you had already taken care of it?" he said, a prickle of irritation needling him as Alexus pulled away.

"Those were for the garden, I still need your help with the house lights."

Christen sat and grabbed the TV remote. "Later," he said, pouring another shot. "I will do it later."

"So long as it gets done by tomorrow morning."

Christen flipped in an aggravated manner with no desire to land on anything to hold his attention; channel surfing was an activity born from frustration; a soothing distraction, similar to trawling through his Facebook posts or Twitter feeds.

"Go back to that," Alexus said, waving her hands. "I want to see the news."

Oakland's Chief of Police, Martin C. Dugdale, was

addressing the cameras, the text scrolling along the lower third of the screen paraphrasing his speech:

"The body of a seventeen-year-old missing Oakland high-schooler, Catalina Gomez, was discovered yesterday morning. We are asking anyone with any information to please come forward. We are especially eager to locate Catalina's cell phone, a white Samsung Galaxy 8, with a case similar to this one."

The video cut to a shot of a phone case with a Black Lives Matter logo embossed in gold lettering on the back.

"Her parents will be speaking to the press later tomorrow, for now they ask for privacy and for you to keep them in your prayers at this time."

"Isn't that our gardener, Francisco?" Christen asked, as Catalina's parents stood, heads bowed, next to the Chief as he spoke.

Alexus shivered. "That poor family. I can't imagine what they're going through. Losing a child, I can't even go there."

But Christen wasn't listening. He was transfixed by Catalina's photograph. As the video zoomed into a close-up of her eyes, he wiped a hand across his face, a dense wave of nausea pushing him into his seat.

"Christen. Christen, are you okay?"

"Yes, of course," he said, patting Alexus's hand. As the news report cut back to the studio, Christen somehow found the strength to stand. "I forgot, I have to check in at work," he said, grabbing his jacket from the back of the kitchen chair.

"Seriously, tonight?"

"Yes," he said. "It has to be tonight. Anyway, you won't miss me," he said, gesturing at the paperwork.

As Christen pulled the door shut, Alexus reached for the vodka bottle. "Definitely not a good idea," she mumbled, gripping the neck of the bottle and taking a sharp, determined slug.

12

Christen pulled up his metallic gray Tesla Model S outside the warehouse at Brooklyn Basin and stepped into the warm evening air. Fireworks crackled through the nearby streets with an anxious menace. The warehouse looked deserted; the windows dark, a sliver of moonlight reflecting off the roof. But that was the intent of the Rat House; it wasn't designed to draw attention. Typically, a single blue light in a top story window would signal it was operating, along with a clutch of expensive cars tucked away in the shadows at the dockside.

He jogged towards the entrance. A gleam of a flashlight scurried around the door, then switched its attention across the gravel to Christen's face. A voice: "Who the fuck's there?"

Christen shielded his eyes from the glare as the flashlight examined his face, then pulled back to the doorway.

"Oh, it's you," Nelson said, pulling the key from the padlock and testing the chain. "Girls all gone home, bro."

"All of them?" Christen asked, looking up to a second-story window where he was sure he glimpsed a flicker of light and a figure moving behind the glass.

"Ain't nobody working, ain't nobody buying."

What Follows

"Hector here?" Christen asked, glancing up at the window.

Nelson shook his head. "Like I say, you gonna need to find your kicks someplace else."

"I wasn't looking for kicks, I was looking for Hector."

"Don't make no difference to me," Nelson said, securing a second padlock to the door. "Try tomorrow night."

"Tomorrow night?" Christen muttered, tightening his fingers around the steering wheel. He needed to talk to Hector tonight: now. He'd already left several messages, none of which Hector had deemed worthy of a reply. The news report had unnerved him enough to compel him to drive the three miles from Rosemont to confirm his suspicions. He was sure she was the same girl he'd seen arguing with Hector in the parking lot of the Rat House.

The Tesla's suspension snapped over the potholes as Christen drove past the shells of abandoned buildings marking the hinterland of Brooklyn Basin. The neighborhood gathered scant attention from Oakland PD. With only seven hundred officers responsible for seventy-eight square miles of the city, they rarely ventured that far south, taking the *"if it ain't squealing, it don't need oiling"* approach to policing.

Even if the Rat House had been open for business, he hadn't intended to partake in the entertainment, he just wanted to talk to Hector. But standing outside the building, the heavy sense of a lost opportunity carving a hole in his belly, Christen sensed a familiar, resolute force tighten its fist around him, just like it always did.

Taking the Embarcadero exit, he drove past Jack London Square towards the half-darkness and promise that lingered on the edges of East Oakland. He'd vowed to stay away, curb his appetite for a few days; test his willpower in the face of temptation. But, one look at the Rat House, the smell of the place catching like firework powder in his nostrils, his resolve had disintegrated to dust.

Promises you made to yourself were easy to make, even easier to break. He imagined his own addiction was like an itch. An itch that, once satisfied, would start up again days, sometimes even hours, later. He hated himself for it; every dependent, weak-willed part of it. That was the flip side to his addiction; the self-loathing that made him want to crawl out from under his own skin. The thought of Alexus finding out was sickening, but never sickening enough to make him stop. But maybe that was the nature of his addiction; any addiction. Cravings that would never be wholly satisfied; self-hatred that ate him up like a tumor, and the sheer thrill that someday, somehow, he'd be caught out in the lie.

It was slim pickings, Christen thought as he drove past the six young women standing with their backs against the overpass pillar. None of them were motivated to walk the few steps to the sidewalk, probably imagining Christen was just another tourist, window shopping with no intention to purchase. As he pulled up, one of the women, mid-twenties, Asian, wearing a tight red spaghetti-strap top approached the car.

He wound down the window.

The woman leaned in, curled her fingers around her top, and tugged down to reveal the firm cut of her breasts against the frills of her black bra. "Hey, handsome. You ready to party?"

A sharp pulse of electricity shot through Christen.

He took a moment to check out the jewelry on her wrist,

then reached out his hand, taking the bracelet between his fingers, and read the name. *Wendi*. "Is that your real name?"

"If you're paying, call me whatever the fuck you like," she said, gently brushing his hand away.

Christen unfurled a wad of dollar bills from his pocket.

Figuring Christen was for real, she gave him an extra wide smile. "Two hundred straight up. Freaky shit's extra. No bareback," she said, twirling gum suggestively around her tongue.

Christen peeled off ten twenties, settled them on the dashboard, then grabbed her firmly by the wrists.

"Hey! I already laid it out, asshole, you pay extra for that kinda shit," she said, struggling to break away, but Christen's grip was unrelenting.

"Turn them over," he insisted.

Familiar with the routine, Wendi rotated her arms. Under the spill of the streetlights her skin had a tawny, soft complexion like mocha. "See, clean as fuck," she said, pulling back her arms. "Now, you want to party or not?"

"Get in," Christen said, rolling up his window. His body arced with electricity as he caught the scent of the girl's cheap perfume, the sheer thrill of anticipation shuddering through him. She scuffled her thin body into the passenger seat and told him to drive.

Behind them, a pair of headlights peeled from a side street, following several car lengths back, maintaining a steady speed, just like it had for the past fifteen minutes since leaving the Rat House.

13

Roscoe Tanner sat in his pea-green 1987 BMW 325i station wagon and looked over the anxious flickering of the Bay Area skyline. He was parked at his favorite vista point on the apex of Grizzly Peak, nibbling on a bland and now wilted sandwich as he concentrated on Catalina's preliminary autopsy report. The image of Francisco and Marta Gomez, heads bowed low, walking hand in hand down the steps of Oakland Police Headquarters, came back to him.

"No comprendo. No comprendo," they'd kept repeating as if the mantra might somehow manifest their daughter. The sight of them walking from the station reminded Tanner of the hesitance of death-row inmates shuffling toward the execution room, hoping the phone would ring informing them their appeal had been successful. In the one execution Tanner had witnessed, it hadn't happened. He guessed it rarely did. It would be the same with Francisco and Marta. No matter how reluctant their steps or however strong their conviction that this was all a bad dream they would soon wake from, their world had changed forever.

Tanner felt a tightening in his throat. Thirty-five years on, he'd expected the work would have become easier: it didn't. The opposite was true. Every case and every year seemed to bear down on him a notch harder and heavier than the one before.

As Shaughnessy had so efficiently pointed out, it was closing in on one year since his wife's death; maybe that was a factor, but it was one of many. More than likely it was the promise Teresa had resolutely urged Tanner to keep in the final weeks before the cancer had ravaged her so completely she was barely recognizable. A year to mourn, she'd insisted, *"then get back in the darned saddle, Roscoe. You're still young, don't be alone for the rest of your life."*

Teresa had always been the practical type. She'd even compiled a list of single women he should consider dating after she'd passed. It was a short list, and he'd barely glanced at the names. If he was going to keep his promise (and there was no doubt in his mind that he wouldn't) he'd extend his attentions far from the immediate circle of friends. It would be too harsh a betrayal of Teresa's memory to date someone they both knew.

The internet had been his first port of call. He'd browsed a dating site for the over fifties, though had yet to complete his profile or upload a photo. The only pictures he possessed all featured him with Teresa, or with their two grown children, Carter and Diane. He figured posting his official OPD ID wouldn't be the most effective advertisement. But a promise was a promise, and this was one he was going to keep; he owed Teresa that much.

Tanner blew his nose on a napkin and checked out the details in the report. Heroin had been found in Catalina's bloodstream, though not enough to prove an overdose as the primary cause of death. No visible signs of trauma or contusions, sexual activity or abuse pre- or post mortem. The report concluded she'd been in the lake for at least seventy-two hours, making it likely she was killed the night she vanished and her body dumped soon after.

Tanner slipped the autopsy photographs from the envelope and compared them to the pictures from the crime scene. The bruise on Catalina's calf was still noticeable, but the autopsy photographs showed the bruising had subsided considerably; more than he would have expected in a twenty-four-hour period, certainly a more aggressive fading than he would have expected from a hardcore addict who would have punctured around the same area several times a day.

He put the file back on the seat. Something stuck in his craw. Why would a straight-A student with her whole future ahead, inject herself with heroin? He'd expected the usual laundry list of narcotics; some form of methamphetamine the school kids swallowed like candy these days, weed would be a given, edible or smoked. Heroin was a tougher sell. If she was a regular user, she wouldn't be posting straight-As, that was for dang sure.

He checked the photographs of the shoes Catalina was wearing when they found her and conducted a quick search on his phone to confirm Madeline Ambrose's claim. The Crime Scene Leader was right. Jimmy Choos cost a small fortune. How could a high-school student working ten hours a week afford shoes the price of a week's vacation in Mexico?

He slipped in his favorite Waylon Jennings CD and reached for the brochure he'd ordered promoting an Outlaw Country Cruise: a long weekend of rabble-rousing on the Norwegian Pearl from New Orleans to Costa Maya, Mexico. Teresa had always laughed at the suggestion, calling him crazy if he thought she was going to spend a weekend with a bunch of drunken old men line dancing. She was a more traditional rock fan; Aerosmith, REO Speedwagon and their ilk. It might have been the single bone of contention between them in their thirty-two years of marriage.

Twenty minutes later, as he navigated the steep twists and turns of Old Tunnel Road leading back onto Highway 24 and towards downtown Oakland, he thought back to something Shaughnessy had told him; that she'd *"followed"* Dugdale to Oakland. *It was a strange choice of words*, he thought. Why not "transferred" or even "headhunted"? It wasn't unheard of for other cities to poach smart officers; yet more evidence of American corporate culture seeping into law enforcement. She'd also called him Marty, twice. Maybe he was just overanalyzing. He'd been doing that a lot recently, or maybe that kind of skepticism was woven into his being now, as natural as the skin on his bones.

14

Gérard Rosseau's hangover was a thing of violence. A merciless stab of pain that appeared to have hijacked his entire body and was, at 4pm, intent on inflicting more damage. Listening to one of his students, Mason Arnett, practicing his scales wasn't helping. The squeak of the 12-gauge steel strings rubbing against Mason's fingertips as he travelled the frets was like a sharp drill digging somewhere in his frontal lobe.

"Play those new chords I taught you," Gérard said, chugging 800 milligrams of ibuprofen, washed down with a slug of his homemade red wine. "The minor sevens, not just the major shit, you should be past those by now."

"Sure, G-Man," Mason said, brushing the lank strands of hair from his face and settling the guitar further in the crook of his arm and rearranging his hand position.

As Mason strummed, Gérard looked out over his back deck to his yard. The sun was dipping low over his magnolia tree, dappling the rows of plants with a faint golden haze. He felt a sudden pang of sadness. This year's drought, relentless and severe, had decimated most of the vegetables he'd been tending to. He could have taken the risk, watered in the dead of night, but his new neighbors seemed the kind of people who would have reported him without a second thought; the last thing his bank account needed right now was the hit of a $350 fine. He was already bleeding his credit cards dry, and teaching one guitar student a week was hardly going to stop the hemorrhaging; neither was his day job, bagging groceries at the local Natural Foods Market for minimum wage.

"Everything I touch turns to shit," Gérard muttered to himself as he took stock of the parched garden. Drinking was the only vice he could afford these days; that and the occasional joint which Mason seemed happy to provide.

"All done," Mason said, laying down his guitar and reaching into his backpack for a ziplock bag full of pre-rolled joints. "You're partaking, I assume, G-Man?"

Gérard turned and looked at the skinny, awkward kid, his face a hot mess of acne. "How old are you, Mason, seventeen?"

"Old enough, man," he said, handing Gérard the bag.

"No, no you're not." Gérard reached for the joint and set it between his fingers. "I could get in some serious fuckin' shit for this, you know, smoking weed with a minor."

"S'all good," Mason said, taking a hard pull. "Ain't nobody minding none."

"At least come away from the damned window," he said, ushering him to the back deck.

"Man, looks like a freakin' apocalypse or some such shit," Mason said, looking over the garden. "Ever think maybe you just ain't the green-fingered type?"

"Ever think you're a shitty guitar player?"

"Nah. I know I'm good, man. Confidence. Gotta fake it till you make it."

Gérard took a deep inhale. "How's the band? They kicked you out yet?"

"Got a gig booked for next week, you should come. I'll put you on the guest list."

"What is it you play again?"

"Post-punk southern rock. Sex Pistols meet the Drive-By Truckers."

"Tempting, but I'll give it a miss. Thanks all the same, Mason."

"It ain't for everyone," he said. "And don't call me Mason, only my pops calls me that. It's Moonshine, like in Moonshine Fever, my band."

"Nobody calls me G-Man either, so I guess that makes us even, Mason."

Moonshine shrugged. "So, am I your only student? You know, after that whole shitshow?"

Gérard leaned over the rails of his deck. "Seems that way."

"That chick was crazier than a bag of pissed rattlesnakes, everyone knew it."

"Severe bipolar disorder," Gerard confirmed. "I'm surprised your folks didn't cancel, like the other parents."

"My pops ain't around much so he don't care none." Moonshine leaned back on the table and giggled. "Anyone tell you, you look like that dude from the Grateful Dead?"

"You're the first today," Gérard said, stroking his thick, gray moustache which drooped down in the handlebar fashion.

"Yeah, David Crosby," Moonshine said, cocking his head and studying Gérard's long grey hair which rested on his shoulders. "But he ain't losing his hair, like you."

"Fuck you, Mason," Gérard said, taking a sharp toke.

"No. Fuck you, G-Man."

There was a moment of silence before they both cracked up laughing.

"Wanna jam?" Gérard said. "If you can keep up."

"You serious? You do know I only come here out of pity, but

if you're up for the punishment, then I ain't averse to dishing it out."

"If your guitar playing was as smart as your mouth, then I might be worried. Go and choose your weapon."

Moonshine headed into the house and returned to the deck with a Martin D-28 acoustic. He sat, rested the guitar on his lap. "So, you do it, G-Man?"

"Do what?"

"What that crazy chick accused you of."

Gérard shifted uneasily in his chair. "What the fuck do you think?"

Moonshine strummed an open D chord, the sound resonating and fading into the hills where the final shadows of the day folded across the peaks. "Chicks fuck with your mind, that's what I think."

"What's that mean?"

"Means if you did do something, I'm not one to judge. Sometimes shit goes down, ain't nobody's fault, just the way it is."

Gérard stood, reached for the guitar from Moonshine's lap. "Lesson's over for today, you best be getting home, Mason."

15

The following day, the heat had notched up another two degrees, with the prospect of rising temperatures over the next few days. Tanner peered through the artificially darkened windows of the 3rd floor of the Oakland Police Department and watched a trace of gunpowder snake skywards. Over in Chinatown, the spittle and crack of firecrackers echoed off the downtown buildings. Tanner tended to avoid the Fourth of July traditions and would book himself and his dog, Stanley, into a quiet log cabin in Cloverdale, three hours north of the city. With the Catalina Gomez case dominating the news, he figured he and the mutt wouldn't be traveling anywhere anytime soon.

Returning to his desk, he checked out the archive of Catalina's Instagram postings the digital forensics team had sent over that morning. She was a stunning girl, her complexion unblemished by any of the expected flush of teenage acne, her eyes dark and almond-shaped, her hair jet-black and straight, trailing the length of her back.

For a seventeen-year-old girl, she seemed unnaturally confident, maybe even sexually mature beyond her years. The word *jailbait* came to mind as he browsed: Catalina posing in her bathroom mirror, pouting in a white bikini; looking pensively out to the horizon on some beach, her shoulders bare and reflecting the day's final offering of sunshine. She had just short of seven thousand followers. He wondered how many of those were the kind of men with an unhealthy obsession for girls of that age. The internet was like Macy's storefront window at Christmas for men of that persuasion.

The local news had jumped on the story. If she'd been a sex worker or another overdosed junkie, he suspected the story would have barely made the tail end of the news. Catalina Gomez, however, was beautiful and popular. A straight-A student with scholarship offers from the best colleges in the state. It was a headline story that sold papers and ratcheted up the viewing figures.

The autopsy report highlighted a significant bruise on the great saphenous vein in her calf, consistent with a needle puncture. Tanner was familiar with the routine. The girls working the corners of 50th Avenue and East 14th would pierce themselves around the calf so as not to put off the more discriminating Johns who would flip over a girl's forearms before negotiating any transaction. He was sure as eggs were eggs, Catalina was not one of those girls.

Her close friends had provided statements directly after she was reported missing. No indication of unusual behavior; no enemies, nobody had threatened her or made her suspicious or scared. That wasn't unusual in a missing person's case, especially if the person intended to stay missing. But they'd found Catalina, her death suspicious. That changed everything.

Tanner rechecked one of the original witness statements. Catalina had finished her shift at the Boba Lounge at ten o'clock on Friday, June 27th. The place was owned by Bruce Ho, a small-time entrepreneur who owned a string of Boba Lounges in the East Bay. There was something in Bruce's alibi for that night that caught Tanner's attention. It was probably nothing, but he could do with some fresh air and a change of scenery.

"Hey," Tanner called over. "I'm headed out."

"Cool," Shaughnessy said, distractedly. "Coffee run?"

"No, not a dang coffee run."

"Right on," she said, grabbing a sheet of warm paper from the printer. "You might want to check this guy out."

Tanner checked the name.

"HansenBoy420. Seems he commented on most of Catalina's postings. I traced him back to his Facebook account, which is a freakin' miracle because how many teenagers do you know with active Facebook accounts?"

"Don't think I know any teenagers, period," Tanner said, grabbing the slip of paper.

"You're welcome," she said, as Tanner flung his jacket over his right shoulder and headed out.

16

Tanner set a hand across his brow and stared past his reflection into the Boba Lounge. Sweeps of bright orange offset the lime-green walls and luminous yellow tables. Stuck to the door, a handwritten sign that read, *"Help needed. Ask for Bruce."*

A thickset Asian man with a harried expression mouthed at him through the glass, "Come back in one hour."

Tanner stuck his ID against the window. The man wiped his hands down his jeans and unlocked the door. "You Bruce?"

The man glanced furtively down both directions of Oakland Avenue before cracking the door barely wide enough for Tanner to squeeze himself through.

"Worried you're being watched?" Tanner asked, stepping into the welcome blast of air conditioning.

"If the kids think we're opening early, there'll be a line down the street, I don't need that shit today."

Bruce was built like an overdrawn comic book character. Thick biceps bulging from the sleeves of his T-shirt, his hair shorn to a number one buzz on the sides, his fringe left to grow long, with a blond streak like the markings of a skunk.

Tanner quickly scanned the establishment. A bunch of Boba Lounges had recently opened up around Oakland, typically close to high schools where they were guaranteed long lines snaking out of the door come dismissal. Last year, frozen yogurt shops were all the rage but Tanner guessed the young were naturally fickle and had shifted their allegiances to Boba, which seemed to him nothing more than cold, milky tea infused with tapioca that floated in its muddy depths like frogspawn.

On the wall closest to the window was a space reserved for customer photographs that all featured a selfie of some fashion, reflecting in a six-feet-by-nine-feet corkboard Oakland's cultural diversity: Caucasian, African American, Hispanic, Asian, and every mix in between. Tanner was immediately drawn to the photograph of Catalina set in the center, the unrealized potential of her thousand-watt future outshining the other, less luminous kids that had pressed their way into her frame.

Bruce made a big deal of clattering utensils and poured a jug of batter into the mixer. Sliding a knife from the block behind him, he began slicing oranges. "I already spoke to the OPD," he said. "Nothing's changed."

"Last week she was missing, this week we found her body in the lake. That changes everything." Tanner flipped open his notebook. "So, tell me about Catalina."

"Not much to tell. She worked here four days a week, didn't piss off the customers, didn't steal my money."

"Not exactly a glowing reference."

"Look," he said, rubbing a towel along the blade. "Churn's fast here. Kids come and go, I don't get attached. They work, I pay them, they leave, it's not a career path."

"But I'd guess you get to know the kids, working with them and such?"

Bruce put down the knife. "I heard Catalina liked to party."

"Drugs? Alcohol?"

"She didn't bring that shit in here, I'd have fired her ass."

"I'm surprised a busy girl like Catalina had time to party, what with all her school and working for you."

"If you like to party, I guess you find a way."

"And the night Catalina disappeared, where were you?"

"Already told the other cop, I was with my fiancée. She wasn't feeling well, took her some medicine, stayed with her until I opened up in the morning."

"What kind of medicine?"

Bruce shrugged. "The kind that makes you feel better."

Tanner checked his notes. The officer investigating Catalina's disappearance had interviewed his fiancée who had confirmed Bruce's account. He felt a familiar twinge of irritation. The alibis provided by relatives, boyfriends, girlfriends, fiancées, irked the bejesus out of him. At best they were untrustworthy, at worst plain fabrication. Sometimes, the lie would mercifully crumble under the cold light of an interview room, but mostly the alibis held water until more compelling evidence came to light.

"What did you guys do that night? Watch TV? Play chess?"

"TV."

"What did you watch?"

"Some reality show. *Real Housewives of Atlanta* or some such bitch shit. I wasn't paying attention."

Tanner referred to his notes; they tallied with Bruce's account.

"When did Catalina leave?"

Bruce set to work slicing another batch of oranges. "She finishes her shift at ten. I give her the code for the alarm. She shuts up, goes home. I figured she did the same that night."

Tanner pointed to the ceiling. "What about your CCTV cameras? Would they tell the same story?"

Bruce shook his head. "Fake. If the kids think they're being watched they won't steal my shit."

"So, Catalina was working by herself the Friday night she disappeared?"

"No, I already told the other cop. I was here until nine. When business slowed, I left."

"So you have no idea where Catalina was headed after leaving here on the night she disappeared?"

"I gotta say it again?" he said, firing up the juicer. "No."

"Got it, thanks for your cooperation, Mr. Ho," Tanner said, reaching into his jacket pocket and handing over his card. "I expect you'll call me if you remember anything else about that night, because the way things stand, you were probably the last person to see that poor young girl alive."

17

Mornings at the tent encampment followed a similar pattern: a constant and exhausting hustle for food, drink, drugs, sex; anything to break the monotony and carry them through to the next morning. If luck had rolled their way, Marigold Mary—so named because of her insistence on always wearing bright-yellow Marigold kitchen gloves—would have guilt-tripped a local coffee shop into donating a couple of gallons of drinking water and coffee grounds, which she would boil in a large cauldron in the center of the camp. As Mary hollered the coffee was ready a pageant of bodies slunk out from the tents and stood clutching at their takeout coffee containers they'd dug out from the trash the night before.

Jessica Swift observed the morning routine from her car. "You don't have to do this."

Sabine hauled the Discount Grocery bag from the back seat. "Part of my school community service hours anyway," she said.

Jessica smiled. Sabine was the one positive outcome of a terrible decision in the husband department. "There won't be anyone to sign off. These camps aren't legal, they pop up overnight."

"That's okay," Sabine said, resting the bag on her lap. "Charity begins at home, right?"

"Is that you asking me for a favor sometime down the line?"

For a moment Jessica thought she recognized the same mischievous twinkle her ex-husband often had, though Sabine's eyes were more guarded. Like most teenagers, she didn't quite trust the world yet.

"Could be," Sabine said, smiling and opening the car door.

"Hi, Mary!" Jessica called out, as she and Sabine walked. "I hear they're hiring over at Starbucks."

Mary gazed into the dark slosh of coffee and stirred it in long, slow movements. "I ain't working for the man. He can kiss my ass, him and that goddamn mermaid."

"Got some groceries," Sabine said.

Mary nodded. "Put 'em by there, I'll share them out later. Don't want too much excitement at one time, gets everyone all riled up. I ain't in the frame of mind for that today."

"OPD moved you from San Pablo?"

"Last week, middle of the freakin' night," Mary confirmed. "Give 'em another few weeks they'll move us from here too."

"Everyone okay? No health crises?"

"Ain't no one passed, if that's what you're asking."

"Good enough," Jessica said.

As Sabine laid down the groceries, a loud blast of rap music echoed off the thick concrete of the underpass, followed by a squeal of burning rubber. A white Ford Mustang came to a violent stop at the sidewalk.

The doors swung open, four young men jumped out. They ran into the camp, whooping as they launched fistfuls of firecrackers and smoke bombs into the tents. The residents who had slept in, ran from their shelters, half-naked, imagining the world had come to a sudden and ferocious end. The chaos lasted a few more seconds before the men ran back, leaned against their cars and laughed.

As Jessica contemplated marching over and giving them a sharp piece of her mind, she thought she recognized one of them; a young boy, who was reaching into his pocket. He drew back his arm like a little league pitcher and lobbed a bottle rocket into the camp. "Happy Fourth of July, motherfuckers!"

As the firework exploded in strobe-like flashes and a loud rat-ta-tat-tat crackle that ricocheted through the camp, the kid leapt back into the car and glowered at Jessica through the window and made the same handgun symbol and half-wink of his eye he'd made at her two days ago when she saw him on his bike.

Tyler's gesture sent a chill to her marrow. She took a deep breath. It was bravado, that was all. The kid was showing off, proving himself worthy of inclusion in the gang; acting how he thought a man should act.

"You all right, Mom?" Sabine asked, touching her arm.

Jessica smiled. "Sure, I'm okay," she said, patting her hand. "Takes more than a few fireworks to scare off the Swift girls, right?"

From the north of the camp, where the residents were expected to dig holes and bury their excrement, came a loud scream. An elderly woman stumbled towards the tents, flaying her arms. She was barefoot, a wildness in her eyes. A long trail of tissue paper hung down like a ribbon from between her legs to the crotch of her jeans, which she was struggling to pull up past her ankles. She fell to her knees, tugging at the tissue and throwing it to the ground.

"Oh, Lord Jesus! I ain't ever seen such a thing," she said, bringing her hands to her face and shaking her head as if the motion might dislodge the image imprinted there.

"What it is, Jazmyn?" Marigold Mary asked. "What's wrong?"

"The devil's work. Ain't nothing but the devil's work. Lord have mercy on her poor, sinful soul," Jazmyn hollered, directing her gaze heavenward and clasping her hands in prayer.

Jessica turned to Sabine. "Stay here," she said.

"But, Mom..."

"I said here, Sabine. Do not move."

"Come with me," Jessica said, urging Mary to follow.

The stench of feces and urine was already fermenting under the glare of the morning sun as they walked over the empty fast-food containers and discarded soda bottles.

Mary and Jessica stopped at the camp boundaries, where the garbage was piled high against one of the freeway supporting pillars.

"Oh, Christ," Jessica said, stretching out her arm. "You don't want to see this."

Mary brushed her away. "The hell I don't."

She looked down. "Holy fuckin' shit-sticks!" she said, a hand bolting quickly over her mouth.

The body of a young girl was spread out over the dirt, her legs set out at right angles to her hips, her clothes torn; her lips blue and cracked like broken porcelain.

"Do you know her?" Jessica asked, her legs barely supporting her body weight.

Mary took a tentative step closer and shook her head. "Ain't one of ours, looks too clean, and anyway we don't have no residents missing their hands."

Jessica looked closer. She had assumed the girl had maybe fallen backward, her hand hidden under her back. But Mary was right. The girl's left hand was missing, leaving nothing but a dry, bloodied stump, a squadron of anxious black flies circling the wound. Jessica's stomach roiled. She stepped back as six fat rats scurried from the undergrowth and crawled over the body.

18

Tanner and Shaughnessy walked across the scrubland of the tent encampment back towards the car. The body had just been zippered into a body bag and hauled into the coroner's ambulance. Around the camp, people wandered around dazed, muttering to themselves. Others had already packed up their belongings, ready to move on some place where dead women's bodies didn't suddenly appear overnight.

"What do you think?" Shaughnessy asked, leaning on the car hood. "Connected to the Gomez case?"

"Doubtful," Tanner said, brushing a dusting of dirt from his pants. "Catalina's hands were still both attached when we found her, and I bet you a dime to a dollar those two girls weren't associating in the same social circles."

Shaughnessy reached in her pocket for a single Marlboro Light and set it between her lips. "You know that for sure?"

"For sure? No. But the way this girl was dressed? Two hundred dollars cash in her purse and a handful of unused condoms? She's not out here doing charity work, that's for dang sure."

"You told me Catalina liked to party," Shaughnessy said. "And if she died of an overdose—"

"If," Tanner interrupted, focusing on the unlit cigarette flicking anxiously at the corner of Shaughnessy's lips. "Until we get a COD, this case is like my liquor cabinet on Christmas Day, wide open."

Shaughnessy kicked at the dirt beneath her boots. "She had secrets. Thousand dollar shoes and a taste for the brown stuff. Just makes me think what else they didn't know about their daughter. Wouldn't be the first time a teenage girl lied to her parents."

"Whatever secrets she had, I'm dang sure prostitution wasn't one of them. And, are you going to light that dang thing, or not?"

"No, I'm quitting."

"Sure doesn't look like you're quitting."

"One step at a time," she said, batting away a fly buzzing around her face.

"We'll need a statement from the person who called this in." Tanner checked his notes. "Jessica Swift. And make sure you ask anyone who was in the camp last night if they saw or heard anything suspicious."

"Probably too high or drunk to notice anything," she said, taking the cigarette from her lips and slipping it back in her pocket.

"Judas Priest, Shaughnessy," Tanner said. "They're still human beings. Treat them with some dang respect."

Shaughnessy shook her head. "*Judas Priest?* Are you for real? Have it your way, Tanner, you've got seniority here, but if this is connected to Catalina Gomez, Dugdale's gonna be on both our asses. You might want to think on that."

19

Saint Mary's cemetery had become the preferred hangout amongst Rosemont's teenagers. It was as if they enjoyed taunting death, sitting close to it, confident that it wouldn't dare touch them--the young were naturally entitled to consider themselves immortal.

He was the same once, Tanner imagined, as he trudged the path between the gravestones. Recently, he'd been reflecting on his own mortality to an unhealthy degree. He attributed this dark state of mind to the relentless reports from the local news stations, each trying to out-shock each other with what some wry blogger had termed "drought porn". The footage of the lifeless riverbeds brought to mind the body they'd found at the tent city. The woman's face had the same arid, gray pallor. The only difference being the reservoirs would one day teem with life. For the young woman, that hope had long passed.

He continued navigating the narrow pathway between the gravestones. The temperature nudged the high seventies; way too warm for his wool suit, which scratched uncomfortably against his inner thighs. On the hillside to the east, he spotted a group of four kids. The sweet fug of marijuana floated like a smoke signal over the hilltop. They didn't notice Tanner until he was a few feet away.

"Any of you know someone by the name of Jonas?" he asked.

One of the teenagers brushed a curtain of greasy blond hair from his eyes and examined Tanner's brown suit, which had three rollerball pens sticking out from the breast pocket.

"Yeah? And who are you, his physics tutor?" he said, taking a deep drag on a joint and laughing. The boy had a pale complexion, his face shot with acne.

Tanner showed his badge. "Detective Roscoe Tanner, OPD."

"Crap!!" one of the girls, Century, yelped, flicking her joint into the scrubland behind her.

"Now, would you look at that," Tanner said. "By rights I should write you up for littering with intent to start a wildfire, and that there's a misdemeanor you'd have to disclose on your college submissions."

Century shrugged. "I'm already accepted, Brown."

The other boy, over six feet tall and with what Tanner guessed was a hundred-dollar haircut and a five-thousand-dollar smile, got up and extended his hand. "Jonas Hansen."

"That right?" Tanner said, looking over the kid. *Bi-racial, overconfident and too dang smooth for his own good*, he thought.

Jonas flashed a high-wattage smile. "What can I help you with, detective?"

"Catalina Gomez," Tanner said, letting the name hang for a moment. Jonas's face was composed, unreadable. "We're reaching out to her social media contacts. Your name came up a few times; HansenBoy420? You followed Miss Gomez on Instagram, seemed you commented on a lot of her posts."

"Yeah, me and a few thousand others."

The pale kid nodded in agreement. "A girl looks like that she's gonna attract some serious attention. Like bees to a honeypot."

Tanner squinted. "And you? What's your name?"

"Moonshine."

"That's a heck of a name to live up to. You got a real name?"

"My given name? Unless you got probable cause, I don't think I have to provide you with that information, sir."

Tanner's left cheek twitched. The kid was a smart-ass. "Don't sound like you're from around these parts, Moonshine?"

"Kentucky born and raised. Also, I ain't turned eighteen yet, in case you were fixin' to interrogate me some more."

"I could be fixin' to arrest you for smoking weed under the age of twenty-one in the State Of California. How's that for starters?"

Moonshine raised his hands. "Apologies, you just keep doin' your job like I ain't even here," he said, settling his headphones over his ears.

"Back to you, Jonas. Did you see Catalina on the night of Friday, June 27th? The night she disappeared?"

"Should you be questioning me without my parents?"

"You turned eighteen two weeks ago, that right?"

"Sure," Jonas confirmed.

"Well, legally you're an adult. Now, your call if you're willing to co-operate right here, or spend some quality time at the station. Don't make a lick of difference to me."

Jonas kicked the soil around his feet. "I heard she lives on International. You know how it is, we hang with our own, don't make it east of MacArthur. Our parents get nervous, don't want us mixing with the wrong crowd." Jonas gave Tanner another five-thousand-dollar smile.

"When was the last time you saw Catalina?"

"Probably at some party someplace, she was like hardcore, you know?"

"No, I don't know. Hardcore?"

"Liked to party, big time. Drugs, alcohol, the routine shit."

What Follows

"She didn't seem the type, smart girl like that."

"How she liked to blow off steam, I guess."

"And where were you the night she went missing?"

"Bunch of us went to First Friday, downtown. Hung there most of the night, listened to some bands, the usual."

"Gets busy there, I'm guessing there's no one to confirm that?"

"Just my crew here."

"Right you are," Tanner said, handing over his card. "Just in case something you forgot comes to mind, Jonas."

He turned to Moonshine, who was amusing himself playing air guitar. "And you, Kurt Cobain," Tanner said, reaching for Moonshine's still-smoldering joint and stubbing it out on a gravestone. "I assume you weren't smoking this in the presence of a police officer?"

"That would be illegal, sir," Moonshine said, smirking.

"Dang right it would be, son," Tanner confirmed. "You young'uns take care now, this ain't no place to hang out after dark."

With Tanner safely in the shadows, Jonas sat back and lit up another joint. "Fucking OPD," he said, taking a deep draw and kicking one of the gravestones. "Assholes."

The other girl, a wafer-thin senior called Peyton, put her arm across his shoulders in a soothing, motherly fashion.

"Leave me the fuck alone," he said, elbowing her away.

"Geez," Peyton said, rubbing her ribs. "That hurt."

"Yeah, chill the hell out, Hansen," Moonshine said. "You been mixing your meds with the weed? That's a fucked-up recipe right there."

Jonas's jaw tightened. Moonshine was right. But he wasn't

about to give him the satisfaction. He'd taken twenty milligrams of Adderall this morning and another eight later that afternoon. If he smoked with the methamphetamine still in his system it made him irritable, as if all the attention that should have been directed towards his studies was instead laser-focused on whatever was pissing him off. And right now what was pissing him off was everything.

"You got a plan, Jonas?" Peyton asked, her pupils pinpricks.

Jonas threw his joint to the floor, grinding the heel of his SeaVees sneakers into the embers. "Yeah, I got a plan," he said, extending his hand. "You guys like to party?"

Peyton took his hand. "For sure, we like to party."

Moonshine and Century followed close behind. No one asked where to or why. It was like that around Jonas Hansen's orbit; you tagged along as if it were the most natural thing in the world.

20

The location of the Badge Belforts was kept under wraps until two hours before the event, when a communication would be sent to the elite circle of "investors". Location and time was all the information required. The rest you were expected to know. You were either familiar with the drill or you weren't; and if you weren't, you probably weren't hot enough nor chill enough to be invited. By the same measure, if you had to ask *"what's a 'Belfort'?"* you were equally clueless the parties were named in honor of Jordan Belfort, the penny stockbroker, who had, after repeated late-night screenings of *The Wolf of Wall Street*, become a folk-hero amongst the sons of the more hardcore libertarian-leaning parents in Rosemont––the breed of parents who religiously read a passage from their first edition *Atlas Shrugged* at least twice a week and attended church every Sunday.

Jonas strode up the footpath towards the two Badge Brokers assigned to collect payment. Drugs were the accepted currency; weed, edible or otherwise, mollies, buzz bombs, prescription amphetamines such as Ritalin or Adderall. The party drugs would be distributed throughout the evening, with the majority share passed out to the host who would be referred to as "The Wolf" for the evening.

The Badge Brokers rarely acknowledged Jonas's presence as he approached. They were busy pawing two Baby Bonds–– overly made-up girls who barely looked eighteen, and under the deposits of thickly applied makeup were too young to know any better.

Jonas flashed them the text on his phone. "They're with me," he said, gesturing at Moonshine, who had his arms looped over Peyton and Century's shoulders. "Moonshine, pay the guys."

"USDA grade, motherfuckers," he said, handing the guys a ziplock bag of cannabis buds. "Grew that shit myself."

They sniffed the contents and nodded their heads in the "go right ahead, bro" manner.

"Jesus H. Christ," Moonshine said as they entered the cavernous foyer with a glass chandelier the size of a rowboat hanging from the ceiling and a long, curving double staircase that looked as if it were created for a movie set. "This is some sick shit."

Jonas gestured to his left. "Refreshments and snacks outside."

"I'm down with snacks," Moonshine said. "Where you going?"

"Got to talk to someone. I'll come find you later."

Jonas pushed his way through the crowd. He recognized most of the guys: they were typically drawn from the same limited gene pool. A new face would occasionally be invited, but only after a series of stringent background checks. The girls, however, were subject to a less rigorous initiation. If they were hot, partied hard and had enough "investment product" to satisfy the Badge Brokers, entrance was guaranteed. Those without the necessary "investments" could always find other means of payment; it was one of the benefits of being elected a

"Badge Broker"—what you lacked in product, you could make up for in sexual favors. It was known at the Badge Belforts as a "win-win".

Most of the girls were high-school seniors, the rest he figured were U-Bunnies: girls who required an Uber to drive them to Rosemont. They'd arrive in packs, stumbling from the backs of Priuses or Camrys already drunk or high. For the U-Bunnies, the parties were an opportunity to showcase their wares; tops cut low and designed to show maximum cleavage; skirts cut high above the thighs; heels that added four inches to their height, and makeup that betrayed their true age. They came for the free drinks, the hired DJ and the opportunity to break free from the confines of their small, uneventful worlds.

The sudden blast of a grinding bass riff rattled the light fixtures. *"Jordan Belfort"*—the party's signature tune set the kitchen pumping. Jonas swiped a beer and shoved through the sweating mass. A couple of guys he knew informed him tonight's Wolf, Bristol Hadleigh, was outside. He cut through the kitchen and into the warm evening.

"Jesus, standards, bro! What's up with those Badge Brokers?" he said, pulling Bristol in for the obligatory bro chest-bump.

Bristol threw back his head and slugged his beer. At six-feet-three, he matched Jonas in height, but Bristol was stockier with a wide, petulant face that reminded Jonas of an overgrown toddler. "Those two jerkoffs are killing me. They take your investment?"

"Nah, they were too busy feeling up a couple of Baby Bonds."

"Dumbasses." He extended his hand. "Wolf's share, you know the rules."

"You don't need to explain shit to me," Jonas said, "I'm alumni." He reached into his pocket, handing Bristol what looked like a candy bar. "Edibles," he said. "Don't go sharing that shit. Personal consumption only, it'll fuck you up if you're not used to it."

He tore at the package with the ferocity of a small child opening a birthday gift and took the chewy substance between his teeth, bit off a dime-sized chunk and swallowed it down with a throat full of Corona Light.

"Bruce here?"

"Huh?"

"Bruce? The Asian dude? Brings the U-Bunnies?"

"Barbell Bruce?"

"Yeah. You seen him?"

"Can't remember," Bristol said. "Got fucked up earlier."

"It's cool," he said, patting him on the shoulder. "I'll find him."

He didn't need to. He could hear Bruce's deep, grating voice from across the garden. It was as if he'd caught Jonas's scent in his nostrils. Jonas had never seen Bruce wearing anything other than a pristine white crew-neck T-shirt tucked into perfectly pressed, dark-blue Levi 501s and bright, white, high-ball basketball shoes. Tonight was no different.

"Yo, Hansen! We got some shit to discuss," he said, brushing his fringe from his face. Jonas caught the powerful aroma of deodorant and coconut oil as Bruce approached.

"Your buddy just puked all over me," he said, gesturing at the damp, yellow stains across his sneakers. "Look at that shit."

"Why are you telling me? Get him to clean it up."

"I'm telling you because you vouched for the dude. If he can't hold his shit together, he shouldn't be asking for Grade A product."

Jonas stiffened. "You sold him H?"

Bruce stepped closer and poked Jonas in the chest. "I don't sell to dipshits who can't keep their shit together. What's his deal anyway? Got a death wish or something?"

What Follows

"He's into the whole rock star thing. Live fast, die young."

"Don't you have to be fucking famous already before you do that shit?" Bruce shook his head. "Fucking dumb fuck."

Bristol, who had been carefully studying the plaid design on his shirt like it were a puzzle that needed solving, spoke, "Hey, Bruce, Jonas is looking for you."

Bristol's vision blurred in and out of focus. "Shit, I gotta lie down," he said, throwing himself at the mercy of the outdoor couch. He looked up at the night sky with a large grin as if he'd just noticed its existence and was wondering why the fuck it was full of holes.

Bruce pulled Jonas aside. "We all good?"

"I already told you, I'm not stupid."

"Yeah, you keep on not being stupid. The people I do business with, you don't want to fuck with, understand, Hansen?"

Jonas felt a tight twist of anxiety. He'd heard rumors that Bruce beat up on a couple of seniors when they tried to stiff him out of what they owed him. He wasn't a guy you crossed, that was for sure. And the girls he brought to the Belfort's? He'd never really dug too deep there either. Jonas was still carrying a scar on his cheek from the last party when one of the U-Bunnies Bruce introduced him to went ballistic all over his ass for no reason. Jonas scratched the back of his hand.

"You nervous, bro?" Bruce asked.

"Poison oak, caught it down by the lake."

"Maybe you should be nervous," Bruce grunted. "Go look after your buddy, we don't need another dead fucking body. We clear?"

Jonas nodded. But he wasn't clear. Was Bruce talking about Moonshine, or was he threatening Jonas?

As Bruce turned to leave, Jonas called out, "Did you drive me and Cat home that night?"

"I keep telling you, nobody saw the chick that night."

"You didn't call me an Uber or anything?"

"Call you an Uber? Who do I look like, your fucking mom?"

Jonas tried to force back the memories from that night, but the glitches were still noisy and unreadable. The back of a car, an argument? Did any of it even happen?

"I need some smoke," he said, hoping a hit of weed might stop the torrent of confused thoughts cascading through his head. "Want some?"

Bruce slurped from the water bottle. "I don't do that shit, pollutes my body. You go ahead, go get fucked up."

As he walked towards the house, Jonas heard a loud scream. "Someone's in the pool! I think he's dead!"

He recognized the shrill, anxious voice: Peyton.

"Fuck," Jonas said, running to the far end of the garden.

21

The pool lights cast a soft, milky complexion over the water. At the pool steps, Jonas immediately recognized the ratty T-shirt and the body lying face down in the water, arms stretched wide, straggly blond hair swept outwards as if it were drifting to the shallows.

"Fuck!" Jonas waded into the pool, gesturing to Peyton to help.

"Is he dead, is he dead? Fuck, my parents will kill me!" Peyton grabbed her cell phone. "I can't be here," she said, running back towards the house.

"Peyton!" Jonas shouted. "Jesus, some help here?"

Behind him, Bruce had already removed his shoes. "Take his legs, I'll take his arms."

Jonas nodded and grabbed Moonshine's ankles, dragging him back to the shallow end. "Is he still breathing?" he asked, as he and Bruce lifted Moonshine onto the lawn.

"Do we do CPR, or what?" one of the other kids asked, poking at his screen. "I can search YouTube."

Bruce shoved the guy out of his way. "Fucking amateurs." He

knelt down and pressed a palm across Moonshine's chest. He was about to apply pressure when Moonshine let out the breath he'd been holding for the past minute and smiled.

"You're a fucking dick!" Jonas said, barely resisting the urge to kick his friend hard in the ribs.

Moonshine sat up. "Just in the mood for a midnight swim, that's all," he said. "Don't know why ya'll so bent out of shape."

Bruce leaned deep into Moonshine's face. "Next time, I drown you myself, motherfucker," he said, walking off.

Moonshine called out, "Yeah, do the world a favor, right?"

"That was a pretty dick move, Moonshine, even for you."

"Yeah, I hate that, shithead."

Jonas sat on the damp grass. "Fuck, all this Catalina shit's messing with my head."

Moonshine faltered for a moment, looking over the pool as if he was contemplating throwing himself back into its milky depths. "Yeah, kills the party vibe, right?" he said, watching as people filtered out from the backyard and into the house.

"Is that all you've got to say?"

"Ain't nothing I say gonna bring your girl back."

"She wasn't my girl."

Moonshine slicked back his hair. "Like you told that cop, right?"

Jonas felt his blood flow ice cold for the second time that night. Cat was dead, and he'd lied to the police. But what else could he have done? That night was still one massive, unreadable glitch.

"Hey! You wanna dump this shitshow?" Moonshine asked.

"And do what?"

Moonshine wrung the water from the bottom of his T-shirt.

"Go fuck something up?"

"Like what?"

"Like the Rosemont Parade. You in?"
"Will it piss off my mom?"
"Big time." Moonshine smiled.
"Fucking A," Jonas said, grabbing his car keys. "Let's bail."

22

The morning of July 4th, the air pressing down over the Bay was heavy and dry. The fog had burned off quickly, and for the remainder of the day the sun would beat down hard and unforgiving on Rosemont's parched lawns.

Christen stepped out to his backyard patio, breathed in the sweet smell of ripe jasmine and watched the sunrise over the tall palm trees. Alexus had woken him early, insisting he helped with the final arrangements for the parade. He was finding it hard to muster any enthusiasm: didn't people grow tired of it? The mind-numbing receptiveness? The same goddamn thing year after year. It was like people he knew who vacationed at Disneyland every summer, even after their kids had left home. He'd read their Facebook postings and feel nothing but an overwhelming sense of melancholy at the sheer lack of imagination or curiosity for anything beyond their immediate comfort zone.

As he looked over the miserable state of his backyard an old memory, as colorless and faded as his lawn, came back to him. He was watching his father on their small plot of land behind the house where he grew up; he was still young enough to imagine his father as some heroic, invincible figure. It was spring, the frost having finally relented its wintry grip. His father was turning over the topsoil, preparing it for the vegetables he intended to plant in late spring. Watching his father slice into the earth with his shovel had always made Christen feel safe; a routine that assured him the world was as it should be. Maybe that's what he needed to break his own rotten pattern, he thought, as he reached into his pocket, took out a joint; a tether back to something real, to feel dirt and grit under his fingernails again.

He flicked open his lighter and brought the flame to the paper, making sure Alexus wasn't within sniffing distance. He held a long breath, then exhaled a thick, white plume.

Fuck all that mindfulness, hygge crap, he thought as the cannabis flooded his bloodstream. FiltrD had pumped out enough stories on that subject that his skin recoiled at the mention of the word *hygge*. Even though he was Danish, he'd never experienced that mythical state, which to him seemed nothing more than a cynical marketing ploy to sell meditation candles, wool slippers, and crocheted bobble hats to people who didn't know any better. No, this was mindfulness, right here, wrapped in four inches of Zig-Zag paper and inhaled in long, considered breaths.

He drew again. A red-and-grey hummingbird darting around the bird feeder caught his attention. Had he ever seen anything so perfect? The way it hovered in place, as if the creature was a cut-out, superimposed on the world for his pleasure. He studied its wings, which seemed to move so fast that they were hardly moving at all.

From somewhere in the back of his mind, or was it someplace else in the far, unfathomable distance, he heard a scream, followed by someone's name. It took him a few seconds to realize it was his name and the person screaming was his wife.

"Christen!" Alexus shouted, marching out to the patio, an angry wind at her back. "Christen!"

He turned, raising his eyebrows in the "what's up" manner and tried to disguise the joint by flipping it into his palm.

"Oh, that's just great!" Alexus said, watching the trail of smoke rise behind him. "Today of all days. There's a situation."

"Is there?" Christen said, the word "situation" killing his buzz. There was a "situation" at least once a day, sometimes twice, and the Fourth of July it seemed, would be no exception. "What is it? Has Dave Maddens-Smith turned on his lawn sprinklers again? Ignore him, he is an ass, people like him do not change."

"No, I will absolutely not let it go, it's a matter of principle," she said. "Anyway, it's not that, it's more serious, come look."

Christen sighed, and followed her to the front lawn.

"See, I told you, a situation."

Christen looked to the small park across the street and laughed.

"You seriously think it's funny?" Alexus said, glowering.

"No, sorry. Must just be, you know..." he said, waving the joint aimlessly in front of him.

"Well, aren't you going to say something?"

"I suppose it could be worse," he offered, shrugging.

Alexus put her hands on her hips. "How the holy hell could it be any worse, Christen?"

"They could have set them on fire," he said, gesturing to the pyramid of multicolored lawn chairs stacked around fifteen feet high, like the twisted skeleton of a bonfire.

"They didn't leave one, not one," she said, checking out the naked sidewalks of Lansing Avenue.

A few moments later, their daughter, Sydney, joined them, Luna following close behind. "Holy shit!"

"Language, Sydney!" Alexus snapped.

"So fucking sorry," Sydney snapped back.

"Where's your brother. Did he do this?"

"How should I know?"

"Well, is he in his room? Did he come home last night?"

Sydney rolled her eyes. "This whole family's freakin' insane," she snapped, stomping back inside.

Several neighbors had gathered around the stack of lawn chairs, muttering to each other. Dave Maddens-Smith, their immediate next-door neighbor, stepped from his front door, nursing a mug of steaming coffee.

"That'll get a few people riled up," he said, turning to Alexus. "Wasn't one of your lot was it?"

"No, it wasn't," Alexus said. "And what exactly do you mean by 'your lot?'"

Dave ignored the insinuation. "You sure it wasn't one of your kids?"

"Yes I am," Alexus said. "Nice lawn, by the way. I guess you didn't get the notification from the State outlawing all non-essential residential watering?"

"Oh, I got it," Dave said, taking a gulp of coffee. "I just chose to ignore it, free country after all."

"Well, I've got evidence," Alexus said, pointing at the security cameras above her front porch, which she'd positioned to record the immediate vicinity of Dave Maddens-Smith's front lawn. She reached into her pocket and pulled out a thumb drive, waving it at Dave. "I'm sending this to the OPD, they'll get Sacramento involved. I might even call the local news."

Dave smiled. "Knock yourself out. I'm already suing the goddamn State, I could do with the publicity to rally support."

Alexus took a calming breath and directed her attention to a situation which she had some immediate control over. She'd deal with Dave later, right now there was a more urgent matter to address. She snapped into "situation critical" mode.

"Christen, come. Two hours, we'll have them back like nothing ever happened."

"I'm not..." he began, but Alexus had already nailed him with "that" look; a stare that defied any dissension or contrary opinion.

"What?" she said, glaring. "Not high enough yet?"

Christen took a sharp drag, laid the joint next to the porch steps, and followed three paces behind his wife as she addressed the neighbors with a fierce efficiency, directing them as how best to untangle the chairs and set them back in an orderly single file along the sidewalks.

23

"Cougar juice," Gérard Rosseau said, examining the $38.99 Rombauer Chardonnay he was packing into the man's grocery bag.

"Sorry?"

"Cougar juice. Third one this week, right?"

The man, late forties, lean with a permanent tan, blushed.

"Buddy," Gérard said, with a conspiratorial wink. "You're not buying forty-dollar bottles of Chardonnay to serve at the family cookout. That Chinese guy recommend this?"

"Yeah, what of it?"

Gérard nodded. "As I said, cougar juice. Those older ladies, they go crazy for the high-end stuff. Listen, chill it for only an hour or all you'll taste is the cold, and with the alcohol at fourteen-and-a-half percent that's going to get someone passed out or pretty frisky in this heat. Either way you win, right?"

He winked at the man as he packed his final items; a block of tofu and two pre-made salad boxes. "Have a nice day."

The man walked to the parking lot and placed his groceries in the trunk of his two-seat, convertible Mazda Miata.

"Nailed you, motherfucker," Gérard muttered.

The store manager, Gregory Ansel, walked over and tapped Gérard on the shoulder. Greg was built wide and square, like the cab of a Peterbilt truck, with a thick beard and a nose piercing, "All good?" he asked.

"Apart from working a job a monkey could do, I'm freakin' peachy, Greggo."

Greg whispered, "Listen, bro, Cheung says you've been giving him looks again."

"Looks?"

"Like you want to kill the guy or something. We don't tolerate haters here, it's against company policy."

"You can't police against personal feelings, bro. You and I both know who should be running that wine department. Eight freakin' months I've been here. You promised."

"I've told you, head office wants qualified wine associates."

"He's got some certificate from UC Davis, that's all."

"Wine Educator."

"Bullshit. I took my sommelier test."

"Yes, three times and you failed. Old news, Gérard."

Gérard pumped his fist at his heart. "It's not in books, it's in here, in my blood. I'm a freakin' garagiste."

"Because you make wine in your garage?"

"No, because I'm from a long line of garagistes from fucking France, Greggo! Give me one shift or put me out front on the Friday wine tastings. I'd kill it, man, you know I would."

"We're circling," Greg said. "Hang up your apron, we're closing in ten. You got any plans for the afternoon?"

"Spending it with my daughter, then cracking open a couple of bottles. Come over later if you like."

"Nah, got family in town, my wife wouldn't be happy."

"In my experience, wives never are, especially the ex variety."

"Well, I hope never to confirm that," Greg said, wiping a

palm across the back of his neck. "Mave's already bugging me to move out of the apartment and find a house, but the rental market's crazy right now. Must be her nesting instinct kicking in or something."

"Yeah, pregnancy, best not fight it, just go with the flow."

"Is that what you did, go with the flow?"

Gérard paused. "Nope, fought that shit all the way to divorce town," he said, slipping off his apron, throwing it across the bagging area. "Ended up with limited custody of my kid, living by myself in a two-bedroomed craftsman and bagging groceries like a freakin' teenager. Take it from me, go with the flow, and don't expect happiness, it's way fucking overrated. Best you can hope for? Good health and a decent bottle of wine at the end of the day. That, Greggo, is life."

"You all right?" Greg asked, noticing Gérard's gaze had settled somewhere far beyond the store windows. "Looks like your daughter's here," he added, gesturing to the teenager leaning on the hood of a worse-for-wear, shit-brown Toyota Camry in the parking lot.

24

The sickly sweet aroma of candy apples, grilled onions, and stewed hot dogs wafted over the fairground which occupied a patch of scrubland off the 880 Freeway. The Fruitvale Carnival was a tradition that lasted only a few days over the Fourth of July weekend, before moving several miles west to the larger, more lucrative Alameda County Fair.

"Why do we always come here?" Sabine asked, raising the sights and firing the last of her pellets at the balloon; another fail. The young carnie shrugged and took back the rifle.

"Tradition, Sabine," Gérard said. "Been doing this since you were what, five?"

"You do realize it's completely lame, don't you, Dad?"

"Sure. But tradition's important. Why do you think we celebrate Independence Day every year?"

"Oh, not again," Sabine said, rolling her eyes in a manner only a teenager could pull off with any credibility.

"Some people will tell you all this is a throwback, not me. I'll celebrate the Fourth of July until I'm dead or too senile to know what's going on. And do you know why?"

"Because of the Brits," she said wearily, having heard some variant on her father's lecture since she was five years old.

"Not the Brits, the English," Gérard clarified. "Two hundred years ago we told them where they could stick their monarchy and we celebrate by blowing shit up. Not to mention the goddamn English massacred most of our relatives in Northern France, Sabine, don't forget that."

"Yeah, like back in the fourteenth century, get over it already."

Gérard stopped for a moment, watching the gleeful faces of toddlers being carried around slowly on a miniature train. "Got plans to travel there in the next few years," he said. "Track down my family lineage and drink my way through the Loire Valley."

"Really? Am I invited on this family pilgrimage?"

"'Fraid not," Gérard said, walking on. "Some journeys a man needs to complete solo, reconnect with his roots."

"Yeah, sure, got it, Dad," she said and gestured at the Ferris wheel. "Want to ride, or are you too chicken?"

Gérard looked suspiciously over the groaning metal as it clanked through its gears. "Are you sure it's safe? Looks kind of beat up, like your mom's car."

"Only one way to find out," Sabine said, handing over two tickets and jumping into a carriage. "Coming or not?"

Gérard waved his finger at the young carnie as he clambered in. "This better be safe. Precious cargo here, buddy."

At the peak of the first revolution, the wheel jarred to an abrupt stop, rocking the carriage back and forth. Gérard grabbed onto the metal bar, his knuckles peaking white.

"Sure you're okay, Dad?"

"Yep," he said, the familiar sensation of vertigo making him queasy as he took in the view that spread from the East Bay over to the outline of San Francisco, barely visible through the early afternoon haze. "Never been better."

Sabine laughed. "You don't have to pretend, Dad, I know you hate heights. I was just testing, I didn't think you'd actually do it."

Gérard relaxed his grip slightly. "Anything for my girl, right?"

Sabine turned. "If you're going to be sick, just do it over that side, this is a new top."

"Yeah, yeah." He nodded anxiously. "I get it, you inherited your mother's sense of humor, nice."

As she leant back, enjoying the view, Gérard stole a glance Sabine's way: his daughter was changing so quickly it almost took his breath away. Her features were becoming more defined; more like her mother's, strong and determined. Her skin was a lighter hue than Jessica's, though working at the pool had given her a deep tan. Her eyes the same bright blue, but with flecks of brown around the iris. *Sabine could do anything she wanted, be anyone she wanted*, he thought, a huge knot tightening in his throat.

A gust of wind shook the seat, sending a wave of nausea through him. Gérard felt Sabine's hand settle over his. The gesture caught him by surprise. Had it come to that already? The inevitable slide into the child eventually becoming the parent? The days when he could haul Sabine on his shoulders when she was tired of walking, or heal her tears with a funny face were long gone. He was happy back then; he was sure of it. And Jessica? Maybe she was happy for a while too; he'd never taken the time to ask. Maybe if he had, things would have turned out differently.

As the motors cranked as if it were their last gnarled gasp, Gérard held on tight to the safety barrier, his stomach flipping as the wheel lurched forward. The sensation brought him right back to six months ago; the girl's accusations, the police interrogation; his insistence it was all a misunderstanding. It took three months for the girl to finally retract her statement;

the lawyer blaming the meds she was taking for her lapse in judgment. Gérard hadn't pressed charges, he wanted to put the whole episode behind him, get back to some kind of normality. But then there was the missing girl, now the dead girl, and what followed that, he was sure, would be a knock on his door from the OPD. The free-falling sensation he had as the Ferris wheel continued its downward trajectory only seemed to confirm that suspicion.

25

Luna, caught up in the excitement of the morning, bounded around Rosemont Park. Thirty neighbors had now joined Alexus and Christen, helping untangle the lawn chairs and setting them back on the sidewalk. As they reached the final few at the bottom of the pile, Luna began to whine loudly and scrape her nails through the grass to the brown dirt below.

"Luna!!" Alexus snapped.

The dog ignored the command.

"Christen, can you please get her back to the house?" she said, handing a chair to one of her neighbors.

"Sure," he said, standing and stretching out his back. It was the excuse he'd been waiting for to steal a quick draw on the joint he'd left smoldering on the front porch earlier. He reached and grabbed Luna's collar. She flicked her head around, snapping at Christen.

"Hey, calm down. What have you got there, girl?" he said, peering under the tangle of metal and fabric. As he pulled away a chair, he saw something sparkling in the sunlight. Luna

What Follows

barked, nudging his hand out of her way. She set her front teeth around the object and dragged it from the undergrowth.

Christen barely had time to register what was in the dog's mouth before she ran off to secure a safe burial spot. "Luna! Come!" He jogged over to where she was digging up a flurry of black dirt in the shade of a large redwood tree.

"What the fuck?" Christen said, kneeling. At first, he thought it was maybe a slab of hide, or a discarded kid's baseball mitt; but hides and mitts didn't have perfectly manicured, purple fingernails. He picked up a twig and poked at the object. It was clear this was a hand. A woman's hand.

The skin, which he was certain once had a tawnier hue, was now a mottled gray. At the point where the wrist should have connected to the forearm, the severed veins and shredded sinews were pitted with dirt. Using the twig, he flipped over the hand and reached to untangle the bracelet, separating the cheap metal from the dried clumps of blood. As he did so, his stomach lurched, his world telescoping to the dimensions of a pinprick as the letters on the bracelet came into focus. *Wendi.*

He let it fall back onto the wrist and placed his hands flat on the ground, his head humming like the feedback from a speaker. Instinct told him he should let Luna bury the trinket; maybe even bury the hand himself, but he was out of time; Rosemont's Mayor, Ben Strauss, was standing directly over him.

"You all right there, buddy?" he said, laying a hand on Christen's shoulder and looking down at the hand. "Is that what I think it is?"

Christen nodded.

"Jesus," Ben said, scratching an eyebrow. "That's going to blow an almighty hole in the day's proceedings."

26

The tremor that rumbled through the Bay Area that evening was a momentary jolt; just the earth saber-rattling its intentions for anyone who was paying attention. It happened just after the grand finale of the display over San Francisco, and the last patriotic burst of fireworks shattered into ashes and showered down in a weeping-willow of red, white and blue.

Alexus was sitting at her bedroom mirror, her mind numb from the day, her body still buzzing from the bottle of red wine she'd drunk that evening. She wiped off her makeup with slow, determined strokes, her eyes blurring in and out of focus as she worked. The matter-of-fact statement, like it was no big deal, spoken by that officious detective from OPD came back to her. *"No parade today. Not all over my crime scene."*

The words had landed with the brute force of a sucker punch. She pressed the cotton wipe harder against her cheek. And that woman detective––the snippy one who'd insisted they interviewed every neighbor in a three-block radius––she was just as severe and belligerent. Even Ben Strauss, the goddamn Mayor, had backed them up. *"There was no way to get an injunction at this short notice, and it was a crime scene, after all, Alexus,"* he'd insisted, giving her that peevish look that made her want to knock the horn-rimmed glasses off his face.

She felt a tear prickle at the back of her eyes, but quickly dismissed the sensation, took a deep breath, and reached her fingers inside a tub of moisturizer. *"Don't. Do not be an idiot,"* she said to herself. This wasn't how she did things; not Alexus Hansen. She didn't cry, not at stuff like this. It was at that moment, as she applied her night cream across her chest, she decided. The elections were still a few months away; maybe there was a way to redeem herself, cast off the shadow of what had gone down today. The Rosemont Parade cancelled, the first time in fifty-three years, and it had happened on her watch.

As Christen walked into the bedroom, the tremor startled them both. It lasted less than a second or two; a tiny nudge that rattled the jars of cream on Alexus's vanity, and just for a moment, blurred Christen's reflection into something unrecognizable before focusing back to normal again. He walked behind her, laid his hands over her shoulder and smiled. It was probably the wine playing tricks, but for a moment, Christen's smile seemed disconnected, and like the tremor, fleeting and unknowable.

Three blocks away, Ben Strauss was lounging in one of his four Adirondack chairs arranged in a circle around a firepit, the flames flickering in time to the breeze playing around the deck. He was alone, sipping on a hot mug of herbal tea. He didn't mind being alone; what he minded was being lonely. But he didn't feel lonely, not happy nor sad either, just a constant hum of indifference that buzzed around him like an impenetrable aura. The clinic had advised him of the drug's side effects and he'd signed the consent form in full recognition of that fact. He was fine with it. Feelings often got in the way; made things messy and unpredictable. The vibrations from the tremor passed through the redwood timbers on the deck and seemed to reverberate from inside the wood and pass through his bones. He set his mug down and gripped the sides of the chair. For a moment, he was defenseless, impotent and at the mercy of a power much greater than himself; greater than anyone. It wasn't God you surrendered yourself to--he'd realized that sitting at the first and only AA meeting he'd attended--no, what you surrendered to was your true self; only then could you be free.

Eight miles north, at the old pier at Point Richmond, Gérard and Sabine sat on the hood of Gérard's old truck, just as they did every year, and watched the sky over San Francisco bloom into a sparkle of noise and color. Sabine was leaning close to her father, feeling safe in his familiar smell of wine and old leather. She was thinking about Jonas Hansen, how someday they might both do this together--if he'd ever reply to any of her damned texts.

Gérard's thoughts were more of a practical nature. He looked at his daughter, Sabine, so beautiful, perfect in so many ways he could never be. He wiped a hand across his eyes; he was glad it was dark, where tears were safe, hidden. The tremor seemed to ripple along the soft ground and vibrate through to the undercarriage of the car. They both looked at each other, waiting for something more, but it didn't happen, at least not then.

In the family room of a mock-Tudor mansion in Rosemont, Jonas Hansen was watching the end credits of *The Wolf of Wall Street* on a flat-screen TV positioned above the red stone fireplace. Beside him on the couch, Moonshine had fallen asleep, sedated by his own weed. Bored, Jonas scrolled through his Instagram feed for a few minutes before stopping at a post from Sabbi2000. He flipped through several selfies she'd posted yesterday. Sabine was posing in a red bikini at the Rosemont pool. *When did she get so hot?* he thought as he zoomed in on the long stretch of her legs and her lips which were pouting suggestively to the camera, though her eyes seemed to smile, like she was in on the joke.

"*What the fuck was that, bro?*" Moonshine said, sitting bolt upright as the glass chandelier in the kitchen rattled in its fixture. "*Nothing, just a tremor,*" Jonas replied. Just another tremor. He'd felt enough of them to know this one would pass; they always did.

In a basement of a faded Victorian house in Alameda, Bruce Ho stood naked under the lamplight, his hands gripped around the head of someone he'd met earlier that afternoon, Fallon, if he recalled correctly, though the name wasn't important. Fallon was knee-bound, fingers wrapped around Bruce's buttocks, face anonymous and sweating. The tremor was like a jolt traveling from his bare feet, rocking the bookshelves and shaking a photo frame to the floor. Bruce looked down. A photograph of Fallon with a woman; they looked like a couple, smiling, arms draped around each other, comfortable in their own skins. He jerked harder on Fallon's head, then pushed it away in disgust. As Fallon looked up, hand wiping cleanly across lips, Bruce detected a trace of fear, or was it pity? Sometimes he found it hard to tell. He leaned over, drew back his arm and pounded his fist into Fallon's face until his knuckles bled raw and Fallon's pathetic look was hidden under a wash of blood, mucus and splintered bone. *"Fuckin' faggot,"* Bruce said as he scrambled to pull up his jeans, giving Fallon a parting kick to the ribs as he left.

On the borders of Lower Rosemont, Jessica Swift switched on her local NPR station and sat at the small desk in her living room. The correspondent's voice had a hypnotic quality to it as he talked about the ongoing drought and its wider implications for the California ecosystem. The tremor seemed to happen right on cue, as the correspondent mentioned the words *"climate change"*—as if the earth itself was shrugging in agreement, adding its own exclamation point. The full cup on her desk rattled, spilling some coffee over the papers she was intending to read that night. She blotted them with a towel and flipped through the college application forms Sabine had given her to look at at the beginning of summer. As much as she might have wanted to, she couldn't delay it much longer. In just over a year Sabine would be in college. It was a reality she'd been able to push to the back of her mind, but now it was time to face the inevitable; Sabine had worked hard, Jessica had made sacrifices, it was what was expected, but the rationalization did little to blunt the pain. She looked around the tiny apartment as if waiting for another tremor; but one, she figured, was enough for one night.

What Follows

In the Glenview district of Oakland, Detective Moira Shaughnessy was slowly unzipping her hoodie under the spill of street lights that bathed her bedroom with a soft glow. Slipping off her jeans, she placed her knees on the edge of the bed, reached back to untie her ponytail and ran her hands through her hair until it fell over her face. The tremor—a bullet releasing under the pressure of a trigger pull—shook the foundations of her apartment building. She held her breath, expecting another release of pressure, which never came. Instead, it was the footsteps crossing the creaky floor of her apartment that sent a jolt of energy through her. His arms were strong and forceful, his cologne expensive and exotic as he positioned himself behind her. She was *"the most goddamned beautiful thing,"* Martin Dugdale said, leaning deep into her neck, and reaching to unclip her bra. For the time it took the tremor to pass, she believed him.

Roscoe Tanner had parked at his favorite lookout point at Grizzly Peak, classical FM turned to full volume as he watched the fireworks bloom and fall over the San Francisco skyline. He liked the colors, but could live without the noise; it reminded him too much of gunfire. He sensed the tremor as the pine air freshener dangling from his rearview mirror shook. Looking over the houses dotted precariously on the hillsides, he was sure they shuddered, as if from the cold. He'd always considered these kind of tremors nature's elbow nudges; there to remind everyone of their insignificance in the world. He glanced at the photograph of Teresa he'd placed on the passenger seat. They drove up here most weekends when she was alive. Teresa loved the view; loved to see the world spread out below her like she had some dominion over it. The last time they were both here, the doctors had given Teresa four weeks to live; she survived three. That night, overlooking the Bay, she'd made him swear to her that he wouldn't die alone; that, when the time came, he would have someone care for him with the same love and dedication he'd shown her. They'd both cried hard that night, maybe harder than they'd ever cried.

He took the photograph and held it in his hand. *"You and your dang promises,"* he muttered, wiping his tears. Christ, he hated how grief seeped into your bones like it belonged there. Grief, he'd come to believe, wasn't something you passed on your way someplace else—it was the journey and the destination. He lived there now in Grief Town, had himself a studio apartment on the main street and neighbors he never spoke to. But what followed grief, he had no business predicting, he could only hope it was something better than this.

PART II

TREMORS

27

Come Monday morning, there was no respite from the heat. News reports called it the longest Californian heatwave since records began. For the past several weeks, one of the local news stations had been broadcasting segments on Urban Survivalist, mostly retired men residing in the outer suburbs of the Bay Area, who had constructed military-grade fallout bunkers stocked with five years' worth of canned food, water, and an arsenal of weaponry to defend themselves against the hordes of the hungry underprepared they were certain would come knocking at their reinforced steel doors. *These idiots were watching too much* Walking Dead, Roscoe Tanner thought. He could barely shop for the next two days, let alone half a decade from now. *"Darned numbnuts,"* he muttered as he clicked off the TV and headed out. He was sure as eggs were eggs, Francisco and Marta Gomez weren't fretting about climate change, the unremitting drought or some fabricated Armageddon.

Detective Shaughnessy handed Tanner a stiff brown envelope as he walked by her desk.

"Gifts? You shouldn't have."

Shaughnessy offered him her usual "almost" smile. "That woman in Rosemont, the lawyer with the shitty attitude?"

"I recall," he confirmed, opening the envelope and slipping out a small thumb drive.

"Some footage she wants us to look at."

"Pertaining to my homicide investigations?"

"Doubtful," Shaughnessy said. "Something about her neighbor watering his lawn in the drought. Bullshit, right? I wouldn't even bring it to your attention, but Dugdale's all up in my face about it."

"You got a hotline to the Chief all of a sudden?" he said, examining the drive.

"Saw him on my way in, that's all. If I knew there was a dedicated chain of command protocol, I'd have called you down three floors to take the envelope yourself."

Tanner huffed. "Shouldn't this be Rosemont PD's purview? It's not like they're elbow deep in homicides over there."

"Dugdale's of the opinion it shows our support for the larger community, not just Oakland."

"Dugdale said that?"

"Those exact words."

"Fudge. You know what they call this?" he said, tossing the envelope onto his desk. "First World problems."

"Damned straight. Oh, and Mrs. Gomez is here. I put her in the interview room."

"You did? When?"

"Ten, fifteen, maybe."

"Did you offer her some tea or coffee?"

Shaughnessy shrugged. "Didn't cross my mind."

Tanner shook his head as he scrambled to gather his

paperwork and grab a plastic bag he'd signed out of the evidence room earlier that morning.

"Mind if I tag along?"

He hesitated. "Em, I'm..."

"We are meant to be partners. Or was there another chain of command memo I missed?"

"Sure," he said, shoving the bag into her hands. "Knock yourself out."

"Your husband's not with you, Mrs. Gomez?" Tanner asked, as he and Shaughnessy sat across from Marta. Her eyes were foggy and red, as if she'd been rubbing them and hoping that when she took her hands away all of this would have just been a terrible dream.

"He is very upset, Detective Tanner," Marta said, taking a handkerchief from her purse and dabbing her eyes. "He blames himself for not being a good papi."

Shaughnessy spoke. "We do prefer to talk to both parents in these situations, it saves us a lot of interview time."

"This is my colleague, Detective Shaughnessy."

Marta nodded, studying the stern face of the detective, before turning her attention back to Tanner's kinder, softer bearing.

"We understand it's hard," he explained, "but the more information we have, the sooner we can figure out what happened to your daughter."

"And you find whoever did this to Catalina?"

There was a steel to Marta's voice that sounded more like a demand than it did a question. Tanner let it go. "Tell me about Catalina."

Marta smiled. "She was smart, you know, straight-A student. Always worked very hard, very hard."

Tanner leaned forward, spoke softly. "What was your daughter like, Mrs. Gomez? Who did she hang around with? What did she like to do?"

"She was a good girl, always, never got into any trouble. I don't know why someone would do this."

"Anyone that might have been a dangerous influence on Catalina?"

"No," Marta said. "I would know."

"Were you familiar with all of her friends, Mrs. Gomez?" Shaughnessy asked. "It's just with all this social media these days it's hard to keep track of everyone your kids are making friends with."

"Catalina was a good girl," Marta insisted. "We told everything to the police when she went missing. You have all the names," she added, pointing at Tanner.

"It might seem like we're treading the same ground, but it's important. Tell me about the last time you saw Catalina."

Marta wiped a tear from her eye. "Friday last week, in the morning. She kissed me before she left." She ran a finger along her cheek. "Catalina said she was going to the charity."

"The Rock Paper Scissors Art Cooperative?" Shaughnessy asked, checking the notes.

Marta nodded.

"What did she do there?"

"She helped with the children. She was always good with the little kids, they connected with her."

"And after that?"

"She has a guitar lesson every Friday, then she told me she was going to the Boba Lounge," Marta said. "She works there until ten. The owner, he trusts Catalina to close up, do the cash, everything. I kept telling her she should ask for a raise."

"So she didn't come home that night?" Tanner asked.

Marta wiped her eyes. "We called the police Saturday morning."

"You didn't think to contact us the night your daughter went missing?" Shaughnessy asked.

Marta shook her head. "Francisco, he think I worry too much. He said she was with her friends, she would come home later. We were both very tired, we fell asleep. When her room was empty that morning, I felt like I would be sick. That's when I told Francisco, I don't care, now I'm calling the police."

"You did the right thing," Tanner said. He pulled out the evidence bag, carefully removed the shoes and placed them on the table. "Do you recognize these?"

Marta glanced and shook her head.

"They're Jimmy Choos," Shaughnessy explained.

"Jimmy's shoes?" Marta asked, confused.

"Choo, Jimmy Choo," Shaughnessy said. "Where would Catalina find the money to buy two-thousand-dollar shoes, Mrs. Gomez?"

Marta picked up a shoe, examining the bottle-green leather with a python-coat design and a crystal anklet that sparkled as she turned them. They were the kind of shoes those trashy women she'd seen walking the underpass at night wore, she thought, flipping them over in her palm. She shrugged. "They are not my daughter's."

"She was wearing them when we found her," Shaughnessy insisted.

"No. Catalina would never wear shoes like this. She is a good girl. A mother knows." Marta threw the shoes back on the desk as if they were garbage. "Do you know how she—?"

"We're doing everything we can to find out," Tanner said.

Marta knotted her handkerchief around her fingers like a

rosary. "When can we get our daughter back? She needs to come home now, be with her family."

"Well, we still need to—" Shaughnessy began.

"Soon, I'll make sure of it myself," Tanner interrupted.

"Thank you," Marta said, reaching out to grasp his hand. "You are a good man. You'll find whoever did this, I know you will."

Tanner felt her grip tighten as she spoke, sensing his hesitation. "Please. Please try."

Tanner nodded as Marta's fingers wrapped tighter around his hand, holding on, as if it were the only thing keeping her from drowning.

28

"Got a live one," Alyssa Bennett said, looking over the man with a glare of suspicion she reserved for young men hovering over her desk and refusing to surrender their names.

Jessica peered through the corridor window. She could make out the man's back, a black hoodie pulled tight around his head.

"Did he give a name?"

"Says he'll only talk to you."

Jessica hung up and buzzed herself into reception. "Jessica Swift, can I help you?"

The man turned. She recognized the young handsome face. He looked a lot less dangerous than he did a few days ago when he'd thrust a gun against her temple.

"Nelson," she said, showing her best *"trust me"* smile. "How have you been feeling?"

Nelson took his hands from his pockets and showed them to Jessica. The skin was raw and peeling; red blisters spreading uniformly from his wrists to his knuckles.

"And there," she said, gesturing at his crotch. "The same?"

Nelson thrust his hands back in his pockets and nodded.

"It's good you came, but you shouldn't have left it this long."

"I'm here now, ain't I? You got something to cure this shit? A shot, pills, something?"

"Maybe," Jessica said, "but I need that list, like I asked for."

Nelson shook his head. "You always been a cold bitch?" he said, handing Jessica a crumpled sheet of paper.

"Is this all of them?"

"Yeah. Don't have no addresses, just names."

"It's a start," Jessica said, taking the paper.

"So, do I gets my treatment now?"

Jessica gestured for him to sit, which he did so, reluctantly.

Jessica sat in the chair next to him. "Let me explain how the course of treatment works."

"Course? I don't got time for no course, bitch."

"You call me bitch one more time," she said, gesturing at his crotch, "and you'll be scratching until it falls off. Are we clear?"

Nelson shuffled the heels of his high-ball basketball shoes across the carpet.

"The treatment consists of two shots. In the meantime, no sexual activity. No penetration, no oral. Keep your pecker in your pants, Nelson. Can you do that?"

Nelson nodded, scratched the back of his hand. "So, we gonna do this or what?"

Jessica hesitated. "Em, not for a couple of days."

"Fuck that!" Nelson leapt up, spun around and spread his hands either side of Jessica's chair. He pushed his face close into hers. "I gotta gets this fixed. Now. Like today."

He pulled back, placed one hand on the wall and scratched hard at his crotch with the other. "Motherfucker!"

"We don't have any of the vaccine here, it's on back order from the manufacturers."

He kicked the chair leg. "That don't gonna work for me."

Jessica stood. "It's going to have to, I'm sorry," she said, placing her hand on his back.

He shrugged it off. "How abouts I take my list back until you get those motherfucking shots? How's that work for you?" he said, making a grab for the paper.

Jessica pulled it back, tucking the paper behind the waistband of her pants. "I wouldn't recommend it." She pointed at the CCTV cameras. "Security takes seventeen seconds to get here and three seconds to drop you and cuff you. We have drills every week."

Nelson stepped back. "Wouldn't have made no difference, right, coming here when you told me? If you don't get the shots ain't no use. The system's fucked, bitch."

He swiped his arm across the reception desk, sending a stack of files and boxes sprawling to the floor. Alyssa moved her chair back, settling her finger on the emergency buzzer. Jessica looked at her and shook her head. Alyssa complied, but hovered her fingertip around the buzzer, just in case.

"Where are you going?" she asked, as Nelson reached for the door.

"Find out which one of those bitches gave me this fucking shit."

"Two days, Nelson," she pleaded. "Come back in two days, we'll figure this out."

There was no answer, just the sharp draft from the door slamming into place.

In her office, Jessica unfolded the list of twenty-two names, and flattened it on the desk. She reached for her clipboard and cross-referenced the names with the names on her spreadsheet. There were at least seven matches—hardly good news—it meant there were another fifteen infected girls that were off their radar. Studying the bottom of the list, one name caught her attention. She glanced over to today's *Oakland Chronicle* on her desk:

> *Every parent's nightmare. Teenager's body recovered from Lake Temescal. Will there be justice for Catalina? OPD's Chief Martin Dugdale on the record.*

Jessica's thoughts immediately turned to her own daughter, Sabine, as she studied Catalina Gomez's eternal smile beaming from the front pages.

29

The kid, sixteen, with a whisper of facial hair on his chin, leaned back in the interview room and stretched out his legs. He looked up with an arrogant tilt of his head as Tanner and Shaughnessy pulled up a couple of chairs.

"So, let me get this straight," Tanner said, adjusting his pants belt as he sat. "You're confessing to selling Schedule One narcotics to Catalina Gomez on the day she died?"

"I don't know shit 'bout the day she died," the kid said, turning to his attorney.

"My client is correct," the young woman explained. "You have no evidence the drugs that ended Miss Gomez's life were sold to her by Mr. Debose."

The woman was fresh out of law school, Tanner guessed, a certified student attorney finding her feet on the lowest rungs of a mid-sized law firm.

"Is that right?" he said. "And you recall the exact details of this transaction, Shawn?"

The kid shrugged. "She had to have it, you know? *Please, please*," he said, affecting an effeminate tone. *"I'll do anything, Shawnie, just get me some junk. Your da man, Shawnie."*

"Junk? Heroin?" Tanner asked.

"Them junkies?" Shawn said, leaning across the table. "Can't crush their Oxy for a quick hit, no more." He ground his thumb into the desk for effect. "Turns the pills into some fucked-up paste or somethin'. The drug companies ruined it for us all, man. But brown sugar? Inject that shit," he added, tapping hard on his forearm, "and that monkey's gone to heaven."

"Did Catalina strike you as an addict? A habitual user?" Shaughnessy asked.

"Like a habit, what?"

"A junkie. Did she act like she knew what she was buying?"

"I just sold her shit, I ain't no damn social worker."

"But you know the type, right, seeing as you're such a big man on the streets," Shaughnessy said, checking her notes. "Strange we haven't seen your name come up as a suspect or a known dealer. Maybe you're not as big a deal as you think you are, Shawn."

Shawn frowned and bit on his thumbnail.

"No record of any Shawn Dubose in my notes either," Tanner said, flipping his notebook closed. "You're a ghost, Shawn, either that or you're just serving us both a steaming bowl of fresh crapola."

"Ain't lying," Shawn protested.

Shaughnessy leaned forward. "Tell us one thing that would convince us otherwise."

Shawn shrugged, scraped his heels across the floor.

"Here's what's sticking in my craw about this cockamamie story of yours, Shawn," Tanner said, pacing the room. "Why admit to the crime? What's in it for you?"

Shawn shrugged. "Jesus told me to. I'm redeeming myself."

"For the love of Pete. Let me ask your lawyer here. What's your name again, ma'am?"

The attorney, prim, with an anxious demeanor, looked up. "Emily. Emily Scheve."

"Miss Scheve, please advise your client on the penalty as a juvenile offender, for possession with intent to sell Schedule One narcotics in Alameda County."

Emily paused. "It's Shawn's first offense. With a lenient judge combined with the pressure on the courts to incarcerate fewer young African American men, I'd plea for twenty-four months in a Juvenile Detention Center with three years' probation."

"Geez Louise, that's a heck of a deal, right?" Tanner said, dropping back in his chair. "You know what we call the JDC around here, son?"

Shawn shook his head.

"Prep School," Tanner said. "You'll be incarcerated in a segregated area with gang members a couple of grades ahead of you where you'll serve a kind of apprenticeship. With good behavior, you're back on the streets in twelve months and a few thousand in the bank for taking the rap for a crime you didn't commit and an advanced degree in dealing and pimping. Hardly a career path."

Shawn picked at the skin on the back of his hand. "You got a better offer?"

"I don't think we need to detain my client any longer, Detective Tanner," the lawyer said. "And these bullying tactics? Is this how you always conduct interviews with minors?"

"Not always," Shaughnessy said. "We made an exception with Mr. Dubose."

Tanner leaned his palms on the table. "Tell me, Shawn, what if your very young, very green attorney here doesn't secure you the generous deal she just pulled out of thin air…"

"I didn't––" the lawyer began before Tanner interrupted.

"What if the DA prosecutes you through the criminal courts,

tries you as an adult? Then what? You think whoever you're protecting's going to come save your dang patootie then?"

"Patootie? You talk like a motherfucking hick," Shawn said, bouncing his leg. "We done here?"

"One thing, Shawn," Shaughnessy urged. "One statement or piece of information that proves this story of yours."

Shawn thought for a moment, bit his lower lip. "The chick," he said, rapping his fingers on the table. "She always shot herself up in the leg, like here." He pointed to the back of his calf.

Tanner and Shaughnessy looked at each other.

"Didn't want nobody know she had a problem. I figured it was some vanity shit. That a good enough statement?"

Outside the interview room, Tanner and Shaughnessy leaned against the wall and watched Shawn and his lawyer, escorted by a uniformed officer, walk towards the processing room.

"What's your take?" Shaughnessy asked.

"Like I said, bunch of horse-hooey. He's been paid by someone to take the rap. Someone who doesn't want us poking around whatever's going on here. There's always a chain in these things, Shaughnessy, a line of command that leads to the top dog. My guess, they've sent the runts of the litter to nip at our heels, keep us occupied."

"But the back of the calf?" Shaughnessy said. "We didn't release that to the press. What if the little prick's on the level?"

"Doesn't really matter if he is or isn't. If Dugdale and the DA buy his story, it's just another teenage overdose, accidental death. The case gets solved before the election and the Mayor's record looks one homicide cleaner."

"If Shawn goes down, that's some kind of justice."

"That's not justice, Shaughnessy, it's just good PR."

"That's some pretty cynical shit, right there."

"If you find something to be optimistic about in this dung-show, be sure to let me know," Tanner said, walking away. "I need a dang coffee."

30

Jonas parked his Jeep Wrangler at the parking lot under the 580 Freeway and walked towards the park at the north of Lake Merritt. He knew Bruce came here most afternoons after his lake run and worked out on the pull-up bars positioned along the running trail.

"What the fuck do you want?" Bruce said, his face flushed, his body pumping like a fierce piston on the bar.

"Just talk," Jonas said.

Bruce executed one last haul, launched himself nimbly from the bar and landed on his heels, gymnast-perfect, on the grass. He scouted the road. "I can't sell you shit out on the street. Get the fuck out of here," he said, wiping a towel under his armpits.

Jonas tensed and wondered if it was a good idea coming here at all. Bruce always stared at him as if he were waiting for him to say the wrong word, or look at him the wrong way; any excuse to punch him in the face, Jonas thought, or worse. "I'm not buying gear, I need some information."

Bruce sized him up. "'Bout what?"

"The night Cat disappeared."

"I heard you got real fucked up," Bruce said, stabbing his

finger in Jonas's face. "And if anyone asks, I didn't sell you nothing, we clear?"

"Yeah, sure, whatever," Jonas stammered. "About Cat, did you like drive us both home that night?"

"I had my own shit to deal with."

"How did I get home then?"

"Magic carpet ride? How the fuck do I know?"

Jonas looked over at the calm shimmer of the lake. "I should tell the police," he said. "That I was with Catalina that night."

Bruce snapped the towel tight between his hands. "You sure about that? Maybe you imagined it, like some hallucination or some shit."

"I guess... I don't know..." Jonas stammered.

"If you don't know, then what the fuck you going to tell the police, Hansen?" Bruce said, stepping closer. "Officer, I think I was with Catalina Gomez that night, but I was too stoned to know what the fuck went down. Good luck with that."

"The police already questioned me."

Bruce's eyes narrowed, his fingers wrapping tighter around the towel. "Yeah, what'd you tell them?"

"Said I followed her on Instagram, never really met her."

"Any pictures of you guys? You weren't dating, right?"

"She was careful about protecting her brand or whatever, said she got less followers when she posted photographs of herself with a dude."

"She was a smart girl," Bruce said, poking Jonas in the shoulder. "You be the same kind of smart. Now, get the fuck away from here before someone sees us talking. I don't need that kind of attention."

Jonas nodded. "Sure, yeah, whatever you say."

Bruce smiled, his eyes leering over Jonas as he pressed his index finger gently on Jonas's lips. "And keep that pretty mouth of yours shut, we clear?"

Jonas's stomach churned as Bruce's finger lingered on his lips for a second longer than was necessary before he wiped the tip along the scar on Jonas's cheek as if he were rubbing off a stray crumb of food. *Shit*, Jonas thought, maybe Bruce wasn't waiting for an excuse to punch him in the face after all.

Watching Bruce jog back towards his truck, Jonas relaxed. What did he really know about Catalina? He'd only hung out with her a few times, he didn't know her at all, not really. Maybe she was into hardcore partying, just like he'd heard. That kind of gear was easy enough to source around Oakland if you knew the right people; people like Bruce.

Speaking with the police would be a mistake; there'd be too many questions he couldn't answer, too many blank spaces in his memory. Nobody remembered seeing him and Cat together that night and for now, that was good enough.

31

The following Thursday, Tanner sat at his desk rereading the case reports. Shaughnessy was interviewing Wendi Chee's colleagues––at least those willing to talk. Tanner didn't have the stomach for interrogations today, and anyway he figured his partner would cut through them quickly with her trademark brusque efficiency.

He was still unsure about Shaughnessy; whether he admired her no-bull crap, tell-it-like-it-is attitude, or did he want to take a chisel and burnish off those sharp edges? Or maybe his own edges were eroded to such a smooth polish these days and Shaughnessy's bluntness just highlighted the fact.

Refusing to let his mind wander too far down that highway, he opened Wendi Chee's file; it made for thin reading. Second-generation Korean, mom left while Wendi was still in diapers, father unknown, no extended family, and a series of foster families until the age of sixteen. It was an all too familiar story.

Tanner turned his attention to the autopsy report: evidence of sexual activity before death, with deposits of lubrication from the same condom brand they'd found in her purse. A partly smoked joint in her handbag had thrown up another DNA sample, male according to the marker, but there was no match found in CODIS. Judging by the clean cut, her hand was severed with a sharp instrument; maybe a cleaver or a chef's knife.

He flipped the file closed and glanced over at the newspaper on his desk. Catalina's death was still making headline news, while Wendi's death had barely made the back pages. Disturbingly, Tanner had also noticed an unsettling shift in the media's reporting of Catalina's case over the past two days. It was the nature of the twenty-four-hour news cycle, a machine that demanded fresh meat, new perspectives, opposing views. OPD had no new evidence to share with the press, so the press grew tired of asking and instead poked around the Alameda County DA's office until they found someone, who for the right price, was willing to talk. A junior administrative assistant with a history of bad debts had leaked the submitted evidence, adding his own flourish and embellishments.

"A juvenile was in custody, had confessed to selling narcotics to Catalina Gomez on a regular basis. She was a user who performed sex acts to satisfy her addiction. She had a dark side, evidence of which the police had suppressed to garner more public sympathy and press engagement."

It was the narrative twist the press was hungry for. If there was one story juicier than the murder of a beautiful young girl, it was the story of a young girl whom no one really knew. A girl who ran in the wrong circles, hid her secret life from those closest to her; lived a double life where she'd rolled the dice with death and lost.

One of the more hysteria-mongering online news sites had secured screen grabs of Catalina's Instagram account before it was taken down and posted a handful of photographs. They'd seen fit to blur out some of her body parts, which only added to the risqué nature of the photographs, which were in reality no more than the postings of a young girl confident in her own body. The argument made no difference—Catalina's death was no longer the headline: it was Catalina herself, her reputation questioned, her narrative spun to suit the headlines of the day. It made Tanner sick to the stomach. Whoever Catalina was, he was dang sure she wasn't the person the press were painting her to be.

As he pushed the newspaper across his desk, a young officer approached, alerting him that there was a woman in reception, insisting she had important information to share concerning the Catalina Gomez case.

"Sure, send her up," Tanner said, slipping on his jacket. "My day ain't complete without one more wingnut theory to chew on."

32

Shaughnessy had been interviewing for three straight hours; a cheap pageant of perfume, bright lip gloss and spray tan. Several of the women had asked for money in exchange for information––information Shaughnessy guessed would turn out to be false or a waste of her time. Several women had offered the obligatory *"no comment," "fuck you,"* or *"go fuck yourself."* She'd been propositioned three times, the last offer came from an Asian transgender by the name of China Jade, who looked up and down the length of her as if they were about to eat Shaughnessy for dinner––*"as they say, honey, everything tastes better on a cracker."*

When an anxious black girl in her early twenties sat across from her, Shaughnessy caught something in the girl's eyes she hadn't seen in the others. Fear.

"You were friends with Wendi?"

The girl nodded, scratching at her stick-thin forearm.

"And you were with her that night, at the underpass?"

"Yeah. I wanted to go to the House, but Wendi said it was closed."

"The House. What's the House?"

The girl shuffled uncomfortably.

"Tiffiny?"

"I shouldn't have said nothin'," Tiffiny said, her body language stiffening. "I came here to talk 'bout Wendi, that's all. If you're gonna push me to talk about other shit, then I gots places I need to be." Tiffiny grabbed her bag and stood.

"Unless where you've got to be is an OPD processing room, you'd better sit your ass down."

Tiffiny flopped herself back in the chair with a resigned sigh. "Why you so cold, bitch?" she said, leaning her arms across the table. "I didn't have to do this shit, none of us did, but we're here, ain't we? So where's the fuckin' respect?"

Shaughnessy checked her notes. "You saw someone pick up Wendi?"

"It was like ten," Tiffiny said, wiping a hand under her nose. "This guy's driving past like he's checking what's on offer. I figure he was another pussy tourist, but Wendi thinks he's on the level."

"Did you see the man she approached?"

"Nah, but he's driving one of those expensive electric cars."

"A sports car?"

"Longer, like a sedan but sleek, you know, curves down real low at the back."

"If I showed you some pictures, do you think you could recognize the brand of car?"

"Maybe."

"What about the security cameras at the underpass?"

Tiffiny laughed. "The kids use that shit for target practice, they ain't worked for years."

"Okay," Shaughnessy said, pushing her chair back. "Let me get some photographs of those cars to look at. Maybe that'll jog your memory."

"A coffee, two sugars, be freakin' nice," Tiffiny called out as Shaughnessy pulled the door closed.

33

"How can I help you, Mrs. Swift?" Tanner asked, offering his hand as Jessica stood at his desk. The woman had a confident grip and her eyes held a steely intelligence that seemed to be taking the measure of him as he greeted her.

"It's Ms. Swift." Her tone was equally firm and efficient.

"My mistake," Tanner said, brushing a scatter of cookie crumbs from the seat and standing, as if to attention, as he pulled back the chair for her.

"Oh, right, thanks," Jessica said, sitting. Tanner's old-school politeness had caught her off guard. She was expecting either a gruff, impatient pen-pusher, like she usually encountered at the OPD, or someone like the spikey female detective they'd sent to interview her and Mary at the tent encampment.

"Swift?" Tanner said. "Haven't I heard that name before?"

"Taylor. I get it all the time. I'm her sister from another mother," she said, smiling.

Tanner shook his head. "Nope, you were at the encampment. You talked to my partner, Shaughnessy."

"I remember, she was hard work. Wouldn't want to be across the table from her during an interrogation."

Tanner studied Jessica as she tugged at the front of her blouse, which was in his opinion, opened one button too low; not that he was about to complain. She was a striking woman, unusually so, with eyes that held a smoky, cornflower moodiness and stood out like bright blue pebbles next to her light-brown skin.

"So, how can I help?" he asked, catching himself staring a little too intently as she reached into her bag.

"Jessica Swift, Senior Health Investigator, Alameda County," she said, sliding him her card. "I'm sure the OPD is very aware of the serious epidemic in our city."

Tanner's stomach dipped; another liberal leaning do-gooder with an elevated social conscience. "Which particular epidemic are you referring to?" he asked. "The homeless epidemic? Gentrification? Narcotics? Handguns? Boba Lounges? We're kind of backed up on epidemics at the moment, I doubt we have the resources to tackle another one."

"Syphilis," Jessica said, without missing a beat.

Tanner scratched the back of his head. "That's a new one."

"No, actually, it's not. We notified the OPD last year when the first cases came to our attention. Not that anyone had the time or inclination to follow up."

"Communicable diseases are not OPD's purview."

"Not your purview? Are you aware which segment of the population is most affected by syphilis?"

"Sex workers?" Tanner offered.

"Amongst others, yes," Jessica confirmed, taken aback by the accuracy of his answer. "But it also spreads rapidly to addicts, mothers and their unborn children. It only takes one person with the infection and within a few months it's an epidemic."

"And what do you propose law enforcement do?"

"Oh, nothing. I've been working with the county too long to

expect the OPD to lift a damned finger to help the poor and desperate in our community."

"So, why are you here?"

Jessica unraveled the paper Nelson had given her. "That young girl, Catalina Gomez? Her name came to our attention."

"Came to your attention?" Tanner asked, as Jessica pushed the paper back in her purse. "If you have information pertaining to the case, it would be your legal duty to share it with us."

"I'm well aware, thank you, detective," Jessica said, choosing her words carefully. "Catalina's name was on a list we received."

"What kind of list?"

Jessica set her hands on the table. Tanner quickly checked out her ring finger; it was bare, with only a faint ghostly circle of a wedding ring past.

"If we suspect a member of the public has symptoms we ask for the names of their most recent sexual partners so we can contact them for treatment."

"And Catalina's name came up on one of these lists?"

"I recognized the name as soon as I saw it."

Tanner opened his notebook. "Who provided you the list?"

"I can't say. It's a public health matter."

"It's also a police matter," Tanner insisted.

Jessica's steely-eyed gaze returned as she folded her arms. "And tell me, detective, how does the Health Department maintain trust if we surrender confidential information at the drop of a hat? It's critical these people come in for treatment. If the OPD starts asking questions, rounding them up, they'll go underground, the epidemic spreads, no one wins."

Tanner paused. Maybe the woman had a point. "I'm struggling with how this information helps my case any."

"That's not my job. I felt it was my duty to tell you what I know."

"It wasn't mentioned in the autopsy report."

"Unless they were testing specifically for syphilis, it wouldn't be. It's a tricky disease to confirm. Even after we treat patients, they can still test positive afterwards."

"I guess the lab could run some tests, see if it's fact or fiction."

"Oh, it's a fact," Jessica said, scraping back her chair. "The question is what do you intend to do about it?"

Tanner sat back. She wasn't giving up without a fight: the kind of woman his father might have called a firecracker; the kind of woman he'd spent the best thirty-two years of his life married to.

As Jessica stood to leave their eyes locked for a second too long, their handshake lasting a few beats longer than officially necessary. Tanner glanced at the photograph on his desk. *This one's for you, honey.* He took a deep breath and jumped in feet first.

"Ms. Swift, one moment," he said, tugging at his jacket sleeves.

Jessica turned and smiled. It seemed to radiate warmth into every pore of Tanner's skin, urging him to finish what he'd started.

"Em, I was wondering if you'd like to discuss this further, maybe over a coffee or maybe some wine?" Tanner felt his armpits sweat. "That's if you're into that sort of thing."

Jessica tilted her head. "Discuss this further?"

Tanner ran a finger under his shirt collar, sensing his neck was flushed. "Em, it doesn't have to be about the case, we could discuss the other thing you mentioned." *Judas Priest!* He was bad at this. But there was no turning back. He was saddled up, riding into the wilderness, secure only in the fact he was keeping his promise to Teresa.

"The other thing?" Jessica said, feeling a tug of unexpected empathy towards the awkward but well-mannered detective.

"You'd like to discuss syphilis over a glass of Chardonnay? Are you always this compelling when asking women out on a date, or am I special?"

Tanner felt the flush rise to his cheeks. "We could discuss herpes maybe? Gonorrhea? Expand the subject matter," he stammered.

Jessica laughed out loud. It had been a while since a man had inspired that reaction in her. "You have my card," she said. "But, just so you know, I require a full screening. Nothing unusual, just the regular communicable diseases, STDs, that sort of thing."

"Jeepers, em..." Tanner began.

"Relax, I'm teasing," Jessica said, flashing him another radioactive smile.

"Yes, ma'am," Tanner said, sensing the woman had just put him through a test where he'd barely scraped a passing grade.

As Jessica walked out, he picked up the phone. "Ambrose, get the lab to run another blood test on Catalina Gomez. Syphilis. Yep, you heard me right. Much obliged."

34

Tanner and Shaughnessy sat in the reception area of The Rock Paper Scissors Art Cooperative, located in an abandoned warehouse on San Pablo Avenue. The non-profit provided workspace for a loose affiliation of artists, writers and aspiring musicians, with free after-school and summer programs for kids in the Oakland School District.

"Never had much time for art," Tanner said, looking around the warehouse which had the whiff of untreated dampness mixed with the oily secretions of fresh paint. "My wife, Teresa, was a teacher, she was more into this kind of thing."

"I went to Burning Man one time," Shaughnessy said, studying a large, cubist metal sculpture which she guessed represented a pregnant woman––the abdomen was shuffled to the side of the body and the head lay sideways across the shoulders. "Too much dust, too few toilet facilities. Sharing a yurt with bunch of over-medicated hippies for a week was not my idea of a vacation."

"You don't seem the type."

"Yeah, that whole scene played out before I turned twenty-one and got my shit together."

"Careful, you're treading dangerously close to oversharing, Shaughnessy."

"Hey!" Shaughnessy called out to the receptionist, who was laser-focused on her cell phone. "Can we get this shitshow started already?"

Two minutes later, Cassandra Winters, an African American woman wearing a bright-yellow tribal-style dress that gave the impression she floated rather than walked, escorted them into a conference room lined with a gallery of framed photographs. She gestured at the man stood in the corner whispering into his cell phone. "This is our chairman and one of our most generous donors, Ben Strauss," she said.

Ben hung up, walked towards them, hand outstretched.

"I've met you before," Shaughnessy said, narrowing her eyes. "Rosemont, last week. You threatened us with an injunction for cancelling the parade."

"I'm the Mayor. I had to give some kind of pushback. You didn't take it personally, I hope. Please, sit."

"We'd rather stand," Shaughnessy said.

"You stand if you want," Tanner said, pulling back a chair. "My knees don't take kindly to being vertical for too long these days."

"How can we help Oakland PD this morning?" Ben asked.

"Catalina Gomez––" Tanner began.

"Such a tragic loss," Cassandra interrupted with a solemn shake of her head. "She had such a big heart, her aura was always so warm," she added, with a distant look in her eyes as if she were attempting to materialize Catalina into the room.

Reluctantly, Shaughnessy sat. "Catalina volunteered here, correct?"

"She was a rare find," Ben confirmed. "Dedicated, good with the kids, she'll be sorely missed."

"Did anything strike you as unusual about her behavior in

recent weeks? Did she seem more distracted than usual? Unduly worried or stressed about anything?" Tanner asked.

"I'd have felt that," Cassandra said, nodding. "In her aura."

Shaughnessy leaned back and smiled. "And this aura of hers, did it tell you anything else, like where she was headed after finishing up here? Or if she was meeting someone?"

Cassandra stiffened. "That's not how it works."

"All right, let's haul the pony back on the track here," Tanner said. "There are some inconsistencies surrounding Catalina's death. Did you ever know her to take drugs? Anybody she met here that might have seemed suspicious or threatening?"

Cassandra shook her head. "Catalina hated drugs. I didn't even see her smoke."

"Doesn't mean she didn't," Shaughnessy said.

Ben cleared his throat. "I agree with Cassandra, we never saw Catalina take anything, at least not on the premises, but you can never really be a hundred percent sure. We cater to a diverse cross-section; schoolkids, artists, musicians; I doubt it would have been hard for her to buy whatever drugs she wanted, if she put her mind to it."

"She was volunteering here the day she disappeared?" Tanner asked.

"She was scheduled but she didn't turn up. I guessed she was busy with her family or something," Cassandra said.

"You didn't try to contact her?"

Cassandra smiled. "It's not a job. We don't fill in time sheets. Sometimes volunteers turn up, sometimes they don't."

"Did Catalina usually bail on her obligations?"

"Not once that I can remember."

"So, Catalina failed to turn up for work, might or might not have taken drugs, and if she did, they would have been easy for her to source from someone on the premises," Shaughnessy said. "Certainly paints a different picture."

Ben sat forward in his chair. "I doubt we can ever fully know anyone, can we Detective Shaughnessy? Now if that's all?"

"For now," Tanner said, easing to standing. He studied one of the framed photographs—several teenage boys standing in front of Lake Merritt Boat House. "When was this taken?"

"Last week, a Leadership Training field trip," Cassandra confirmed. "We like to keep our publicity current."

Tanner slipped on his reading glasses. "This boy," he said, tapping on the glass, "you know him?"

Ben walked over. "Yes, vaguely, Shawn Dubose, I think."

"Did you ever see Catalina and Shawn together?"

"Not that I recall," Ben said. "But then again, I'm not involved in the day-to-day, that's more Cassandra's thing."

"His mother signed him up for the art camp but I haven't seen him in a few days. It happens," Cassandra offered. "The kids get bored, drop out."

"Sign of the times, right?" Tanner said, handing her his card. "If you, or Mr. Strauss remember anything else, please call me."

Cassandra nodded. "Are you any closer to finding out who did this to Catalina?" she asked, placing her hand across her heart.

"Getting closer by the hour," Tanner said a little too brightly, as if he were trying to convince himself it were true.

35

Outside the Awoken Café, a homeless man handed out copies of Street Spirit to the scurry of evening commuters who had better places to be and were in a hurry to get there. They had no interest in reading about Oakland's homeless crisis; they witnessed it every morning, wrapped in newspapers and blankets in the shop doorways, and smelled its urine-soaked presence as they emerged from the escalators at the BART station each night.

Jonas was waiting outside for Moonshine Fever to finish up this evening's set. An all-ages venue, the Awoken Café was a hangout for teenagers too young to enter the local bars and clubs. As the band ended their set with the self-penned, "Biscuit Chokehold," Jonas checked his cell phone. His Snapchat alerts were still circling around Catalina's death. It was the usual circus of hysterical postings that typically began with OMFG! or WTFF? Someone had forwarded a posting from what he guessed was a White Supremacists website––a screen grab of Catalina with the misspelled caption, *"One less immigrunt. One more job for an American,"* splattered in thick, white font across her face.

How could someone hate that much? It turned his stomach, but he guessed trolls of all flavors slithered out from under their rocks at times like this. Catalina was a hardcore partier, took hard drugs, slept with older, rich dudes. On the other hand, she was a straight-A student, did charity work; helped in church on Sundays. Or maybe she was all those things? No one was ever wholly good or bad. At the end of the day, it was down to whose version of Catalina you believed. Reputations were handed out and chewed on like Halloween candy when it came to social media, and Catalina's reputation was being passed around as if it was everybody's right to comment on. *People posted that shit because it made them feel better about their own crappy lives*, he thought. Catalina didn't deserve this, no one did; except maybe rapists, child molesters, and murderers. He'd throw in fans of the Dave Matthews Band in there too, just for kicks.

Moonshine mumbled, "*Thanks a lot, fuckers,*" to the audience. Jonas pushed through the crowd and caught up with him as he laid his Gibson Les Paul into its case.

"We slayed it, bro. They loved us. Even the new stuff," Moonshine said, raising his hand for a high five.

"There was new stuff?" Jonas asked.

"Asshole. I wrote three new songs last week."

"Sorry, dude, I came late."

He snapped the case clasps shut and tugged the greasy strands of hair from his face. "You can buy me a latte for being a douche."

"Seems fair," Jonas agreed. "I need to talk. Important shit."

"That'll cost you a donut, Hansen, two if it's like super extra."

They headed towards an empty table at the far end of the café.

Moonshine set his teeth around a glazed donut. "This about Catalina, the dead chick?"

"Way to go on the sympathy, Moonshine."

"She the same one that gave you that?" Moonshine asked, gesturing at the scar on Jonas's cheek that was taking its time healing.

Jonas ignored the question. "The news said she overdosed. That's fucked up. Never had anyone I know die before."

Moonshine shrugged. "You gotta let that shit go. Like my pops says, life's as short as a gnat's ball sack."

"What? So your dad's a philosopher? Thought he ran a liquor company," Jonas said with a smile.

"Fuck you, Hansen. Now what's this important shit that cost you two donuts?"

"Talk me through what went down."

"You don't remember shit?"

"I remember Bruce sold me edibles, real trippy stuff. Catalina came later, I think… I don't know, it's fractured, like when you lose your connection on an online game, all glitchy."

"We had a gig that night. When I arrived at the party you were already fucked up on the front lawn like some redneck meth head."

"And Catalina?"

Moonshine rubbed his hands down the side of his jeans. "She was a no-show, dude, I'd have remembered."

"You didn't see us together, arguing or something?"

"You weren't in no state to argue with nobody."

Jonas wiped a hand across his face. "I keep thinking I maybe did something, something fucked up to Catalina."

Moonshine put his cup down and shook his head. "Man, I think you need a drink. Another of that Kombucha shit?"

"How did I get home?" Jonas asked.

Moonshine rubbed his shoulder where the guitar strap had dug into the skin. "You're asking the wrong man. I was making out with some U-bunny. She was hot, too, like an eight at least."

Jonas had a flashback, a glitch of static. Riding in the back of a car, him insisting on having the window open, someone shouting at him that it was too cold and demanding he close it up.

As Moonshine headed to the bar, Jonas noticed an alert ping on Moonshine's phone. He glanced down––someone asking for details of the next gig. As the alert faded, he noticed his screen saver was a photograph of Moonshine with his arm around Catalina.

"Dude," Jonas said, as Moonshine sat. "Didn't think you were into her."

Moonshine grabbed back the phone. "Like you rightly said, the girl had an appetite for partying. Met her at a couple of gigs, that's all."

"And?"

"And nothin'," Moonshine said, brushing his hair behind his ears. "She wanted a selfie with the lead singer, I ain't gonna object."

"You might have mentioned it."

Moonshine looked down into his coffee. "You won't get this, being who you are and all, Hansen, but chicks like Catalina, they ain't for the likes of me." He lowered his voice. "Why do you think I started the band? Ain't for the fucking Spotify streaming royalties, that's for shit sure. Now, you need a ride home?"

"What, on your Lime scooter?"

"Fuck you," Moonshine said. "My pops thinks I don't know where he hides the keys to that truck he's always waxing like he's getting off on it. If you're up for smoking a couple of J's, *mi casa su casa*, but you gotta help me load the gear."

"What am I, your roadie?" Jonas said, slipping on his jacket.

"If you want a ride home," Moonshine said, handing Jonas his guitar case, "you're my freakin' roadie."

36

"Your dad really remodeled this place for you?" Jonas asked as he looked around the cavernous basement which housed an 89-inch 4K TV, several gaming consoles, state-of-the-art surround system, and a band rehearsal area.

"That's my pops. Generous as fuck."

"Don't think I ever met him."

"And you won't, not tonight," he said, clicking on the Sonos wireless speakers and blasting out the Orwells' "They Put a Body in the Bayou". "He's back in Kentucky. Some bullshit issue with the liquor transportation company, probably screwing some truck-stop pussy out on the sixty-five, right about now."

"Is that why your parents divorced?"

"Shit no," Moonshine said, laughing. "It's how they met. Romantic it ain't."

Jonas patted the walls. "Soundproofed?"

"Yep, pops didn't want no hassle from the neighbors, but if we get complaints," Moonshine opened a cabinet containing a pair of gleaming black-and-silver 85 Finnlight hunting rifles, "I got these suckers. Father and son edition."

Jonas glanced at the guns with a shrug. He was drawn to the

small rehearsal area in the opposite corner, stacked with drums, microphones and three guitars. "I guess he's supporting your career," he said, twanging one of the guitar strings.

"Either that or the shithead's tired of hearing my bull and figures this way he don't need to listen no more," Moonshine said, handing over a joint.

Jonas twisted the dry, loosely packed paper around his fingers. "You still smoking this hillbilly shit?"

Moonshine opened an old cigar humidor, around four feet high and two feet wide, with several built-in drawers filled with ready-rolled joints. "Got a major supply to blow through yet, Hansen."

"Sell it, bro, make some money, buy some grade A shit."

"Nah. This has sentimental value, vintage. Once this is gone, ain't no more, be like losing a part of my heritage, you know?"

"Not really."

Moonshine lifted the joints to the light. "Nurtured this myself on Grandma's land. She was too far gone on the Alzheimer's express to know what the fuck I was cultivating. Harvested the whole shitshow before moving. Heritage, bro, got to keep true to your roots."

Moonshine lit the joint and passed it over. Jonas took a drag, coughed, passed it back, waving the smoke from his face. "Dude, you'll be freakin' dead before you smoke all that shit."

"Got something on the more alternative scale, if you prefer," he said, sliding open another drawer.

Jonas peered inside and examined the syringe and open pack of what he guessed was heroin. "Shit. Did Bruce sell you that?"

"Open only in case of emergencies, bro," Moonshine said, pushing the drawer closed.

"You do know that shit will fuck you up, right? Catalina? Jesus, Moonshine!"

"Save the lecture. Been there, told it to go fuck itself. You down for a screening?"

"Sure, but put that shit away," Jonas said, laying the joint in one of the ashtrays around the basement and looking at his friend as if he were seeing him in a new light, and wondering what he really knew about him. Moonshine was a loner, had transferred from out of state in his sophomore year, but had enough smarts and attitude to ingratiate himself with the right school clique. Maybe that's what had attracted Jonas in the first place. Moonshine wasn't your regular Rosemont catchment area stiff; he probably wasn't any place's regular catchment area stiff.

"What you got?" Jonas asked, deciding that at least if he was here, Moonshine might be tempted to lay off taking the heroin.

"Wolf of Wall Street?"

"Unrated?"

"Unrated?" Moonshine said, stabbing the remote. "I was born freakin' unrated. Now, pass the J, and stop looking at me like I'm toxic, bro, I get enough of that from the old man."

37

"There's no sense to be made of it," Tanner said, returning the file back to Madeline Ambrose.

"Here, let me look," Shaughnessy said, joining them at Tanner's desk.

Ambrose smiled. "As Shakira predicted, the tox don't lie."

Tanner raised his eyebrows. "Doesn't it look suspicious to you? Our victim had no history of drug abuse, no puncture marks other than the one on the back of her calf. Addicts begin shooting up in their arms, the legs are a secondary location when they've wrecked all other points of entry."

"Suspicious, yes, unusual no," Ambrose said. "What if she was a first-time user? Wanted to play it safe. Miscalculated the dosage?"

"That'd be some darned bad luck."

"Like getting pregnant the first time you have sex," Shaughnessy said. "Bad shit happens to good people."

Tanner sighed. "So, what's the official COD?"

"The medical examiner confirms a coronary embolism," Ambrose said. "The heroin was contaminated with an unidentified cutting agent, probably some kind of powder which solidified in her bloodstream. We're still investigating the source."

"A dang heart attack?" Tanner asked, wiping a palm across his face.

"The cutting agent clotted close to the arterial veins blocking the flow of blood to the heart. It would have been mercifully quick."

"Not much of a blessing, is it?"

"It gets worse. The girl at the camp, Wendi Chee? We found the same contaminate in her bloodstream."

"Same COD?" Tanner asked.

"Negative. Wendi Chee was strangled. Had a string of ligature marks around her neck."

"Why would someone pollute their product? Don't you want repeat business?" Shaughnessy said.

Ambrose shrugged. "They either didn't realize the cutting agent would clot the way it did, or they did it on purpose."

"Could be someone's out to make an example," Tanner offered. "The way Wendi's hand was severed could be a warning of some sort."

"Or he could just be a sick fuck and used her hand to jerk off with," Shaughnessy said.

Ambrose and Tanner both looked at her.

"What? Like that hadn't crossed your mind?"

"Any leads on why the hand was planted where it was?" Ambrose asked.

"Nothing solid. But I doubt anyone's going to pile up a bunch of lawn chairs just to cover up a severed hand."

"So, placed there after the fact, knowing we'd find it."

"No doubt," Shaughnessy confirmed.

Tanner sat on the edge of his desk. "If this report stands, it's what, accidental death? I'm not buying it." He reached under his table and placed the Jimmy Choo shoes on the desk.

"Bit flashy for you, Tanner," Ambrose said.

"The mother insists our victim would never have worn them, let alone have the money to buy two-thousand-dollar shoes."

"Then they're a gift," Shaughnessy said. "Rich, older boyfriend she didn't want her parents finding out about. It's not like they kept tabs on their daughter. Seventeen-year-old girl taking heroin and hanging with the wrong crowd. Hardly model parenting."

"Based on your extensive experience of child rearing?" Tanner snipped.

"Just calling it as I see it, that's all."

Tanner turned over the evidence bag in his hand. "Maybe she borrowed them, or just wore them for a short while, dancing or something, or in a club?"

"You think these are dancing shoes? You don't know much about women, do you?" Ambrose said.

"Barely enough to get me into trouble," Tanner confessed.

"Could be cosplay, some fetish maybe," Shaughnessy offered. "BDSM, bondage, dominatrix?"

"Mother of pearl, Shaughnessy, the girl was seventeen."

"Just a theory."

Tanner balanced one of the shoes in his hands, his imagination still unable to make the leap. "Maybe they're not even hers."

"So, what's the plan?" Ambrose asked. "Play like Prince Charming and slip the shoes on the feet of every damsel in the land?"

"Cute. Don't you have a retirement you should be planning for?"

"That I do," Ambrose said, standing. "Next month. There'll be a party."

"That'll be something to look forward to," Tanner said.

"If you're invited," Ambrose said, turning to face

Shaughnessy. "But you, I like you. You'll get an invite, but you've got your work cut out partnering with this sentimental vintage edition."

Shaughnessy nodded. "I don't do sentimental."

"No shit," Ambrose said, walking away.

"So, what next?" Shaughnessy asked, skimming the report.

"Catalina's guitar teacher," Tanner said, grabbing his jacket. "The officer who took his original statement didn't do his homework."

"I meant about the report. If it's an overdose with no signs of malicious intent by a third party and the prosecutor agrees on accidental death, it's game over."

Tanner grabbed his keys and a file from his desk. Glancing briefly at the envelope containing the flash drives Alexus Hansen had sent in, he shoved it further under a pile of stray papers. "It ain't over till the obese lady sings, Shaughnessy, didn't they teach you that at that academy program you told me you aced?"

"Must have been sick that day."

Tanner grabbed his jacket. "Let's go talk to this Rosseau character, see if we can't shake his tree."

38

As Gérard Rosseau yanked open his rusting garage door, the late morning sunlight struck the cement floor in bright swathes of white. On the opposite side of the street, a group of cyclists had gathered. MAMILS––*Middle-Aged Men in Lycra*, Gérard reckoned. He'd read the acronym in some online article on the benefits of cycling for the over fifties. He patted the wide girth of his belly still bloated from the pot of coffee and pancakes he'd had for breakfast. He wouldn't be squeezing his ass into any Lycra anytime soon, that was for damn sure.

As he watched the men clip cleat to pedal and cycle towards Martin Luther King Boulevard, he felt a familiar itch of irritation. Five years ago, nobody was cycling to North Oakland for shits and giggles. He had hoped his neighborhood could have resisted the relentless march of gentrification a while longer, but he'd already noticed its slow, insistent creep. It would always start in the same benign manner: the opening of an artisanal coffee shop followed by the *"Off-The-Grid"* food trucks on the weekends. By the time the store selling *"I Hella Love Oakland"* T-shirts had opened between the vegan bakery and wood-fired pizza restaurant, the transformation was all but inevitable. There was one upside. His house had doubled in value and the rental value was twice what he paid in mortgage. But he was still house rich and cash poor, and with home prices in the Bay Area skyrocketing, there was no place else he could afford to move to, unless he headed further east into the depths of suburbia, which would have felt like a long, slow death.

He dragged a large, plastic wine vat, swishing with the weight of the Malbec and Mourvèdre blend he'd been fermenting for the past three weeks from the back of the garage and set it at the entrance to what he called his "wine cave". The name was a stretch. It was little more than a basement lined with racks groaning under the weight of several hundred wine bottles. As he walked back, he noticed two long shadows cast along the garage floor.

"We got a problem here?" he called out, reaching for one of the five baseball bats he kept around the house. His neighborhood might have been changing, but that didn't mean shit, it just made it more attractive to the addicts and lowlifes looking to make a quick buck on anything they could steal and sell to satisfy their next fix.

As the figures moved closer, he tightened his fingers around the bat; he wasn't about to let another couple of opportunist punks make off with another one of his vintage guitars. "Don't think I won't use this, motherfuckers."

"That won't be necessary," Tanner said, stepping into the garage and showing Gérard his badge. "I'm Roscoe Tanner, this is Detective Moira Shaughnessy."

"Gerald Rosseau?" she asked, stepping into the welcome shade of the garage.

He laid down the bat. "Gérard," he corrected her. "It's French, like in Gérard Depardieu?"

A blank look from Shaughnessy.

"The French actor? Looks like a pissed bear?"

She shrugged and took a swift inventory of Gérard's garage.

"We're interviewing anyone who had contact with Catalina Gomez in the days before she disappeared," Tanner explained.

"Fucking tragedy," he said. "Young girl like that."

"Catalina came here for guitar lessons, is that right?"

"Used to. Haven't seen her for months. Said she had too much schoolwork, what with this being her junior year. Always happens."

"Really?" Shaughnessy tugged back the bottom of her jacket to reveal her gun and badge. "What if we told you her parents were under the impression their daughter had been coming here every Friday evening for the past year?" she said, flipping back through her notebook. "The last time was the night she disappeared."

Gérard rocked back on his Cuban heels, stuffed his hands in jeans pockets. "Then I'd say someone's spinning you a big fat one, detective."

Shaughnessy gestured to the three dresses hanging from the garage shelves. "Are you in the habit of collecting women's clothing?"

"They're my daughter's," Gérard snapped. "She stays with me every other weekend. Now, if that's all you got, this wine's not going to bottle itself." He bent down and dragged a second vat of fermenting wine towards his wine cave.

As Shaughnessy studied her notebook, Tanner sensed she was set to volley another hardball question at Gérard. He placed his hand on her forearm in the "back off" manner.

"So, Mr. Rosseau, did Catalina show any talent for the guitar? I play some myself, just a few chords. Well, three actually."

"So long as they're the right three," Gérard grunted, shoving the vat over the lip of the doorway. He stood and stretched his back. "Talent? No. She was impatient, like all the kids these days."

"Blame Guitar Hero, right?" Tanner said.

Gérard chuckled. "Ain't that the truth. If they can't rip a Van Halen solo after the first lesson, they want a damned refund."

"Was Catalina like that?"

"She was into the singer-songwriter stuff, seemed happy enough learning the basics."

"Any thoughts as to why she stopped coming?"

"Why do any of these kids quit?" he said, wiping his brow. "Shit gets too hard."

"Why would Catalina lie to her parents about coming here?" Shaughnessy asked. "Was she hiding something maybe?"

"No idea. That's your job, isn't it?"

"Your daughter? Would she have ever met Catalina?"

"Maybe. Sabine sleeps over if her mom's working late."

"Where were you the night of June 27th?" Shaughnessy asked, tapping her pen impatiently on her notebook.

"I was working at Natural Foods, like every goddamn Friday."

"Doing what?"

"Bagging groceries for the fucking one percenters, that's what."

"And when do you leave?"

"After eleven. I was helping with the stocktaking."

"And after that?"

"Came straight home, opened a bottle, slept like a baby."

"Anyone else in the house that could confirm that?"

"Nope."

"That your truck?" Tanner asked, gesturing at the cream, 1988 Toyota pickup outside.

"Use it for transporting my grapes."

"Dang noisy beast, right? Big V8 like that. I bet your neighbors must hear you coming five blocks away."

Gérard thrust out his chin. "Go ahead, ask them. It's not exactly party central around here these days. Lights out before ten, not like in the old days, noise all damn night long, but you gotta move with the times, right?"

Shaughnessy, impatient, tapped on her notebook and stepped closer to Gérard. "You like young girls, Mr. Rosseau?"

"What the fuck is the right answer to that question?"

Tanner checked his notes. "In July of last year, a student of yours accused you of inappropriate behavior."

"Fuck you! Shit sticks no matter what, right?" Gérard said, shaking his head. "I said all I got to say to OPD. It's not a time in my life I want to revisit anytime soon."

"I'm sure the young girl––how old was she, fifteen?––would agree," Shaughnessy said.

"No evidence, no charges. The girl was mentally unstable, been on medication since she was nine. I did nothing, still paid the price."

"Still, there's no denying the coincidence, right? A student of yours is found dead not two miles from here and, last year one of your female students accuses you of inappropriate behavior. We wouldn't be doing our job if we didn't follow up."

Gérard crossed his arms. "Unless you've got some proof or a warrant, then get the fuck off my property."

Tanner flipped his notebook closed. "Right you are," he said. "Just doing our job. We'd do the same for anyone's daughter," he added, gesturing at the dresses hanging off the garage shelves. "You have a nice day now."

39

Sabine often wondered about the blueness of the sky on days like this. Was its color comparable to anyplace else on the planet, or was that deep and unforgiving shade of blue reserved only for California? She'd never traveled out of state (jumping over the state line into Reno for a quick selfie in front of South Lake Tahoe's casinos hardly counted). Having never left the country, even though her father had insisted she acquired a passport the week she was born, she had little to compare California to apart from the curated Instagram postings of her well-traveled friends, whose trips to Europe had become an expected summer family tradition, and as such were bitched about for several weeks beforehand.

WTF! Italy again. Yawnsville!

Three weeks in Spain. So not going to be fun.

OMFG Greece, ugh! Sucky Wi-Fi!

They had no idea how freakin' lucky they were, Sabine thought. The only vacation her parents had taken her on was to Disneyland when she was five years old. After the divorce, her mom rented a small cabin in South Lake Tahoe for a week each June. After seven years of the same glass-calm lake that was too cold for swimming, casinos she was too young to enter, and her mom's insistence on visiting Costco to stock up on groceries to avoid the expense of eating out, the tradition had worn painfully thin. She may as well have stayed home—*different location, same shit*. Maybe she could persuade her dad to take her to France with him one day, unless that too was doomed to his *"could have, should have, would have"* pile.

She blew her whistle at two young boys hurtling down the side of the pool. They looked sheepishly at Sabine, then cannonballed into the water. She waved her finger at them; they smiled, snapped on their swim goggles and dove under the shimmering blue.

Sabine took a sip of water and felt a light tap on her ankle.

"Hey, Lower Rosemont, what's up?"

"Lower Rosemont"—the phrase was a scrape of fingernails down chalkboard for Sabine. Lower Rosemont skirted the Oakland city border and consisted mostly of older buildings and rent-controlled apartments. *"Lower Rosemont"* was a phrase used to ensure the kids understood their pecking order in the school hierarchy. The fact it was Jonas Hansen speaking to her softened the blow, but only slightly.

"I'm working," she said, electing not to look at his broad, suntanned shoulders nor his eyes, which she knew would be sparkling like the afternoon sunlight reflecting off the pool.

"Yeah, I see that. You getting off soon? Bunch of us heading down the lake if you want to hang."

"What's the occasion?"

"Just hanging."

"You're sure a Lower Rosemont wouldn't cramp your style?"

Jonas laughed. "I'll make an exception."

Sabine looked to the floor, avoiding staring too closely at the symmetrical sculpt of his abs and the light wisp of hair poking from the waistband of his orange board-shorts.

"You hear about that girl, Catalina?" Sabine asked.

"Yeah, it's all over my feed. You knew her?"

"Met her a couple of times, I think, at my dad's house. She was always posting on Instagram. Police say it was an overdose, but a bunch of people reckon she was raped and murdered."

Jonas stiffened. "People don't know shit."

"Yeah, probably just posting lies and shit to get more followers," Sabine said, blowing her whistle at a small boy launching his lunch into the deep end of the pool. "Shit, I'll have to go fish that out," she added, jumping down from the steps.

"Tonight, Lake Merritt boathouse," Jonas said, walking backwards and throwing her a cocky smile.

"I'll consider the offer," Sabine said, grabbing a long pole with the netting attached and scooping under the surface.

"See you there, Lower Rosemont."

He flashed another smile at her; it reminded her of the first time he'd smiled at her, during chemistry class some two years ago. It still had the power to make her feel funny, like she was being tickled gently from the inside out.

40

Sabine and two other girls, whom she vaguely recognized from school, peered through the wire gate at the entrance to Lake Merritt boathouse. Jonas was stabbing at the numbers on the lock while Moonshine read off the combination from his cell phone.

"Isn't this like, illegal?" Sabine asked, as the guys high-fived and pushed the gate, which opened with a loud scrape across concrete.

Moonshine turned to Sabine, swatting thin loops of hair from his face. He was wearing a baseball cap with the words John Deere embossed across the front and the peak pulled down low. She'd seen him around school; the kind of kid who hung around the fringes and never seemed to settle in one place or with any one group.

"Ain't illegal if we don't get caught," he said, adjusting the peak of his cap to afford himself a better view of Sabine.

He sounded like one of those lost boys from a TV series she and her mother had once watched, set in some rural American state she'd never visited. "That doesn't seem right."

Moonshine laughed. "I'm fuckin' with you. The owner's a friend of ours, he's cool so long as we don't fuck up his fleet."

"Fleet?"

"Boats," Jonas said, ushering the other girls onto the jetty.

Sabine craned her neck to the dockside and checked out the sleek, black gondolas rocking gently in the lake water. "Can you even drive one of those things?"

Moonshine and Jonas doubled up in laughter. "Drive? It's called rowing. And yeah, we row. Summer jobs, me and Moonshine, thirteen an hour, plus tips."

"Beats flipping burgers, but you gotta get used to the goose shit and the overabundance of wildlife," Moonshine said, running ahead. "Mind you, don't step your expensive sneakers in all the crap, I ain't inclined to fish your ass out of the lake."

"I don't have expensive sneakers," Sabine called out.

"I wasn't addressing you," he shouted back, catching up to the other girls and throwing his arms around their shoulders.

Sabine followed a few steps behind as they ventured towards the boats. They were a recent addition to the lake's activities: thirty-five dollars for a thirty-minute ride in a Venetian gondola, plus an extra twenty dollars for an amateur tenor from Oakland's Operatic Revels to serenade you with a medley of Verdi's greatest hits.

As the sun tipped down behind the surrounding buildings, the lake glimmered like a throw of black satin in the twilight. The loop of lights strung fifteen feet above the footpath hemming the lake burned soft yellow, their reflections dancing in the water. They always reminded Sabine of Christmas, as if every Oakland resident had removed a single light from their home and hung it across the lake in a symbol of peace and unity. It was the kind of community-based initiative the Mayor's Office would have passed in a heartbeat, she thought.

Jonas called to her from the rear of one of the gondolas.

"You're riding with me, Lower Rosemont." He was arranging the cushions and flicking the oar back and forth through the water, sending a cascade of ripples along the black satin.

"You're not like going to try and sing to me or something lame like that, are you?" she said, stalling for time and glancing nervously around, sure that someone must be watching. "And stop calling me that. My name's Sabine, it's French."

"Well, pardon freakin' moi," Jonas said, stretching out his arm.

She hesitated.

"You can ride with Moonshine if you prefer, but his shit's like hillbilly weed. If you want to hack your lungs out, go for it."

"Fuck you!" Moonshine called, as the two girls stepped onto the adjacent gondola.

"No, fuck you, Moonshine," Jonas said, gesturing at Sabine. "What are you waiting for, Frenchie, a formal invitation?"

Sabine took a step towards the dockside. If they were caught and her mom found out, she'd surely be grounded. But at the same time Jonas was beckoning her with that easy, carefree smile that seemed to promise everything would be all right. Junior year had been a grind; prepping for SATs, four after-school swim meets a week, and she'd been working most of her summer just to earn spending money. The week in Tahoe had come and gone in a blink of an eye, though while she was there it dragged on for what felt like a lifetime. Didn't she deserve some fun? And Jonas was there, smiling at her, holding out his hand, assuring her it was all good. She took it. It felt warm as he helped her from the deck and onto the gondola.

"First time?" Jonas asked.

Sabine coughed, the smoke grated on her throat, gripping at

her lungs like tight balls of barbed wire. "Just stronger than I'm used to," she said, handing back the hissing blunt.

"No doubt," Jonas said, leaning back into the cushions at the opposite end. He dipped his fingers in the water. "Got a friend who sells me A-Grade medicinal. Moonshine, on the other hand, smokes a bunch of worthless shit he grew in his grandma's backyard."

"Why do you call him that?" Sabine asked, looking over to the other gondola as a shriek of laughter traveled fast over the lake.

"He transferred here last semester from some redneck shithole," Jonas explained. "His father's rich as fuck, runs a liquor distribution company, so we called him Moonshine."

"He's okay with that?"

Jonas leant forward. "Here's what you need to know about Moonshine, he doesn't give a shit about fitting in. He pretends to be this dumb redneck, but he's like supersmart."

Sabine nodded but couldn't relate. She'd never wanted to stand out. She was happy blending in, navigating the minefield of high school and affecting as few ripples as possible.

"But his real name? Is it like, John Deere?" she asked.

Jonas, mid-drag, swallowed a lungful of smoke. "John Deere? You're shitting me, right?" He brought his hand to his chest, laughing and coughing at the same time. "You're a crack-up. Hey!" he shouted across to the other gondola. "Frenchie here thinks your real name's John Deere. Can you believe that?"

Moonshine stood up, removed his cap and looked at the writing.

"Simple mistake for a city girl to make," he said.

Sabine felt herself blush.

"John Deere is a brand of tractor, and they make those big-assed lawnmowers you can sit on."

"Oh right, I forgot," she said as Jonas passed her the joint.

She took a shorter, less intense drag this time, letting the smoke ease itself through her bloodstream. "It's beautiful here," she said, sensing the weed was getting right down to work.

"Yeah, downtown Oakland, can you believe it?"

She gestured to the flicker of car lights snaking over the off-ramp. "There's like this huge tent city for the homeless just under the freeway," she said. "Then on the hills there's like all this wealth and privilege? It's like two different cities in one."

"Yeah. I heard you do a ton of charity work with your mom."

Sabine hesitated. She wanted to sound offhand, but at the same time not betray her true feelings. She genuinely enjoyed the work. It made her feel good, like she was giving something back. Instead, her words came off callous and glib. "Yeah, she drags me along, I hate it."

"Gotta be good for your college applications, right? I've still got twenty hours of community service before I graduate. My dad can probably get me a gig over at the A's Baseball field picking up litter or something. He knows the owner."

Picking up litter at the A's stadium? Sabine was about to make some flippant remark but held her tongue. Her mom wouldn't have let Jonas off so easily, she was sure of that.

"We should do like a vigil," she said in a moment of inspiration, looking across the flat darkness towards the pillars at the north end of the lake. "For Catalina."

"Thought you didn't know her," Jonas said, with an edge to his voice.

"I didn't, not really, but I was thinking we should do something. We could light candles, have people speak, music—"

"Why would you even want to do that?" Jonas interrupted. "You just said you didn't know her. Why would you do that if she wasn't your friend?"

"Just seems like the right thing to do. We could do one of those candlelight vigils. It'd be super cool."

Sabine's brain ticked over with the seeds of the idea. Maybe all the lectures her mother had given her on the effects of weed on the teenage brain was all bullshit. It didn't make her feel unmotivated, in fact she hadn't been as motivated about anything for months.

"Okay if I join you?" Jonas asked, easing his way from the opposite end of the gondola.

"Sure," she said, her stomach fluttering. It could have been the faint aftereffects of the weed, but she doubted it.

Jonas's thigh pressed against hers as she sat. She shivered.

"Here," he said, taking off his Vineyard Vines sweater and settling it across her shoulders. "Better?"

Sabine nodded as he drew her close. His body was warm. They sat in silence for a moment before Jonas took her cheek in his hand. She managed a weak smile, though her legs felt as if they would give way if she'd attempted to stand.

"Why me? You must have a ton of girls you hang with."

"I like you, you're different," Jonas said, kissing her cheek.

"Because I'm Lower Rosemont?" she asked, running a finger down the scar on his cheek, a faint imperfection that seemed to complicate his handsomeness; an added, mysterious dimension.

Jonas laughed. "No, because you care about stuff, and you think John Deere is actually someone's name."

"Still could be," she said.

"I guess it could."

Jonas pressed his lips against hers, warm and soft, sending tiny spasms of electricity through her skin.

"I didn't think you even noticed me."

"Oh, I noticed," Jonas said. "Freshman chemistry, we were partners on some lame experiment."

As he leant in to kiss her again, she noticed Jonas scratching his hand. She took it in hers and turned it to the light.

"Probably brushed against some poison oak in the backyard or something," Jonas said, pulling it away.

"Yeah, it's a bitch to get rid of," Sabine confirmed. "Caught it in Tahoe one summer."

Jonas smiled and kissed her again. It was less hesitant now, like she'd always been kissing Jonas Hansen, but he hadn't noticed until now.

41

"You know Patricia Hearst was incarcerated there, served twenty-one months before Carter commuted her sentence?"

"Read that on Wikipedia, detective?" Jessica asked, navigating the sweeping exit curving down to the flat roll of Highway 580.

"Hobby of mine," Tanner explained. "I like reading about old police cases, solved and unsolved."

"And you do that for fun?"

"Passes the time. Heidi Fleiss served twenty months there too. The Hollywood Madam?"

"I am unfortunately old enough to remember Heidi Fleiss."

"It also happens to be one of only three federal prisons for women in the country."

"Did your homework then."

"Yes, ma'am."

Tanner glanced towards the hills that shaped Castro Valley. They had a rough, dirt-brown complexion, as if the life had been scrubbed out of them. On the south-facing slopes, a grid of industrial-grade solar panels were reflecting the day's sunlight with a playful glint.

"What about you? Any hobbies? Interests outside your work?"

Jeez Louise! The lameness of his inquiry hit Tanner the moment it catapulted from his lips.

"Apart from managing several bordellos of my own in downtown Oakland?"

Tanner blinked twice before noticing Jessica had turned with a smile he was certain could have powered the surrounding solar grid with its glow. "It might take me some time to get used to your sense of humor," he said, avoiding staring too long into her eyes. Trouble lay there, he was sure of it. Trouble, or some form of salvation. He wasn't sure he was ready for either.

"That's if you're invited to stick around."

"I'll have you know I'm on my best behavior."

"I'd expect nothing less from a gentleman."

Tanner smiled. Teresa had always said that about him. *"No matter how much you annoy the bejesus out of me sometimes, Roscoe, I know you're a good man, a gentleman."*

"This sure wasn't what I had in mind for a first date," Tanner said.

"Well, you know what they say, you only really get to know someone when you spend an afternoon with them at a low-security Federal Correctional Institution."

"Is that right?"

"Cosmopolitan swears by it."

Tanner laughed. Jeepers, he was as nervous as a teenager and sweating through his suit jacket, sure there were telltale damp patches flooding the armpits of his shirt. "So, what exactly are you hoping to gain by bringing me along?"

"A woman on the list of names I mentioned is serving

twenty-four months for engaging in the act of prostitution," Jessica explained. "In fact, several acts according to her record."

"And you think it might have a connection to my case?"

"That would be your department. I'm only here for a blood sample and if she tests positive, recommend a course of treatment."

"This list? Sure would be nice if you considered sharing."

"Wouldn't it just," Jessica said, as she took the exit onto Hacienda Road.

Several minutes later they pulled into the parking lot at the Dublin Federal Correctional Institution.

"Hold up there, Detective Tanner," Jessica said, as he tugged at the door handle. "Ground rules. I do the talking, don't ask questions, and do not give her any sign you're OPD."

"Then what the devil am I?"

Jessica gestured at his shirt collar. "Undo your top button, loosen your tie and pull up those pens poking up from your lapel pocket. I'll introduce you as a colleague or something."

"Or a physics tutor?" he said, pulling up his rollerballs and slipping the sliver clips onto the outside of his pocket.

"Whatever floats your boat, detective."

Tanner looked at Jessica's outfit; an elegant dark-blue dress offset by a heavy, decorative necklace.

"That's a nice dress to go visiting someone in prison."

"Well, that'll be coming off soon enough."

"It will?"

"Yep," Jessica said. "But don't be getting any ideas."

"No, ma'am," Tanner said, following her into the stifling afternoon heat.

Jessica strode elegantly from the restroom into the waiting area as if she were about to take a bow at the end of a performance.

"Judas Priest's aunt!" Tanner said.

Jessica was correct. The dress had been removed, folded into her handbag and replaced by leg-hugging black cropped pants, three inch heels, and a white, tight-fitting blouse opened one clasp too low for what Tanner would consider appropriate for a prison visit. As she stepped into the shaft of sunlight streaming through the window, Tanner could make out the silhouette of a black, lacy bra under the thin cotton. She'd also slapped on a generous measure of lipstick and thick, black eyeliner that intensified the magnetic blue of her eyes.

"Tactical," Jessica explained. "These girls relate to me when I apply the warpaint. Whatever else they are, they're still women and women like to see other women as they would see themselves, especially if they're stuck wearing the same grey sweats and rubber shower slides all day. A bit of spit and polish goes a long way in my line of work. That, and a pair of heels you can run in."

Tanner mumbled something incoherent as Jessica reached across, loosened his tie some more and patted his chest.

"So, are we doing this or not, Doctor Tanner?" she said, striding confidently to the reception desk to sign in.

"Wait? Doctor? Hold up!"

Topaz Autumn Coleman was escorted into the interview room by a thickset prison guard with the chalky white residue of a recently stripped moustache above her lip. "You sure about this?" the guard said, unlocking the handcuffs and shoving the inmate with little ceremony into the chair. The young woman smiled and extended her middle finger.

"Topaz and me go way back," Jessica confirmed.

The guard smirked, slapped away Topaz's hand. "Your funeral," she said, pulling the door hard behind her.

"You a cop?" Topaz asked, scrutinizing Tanner's attire. "You dress like a cop."

"Same stylist," Jessica confirmed. "TJ Maxx."

Topaz was little more than air and bone. Twenty-three years-old, milk-thin, and saucer-wide eyes that once had caught something to challenge wouldn't relent their gaze until she'd won the argument. The girl would barely cast a shadow, Tanner thought.

"He's one of our consultants," Jessica explained. "A psychologist, employed by the Alameda County Health Department on an as-needed basis. Very well respected and much better paid than me, isn't that right, Doctor Tanner?"

"Um, yes," Tanner said, looking admiringly at Jessica, yet at the same time taken aback by the sheer ease with which she lied. "Perks of the job, working with people like Ms. Swift."

Topaz chewed on the inside of her cheek, not wholly convinced of the introduction, but happy to go along with the welcome break in her daily routine.

"You know why we're here?" Jessica asked.

"I might be sick, but I ain't stupid."

Jessica took a small pouch from her bag and unwrapped a fresh syringe and needle. "I need two blood samples. If they test positive, we'll make sure the prison medics have the antivirus when it's available. Two shots and you should be feeling a lot better."

Topaz sniffed. "Do your worst, ain't my first rodeo." She rolled up the sleeve of her grey sweatshirt to reveal an armful of bruises and ghosts of track marks past.

Tanner winced as Jessica slipped the needle into a vein. "You're from Oakland, right?" he asked.

"That a problem?"

"It's just we've seen an increase in these cases recently."

"And they come to a psychologist to get cured? Don't seem like they're seeing the right kind of doctor to me."

"Counseling," Jessica said, drawing out the blood and preparing the second vial. "Helps them cope with the stigma."

"Once a whore, always a whore. Ain't no losing that stigma," Topaz said, with a defiant smile.

"Did any of your friends have similar symptoms?"

"You sure ask a shit ton of personal questions for not being a cop," Topaz said, as Jessica drew the final few millimeters of blood.

"Doctor Tanner," Jessica said sternly, "I told you about asking our girls too many questions. He's the inquisitive type, PhD in some damned subject. What was it again?"

"Em, clinical psychology," Tanner blurted.

Jessica packed the samples into the cold box. "I swear, the city makes us bring these guys along just to cover their asses, it's not like OPD's a stranger to lawsuits."

"True that," Topaz said.

"They've got a tough job," Tanner said. "Understaffed 'n'all."

"A sob story for Oakland PD? You can tell who pays his salary," Jessica said.

Topaz rolled her sleeve back down over her forearms. "OPD put me in here. They can kiss my pure white ass."

"So, Nelson gave us your name, Topaz," Jessica said, packing up her equipment. "You know Nelson?"

Topaz's eyes brightened. "Yeah, I know Nelson."

"Nelson?" Tanner asked.

"Nelson provided us with the list. Topaz was right there at the top. You were probably his favorite, right?"

Topaz's eyes softened. "He looks after us, don't stand for no rough stuff."

"Were you attacked, Topaz?" Tanner asked.

Topaz smirked. "Perks of job, doc."

"The street's no place for a young girl," Tanner said.

"What, you're my dad now? Cos I sure as hell don't need another one of those in my life."

"Just saying you're vulnerable out there, that's all."

Topaz slid further down the chair and folded her arms. "Don't matter, ain't much action on the streets no more anyways."

"So, where is it, Topaz, the action?" Tanner asked.

Topaz ran her fingertip across the scar above her left eyebrow. "Wanna know how I got this?" she asked, rubbing at the welt as if it could be wiped away if she worked hard enough. "I told a cop to go fuck himself when he asked for a hand job in the back of his patrol car. He didn't take it so well. Ends up beating me with the ass-end of his gun, throws me out on the sidewalk and donkey kicks me in the stomach just for shits and giggles. So, you want to know where the real action is?" Topaz leant back and yanked up her sweatshirt to reveal a patchwork of bruises, like eight balls across the stark white of her skin. "Every bruise tells a story, right?"

"What doesn't kill you makes you stronger," Jessica said softly.

"Yeah, if it doesn't kill ya first." Topaz narrowed her eyes to a defiant squint. "Analyze that shit, doc," she said, looking closely at them both, her eyes searching for clues, finding nothing conclusive but figuring there was still plenty to be suspicious about. "So, you got me squared away?"

Jessica nodded. "If you provide me the list you promised."

"You ain't listening," Topaz said, leaning forward. "I said, you got me all squared away?"

"Taken care of," she said, patting the girl's hand; it felt featherlight, bone covered with the barest membrane of skin.

"Should be in your commissary account by the end of the day."

"You do Western Union or PayPal?"

"Neither. MoneyGram. The system doesn't accept PayPal, you know that."

Confident Jessica had passed the test, Topaz reached for the paper slipped into the back of her sweatpants.

"One name?" Jessica said, showing it to Tanner.

Topaz folded her arms. "I don't got a credit card reader and my clients ain't too forward with their names."

"Nelson?" Jessica said.

She smiled and shrugged. "Like I said, he was good to me."

"And the others?"

Topaz shrugged. "They drive up, we negotiate, I blow 'em, or whatever, they pay me. Ain't complicated."

Topaz ran the back of her hand under her nose. "I remember there was this party a few months back. Some rich kid's house around Oakland, I figured it was easy money. I get there and this dude's all up in my face, one of those fuckboy types, wants to ride me bareback, offers me twice my regular rate for the privilege. Like I'm gonna refuse, and anyway he looked clean, preppy-assed clean. So we do the deed, but afterwards the kid tries to screw me out of what he owes me. Ain't no answer to that other than screw 'em back, right? So I scratch my nails across his face. Man, there was blood everywhere. He paid up after that. Cheap ass motherfucker."

"You remember his name, Topaz? It's important."

Topaz shook her head. "He was young, like still in high school or college. Why you so interested in him?"

"If you have syphilis, which I strongly suspect, then he might also be infected."

"Well, he ain't my fucking problem," she said, sitting back. "Can I go now?"

Tanner moved to the edge of his chair. "Do you know Wendi Chee? She might have worked the same block as you?"

Topaz cocked her head. "Why? You locking her ass in here too?"

Tanner spoke softly. "We found Wendi's body last week in a tent encampment in Oakland. Our investigation's hit a roadblock, I was hoping––"

"Fuck you!" Topaz spat. "I knew you were a cop."

Tanner caught something in her body language, fleeting but distinct. Fear. A sharp jolt that made her bones stiffen and her eyes flicker.

"I wanna leave. The stink just got real bad in here." She turned and shouted, "Hey! Bull-dyke Annie! We're done."

Topaz nailed Tanner with a defiant glare. "I ain't assistin' OPD with shit."

"Is there anything you can tell us that might help us catch whoever killed your friend, Topaz, anything?" Tanner pressed. "Nelson, is he the connection?"

"Kiss. My. Ass."

Jessica took Topaz's hand and squeezed it tight. "He's right, Topaz, how many dead girls is it going to take? No one will ever need know you spoke to us."

Topaz took a deep breath and tensed her shoulders.

"You trust me, right?" Jessica urged.

Topaz passed a sleeve under her nose. "I trust you to bump up my commissary account some more," she said. "Seems fair."

"Sure," Jessica said. "Consider it done."

Topaz took a deep breath, looked around and leaned in over the table. "The Rat House," she said, getting up. "That's all I got, can't tell you no more, you gotta figure out the rest for yourself."

As she finished talking, the guard returned, cuffed her wrists and hauled her from her chair. At the doorway, she turned. "You two," she said, smiling, "just screw, get it over with."

Topaz's brittle laughter echoed through the corridors as she was led back to her cell.

"You should have told me," Tanner said, as they stood outside the prison, the heat shimmering in thick ripples off the hot asphalt.

Jessica took a wet wipe to her face, removing the excess of makeup. "I couldn't have you jump the gun. It was better you didn't know, that way you didn't scare her off."

"But you paid her for this information?"

"A few months' supply of tampons and Top Ramen. Hardly a payoff."

"And this Nelson character? I'll need to speak to him."

"As I said, detective, these patients aren't too forthcoming with information."

"You already said. And by the way, can you please stop calling me detective, my name's Roscoe."

"Roscoe? Okay, but only if you stop calling me Ms. Swift or ma'am, which makes me feel like I'm a hundred years old. My name's Jessica."

Tanner held out his hand. "Pleased to meet you, Jessica."

"You too, Roscoe."

Their hands lingered a little too long as they shook. Tanner felt himself soften. "Well, I guess it's a lead of some sort."

"Damned right it's a lead."

"So, what does Cosmopolitan recommend for a second date?" Tanner asked. "A guided tour of maximum security penitentiaries? Breakfast at the state's best reviewed Juvenile Halls?"

"That, Roscoe Tanner," Jessica said, striding off towards the parking lot, "is completely your call."

42

The following morning, Tanner and Shaughnessy stood drinking coffee and peering through the thick glass of the mirror separating interview room three from the viewing booth.

"Leave him to stew for a while longer?" Shaughnessy asked, as she observed the man shuffle and scratch impatiently at his face.

"Nah, he's done simmering," Tanner confirmed, throwing his cup into the garbage and hiking up the belt of his pants. "Now let's see if we can't raise his temperature some."

Gérard Rosseau narrowed his eyes as Tanner and Shaughnessy walked in and pulled up a couple of chairs.

"I have nothing new to tell you people."

"You sure about that?" Tanner said, undoing the middle button of his jacket as he sat.

Gérard folded his arms tight and looked to the floor.

"Now, Mr. Rosseau, you're here voluntarily, to help OPD

clear up a few anomalies. No lawyers, and you're not under arrest. You understand?"

"I understand you've got a pony-sized bug stuck up your asses about me."

"So why volunteer to come in?" Shaughnessy asked.

Gérard laughed. "Yeah, like that was gonna play real well if I refused."

Shaughnessy gestured at Gérard's wrist. "You don't wear a watch, Mr. Rosseau?"

"Keep ruining them," he replied, rubbing his hand over his wrist. "Wine juice is real acidic, once it gets in there there's no cleaning it out."

"See, that would explain it," Shaughnessy said, turning to Tanner. "Why he got his times all mixed up."

"Sure might," Tanner confirmed, flipping through his notes. "We spoke to your supervisor, Greg Ansel. He confirmed you left at 9pm, not 11pm, which is what you told us."

"Yeah, well Greg's not always the most reliable, know what I mean?" he said, bringing his fingers to his lips, sucking in then expelling a large gasp of air.

"And were your neighbors all high too?" Shaughnessy asked. "Because three of them heard your truck pass down the street at around 1am. One neighbor in particular, nice couple, up feeding a two-month-old, saw you enter your residence at that time. So, why lie?"

Gérard stuffed his hands in his pockets.

"Look, I've got to be honest, this isn't shaping up too good for you right now," Tanner said, sliding a CCTV photograph across the table. "That's your pickup, license plate, ZINKING, at 10pm that night on the 24 Freeway taking the exit which leads to Lake Temescal, where we found Catalina Gomez's body."

"That don't mean shit," Gérard said, shuffling on the edge of his seat. "It's the feeder road to Broadway Terrace, which is on my route home. So, unless you got some photos of me swimming in the lake at that time, then you don't have shit. You got any of those?"

The two detectives looked at each other.

"Yeah, I figured not," he said, slouching back in the chair.

"But you can see how that raises one heck of a red flag for us, right? Why we asked you to come in."

Gérard stroked his stubble, contemplating his reply. "I was meeting someone."

"Well, there you go," Tanner said. "You just got yourself a solid alibi for the night in question. Who did you meet?"

Gérard sniffed. "A friend."

"Male or female?"

"Female—"

"Let me stop you right there," Shaughnessy interrupted. "This woman you were meant to meet? I'm guessing she's married, so you can't surrender her name in case her husband finds out?"

Gérard smiled. "It's like you're psychic or something. Now, if that's all you got," Gérard said, scraping back his chair and walking towards the interview room door, "I got twenty cases of wine that need bottling. Like you said, I'm here voluntarily."

"For now, Mr. Rosseau," Shaughnessy said, stepping in his path. "But you know how these things play out. One person comes forward with evidence that contradicts what you just told us and I'll be happy to read you your rights myself."

43

Alexus Hansen walked into the wine bar located on a three-block enclave recently rebranded as Uptown Oakland. At 5:30pm on a Thursday night, the place was empty save a couple deep in conversation at a candlelit corner table.

"Quiet in here," she said, as she sat at the bar.

"Early yet," the server replied, slipping her the wine list. "Younger crowd gets in at around eight. We're usually pretty chill at this time, but it gets loud later."

"So, I'm here for the early bird special?" Alexus said. "That's comforting."

"Is that like a happy hour? We don't do those."

Alexus shoved the wine list back across the bar. "I'll take the Alpha Omega Reserve Chardonnay," she said, selecting the most expensive option on the list.

"Glass?"

"No, the whole bottle," she confirmed. There was some comfort in not being twenty-one and broke; she could order a $95 bottle of wine without a second thought.

As the server poured, Alexus looked around and wondered if

this was a good idea. She wanted to tell Ben Strauss herself before he heard it from someone else. There was something to be said for looking your opponent in the whites of their eyes—see what they were made of, though in Ben's case, she figured it was probably more of the same.

She was halfway done with her first glass when she caught the familiar whiff of Polo aftershave as Ben pulled up a stool.

"Drink?" Alexus asked, turning and studying his face for some sort of clue; what of, she wasn't sure.

"Soda water," Ben said, sitting. "Boring, but the piper always names his price, right?"

"How long's it been?" she asked, though she already knew the answer; Ben had spoken of it endlessly in his Mayoral campaign.

"Seven years clean."

"Don't you feel you ever want to throw back a couple of shots?" she asked, taking a long sip of her wine.

"Only at the end of every goddamn day," Ben said, with a rueful smile.

"I—" Alexus began.

"I know," Ben interrupted, lifting his finger as if he were testing which way the wind was blowing. "You're running against me."

"You already knew?"

Ben set his hands on the bar. "I'm the Mayor, I get to see everything that comes across the Commission's desk."

"You didn't expect to run uncontested?"

"I was hoping that would be the case. We started some very significant initiatives which will bear fruit in the next few years, I'd hate to see them wither on the vine."

"Look, I'm not here to trade blows on your achievements, I just wanted to tell you personally, as a former colleague and your neighbor."

Ben shuffled, took a sip of soda water. "Do you know how I quit drinking, Alexus?"

She shrugged. "AA, I assumed. The twelve steps?"

Ben shook his head. "Medication."

"I wasn't aware that was an option."

"Here's the thing," he said, leaning his elbows across the bar. "Those AA types of organizations? They base their whole philosophy on the falsehood that alcoholism's a moral failing. I disagree. It's a disease, like depression or bipolar disorder, a chemical imbalance in the brain. So all that happy-clappy religious surrender they want us to buy into, it's all bullshit. I circumnavigated all of that."

"What kind of medication?" she asked, sensing an edge to Ben; one which she wasn't quite sure what to make of, at least not yet.

"Naltrexone. It's usually administered to opioid addicts, but in controlled dosages it can stop the similar cravings that accompany alcohol addiction."

"Sounds too good to be true."

"It is," Ben said, bringing his fists together at the knuckles. "For every action there's an equal and opposite reaction. If I drank three bottles of that very expensive Chardonnay you're sipping on, I wouldn't feel a goddamned thing, not pleasure, not joy, nothing."

"Jesus," Alexus said. "It all sounds a little extreme."

"It's not for everyone. But if you've got the stomach to go that deep I see it as a gift, because at the end of the day the only reason us addicts drink is to stay one step ahead of whatever's making us so damned miserable. The more we drink, the faster and harder we run, until we finally realize there is nowhere to run to; no safe place, no sanctuary. That's when you find out what you're made of. When you stare your greatest fear right in the eyes and everything you have to lose comes into focus. In my case, that epiphany came too late. My wife made the only choice she could: leave."

"I'm not sure——" Alexus began before Ben interrupted.

"Remember that tremor we had a few days ago? Three-point-eight or thereabouts? It reminded me how fragile everything is. The houses we build? The families we nurture and protect? None of it is permanent, it can all be taken away in a blink of an eye."

Alexus took a gulp of wine. "Good thing you didn't mention any of this in your campaign."

"I revealed what was relevant, what people needed to know."

"But why tell me all this?"

"I'd rather you hear it from me than you digging up some half-assed story and using it against me. *'Rosemont Mayor takes opioid treatment drugs to cure his alcoholism,'* not the most catchy campaign slogan."

"That's not my style. I don't make it personal."

Ben nodded. "Styles change depending on the season," he said. "How's Christen, by the way, after that messy business at the park? Must have been quite the shock."

Alexus sat up straight. "He's okay. Busy as usual."

Ben finished his club soda, swirling the ice cubes around the glass. "Hell of a coincidence though, him finding a severed hand a few feet from your front door, buried under the chairs your son and his friend piled up in the park for shits and giggles."

Alexus stiffened. "You don't know it was Jonas."

Ben took out his phone and tapped the screen. "Dave Maddens-Smith filmed the whole prank. That's your son and that weird kid he's always hanging around with."

Alexus shrugged. "Like you said, a prank, nothing illegal."

"You're a lawyer, you'd know," he said, getting up to leave.

"Was this why you came? To threaten me?"

"I don't need to, Alexus. I think events will play out the way they're meant to, they always do. Have a nice rest of your evening."

44

Gérard walked into the Awoken Café looking for Moonshine. He found him sitting at the corner table, typing on his laptop. He ordered a double espresso and walked over.

"Hey, G-Man, what's up?" Moonshine said, removing his thick padded headphones and looping them around his neck.

Gérard pulled up a chair. "What kind of shit did you get me involved in, Mason?"

"Hey, ease up," Moonshine said. "Wanna tell me what the fuck this is all about?"

Gérard looked around, lowered his voice. "Catalina Gomez. The girl they found dead?"

Moonshine brushed his hair from his face. "Yeah, I'm aware."

"The police hauled my ass in, all up in my face about the night she disappeared."

Moonshine fidgeted with his headphone cable. "So?"

"The same night you called me because you were out of your head on some shit and you needed a ride home? That night?"

"Yeah, and I was grateful, man, I was in bad shape, took

some product that didn't agree with me, hardly knew where the fuck I was."

"I'll tell you where you were, stumbling down Broadway fucking Terrace," Gérard said. "And that's what? Less than half a mile from Lake Temescal, where they found the girl."

Moonshine dragged a length of hair behind his ear. "Don't know shit about that. We had a gig over in Alameda, then attended some party up in the hills."

"Did you know the girl?" Gérard asked, pouring a pack of sugar into his coffee.

Moonshine looked through the window to the stream of people walking past. "Saw her around, you know, but she wouldn't be hanging with the likes of me, ran with her own kind."

As he talked, Gérard caught an edge of vulnerability and maybe fear on Moonshine's face. "If there's something you need to get off your chest, Mason, I'm listening."

Moonshine's face reverted to its customary teenage expression of stoic indifference. "I ain't got nothing to unburden. Maybe you're just projecting."

"Projecting what?" he asked, taking a sharp sip of coffee.

"Your own guilt, G-Man." Moonshine sat up straight and smiled, as if he'd just been struck by the lightning rod of a killer song lyric. "I don't know what you did after you dropped me back at the house. Maybe you saw the chick, picked her up, killed her and threw her ass in the lake?"

"Christ," Gérard snapped. "Are all teenagers clueless morons, or are you just a real special case?"

"Always been special, man."

"If they haul me back in, I'm not lying for you, clear?"

"Sure," Moonshine said. "Like I ain't gonna lie if the cops ask me how much weed my guitar teacher smoked with me."

"That, Mason, is not what happened."

"Yeah? My memory must be all fuzzy and shit, what with all the weed you gave me."

"You're upset, I get it, Mason, but you don't get to fuck with other people's lives."

Moonshine smiled. "Like I said, I'm under eighteen and OPD's already got you on record for some shit with a minor. Just sayin'."

Gérard's hand shook as he laid it on the table, resisting the urge to grab the boy by the scruff of his T-shirt and throw him hard against the wall. "What the fuck happened to you to make you like this, Mason? Your mom? Dad? What was it?"

"You might want to cut back on the caffeine there, G-Man, it's got you all rattled and shit," Moonshine said, setting his headphones back over his ears.

45

"Since when did you start dating Jonas Hansen?" Jessica asked as Sabine dumped her backpack on the couch.

"What, you're spying on me now?" she said, heading to the kitchen.

Jessica couldn't disagree. She'd spent the last five minutes peering from behind the apartment curtains as Sabine and Jonas made out in the front seats of his jeep.

Sabine opened the refrigerator door. "Anyway, we're not dating, just hanging out."

Jessica leant against the countertop. "Just doesn't seem your type, that's all."

"I wasn't aware I had a type," Sabine said, slapping a tortilla on the chopping board and spreading peanut butter across the surface. "Can we stop with the questions now?"

"Sure," Jessica said, as Sabine walked to her room.

Jessica vaguely knew Jonas's mother, Alexus Hansen. She was always heading up the fundraising committees for the high school: the kind of person who'd forget who you were for most of the year, then act like your best friend when she called asking for donations. She figured her son was cut from a similar cloth:

too aware of his own charm and good looks. She knew boys like him; every high school had at least one Jonas Hansen. Inevitably, they'd grow up into Alpha types, overconfident men coasting on their privilege and imagining the world owed them a living. She'd always taught Sabine the opposite was true: that the world owed you nothing, and you owed it to yourself to work and make something of yourself.

That kind of preaching was easier when Sabine was younger, but now she was in the orbit of kids like Jonas Hansen, it was a harder sell. Maybe it was just the natural friction of being a teenager, or maybe the friction was more pronounced because Sabine attended Rosemont High and was exposed to that level of privilege daily. She hoped to God she'd made the right decision sending her daughter there. Not that there was any going back at this point. She had to trust Sabine could see through all that, carve her own path. That was the needle-fine balancing act of parenting; the times you let your kids make their own mistakes and figure life out for themselves were as important as the times you stepped in and saved them from themselves. The trick was always figuring out which was which.

46

There was a connection between both dead girls, Shaughnessy was sure of it as she sat in her apartment re-examining the case notes. It was a gut feeling. She'd always had good instincts. Her mentors at the Academy had made a point of commenting on her clarity in assessing a situation; an uncanny ability to cut through the clutter. But shuffling through the papers, they seemed like a deck of tarot cards that could be flipped over and interpreted differently depending on how they fell.

She could buy into the theory that Catalina had overdosed; maybe it was her first time and it was damned bad luck; the worst of luck. Yet, at the same time, Catalina's picture was fragmented, like the cubist sculpture at the Arts Collective. The parts were all there, but they didn't add up to a clear image, at least not yet.

She was about to rest her eyes and pour herself a strong cup of coffee, when her apartment doorbell rang. "Hold on," she said, squinting through the peephole.

Shit! Dugdale. She wasn't expecting him. Their trysts were typically planned out days in advance with military-like precision. She quickly swapped her old, stained, black T-shirt for a cleaner white one, checked herself in the mirror and patted down her hair.

"It's late, Marty," she said, opening the door. "Shouldn't you be at home?"

Leaning in, he kissed her on the lips. "Rather be with you."

She could smell the alcohol on his breath, mixing with the heavy cologne he'd probably splashed on in the car beforehand. She didn't mind; in fact, it turned her on. There was something deeply masculine about the intoxicating mixture, some clichéd aphrodisiac that before getting involved with Dugdale she would have chided herself for even considering surrendering to.

"You got a corkscrew?" he asked, brushing past her.

"Kitchen. Still on the counter from last time."

As he walked into the living area, popping the cork on a 2015 Barolo, he looked at the papers scattered on the desk. "Homework?"

"Just trying out some theories."

"Then shoot," he said, sitting and beckoning her to join him.

Shaughnessy positioned herself at the far end of the couch. She didn't want to make this too easy for him. "Wendi's death I buy as a homicide, but why sever the hand?"

"Maybe someone found the body, decided to fuck with us. It happens."

"Catalina Gomez though, her picture's real fuzzy. No one person tells the same story, and her parents certainly didn't know shit about her life."

"But you're still hesitant?"

"Tanner's on like some crusade to prove me wrong. Prove us all wrong."

Dugdale shrugged. "Until we have evidence to prove otherwise, that kid Shawn Dubose is going to serve time for possession with intent to sell. If we can connect him to the death of Wendi Chee, the DA might decide to prosecute him as an adult."

"But we'd have to tie the contaminated heroin to Dubose. We searched his place, found nothing."

"And if we can't, Catalina's death is another tragic teenage overdose," Dugdale said.

Shaughnessy swirled the wine glass in her hand.

Dugdale shuffled closer. "How's it going with Tanner?"

"Okay, I guess. He's eccentric, soft round the edges."

"Well, that's why you're sticking close to him, Moira. Make sure those doughy edges don't spill over into Oakland's mayoral election."

"I don't know, Marty," she said, sensing she was both stiffening herself against his advances and surrendering to them at the same time.

"Is it Julia?" he asked, pressing his thigh against hers and tracing his lips along the nape of her neck.

"Your wife? No, I don't get caught up in all that guilt shit, that's your department."

He grabbed a fistful of her hair. She caught her breath, her skin shooting through with a raw, electric energy.

"You're a real piece of work, Shaughnessy," he said, pulling harder, until her follicles tingled simultaneously with pleasure and pain. "I should teach you some fucking discipline."

Her breath was low and fast, her skin trembling. She turned her back to him. "Go ahead," she said, lifting off her T-shirt. "You wouldn't be the first to try."

47

Fallon Young's face was still raw with scars and bruises, as if the beating had happened only yesterday. The older Asian transgender sitting next to her, who went by the name of Skyler Dione, put her arm tenderly around Fallon's shoulder.

"Damn right my girl's reporting this as a hate crime. Why the hell else do you think we're here?" Skyler said, tapping a perfectly manicured fingernail on the interview room desk and giving Tanner and Shaughnessy a defiant stare.

"We need very specific evidence to prosecute a hate crime," Shaughnessy explained.

"And this evidence ain't doing it for you, sweetheart?" Skyler said, hands waving dramatically over Fallon's face. "There weren't no damn love note, if that's what you're looking for."

"So why take two weeks to report this? Why not call the police that night?"

"Fallon's the sensitive type. I'm not. I know how things work downtown. Most of OPD thinks we deserve any beating we get. The rest of them reckon they'd like to take a walk on the wild side, take a trans out for a test drive, see if the ride's all that. And if you're wondering, honey," she said, winking, "it is."

Tanner cleared his throat. "Not in the market for a new model, thanks all the same."

Skyler smiled. "Don't knock it till you rock it, babe."

"Why do you think this is a hate crime and not just a random robbery or assault?" Shaughnessy asked.

"Because he gets me to suck his dick, calls me a fag, then beats the shit out of me," Fallon mumbled, a sliver of saliva dribbling down her cheek. "He didn't take nothing."

"Yeah, nothing but your pride, right?" Skyler confirmed. "And those fine, fine cheekbones." She patted Fallon's hand tenderly. "Don't worry, honey, I got a plastic surgeon down in Encinitas, he'll fix you up real good, cheap too."

Shaughnessy checked her notes. "You were at your own home, so you'd obviously invited him in. Was he paying you for sex?"

"Just because I'm transgender doesn't make me a fuckin' whore," Fallon protested.

"You tell 'em, honey. That monster almost killed my girl. Broke her nose, cracked three ribs, and there's the psychological damage. This is going to mess up the transition real bad."

"Did the man give you his name?" Tanner asked.

Fallon's eyes filled with fear as she looked anxiously at Skyler.

"It's all right, I got this," Skyler said, pulling a newspaper clipping from her purse and flattening it on the desk. "Fallon recognized his face, cried for three hours straight afterwards."

Tanner and Shaughnessy both looked down at the clipping. *"Local entrepreneur, Bruce Ho, to open third Boba Lounge in the city of Rosemont."*

Tanner sat back. "Are you absolutely sure?"

"As sure as the pain right there on my poor baby's face."

"We already interviewed Bruce Ho," Tanner said. "He has a fiancée."

Skyler leaned forward across the desk and raised her perfectly sculpted eyebrows as if preparing herself for a close-up. "They always do, don't they, honey? They always do."

48

"This is like the size of our apartment," Sabine said, walking around Jonas's bedroom as he lay on his bed licking the paper edges of a freshly rolled joint.

He tapped the tip of the joint with a pencil as Sabine took a handful of papers from her backpack. "What's that?"

"Posters for Catalina's vigil. Cool, right?" she said, laying one on the bed.

Jonas quickly glanced it over. "Yeah, s'all right."

"Ease up on the enthusiasm, Jonas."

He passed the joint to Sabine.

"Won't your parents smell it? Or don't they care?"

"My dad smokes this shit all the time. He doesn't know I know. But my mom, she's a hard-ass, which is why we're smoking this on the roof terrace."

"No shit? You have a roof terrace?"

"Yeah, sunloungers, hot tub, the whole shitshow."

"That's why you said to bring my bathing suit. I thought you were taking me on a date to the pool or something lame like that."

"Never said it was a date," he said, taking her hand and leading her up the narrow stairway to the roof.

Sabine caught her breath. "This is amazing," she said, walking towards the roof edge. She looked over the lip and felt a rush of cold to her feet. "Long way down though."

"Better not fall then," Jonas said, removing his T-shirt.

Sabine did the same, slipping out of her shorts and top to reveal her red bikini. Her mother had bought it at Marshalls before they left for Tahoe. It was the only good thing to come out of the vacation. That and the tan she'd acquired lying most of the day on the beach in lieu of anything more interesting to occupy her time.

"You look good, Frenchie."

"Thanks," Sabine said, imagining she was blushing the same deep red as her bathing suit.

"Coming?" Jonas asked as he switched on the jets and climbed into the hot tub which had a wide, fabric shade strung across the top with multicolored lights that pulsed to the beat of the music throbbing through the speaker system.

Sabine laughed. "Disco lights? Seriously? What are you, like some Hugh Hefner character who still lives with his parents?" She slipped slowly into the churning hot water.

"You complaining?"

"Nope," Sabine said, enjoying the rush of heat as she slipped her shoulders under the surface and slicked her hair back.

"But I've got a question." She pulled the wet strands of hair from her neck. "Didn't you like already turn eighteen? Shouldn't you be going to college in the fall?"

"Yeah, well, my parents kind of fucked all that up."

"Because?"

Jonas scooted closer to Sabine. Her skin tingled.

"When I was nine, my dad took us on this European trip for like a whole year. He had this bug up his ass about educating me and my sister to become better global citizens before we went through the American high-school system."

"That's cool," she said. "A year traveling Europe?"

"It pretty much sucked," Jonas said, slicking back his hair. "My dad worked the whole time. My mom tried to homeschool us, but she was like the most impatient teacher, ever. After a few weeks she gave up and just gave us a bunch of books to read, which I don't even remember opening. I got this real bad ear infection after swimming in a lake in Austria that took forever to clear. When we came back, the retarded Rosemont School district said I was a year behind in my education, so they held me back. Total bullshit."

"But Europe?" Sabine glowed with the thought. "For an entire year. That must have been amazing."

"Did you not hear a word I just said?"

"Sure," she said, wiping water droplets from her cheeks. "Sounds like a total nightmare, probably scarred you for life, I hope your parents paid for therapy. I mean an ear infection? I hope you like sued the Austrian government for damages."

Jonas laughed. "You're breaking my balls. You're like totally breaking my balls," he said, passing her the joint.

She took a short, uncommitted hit. "I probably get it from my mother, she's like the maestro of ball-breaking or whatever."

Jonas moved closer. "I like you, you're different," he said, feathering her arms with his fingertips.

"Yeah, you mentioned that," she said, catching her breath and trying not to look too closely into his eyes.

"You should learn to take a compliment," Jonas said, leaning in to kiss her. Sabine responded, less hesitant than last time, like she had the measure of his mouth now.

She watched Jonas's hand as it caressed her gently just under her bikini top, his finger brushing lightly over the thin fabric. She put her hand on his and felt the rough patch of skin.

"You ever get something for that?" she asked, eager to break the flow of the moment, yet equally eager to make sure it never stopped. "Looks like it got worse."

"Poison oak. Should clear up in like two weeks."

Sabine felt a surge of bird wings in her belly as his fingers made their way around the seams of her top. He shifted his hands down over her torso and towards the band of her bikini bottom. Sabine tensed, the spell abruptly broken. She'd never let a boy go that far before. She wasn't ready, not yet, not even for Jonas Hansen.

"Em," she said, removing his hand. "This has been amazing, but I should probably go."

Jonas smiled. But Sabine could tell it was forced. Did he think she was uncool? Too young for him? As she leant in to kiss him, maybe to reassure him, or to reassure herself, she felt his hardness urge itself against her thigh.

"I'm working this afternoon and they get really pissed if I'm late," she said, pushing him away.

Jonas scooted to the far end of the tub. "Sure, Lower Rosemont, go earn those dollars."

"You're not mad, are you? It's just that I can't afford to lose this job."

Jonas blew a trail of smoke into the air. "Like I said, it's not like we're dating."

Sabine's stomach dipped. "Yeah, like who said we were dating?" Goose bumps pricked as she dragged herself from the water. "I mean, who dates, it's like so old school."

Sabine slipped her top over her shoulders and ran a towel across her hair. She stood for a moment, waiting. Waiting for what, she wasn't sure. "I guess I should just show myself out then," she said, an edge to her voice. The same edge her mother had sometimes. She hated herself for how it sounded, but it came out naturally, like something she had no control over.

"Yeah, you do that, Frenchie," Jonas said. "It's been real."

Later that evening, Jonas stood in front of his bedroom mirror. He passed a finger down the scar on his face, which was still tender to the touch, then slid his hand under his boxer shorts. The rash under his pubic hair was just like the one on his hand, but itchier; like he wanted to keep rubbing it until his skin disappeared.

He laid back on his bed and swiped his cell-phone screen. An hour later, he was more confused than when he'd started and had narrowed the issue to either eczema (no history), smallpox (unlikely) and some variant of an STD (highly likely).

He googled, *does my primary care doctor need to...*

The results filtered up rapidly. Even though he was still covered by his parent's health insurance, because he was eighteen, the doctor couldn't say shit to his parents. It made him feel marginally better. He'd call Dr. Beaufort tomorrow, get a prescription to clear the whole thing up without his parents finding out. He drifted off to sleep some thirty minutes later, the sun now long passed under the horizon.

49

"Jesus, I'd put a bullet through my head living in a place like this," Shaughnessy said, squinting through the bleach-white afternoon at the neatly trimmed lawns and rows of identical tract homes on a housing estate above Highway 13.

"Myself and Teresa contemplated it, once," Tanner said, pulling up the car. "Said she'd probably end up on a murder one charge if I made her live out here. After that, I figured we weren't moving any place."

"This it?" Shaughnessy asked, nodding towards the boxy, characterless house across from them. The vertical blinds were shuttered tight, the lawn scruffier than neighboring lawns, suggesting Bruce Ho had little time for gardening.

"Let's go see if the Boba king's in residence," Tanner said, reaching in his jacket pocket to check the search warrant.

As they exited the car, an elderly man, coughing loudly and leaning on a walking stick, shuffled towards them. "You folks lost?"

Tanner gestured to the house. "This Bruce Ho's residence?"

"Sure is. Not here now though, truck's not in the driveway."

"Any idea where he might be?"

The man sucked at his dentures and peered over the rims of his glasses. "And why would you folks be looking for the Chinese guy? He owe you money or something?"

Shaughnessy held up her ID. "Or something," she confirmed.

The man spat a glob of phlegm onto the sidewalk. "Always borrowing my stuff. Lawnmower, stepladder, even borrowed my potato peeler, never returned it neither. I mean, what kind of grown-ass man doesn't have a damned potato peeler in his house?"

The old man laughed; it was thick with mucus and echoed through the street like a sack of bones dragged on the sidewalk. "If he ain't here, he's likely someplace else."

"Very helpful," Shaughnessy said.

"His fiancée," Tanner said. "Ever see her around?"

The man shook his head, walked towards the car, and leant against the hood. "People coming in and out all hours, but I never saw him with no fiancée as I recall. We had a block party few months back, he came alone, didn't stay long, didn't even have a beer, just water. What kind of grown-ass man doesn't have a beer at a goddamn block party––?"

They all turned as the throaty rumble of a large pickup echoed through the neighborhood. The truck slowed, took a right and pulled into Bruce's driveway.

"Warrant?" Shaughnessy asked, holding out her hand.

Tanner passed it to her. "Best play it cool, Shaughnessy, he's not much for talking."

As Bruce jumped from the truck, Shaughnessy held out the warrant and marched towards him. "Bruce Ho?" she shouted. "We have a warrant to search your residence."

Bruce looked around, panicked, and jumped back in the cab, firing up the five-hundred-horsepower Hemi engine.

"Fuck," Shaughnessy muttered, breaking into a sprint.

Bruce slammed the truck into reverse, aiming the tailgate directly at her. She stepped to her right, falling onto the sidewalk. The truck's tire stopped an inch from her face, lurched back into drive and flattened Bruce's mailbox as it thundered back down the road.

Shaughnessy scrambled up from the ground. "Tanner! Start the car!"

"Shoot!" Tanner said, wrenching open the driver side door.

Shaughnessy ran. "Sir, can you please move your goddamn ass," she hollered at the old man, who was still leaning against the hood, enjoying the afternoon's entertainment.

"Sure, just give me a long minute here."

Sliding into the passenger seat, Shaughnessy leant over and pressed on the horn. The old man nodded, waving his hand as he grabbed at his cane and shuffled slowly from the car.

"Left turn at the end of the street," Shaughnessy barked, settling the lights on the dashboard and activating the siren.

"Got it." Tanner whipped the wheel to the left.

"10-80 in progress. Detectives Shaughnessy and Tanner in pursuit of suspect, Bruce Ho, driving a silver F150 pickup, license plate CALI420. Heading west."

Tanner slid the car from the gravel side roads and onto the long, smooth asphalt road leading to Highway 13.

"Got him," Shaughnessy shouted, as Bruce's truck took a wide corner, forcing the car traveling in the opposite direction to swerve and clip the bushes.

Tanner gripped hard on the wheel. As they came to a four-stop junction, he slowed to allow a line of thirty cyclists to pass in front of him in a blur of slow-moving Lycra.

"Shit," Shaughnessy said, her seat belt digging into her shoulder as Tanner slammed the brakes. "We're going to lose him."

With the cyclists finally clear, Tanner accelerated, making up

What Follows

for lost ground. By the time they reached the on-ramp, Bruce was already gone; just another truck swallowed into the endless scroll of commuter traffic snaking west down Highway 13.

"God dang it," Tanner said, slapping the wheel.

"If you'd hadn't let that old geezer hold us up, maybe we'd have caught him," Shaughnessy snapped.

"And if you hadn't gone in, guns blazing, maybe you could have immobilized him before he got the bright idea to hightail it out of there."

They sat for a moment, the only sound the roll of traffic and the static from the police radio.

Tanner turned to Shaughnessy. "Still think Catalina's death was an accident?"

"This proves nothing other than Bruce Ho's got something in that house he doesn't want us to find."

She took a cigarette from her pocket, settled it between her lips and tapped her fingers anxiously on her thighs.

"You could try patches, or hypnosis," Tanner said. "Worked real well for some buddies of mine."

"That right?" She plucked the cigarette from her mouth, crushed it in her hand and disposed of the flaky entrails through the window.

"Or there's always that," Tanner said, slotting the gear lever into reverse. "Back to the house?"

"That's why we got the freakin' warrant," Shaughnessy confirmed.

50

The tract home was under-furnished, as if Bruce had moved in only a few weeks ago. In the living room, a large flat-screen TV loomed over the fireplace, and tucked in the corner a bench press with a shelf-full set of dumbbells stacked in a perfect, symmetrical line.

"Freakin' neat freaks," Shaughnessy said, as she and Tanner walked into the master bedroom. "It's just creepy, all that worrying over what goes where, like there's not more important things in the world to obsess over."

In the bedroom, she wedged open the blinds. The late morning sunlight fell over the militarily arranged bedding. Tanner checked out the trashcan in the en suite bathroom. Squatting, he extracted a syringe and slipped it into an evidence bag.

Moving into the kitchen, Shaughnessy ran her finger along the countertop. "Not one damn dish in the drainer, that's just not normal," she said, opening the refrigerator door while Tanner poked around the cupboards lining the kitchen walls.

"Come take a look," he said, beckoning his partner over to check out the rows of clear plastic containers filled with white powder. Tanner took one from the shelf and examined the green label printed on the side. *Neumi Bio-Tech. Testosterone Cypionate.*

"Shit," Shaughnessy said, "the guy's balls must be the size of raisins."

"Raisins?"

"Well-known side effect of taking anabolic steroids, testicular shrinkage."

"Right you are, add it to the forensics collection."

Tanner moved back into the hallway, scouting the walls. "Basement," he said, clicking his finger and thumb. "I remember when Teresa and I were checking these places out, they all came with built-out basements, usually right here."

He ran his hands over the paintwork and shook his head.

"Maybe it's someplace else?"

"Doubtful. All these houses are identical, down to the last bolt." He tapped on the wall. "Hear that? Hollow."

He passed a finger down a faint seam in the wall. Three feet to his right was another seam, thicker and more prominent. "Help me out," he said, urging his fingers under the lip.

Shaughnessy grabbed under the other seam. As they lifted, the false door slid easily from its housing to reveal another door; the original entrance to the basement.

"Bingo," Tanner said, grabbing one of the three padlocks attached to the door. "Got any bolt cutters in your back pocket?"

She shook her head, walked back to the living room. A few moments later she returned, holding a twenty-pound dumbbell and began pounding at the padlocks with the outer edge. A few minutes later, the three locks lay on the floor, splintered and buckled.

Stepping gingerly onto the first stair, Tanner used his flashlight to guide himself and Shaughnessy down the narrow stairwell.

"Smells like a friggin' zoo down here," she said, as they

reached the basement floor. She gestured to the wall. "There's a light over there."

As Tanner pressed the switch, the fluorescents buzzed to life.

"Christ," Shaughnessy said. "No wonder he hauled ass."

Tanner looked over the long wooden table. Laid across it, at least thirty brown packages with a pairs of scales, eight rolls of brown duct tape, and three large silver-colored baking trays, each filled with power. Next to the baking trays, several bags of the same steroid powder they'd seen in the kitchen.

"The dang clotting agent," he said, grabbing one of the bags. "He was mixing it here. That's a direct link to Catalina."

"Right," Shaughnessy said. "But that doesn't mean Bruce Ho killed her, just that he supplied the product."

"It as sure as heck makes it more likely," Tanner said, laying the bag back on the table.

"What the fuck is that smell?" Shaughnessy said, her nose twitching at the odor which reminded her of wet dog fur mixed with stale feces. She looked to the far end of the basement where a wide green tarpaulin was spread across the wall. "You hear that?" she asked, sensing a faint scratching sound.

"Sure do," Tanner said, placing his hand over the handle of his gun. Shaughnessy did the same as they crossed the basement floor.

Tanner raised his arm. Reaching for the top corner of the tarpaulin, he mouthed a countdown.

On three, Shaughnessy deactivated the safety.

On two, she stood back, holding the gun in both hands.

On one, Tanner pulled down hard on the corner.

The tarpaulin crumpled to the floor.

"Holy fuck," Shaughnessy said, lowering her weapon as the light hit the eyes of the rats; around thirty of them, all in cages set against the wall.

Immediately, they hissed and squeaked; a chain reaction that grew louder. Scrambling across the straw floors, they began scratching and biting at the wire cages until their mouths bled.

51

Tanner and Shaughnessy sat in Dugdale's office, the breeze from the air conditioning fluttering the corners of the papers scattered across his desk. Shaughnessy rapped her fingers along the armrest. "He's not going to agree to it, you know that, right?"

"Don't ask, don't get."

"Won't get," she said, turning as Dugdale strode into the office. He flung a folder on his desk and filled his mug from the coffee maker.

"Tanner and Shaughnessy. A rare pleasure," he said, slurping. "You've got five minutes."

"Right you are," Tanner said, sitting up. He launched quickly into as concise a summary as he could, barely taking a breath as he spoke.

"Hold that thought for a goddamn moment," Dugdale interrupted. "You're asking me to allocate my very limited resources to finding a low-level drug dealer with no priors?"

Tanner cleared his throat. "I also think he may have either killed or had some close connection to both our victims."

"Do you now?" Dugdale asked. "On what evidence?"

"Forensics confirmed the contaminate we found in Bruce Ho's residence was the same one found in Catalina Gomez. He also lied about having a fiancée which means his alibi is worth bupkis."

"He's not the first man to lie about his relationship status," Dugdale said.

"He also halfway killed a young man, Fallon Young––"

"Technically a he, but goes by she, just not transitioned yet," Shaughnessy interrupted.

Dugdale pointed at her. "What's your take?"

"At present, the evidence is circumstantial. There's no proof Bruce Ho supplied the victim with the heroin––"

"We don't require proof because we already have a suspect in custody who's admitted to supplying Catalina Gomez with narcotics," Dugdale said.

"Horse hooey," Tanner snapped. "That boy's being paid by someone to take the rap. Someone who's so far up the food chain in this whole enterprise that we don't even know what the danged enterprise is yet."

"This another one of your square-pegs-round-hole theories?"

Tanner took a breath. "I know I'm running on a gut feeling here, with little evidence but––"

"No shit," Shaughnessy muttered.

"But there's someone driving all this, I'm sure of it."

"Driving all this what?" Dugdale asked. "All we have are two victims, unconnected. One overdosed, the other strangled to death. You're weaving a conspiracy here that no one else is seeing."

Tanner glanced at his partner. "Both Catalina and Wendi had the same contaminate in their bloodstream, the steroid Bruce Ho used to cut the heroin."

"That's not a connection, it's a coincidence," Dugdale said. "You can't secure a conviction on coincidence."

"Thanks for the reminder. Want to teach me the basics of arrest procedures next?"

Dugdale rose, walked to the window. "The DA will sign off on the Catalina Gomez death as accidental before the end of next week, then it's out of our hands, we move on to other things."

Tanner shook his head. "I'm not buying it, too many loose ends, it doesn't feel right."

"Here's the thing," Dugdale said. "I don't much care about your feelings." He turned to Shaughnessy. "Where are we with Wendi Chee?"

"Seems she cut off her own hand just to make our lives easier," Tanner said, his simmer of anger boiling to the surface.

Dugdale's eyes hardened. "You're getting real close to crossing the line here, detective. Unless you're looking to spend the next few months reviewing court evidence until your ass gets numb, I'd recommend staying the right side of that line. Shaughnessy?"

"One of the sex workers, Tiffiny Grant, saw Wendi get picked up the night she died. She recognized the car as a Tesla Model S."

"Great, just a few thousand of those in the greater Bay Area, anything else?"

Shaughnessy hesitated. "She mentioned something about the 'house'? She got real scared when I tried to push her for more information––"

"The Rat House!" Tanner blurted, slamming his fist into his palm. "That's the dang connection."

"What the hell is the Rat House?" Dugdale asked wearily.

"Not real sure, yet. But an inmate at the Dublin Penitentiary mentioned it recently."

Shaughnessy raised her eyebrows "When were you—?"

"It doesn't matter. But what if Catalina and Wendi were both connected to this Rat House? And we found those rodents in Bruce Ho's basement. That's no danged coincidence."

"Might be a private club," Shaughnessy offered. "A strip club, something like that?"

Dugdale frowned. "Adult clubs were banned in Alameda County in the early nineties."

Tanner perched on the edge of his seat, his mind suddenly clear. "Which is why it makes sense. An illegal, underground sex club where men can buy girls like Wendi Chee."

"And Catalina?" Shaughnessy offered.

Tanner shook his head. "Catalina was not a sex worker."

"You sure about that?"

Dugdale leaned back. "It's a damn stretch, any idea where this place might be located?"

"Not yet, but if we assigned more officers—"

"Time's up," Dugdale said, standing and checking his watch.

"And my extra resources?"

"Present me some solid evidence this Rat House place exists and I'll consider it."

Tanner nodded. "But it sure would make a heck of a difference, right, for this year's election? OPD, under your watch, uncovers a major illegal enterprise like that? Could be a career-making bust I reckon."

Dugdale looked at Tanner and narrowed his eyes, not completely dismissing the thought. "Know what would make a big difference to my career right now?" he said. "If you two would do your goddamn job and review that footage I gave you. I'm scheduled to meet with the governor up at the capital and I'd like to show him OPD fully supports the state's policy on prosecuting anyone violating the residential watering mandate."

Tanner shrugged. "Still researching, Chief, been a little busy."

Dugdale leant his hands on the desk. "Understand, this is not a First World Problem, Tanner," he said. "If we need to make an example of someone to get the attention this matter deserves, then that's what we do. I'd like to have a full report to take up with me to Sacramento, we clear?"

"Sure," Tanner said, clenching his teeth. "Like eyes-wide-open clear, Chief."

Heading out from Dugdale's office, Tanner marched towards the elevators, barely able to contain his anger.

"Hey, hold up," Shaughnessy said, catching up to him as he stood by the doors. "We're not going to talk about what just went down in there?"

Tanner stabbed his finger on the elevator buttons. "First World Problem?" he said. "How the Judas did he get that idea. Oh wait, it's exactly what I said to you, wasn't it, Shaughnessy?"

"Look, I'm sorry. It's nothing," she said, her cheeks flushing.

Tanner dropped his voice. "Just pillow talk?"

Shaughnessy was about to protest.

"Don't even try," Tanner growled.

Shaughnessy spoke softly, "You don't understand—"

"Sure, I understand plenty. But here's the deal, you won't come out of this unscarred, nobody ever does. If it gets out, there'll always be questions about any case you're assigned to, any promotion—"

"I don't need a babysitter, I understand the game."

Tanner leaned in close. "I need to know my partner's not running her mouth off to the Chief. Is that why he assigned you? So he could have you keep me in check?"

"Don't act so freakin' entitled. He did it for me, figured the case could help my career."

"Me? You're calling me entitled?" he said, exasperated.

"You want to discuss withholding information?" Shaughnessy snapped. "What about that Rat House? Dublin Penitentiary? When were you going to share that?"

"It's hardly the same."

"Bullshit, it's not."

As the elevator doors pinged open, Shaughnessy looked at the crowd inside. "Sorry, wrong floor," she said, poking the button.

"Why in tarnation did you do that?"

"Because we're not done here." Shaughnessy lowered her voice. "Look, I'm not even halfway convinced the Catalina Gomez case is a homicide. Wendi Chee? I'm thinking there's a connection there, probably Bruce Ho. He's harboring some deep homosexual urges he feels guilty about, which is why he beat up on that trans."

"Fallon. Fallon Young," Tanner said sternly.

"I wish the fuck you'd stop doing that," she growled. "Maybe if we find the location of this Rat House, we'll find a connection."

"How do you propose we do that?"

"Tiffiny? But she's scared shitless of something, or someone."

Tanner pushed the elevator call button. "If she's a frequent visitor to the OPD, there might be some leverage."

"That could work."

"This doesn't mean I've forgotten," Tanner said, entering the elevator.

"Not forgotten either," she said, slumping against the back wall, and noticing how blurred and disjointed their reflections looked in the brush metal finish on the doors.

52

"What's with all the cloak and dagger routine?" Dave Maddens-Smith said, lowering his voice as he slipped into the very back pew of the Rosemont Community Church.

Ben Strauss turned as Dave removed his "Make America Great Again" baseball hat and smoothed his hair. "Alexus Hansen," he said, leaving the name to drift like incense in the chilled air.

Ben spread his arms across the back of the pew and leaned back. "What about her?"

"She won't be a problem, right? You whipped her ass last time."

"I wouldn't call a two hundred vote margin an ass-whipping, more like a rap on the knuckles."

"If you asked me here for my support, it's a given."

"Understood," Ben said, patting Dave lightly on the shoulder.

Dave's flinty, bloodshot eyes narrowed to a suspicious squint.

"Not wavering are you, Strauss? Yielding to the pressure?"

Ben brushed a strand of lint from his chinos. "Too much in motion to ease up on the throttle now."

"Damned right," Dave said, slipping a paper from his jacket pocket. "I took the liberty of bringing along a sample of Alexus Hansen's literature from her last campaign."

Ben glanced at the printout. "I'm familiar."

Dave stabbed the pamphlet with his index finger. "A threefold increase in permits for the construction of rental units, with thirty percent allocated for affordable housing. It's just not how we do things in Rosemont."

"She's progressive, that could swing voters in her direction."

Dave settled his hands on the bench in front of him as if he were about to kneel for prayer. "Did you know my great-grandparents moved out here from the city after the big one in 1906? Hell, most of the population of San Francisco who could afford to, hauled ass to the East Bay after that trembler, built themselves a slice of paradise. Of course, land was dirt cheap back then, but they built a goddammed city from that dirt."

"It's the American way."

"Amen to that. The thing is, Strauss, you don't get to have the best-ranked public schools in the state by building rental properties and low-income housing units. What you get is a transient population who, let's say, don't share the same values as we do."

"You think that's Alexus Hansen's ambition?"

"She's got a liberal agenda. One look at her tells you everything you need to know."

Ben shuffled uncomfortably, an unpleasant taste, like a film of dirt, on his tongue. "Some people might call that racism, Dave."

"I call things as they are. I spent my career negotiating with the Teamsters Union at the Port of Oakland, I don't get intimidated by snowflakes and do-gooder liberals."

Ben, eager for a speedy retreat from the subject, gestured to the sculpture of Christ's crucifixion over the altar. "Do you know my favorite bible story, Dave?"

"Didn't imagine you were the religious type."

"It's when Jesus turns the tables on the moneylenders in the temple."

Dave smirked, his lips curling like squid on a grill. "In my top ten list, for sure."

"I tried to figure out why that was, then I realized," Ben said, turning to face him. "It's the most human thing he does. I mean, everyone relates to that kind of rage, right? All that fishes and loaves, water into wine bullshit? Just fairy tales, but a man reaching the end of his rope and losing control, that's so fucking human, you want to pat the man on the back and buy him a drink."

Dave pointed a crooked, liver-spotted finger at Ben. "The parable speaks to you because it goes against his Christian teachings. He doesn't turn the other cheek, instead he kicks some serious philistine ass."

"Incorrect," Ben said. "At that moment he shows the most basic human weakness. He gives in to his anger, lets his emotions get the better of him. How much more fucking human could the son of God become than in that one moment of surrendering to his true self?"

"Not that it did him much good. He was dead by thirty-three. Maybe if he'd sat around the negotiating table, he'd have been spreading the good word for a few more years."

Ben gestured to the crucifix. "And if he ever does return, there're no shortages to remind him of the error of his ways."

Dave glanced impatiently at his watch. "I'm guessing you didn't ask me here for a bible study class, Strauss."

"I heard chatter that Brooklyn Basin was under offer."

"I can neither confirm or deny. But that would be some privileged information."

"Which, as a former Port of Oakland employee, you have access to."

"I could make some calls."

"Even us small-town mayors need friends in the big city," Ben said. "What is it that separates Oakland and Rosemont? Two blocks at most."

"More like $150,000 per year personal income," Dave said, his cackle echoing off the church walls.

"And if the information was correct?"

"Then you'd want in?"

Ben shook his head. "I'd want out."

Dave sat back, looked Ben over as if sizing him up for a suit. "That, I didn't expect."

"Were my sources correct?"

Dave sucked his bottom lip and lowered his voice. "As we're in a sacred setting, let's just say the Port Authority's preaching from the same hymn book as the city."

"Which means selling to the highest bidder?"

Dave stood and settled his hand on the back of the pew. "The moneylenders are already at the table and there's no sign of the messiah storming the temple anytime soon," he said, pulling his cap down firmly on his brow.

Ben waited until he heard the slap of the church doors before standing. He shuddered, uncertain if it was the cold or Dave's cadaver-like presence that had given him the chills.

He slipped on his jacket and walked down the aisle. He hadn't studied the church to any degree before. The venue had served its purpose as a campaign platform, as had his religious beliefs. The faithful rarely questioned the faithful, they preferred to focus their efforts in converting the non-believers. His atheism could easily be disguised as faith; they were two sides of the same coin after all, one gave breath to the other. He turned right at the step leading to the altar and debated whom he should light a candle for. He couldn't decide. He lifted his head towards the crucifix.

"Any inspiration?"

The answer came in the form of a resounding and finite silence. "Figures," Ben said.

Maybe he'd light a candle for himself. Was that even allowed? Would that anger this God in some way? He lit one candle, then another until all thirty were alight, their flames dancing in the thin draft blowing from under the door. He held up his palms against the faint warmth. There were no accompanying thunderbolts from the heavens; he took that as a good sign. As good a sign as someone like him could expect, he thought.

53

The street lights cast a buttery glow across the wasteland between 50th Avenue and East 14th, anointing the area with a ghostly ambience, as if it were pre-lit for a soon-to-be-shot movie scene. The props were positioned just so. An upturned shopping cart, an empty chip bag fluttering across the asphalt, a torn mattress braced against the fence and a stray dog licking at a discarded Taco Bell container. The players, set on their marks, waited for their cues; seven young women, their wardrobe carefully adjusted to show maximum skin, their makeup strategically applied, their stance constructed to showcase availability and promise.

The arrival of two OPD detectives marching from their service car added the dramatic tension. One of the women spat onto the gravel as Tanner and Shaughnessy approached, while the others turned their backs or shuffled into the shadows.

"Tiffiny working this evening?" Shaughnessy asked.

A thin Hispanic girl stretched a long strand of pink gum from her mouth, wrapped it around her middle finger, and raised it high in Shaughnessy's face.

"Helpful," she said, batting away the girl's hand.

Tanner nudged Shaughnessy and nodded towards a car that had pulled up to the sidewalk. Tiffiny was leaning into the window, her red leather skirt hiked up above her thighs. She was wearing an electric-blue wig, giving the impression of some alien pleasure-creature from a trashy sci-fi movie.

Tanner and Shaughnessy walked across the dusty tract of land, and stood either side of her. The driver, suspecting he was about to become the prime suspect in a sting operation, slammed into drive. The car wheels spun on the loose gravel, his tail lights, like two angry red eyes, vanishing into the twilight.

Tiffiny stood her ground in her four-inch heels, hoisted up her top and growled, "So, you gonna arrest me? Or you gonna compensate me for my revenue loss?"

"Neither," Shaughnessy said.

"Oh, yeah?" Tiffiny said, resting her hands on her hips and curling her top lip as if she'd just tasted something unpleasant. "You wanna hook up for a freaky threesome with Mr. Rogers here?"

"The house, Tiffiny, tell me about it."

"You asking the wrong bitch. Now, if you got nothin' else, I got work."

Shaughnessy grabbed her forearm, glimpsing a faint flicker of fear hiding behind the smoky eyeshadow; the same fear Tiffiny had tried to brush off in the interview room.

"Tiffiny, Wendi was your friend, don't you think—?"

Tiffiny cut her off with a sharp bark of laughter. "You think we all hos together? Like some sisterhood of the traveling ass? It don't work like that, ain't no support groups here."

Tanner cleared his throat, flipped open his notebook. "Seems we've got a pretty thick file on you down at OPD, Tiffiny. Solicitation, drug possession and petty theft."

"They didn't convict me of nothin'."

"You're right," Tanner said, snapping his notebook closed. "I guess the judge went pretty light on you, probably on account of your little girl, what's her name, Kylie?"

Tiffiny's shoulders stiffened, her eyes narrowing to two fine lines. "Ain't nothin' below you motherfuckers, right?"

"We just need your help in finding out what happened to Wendi," Tanner explained.

"And if I don't feel much like co-operating?"

Shaughnessy squeezed her forearm until she felt the thick resistance of bone. "We call our friends in Alameda County Child Services, have them check out your childcare accommodations. Where is Kylie now, by the way, while her mom's *working*?"

"I got friends," Tiffiny said, struggling to free her arm.

Shaughnessy's fingers dug deeper into the bone. "In the same sleazebag motel you're living out of down on International?"

"This ain't legal," Tiffiny complained, trying to twist free. "I could sue your ass."

"Sure you could," Shaughnessy said. "I'll retrieve the paperwork from the car, right after I make the call."

Tiffiny frowned and took a loud inhale of breath. "Okay, I'll tell you what I know, but you gotta promise to keep my kid out of this."

"Acceptable, if the information's on the level," Shaughnessy said.

"Not here," Tiffiny said, her eyes like fireflies darting around a flame. "It ain't safe. These other bitches, they like to talk."

"Where?" Tanner asked.

"The motel, tomorrow morning. Figure I don't need to tell you the room number."

Tanner and Shaughnessy looked at each other.

"I don't got time for you two to debate this," Tiffiny said, shaking herself free from Shaughnessy's grip. "I'll tell you what I know, but we do it on my terms. We clear?"

"Crystal," Shaughnessy said.

"No shit," Tiffiny replied, adjusting the bra strap under her halter top and heading back into the shadows, the click of her heels echoing off the overpass walls.

"Think she'll be there?" Tanner asked, watching her walk.

"Where else is she going to go?"

Tanner took a final look over the scene, and wondered, not for the first time, what damned difference the murder of another young girl made to any of these women, or the men who used them. They were just collateral; debris to be discarded and forgotten. Maybe that's what he'd become now, a cleanup man, sweeping up one crime scene after the next, clearing space for the next one to roll in.

Shaughnessy looked over at Tanner, checking out his slumped posture, as if the entire weight of the overpass was pressing on his shoulders. "You ready to roll, or do you want to stroll around the neighborhood some more, Mr. Rogers?" she asked.

"You're a dang comedian, Shaughnessy," Tanner said, following her back to the car.

54

The motel was located off International Boulevard. The kind of establishment where the rooms were rented by the month, or by the hour. The building, a faded peach color, appeared to sweat under the glare of the sun, its stucco walls glistening with condensation.

As Shaughnessy and Tanner pulled up into the narrow courtyard, a commotion was brewing outside one of the rooms, a group of people shouting and hammering their fists on the door and window. From inside, the shrill wail of a young child.

Shaughnessy flashed her badge. "The manager here?"

"That mother ain't ever around when he's needed," said a stick-thin, African American man wearing a Golden State Warrior's shirt. "Got a lice infestation eating the skin off my bones and mold on the wall that's blacker than my ass. Can you arrest him for that? Endangering my well-being and health?"

"Wrong government department," Shaughnessy said, rapping hard on the door. "Tiffiny! Tiffiny, if you're in there, open up now."

No response, just the child's wailing turned up to eleven.

"You might wanna consider beating down the door," an

older, soft-spoken woman said. "That poor baby been cryin' all mornin'."

Shaughnessy nodded at Tanner and threw her shoulder at the door. It flexed some, but stayed in place. Another shoulder shove and the door began to splinter from its hinges. Before she hurled her full weight against it for a last hail-Mary heave, a loud voice hollered from across the courtyard.

"Hey! Hey! Ease the fuck up, dude!"

A young man, shirtless and shoeless, ran over from a room across the courtyard, buckling up his jeans as he walked. A woman appeared from inside the room, wearing bra and panties. Leaning against the frame of the doorway, she blew thick blooms of marijuana smoke skyward with a nonchalant purse of her lips, as if this was a daily occurrence and warranted nothing more than a shrug of her shoulders.

"You break my door, I'll sue your ass," the man shouted as he reached the two detectives. He smelled of stale weed and cheap bourbon.

"You the manager?" Shaughnessy asked.

"Obviously," he said, jangling the bunch of keys attached to one of his belt loops.

Shaughnessy shoved her badge in his face. "Open the door then step back, please, sir."

"Yeah, yeah," the man said, raising his arms. "No need for all the aggression."

"You didn't hear the crying?" Tanner asked.

"Real heavy sleeper," the manager said. "Anyway, kids crying round here all hours of the day, what makes this one so special?"

"The child's two years old and alone in a motel room," Tanner said, following his partner into the room. He sensed the man was following close behind. "Back up," he said, unholstering his gun. "All of you, stay back."

What Follows

The crowd mumbled some dissatisfaction, shuffled back, then moved to the window as the two detectives entered.

The motel room was as expected: queen bed, sheets tumbled to one side, vanity table, two wooden nightstands either side of the bed, one stacked with condoms and lubrication gels, the other holding several packets of disposable diapers. Next to the window, a chrome clothes rack, and next to that a full-length mirror with a patchwork of photographs taped on the sides. The odor of stale urine and feces permeated the room. The baby's diaper needed changing Tanner reckoned as he looked over to the crib at the opposite end of the room, the words "Kylie" looped in colorful, cut-out letters over the front. Standing on the mattress, the child was still crying, her face sodden with tears and snot.

As Shaughnessy attended to the child, Tanner pushed on the bathroom door. The shower curtain was drawn, the steady slap of water on plastic echoing off the walls. Taking a breath, he cautiously pulled back the curtain and prepared himself for the worst.

Tiffiny's naked body was slumped against the shower wall, her head dropped to her chest as if her neck were snapped. Mascara ran down her cheeks like streaks of black tar, her electric-blue wig, like some grotesque joke, had slipped forward to cover her eyes. He called out, " Hey, you'd better come see this."

Shaughnessy walked over and stood behind him. "Shit," she said, holstering her gun.

"It gets worse," Tanner said, pointing at the bloodied stump at Tiffiny's right wrist, a small trickle of red mixing with the pooled water in the shower well.

"I'll call it in," she said, reaching for her phone and heading back into the bedroom.

Tanner stood for a few moments, steadying himself against

the washbasin. How old was this girl? Barely twenty-five? And her kid? What kind of future had Kylie just been handed? One where she'd be shuffled from one foster home to the next until she was old enough to fend for herself, then follow in her mother's footsteps? As he drew the shower curtain shut with an almost reverential motion he heard Shaughnessy call for him.

"Tanner, something you gotta see."

He walked, almost in a daze, back to the bedroom. Shaughnessy stood next to the full-length mirror, studying the collage of photographs. She rolled on a protective glove and carefully unpeeled one of them from the glass. "Look familiar?" she asked, pointing at the two smiling girls.

Tanner nodded, looking first at Tiffiny's face, bursting with youthful joy at some club somewhere, a spread of multicolored lights in the background. But it was the other girl's face that made him catch his breath: Catalina Gomez. Her smile, beaming and as it always seemed to do, outshining everything in her frame, even the dizzying glare of the silver disco mirror ball caught mid-spin above them like some divine orb predicting and forever entwining their destinies.

55

Later that afternoon, Tanner was feeling the weight of the day pressing down on him. He'd taken a break from interviewing the residents from the motel, at least those who'd agreed to talk. Most had just ignored their requests, others had plain refused. He was standing by the window of the fifth floor, tracking the slow movement of the sun as it edged across the port of Alameda and over towards the San Francisco skyline.

"Couple more, Tanner," Shaughnessy said, calling him from the doorway. She noticed his slumped posture as he ran a hand down his face. "You go home, I can finish the statements."

Tanner sighed heavily. "Ever wonder why we do all this, Shaughnessy?"

"Because it's our job?" she said, checking her watch. "And if we don't do our job, we don't get paid. Now, can we go?"

"Sure," he said, following her out into the corridor. "Lead the way."

The last interview of the day was with the soft-spoken woman they'd met at the motel that morning. She stretched her neck back and looked up at the ceiling as if she were checking for something hidden in the air conditioning ducts.

"Amelia Green, current residence Room 315, Sunnyside Motel, International Boulevard, Oakland. Correct?" Tanner asked.

"You know it ain't safe me being here?" Amelia said, her eyes darting around the room, her hands nervy and clammy.

"And why's that?"

"Surveillance," she said. "Got eyes on me everyplace I go."

Tanner sighed and undid the top button of his shirt. "It's been a long day, Ms. Green, I'd be grateful if you could just tell us what you know about the victim, Tiffiny Grant."

Amelia folded her fleshy arms across her chest, eyes focused on the door as if she expected someone to crash through it. "She was a good kid. Apart from the whole hooker thing, but I ain't gonna blame a girl for tryin' to make a living." She lowered her voice. "I can tell you, them other girls, they'd have aborted, not Tiffiny, she carried that kid full term. Ain't many in her situation would have done that."

"Did you ever watch Kylie for her?"

She shook her head, running her fingers under the table, checking for wires. "Once you start, there's no stopping the favors. I helped when I could, bought her formula, diapers, that kind of thing."

Shaughnessy laid the photograph of Tiffiny and Catalina on the table. "Do you recognize this girl?"

Amelia took it between her fingers and squinted. "Yeah, maybe. She looks familiar."

"You might have seen her on the news?"

"Don't follow the news much. Don't have no TV or cell phone, either. Messes with my head," Amelia said, tapping her temple. "That's how they try to control me. They think I don't know, but I ain't stupid."

"Did you ever see this girl with Tiffiny?" Tanner asked.

"Yeah, yeah," Amelia said, stabbing the photograph. "I remember her. Tiffiny always went to some addict support group every Friday, had to do it to keep her kid, mandatory, she said. I had some stuff to give the kid, but there was this girl in Tiffiny's room when I walked over, said she was babysitting. Didn't ask her name or nothing, just gave Kylie some donated toys I got down at St. Vincent's. She was real taken with this one doll--"

"And you saw the same girl there, on multiple occasions?" Shaughnessy interrupted.

Amelia nodded.

"But only on a Friday?"

"Yeah, I said that already," Amelia insisted. "Friday nights. Some dude in this big ass truck dropped her off."

"You saw him?"

"Nah, just heard the truck," she said, craning her head under the table and running her finger under the surface. "That's how they'll come for me, too. Haul my ass off in some big black truck. That's why I got to be vigilant, see, check out all the vehicles entering and departing the motel. Can't be too careful, I got secrets they want to get outta me. But I ain't talking, they ain't getting nothin' out of Amelia Green, no sir, nothing."

56

An hour later, in the OPD café, amidst the lingering aroma of the day's smoked barbeque special, the two detectives sat across from each other. Tanner was twisting around a plastic cup of tepid black coffee spiked with four sugars, Shaughnessy sipped on a bottle of flavored vitamin water.

"Think she's credible?"

"Credible enough," Tanner confirmed.

"And the whole voices-in-the-head shitshow? That didn't bother you?"

"She's maybe a few loaves short of a breadbasket, but she was lucid enough to recognize Catalina with no prompting. She hadn't seen the news or read the papers."

Shaughnessy leaned back and took a slug of her drink. "Okay, let's assume for a moment she's not batshit crazy, that puts Catalina at the motel until 7pm, before she started her shift, which doesn't help us any because we're still missing any witnesses who saw her after she left the Boba Lounge."

"Then we need to establish who was driving the truck."

"Bruce Ho's top of my list," Shaughnessy said. "He probably supplied her the contaminated heroin. Shit, he had enough product in his basement to supply every junkie in a ten-mile radius of the no-tell motel."

Tanner thought for a moment. "Maybe, but you're missing the big question."

"Which is?"

He laid the photograph on the table. "How the heck did Catalina Gomez come to know Tiffiny Grant?"

Shaughnessy drained the last of her water and placed it firmly on the table. "Like I've always said, Tanner, that girl had secrets. Your crusade here? Trying to prove she was some kind of saint, I'm not buying it, never have."

"You and Dugdale both," Tanner said, with a thin smile.

"Fuck you, Tanner," Shaughnessy said, lowering her voice. "Is this how it's going to be now? You think I'm Dugdale's puppet just because I'm sleeping with him."

"Puppet, no?" Tanner said. "But if you're smart, you should be making up your own dang mind about what's going on here."

Tanner scraped back his chair and gulped down the rest of his coffee with a shudder.

Shaughnessy glared. "Want to tell me where you're going?"

"To do my job, that's how we get paid, right?" Tanner said, swiping his jacket from off the back of the chair.

"Fucking great," Shaughnessy muttered, as she launched her empty bottle and watched it hit the rim of the trashcan before falling to the floor, Tanner's words clattering around her head like a pinball.

57

Tanner pushed gently on Catalina's bedroom door and stepped inside. Her bed was still unmade, a pile of freshly laundered clothes stacked neatly on the duvet cover. It was a bedroom like any other teenage girl's: posters of bands taped to the wall, photos of her friends pegged to a length of string looping along the top of her vanity mirror, and a desk piled high with textbooks and paper. Above her headboard, a long string of lights twinkled warmly as if they were beacons to guide her safely home.

"Did you find who killed my daughter?" Francisco Gomez stood in the half-shadow of the doorway as if he were fearful to step inside and face the cold reality that his daughter would never sleep in her bed again; a threshold he was unable to cross.

"We're working on it, Mr. Gomez," Tanner said.

Francisco nodded. "The other police came twice already, they didn't find nothing. Her phone is not here, they looked."

"I'm sure the forensics team were very efficient. I wanted to ask you and your wife some follow-up questions about your daughter—"

"Catalina was a good girl, always a good girl," Francisco

interrupted. "Her heart had so much love," he said, bunching his hand into a fist and pounding at his own chest to prove his point. His eyes glazed over with tears.

Marta Gomez appeared next to her husband. "Hola," she said. She was ashen, as if the life force had been wrung from her leaving a hollow shell.

Tanner spoke softly. "I hate to have to ask you these questions, but were you aware if your daughter took any narcotics?"

"Did the police find any in her room?" Marta asked.

"No––" Tanner began before Marta interrupted him.

"Or in her school locker?"

Tanner shook his head.

"Then, that is your answer. No, Catalina, she would never take drugs. Never."

Tanner extracted a photograph from his jacket. "What about this girl?"

Francisco and Marta caught their breaths as they looked at the smiling image of their daughter, and shook their heads.

"Tiffiny Grant? Did Catalina ever mention that name?"

"No," Marta said. "Who is she?"

Tanner cleared his throat. "Catalina would babysit for her on Friday evenings."

"No, that is wrong. Catalina has guitar lessons, we give her forty dollars every week."

"Mrs. Gomez," Tanner said. "Catalina hasn't turned up for those lessons for over six months."

Marta wiped a tear from her eye. "Why do people keep saying these lies?"

"We checked with her teacher. Catalina quit several months ago. Maybe she didn't tell you because it might have upset you?"

"So, who is this woman?" Marta snapped.

Tanner hesitated. "A sex worker... we found her body in a motel room this morning."

Marta stabbed her finger at Tanner. "My daughter did not know women like that. She did not take drugs or wear those whore shoes you showed me. Not Catalina."

Francisco put his hand on his wife's. "It's okay, Marta."

"Enough, I listen too much to you already," she said, swatting away his hand.

"Marta--"

"You are no different to the news," she said, jabbing Tanner in the chest. "You want to say Catalina was a junkie because that makes it easier, you don't need to investigate no more? But it is all lies."

"Marta, don't cause no trouble," Francisco said, a nervousness Tanner hadn't noticed before flitting across his eyes. "The police, they are doing all they can."

Tanner studied his reactions; the flickering eyelids, the tensing of the shoulders. "I can assure you we are, Mr. Gomez, but if there is anything you haven't told us, now would be a good time to unburden yourself of whatever it is you're holding on to."

"He is not holding on to anything but the memory of our beautiful daughter," Marta said, shoving the photograph back.

"I understand--"

"No, you do not understand. Maybe if you come to this, you will understand," she said, handing Tanner a pamphlet.

```
        Night Vigil for Catalina Gomez.
                  July 19th.
              Lake Merritt. 7pm.
         Peace Love and Understanding.
```

Tanner sighed. "If they have a permit, there's nothing we can do about it. You don't have to attend, in fact it's probably best not to go, these things can be upsetting."

Marta shook her head. "No, no! See, you do not understand, detective, you do not understand at all. They are doing something good, keeping Catalina's memory alive. Maybe someone saw something and will remember. Maybe this will show people who Catalina really was, not the lies the TV and police are saying. I think you should leave my house now."

Francisco and Marta watched as Tanner exited the apartment building towards Lake Merritt.

"Maybe it is time you tell them," Marta said, resting her hand on Francisco's shoulder. "Catalina has gone now, and we have two boys that need their papi."

Francisco nodded solemnly and put his hand over his wife's. "We will find a way," he said. "But not today, not yet."

Marta slowly slipped her hand away. "Soon, Francisco," she said softly. "For your sons, let it be soon."

PART III

FRACTURES

58

Alexus pulled the cork on a bottle of 2013 Viognier she and Christen had bought from a vineyard in Napa. The taste reminded her of last summer when things seemed simpler, when she still felt like she had some control over events and understood her place in the world. Strange how in just twelve short months the ground had shifted under her feet without her even realizing it. She was lost in these thoughts when Jonas's size eleven feet bounding down the stairs startled her.

"Thought you were out already."

"Leaving now," he said, downing a can of Red Bull from the refrigerator.

"Someplace nice?"

"First Friday," he said, grabbing his keys.

"Oh, right," Alexus said, staring at her son as he slipped on his jacket.

"What?" Jonas asked. "You're looking at me all weird."

"You look tired, that's all," she said, examining the rheumy redness at the corner of his eyes. His eyes had always been bright and unsullied, like hers.

"If the school eased off on the holiday reading list, then I might get some sleep."

"You're not taking drugs, are you? Weed? God forbid those prescription meds? This an important year for you."

Jonas sighed. "This, again?" he said, scratching aimlessly at the back of his hand which was red and raw with specks of blood.

"What's that?" Alexus said, reaching to flip over Jonas's hand.

"Leave it, it's just some poison oak or something," he said, pulling his hand back.

"Both of them?" Alexus said, glancing at the other. "Do you have cream? I think I have some from the last time your dad hiked Muir Woods." She flipped open several cupboard doors.

"I already bought some cream at Walgreens, Mom. Gotta go," he said, brushing past her.

"Jonas!" she called, but he was already out of the door and firing up his jeep.

An hour later, Alexus had made good headway on the Viognier, the first fluttering of a wine buzz dulling her senses. Above her, the fluorescents hummed at the silence. She'd become as useful as that damned robot vacuum cleaner, she thought as she looked down at the circular, docile device locked in its home base and switched on autopilot to navigate its daily routine. For an hour a day the robot would bump against the skirting boards as if looking for a new path to some place where it could roam endlessly, picking up debris until its charge weakened to nothing. They both shared the same boundaries, Alexus imagined, invisibly marked but nonetheless solid and real.

When Christen returned home fifteen minutes later, she was busy dismantling the device with a screwdriver.

"It did something to upset you?" Christen asked, looking at his wife, then to the wine bottle.

"No," she said. "It's broken."

"Well, it is now," he confirmed, as Alexus slipped the end of the screwdriver under the casing and splintered the plastic.

"Leave any for me?" Christen asked, swinging the bottle between his thumb and forefinger.

"Two more in the fridge," she said. "Knock yourself out."

Alexus looked through the patio doors to her backyard, where the parched, yellow grass was illuminated by the glow of the solar lights. The lawn looked like she felt, irrelevant and lacking any significant purpose. Maybe she should put it out of its misery, replace it with paving stones and drought-resistant shrubs. Or, she could just turn on the sprinklers, like her neighbor, pay the fines and give the state the middle finger. She quickly dispensed with that idea; maybe that asshole didn't give a shit, but Alexus Hansen couldn't afford that luxury, not if she was to become Rosemont's next mayor. She needed to take a stand against people like Dave Maddens-Smith, and made a mental note to follow up with the OPD about the video footage, make sure they were doing their damn job.

"Do you think I'm doing the right thing?" she asked, joining Christen at the kitchen island.

"What thing?" Christen asked, distractedly checking his phone.

"Running for Mayor."

Christen sipped at his wine. "Of course."

Alexus poured herself another glass. "I had this weird meetup with Ben Strauss. He revealed some personal stuff, but I don't know why. Then, he told me Dave Maddens-Smith has some video of Jonas and that friend of his stacking up the chairs the night before the parade."

"So, he's blackmailing you?"

"I don't know. I don't think so. That's why it was all so weird."

Christen looked around. "Where is Jonas?"

"Out. First Friday in downtown."

"First Friday?"

"The bands and the food trucks?"

Christen thought for a moment and reached for his hoodie.

"No, Christen. Seriously, you're not?" Alexus pleaded.

"I'm sorry," he said, leaning over to kiss her. "We are in the middle of a very complex product test. I'll be back soon, I promise."

"You better not be having a goddamned affair," she muttered under her breath as the front door slammed into place.

59

Preparations for the First Friday Street Fair typically began at 2pm, after the OPD blocked off a large section of Telegraph Avenue and guided the food trucks into their reserved lots. Several hours later, six temporary stages would be assembled on the sidewalks across from the dive bars and urban beer gardens, which by 6pm, would be heaving with customers.

What had begun as a celebration of Oakland's artists had now transformed into a retail opportunity. The art galleries were now hidden behind the stalls selling tie-dye shirts, artisanal jewelry and pot-smoking paraphernalia. Elderly, soft-looking women tending tables for cat adoptions would strike up conversations with the sweet-natured African-American men with sun-crusted dreadlocks that hung off their shoulders like climbing rope, and who sold oversized beach towels embossed with the faces of Bob Marley, Martin Luther-King, President Barack Obama, and various heroic figures of black culture.

It was 5pm when Francisco Gomez arrived. His eyes were bloodshot, holding on to the same glazed expression they'd had since the medical examiner had slipped the sheet from Catalina's face, then solemnly folded it back again. Francisco shook the image from his mind and followed the chugging spit of a generator towards the rear of Guadalajara Tacos.

He climbed the truck's steps and rapped on the door. As he waited, he caught the familiar aroma of lard and the warm, sensual steam of fresh tortillas slipping across the heat. He craned his head, peered through the square air vent and observed one of the cooks, Nibea, resting the tortillas over the grill with the reverence of a priest placing the Body of Christ across a parishioner's tongue.

The scene took him back to another time; another place far from here. A village, high in the Sierra Sur mountains in Oaxaca, his grandmother exacting a similar reverence as she flattened the tortillas, blessing each batch as she handed them to Francisco. He must have been five or six. He couldn't recall the buildings in the village, or what the sunrises or sunsets were like, but the ritual had stayed with him; as clear as the aromas rising from the grill. An overwhelming sense of sadness cascaded through him as he watched Nibea work; a sense of something lost to him forever.

The bubbling roar of fresh pork skins poured into the deep fat fryer shook him from his thoughts. He knocked again and looked to the front of the truck. There was already a long line, which in an hour would increase three-fold. The door cracked open.

"Cisco? What the fuck you doing here?" Hector Figuerello wiped his brow, looking directly past his cousin to the sidewalk. "I told Marta, take all the time you need, I got Arturo and Nibea tonight, you should be at home, with your family."

Francisco threw back his shoulders. "I'm a good worker."

Hector guided Francisco to a nearby doorway, placing his hands across his cousin's shoulders. "You're the best I got, cuz, but you got some real bad shit to deal with, we don't need you tonight. I'll call Marta to come pick you up."

He brushed away Hector's hands. "I work hard," he insisted.

Hector reached into his pocket, unfurling a wad of five-dollar bills. "Take it, go home, we got you covered."

Francisco contemplated refusing the offer before snatching the notes in case Hector changed his mind.

"Go buy some pizza or something and go home to your family."

Francisco flipped through the notes. "My family is broken," he said, wiping a sleeve across his eyes. "Now, it will always be broken."

He stuffed the money in his pocket and scuttled off before his cousin could see his tears.

60

Friday, 9pm, there was a shift in the evening's mood. Darkness had fallen like a mic drop, bringing with it an edgier crowd. Young men, hoodies flipped over their heads, strutted south down Telegraph Avenue, stopping every few hundred feet to listen to the freestyle rappers and slam poets spit out their latest rhymes. The men would watch for a few minutes and either nod their heads in approval or shuffle to the next stage depending on if they were "feeling it" or not.

Francisco Gomez had already drank half a bottle of cheap tequila. Lurching through the crowds, a thickness, like wet cement, setting in his head, he stumbled into a circle of men who passed him from one set of arms to the next like an unwanted party gift. They shoved him back into the street and into the path of a young woman with a coil of tattoos snaking across her neck. She stepped back, rummaging in her handbag for her pepper spray before realizing it was just another drunken old man; harmless, but it set her senses to high-alert nonetheless.

He mumbled a forlorn *"lo siento"* to the woman, muttering

the apology like a mantra as he staggered back to the sidewalk, *"Lo siento, lo siento, lo siento."*

He didn't know why he was apologizing anymore; maybe now it was all he had to offer. He blundered into another crowd. This mob was ten deep and moving to the beat of a salsa band. The lead singer looked like Catalina; he was sure it was her. He elbowed his way through, but he was stuck fast in the clutch of swaying bodies. He moved forward but the mass of bodies was thick and unyielding. Slowly, he dropped his hands. Maybe it wasn't Catalina after all, and this was just another illusion.

He moved away and fell into the shelter of a nearby doorway. A homeless man, reaching for blankets from his shopping cart, leant over, spit dripping from his cracked lips.

"Hey, my doorway, asshole, get your own."

"Lo siento, lo siento, lo siento."

He was hungry; more than hungry, ravenous. He hadn't eaten for days it seemed. He stumbled back to the truck. Staggering around the back he banged hard on the door.

Hector answered, his brow slippery with sweat. "Shit, I told you man, go the fuck home, we don't need you."

"Tacos. Gimme four tacos. Carnitas," he said, swaying back and forth and fumbling for the scrunch of dollar bills in his pocket.

Hector sighed. "All right, cuz, stay here, I'll get you your tacos, then you'll go home?"

Francisco nodded.

Hector was about to shut the door, when he heard a cool, curt voice call out to him. "Hector, what do I have to do to get you to call me back?"

Hector looked over his cousin's shoulder at the tall, composed Dane he'd got to know as Christen. "I'm busy, you'll have to come back later."

"It's about Catalina. We need to talk."

"Hey, keep your fucking voice down," Hector grunted.

Francisco's senses prickled at the mention of his daughter's name. "Hey, I know you!" he said, waving a finger. "Your wife, Miss Hansen, I work for her."

"Shit," Hector said, brushing past Francisco. "Usual place, two hours."

Francisco stepped forward and poked Christen in the shoulder. "You know her? You know Catalina?" he said, swaying on his heels.

Before Christen could answer, Francisco felt his legs give way beneath him, as if the sidewalk had opened him up and swallowed him whole.

61

Christen walked down the dimly lit corridor. A permanent stench of bleach lingered deep in the brickwork, and he suspected they doused the corridor floor with gallons of the stuff at the end the night. Off the hallway were several soundproofed rooms available to rent by the hour, no questions asked, all monies payable to the management in advance.

He took a right towards what he'd heard called "The Pussy Drome". As he got closer, the dull thud of music thumping through the walls and floor reverberated through his bones. At the entrance he nodded to the bouncer, who returned the gesture and swung open the door.

The Rat House had a temporary, unfinished feel about it; as if it could be pulled down and packed up in a matter of hours, like a circus tent, and pitched elsewhere. The lighting was always sparse and cleverly positioned to ensure the dark corners remained dark; *nothing to see here, just feast your eyes on everything else on offer.* Christen had partaken of those offerings too many times to recall; a blind eye was easy to turn when the shiny objects dazzled so brightly in the other direction. But tonight, as he walked towards the bar, he studied more closely the black drapes hanging from the rafters and wondered what lay behind them; what kind of rot they were hiding.

When he'd first been introduced to the Rat House, the idea had intrigued. An exclusive gentleman's club open to any man with the means to pay the $20,000 per year membership fee and the discretion to keep their mouths shut. He couldn't imagine the place could deliver on its promise; every whim catered for, every desire fulfilled, every perversion satisfied. Of course it had. For Christen, it had delivered exactly what it had promised, though his own desires could be classed as pedestrian compared to the activities the other men bragged about.

Prostitutes were Christen's vice, the more exotic the better, so long as they performed as dirty as they talked, he was happy to pay the price. He could have analyzed why he did this, but why expend the time and money on therapy when, deep in his core, he both recognized and understood his motivation? Like most things in his life, it circled back to his father.

At the age of fourteen, his father had taken Christen to Amsterdam's red-light district when he was on one of his frequent business trips. There, he'd instructed Christen to choose the prostitute of his liking and not to come out of the room until he'd lost his virginity. The entire experience was humiliating. He'd climaxed the moment the young girl––black, with a mean curl to her lips––reached inside his pants. He'd ran out, lied to his father and spent most of that night awake in his hotel bedroom, feeling both ashamed and electrified by the experience. It proved to be both a vicious circle of emotions that had followed him like his shadow; the thrill of the transaction, the satisfaction of the act itself, then the bolt of shame, so searing and deep that it compelled him to want to lose himself in the act again as if, if he performed it often enough, he might somehow purge himself clean; fuck the shame away.

The turgid thought was still rattling around the corners of

his mind as he walked across "The Pussy Drome" floor. *Fuck the shame away?* If only it were that easy. He checked for an empty booth, preferably in the shadows and far from the pole dancers swaying their pale flesh in time to "Pour Some Sugar on Me". He took his time passing, just in case one of them caught his eye. None of them did. They all looked the same: languid bodies with vacant eyes, going through the motions, the only sparkle emanating from the glitter pasted onto their skin, reflecting the spikes of light from the overhead mirror balls.

A pretty Asian girl wearing a green bikini and a coy smile served him his Corpse Reviver No.2. Christen handed her a twenty and gestured she should keep the change. As he looked over the bar, a pack of men were escorted to the lap-dancing tables where they began whipping out fresh dollar bills. Had Catalina been one of the lap dancers that night? No, he was sure she was just a server. He remembered talking to her for a while; the lap dancers would balk at conversation, it slowed down trade. Catalina had served him drinks––the same night he'd seen her and Hector argue out in the parking lot.

He took a large gulp of his cocktail. Seeing Catalina's picture on the news had shaken him, but he wasn't about to show that to Hector; he was the kind of man who, like a rat, could sniff out a weakness and gnaw at it until it bled. He was about to order another drink when Hector strutted in, two young girls hanging off his arms like trinkets. He directed them to wait by the bar and strode towards Christen.

"*Que pasa, amigo?*" he said, gesturing for the server. He was wearing another cheap suit two sizes too large, which by the shine coming from the lapels, looked as if it had been dry-cleaned too often.

"You got something to tell me? Something about Catalina?" Hector flung his arms behind the back of the booth. "Then talk, I don't got all night."

62

Christen took a large slug of his drink; more for fortitude than pleasure and gestured the server to bring him another. "Your cousin, is he okay?" he asked.

"He don't remember shit." Hector leaned close to Christen, his nose twitching as if he were sniffing out something unpleasant. Having detected nothing but the waft of expensive aftershave, he sat back. "You fuck with Catalina that night, give her some bad H?"

"I don't do that shit, just the weed," Christen protested.

"Your son though, what's his name, Jonas? He takes after his father?"

"What's my son got to do with this?"

"Maybe something, maybe nothing. But you already knew him and Catalina were dating. Maybe he invited her over for dinner to meet the family?"

"I have no idea what you're talking about, Hector."

"Maybe Jonas, he supplied her the bad H?"

Christen blanched. "I understand what you're doing, Hector, it won't work. I saw you and Catalina arguing in the parking lot that night. It looked like things got very heated."

"What you saw was a family dispute."

"Did you––?" Christen began.

"Don't fuckin' say it! That girl was family," Hector said, taking a messy slug of his drink, spilling some over his shirt. "You want to know why, I'll tell you. I was protecting you and all the other fuckers in this place."

"What about protecting Catalina?"

"Fuck you! She begged me for a job. She liked the fancy stuff you know, clothes, cell phones, shoes. Who do you think paid for that? Wasn't her parents, they don't earn shit. A few weeks later, someone tells me she's taking photographs. I warned her to stop, but she wouldn't listen. That night, I caught her again, chased her out into the parking lot, made sure she gave me the phone. Then I hear a truck pull up, and she runs off. I didn't chase after her––"

"Bet you wished you had, Hector. She might still be alive."

Hector couldn't bring his eyes to meet Christen's. "No point dwelling on what might have been. I got the photos, that's what the boss wanted. Job done. Shame she got none of you, but that's okay, I got that covered."

He took out his phone. "Family," he said, swiping the screen. "It's important, no?"

A flutter of nervousness settled deep in Christen's belly.

"See, I know you, amigo," Hector said, wagging his finger. "You got secrets you don't want your family to know about."

Christen shuffled, his hands turning clammy.

"Hey, it's all good, bro. I don't know one fucker in here who don't got a secret. But that's why we come, right? To let off some steam in someplace nobody's gonna ask questions?"

Hector turned the screen. "And a man like you, you're into variety, like to taste all the colors of the world?"

Christen felt his body shiver as Hector swiped through the photographs.

"See, that's your car," Hector said. "Real nice. What you do, lease or buy? I'm guessing a man in your position, you lease, you like upgrading, get bored with the same model, right?"

Christen's mouth was dry, his pulse thumping deep in his ears.

"And see that chick? The one leaning her titties into your car window, she's a street ho. You remember her, right? Wendi Chee?"

Hector scrolled to the next photograph. "And this one," he said, pinching the screen to zoom closer. "A real, what did they used to call them? A Kodak moment?"

He continued scrolling. "That's you, leaning out of the window checking out her arms, because who wants to fuck a junkie ho, right? I know you like 'em dirty, but you don't like 'em contaminated."

Hector sat back. "I got a bunch more too, but I figure you got the picture by now."

Christen felt sick. The syrupy finish of the cocktail roiling around his stomach. "I didn't. I would not do that. I dropped her back there, after."

"You did? Let me check on that," Hector said, looking at his screen. "No. I got no pictures of that, my storage must have been full. But if I do find some, I'll send them on."

Christen exhaled, taking in the weight of what Hector was implying. Was this it? The payback he always expected? The reckoning he knew would come someday? How the shame would become manifest?

"Hey, it's not so bad," Hector said, patting Christen's knee. "You're not so special. We got a whole collection of client photos. The boss insists on it, you know, just in case."

"And can I meet this boss, maybe talk to him?" Christen asked, his voice hoarse.

"It don't work like that. The boss, he very particular about who he meets."

"Money then? I can pay."

Hector shrugged. "He don't need your money, he just needs you to keep your mouth shut about what you saw that night with Catalina, about all this," he said, waving his hand. "Then, maybe I need to delete a whole bunch of photos and locate those shots of you dropping off that street ho back where you picked her up. You think on that, amigo."

Christen sat forward, having his first clear thought of the evening. "You said nothing happened with you and Catalina, that she ran off. So why blackmail me if nothing happened?"

"Blackmail's an ugly word, amigo, boss likes to call it an insurance policy," he said, slipping the phone back into his pocket.

"Insurance against what?"

"Above my pay grade. Boss asks me to do something, I do it." Hector downed the remainder of his drink and stood. "Adios, Mr. Hansen, I bet you'll do the right thing in the end, people in your situation always do."

After Hector left, Christen ordered several more drinks. He gazed over at the pole dancers as they became like the ghostly floaters he sometimes saw in the periphery of his vision after staring too long at a computer screen. Using the table to steady himself, he stood and made his way to the door, the room spinning in ever-increasing circles.

Back in the corridor, he traced his palm along the wall as he walked. A few feet ahead, a man, his back turned, walked towards one of the rooms. The man briefly turned to look behind him as if some sixth sense triggered the feeling he was being watched. Christen's own reactions were slow, running several off-beats behind his usual rhythm, but he was certain he recognized the face, maybe from some newspaper article or some promotional literature. Before he could be sure, the man was already gone, faded like a ghost into the shadows.

63

Madeline Ambrose watched Tanner pace in front of his desk for a few moments before approaching. "Am I interrupting your workout?" she asked, watching Tanner stretch out his back with a gruff moan that fell somewhere between pleasure and pain, but settled mostly on the side of pain.

"Got something for me, Ambrose?" he said, shaking his arms out as if drying his shirtsleeves of something he'd spilled on them.

"Sure do," she said, handing him a slip of paper. "The supplemental tests you asked me to conduct on Catalina Gomez."

"Don't tell me, positive for syphilis," he said, slipping on his jacket.

"Negative," Ambrose said. "The results came back negative."

Tanner sat his buttocks on the edge of the desk and sighed. "Dinkelberg."

"I thought you'd be pleased."

"Far from it. You know what this means, don't you?"

"I await enlightenment."

"Someone deliberately put Catalina's name on that list--"

"What list?" Shaughnessy asked, having just walked in on the tail end of the conversation.

"A list..." Tanner began before pausing to carefully choose his words. "A list provided to the Alameda Health Department of suspected syphilis victims in Oakland."

"That right?" Shaughnessy said, placing her latte on her desk. "First I've heard of any kind of list."

"It's confidential, apparently," Tanner said.

"Yet you knew Catalina's name was on there," she said, taking a sip of her coffee.

Tanner's neck muscles tightened. "Besides the point. Someone put her name on there for a reason. My guess, they wanted to tarnish the poor girl's name some more, and we fell for it. What does that say about us?"

"Says we're doing our damned job. We get a lead, we follow up."

"The whole case stinks like last week's sushi dinner," Tanner said, slapping his palm on the desk.

Ambrose cleared her throat. "I should probably go," she said, gathering her files. "Give you two some alone time."

Shaughnessy nodded. "Yeah, thanks, Maddy."

"Maddy?" Tanner said. "Since when did you guys get so chummy?"

"Since she sent me the invite to her retirement party. Got yours yet?"

Tanner shrugged.

"Probably in the mail, or she forgot," Shaughnessy said, reaching for an evidence bag on her desk. "Tiffiny Grant's cell phone. The techs are logging and tracing the incoming and outgoing calls, but I spent last night searching through her photographs."

She swiped open the screen. "Selfies, tons of photos of the

kid, as you'd expect. But then there was this one," she said, turning the phone towards Tanner.

He looked at the screen. Another photograph of Catalina, but this time a young man standing next to her, a guitar hanging low on his hips. His T-shirt had the words Moonshine Fever printed across the front, with the drawing of a Mason jar with large cartoon-like eyes which seemed to be sweating blood. Tanner took a sharp intake of breath.

"You know this kid?" Shaughnessy asked.

"I've made his acquaintance, let's say."

Tanner thought for a moment. "That Instagram thing you did to trace that Jonas Hansen kid? Can you see which friends he's connected to?"

"Already gone one better," she said, gesturing for him to join her at her computer.

"Moonshine Fever has a Facebook page," she said, scrolling down the stream of photographs. "Got a link to a website and an email address."

Tanner leaned back, sensing a minuscule crick of release in one of his lower vertebrae. For the first time in weeks, he felt as if he had something solid to grasp onto; some sliver of hope that he could turn this case around before the DA signed off.

"Dang good work, Shaughnessy, let's see if we can't persuade this Moonshine character to answer a few friendly inquiries."

64

Tanner and Shaughnessy waited at the dockside for Moonshine to row the gondola back to its berth. The morning was muggy; the sun blistering, its white-hot reflection over Lake Merritt. The dry moss and sediment deposits were like bath rings around the shores of the lake where the water had evaporated to reveal the detritus of empty soda cans and food containers that a few weeks ago were submerged beneath the slick, green algae.

A few minutes later, Moonshine rowed into the shallows and helped a young couple off the gondola and onto the jetty.

"Yeah, thanks for the gratuity, fuckers," he mumbled as the couple headed off. He looped the gondola ropes around the mooring posts and looked up. "You two looking for a ride? You gotta pay the bossman back at the boathouse."

"Mason Arnett?" Tanner asked, showing his badge.

"Might be," Moonshine said, his eyes narrowing. "Wait up, I know you. You're the same cop asking questions at the cemetery. You looking for Hansen? He ain't on shift today."

"We're looking for you, Mason," Tanner said. "This is Detective Moira Shaughnessy."

Moonshine laid the oar at his feet.

"Got a few questions, Mason," Shaughnessy said. "About Catalina Gomez."

"What about her?"

Tanner showed him the photograph from Tiffiny's phone. "This was taken the night she disappeared," he said, tapping the date stamp.

"Yeah?" Moonshine shrugged. "Get tons of chicks wanting selfies with the band. Comes with the territory."

Shaughnessy grinned. "Just a regular Justin Bieber, aren't you?"

Moonshine stuffed his hands into his pockets. "Don't the police need my parents' permission to question me about shit?"

"Not if you voluntarily offer to help our investigation."

"Why would I do that?"

"Your call, but if I were to ask you to empty that backpack under that seat right there," Tanner said, gesturing inside the gondola, "what's the likelihood of finding something you'd rather not have us know about?"

Moonshine laughed. "You ain't got probable cause to search my shit."

Tanner checked his notebook. "See, Mason, that's not technically correct. Having already witnessed you and your underage friends partaking in narcotic substances that night at the cemetery, gives me probable cause to search your backpack. And if I find anything in there I don't like the smell of, I'll haul you in for questioning for the next few hours. Then you'd need to source a court-appointed lawyer, which could take some time and contact a parent or guardian so they can be present while you're being questioned. How's that sound for filling up the remainder of your day?"

Moonshine contemplated his limited options, looked over to

his backpack and swallowed hard. "Fuck it. Yeah, I saw Catalina at the gig that night."

"What time?"

"I dunno, ten maybe."

"After she finished her shift at the Boba Lounge?"

"I guess."

"Then what?"

"We finished the gig, then went to a party over at some dude's house in the hills. Don't remember where, one of those big-ass places. Got pretty wasted, don't remember much to be honest, detective."

"Was Catalina with you?"

Moonshine shook his head. "Nah, went solo."

"Anyone else at the party see her?"

"Dunno."

"How did you get home, Mason?" Shaughnessy asked. "If you were so wasted you couldn't recall where you were?"

Moonshine scraped the heel of his Converse sneakers across a crust of moss dried onto the dock timbers.

"Mason?" Tanner prompted.

"I ain't looking to get nobody into trouble," he said, slipping his hands under his armpits. "I called a friend to pick me up."

"Which friend?"

Moonshine dragged a strand of hair behind his ear. "The dude who teaches me guitar, G-Man."

"G-Man? Gérard Rosseau?" Tanner asked, taking a step forward.

"I didn't have no one else to call. He always said if I needed anything, he'd help me out, you know, he's a good guy."

"And?"

"I was hanging around Broadway Terrace, don't remember how I got there. He picked me up."

"That's close to Lake Temescal."

"Yeah sure, maybe."

"Something you're not telling us?" Tanner said.

Moonshine bit his lower lip. "We saw Catalina. She was walking by that big-ass country club, the one with the golf course that cuts across the road? I got G-Man to pull up, give her a ride."

Tanner's "bull crap" radar beeped at the back of his eyelids; a faint but noticeable vibration, like his tinnitus would sound on a good day. "You sure about that, Mason?"

"Yeah," he confirmed. "G-Man picks her up, but she's wasted, ain't making too much sense 'bout nothin'. Keeps talking like she's on coke or some such shit, you know, real fast."

"So why did you lie to us?" Tanner asked.

Moonshine's shoulders slumped. "My dad's a real hard-ass. If he found out he'd ground me for like months. That ain't a good image for the band."

"So, Rosseau picked up Catalina that night. Who did he drop off first?" Shaughnessy asked.

"My place was closest. She lives down on International."

Shaughnessy scratched her eyebrow. "If I'm hearing this right, last person you saw Catalina with the night she disappeared, was your guitar teacher, Gérard Rosseau?"

Moonshine nodded. "I didn't get the dude into trouble or anything, did I?"

65

Hector strode into his apartment and threw his jacket over the kitchen chair. From across the room, Bruce Ho watched as Hector scrubbed methodically over the kitchen sink.

"You bring me some food?"

Hector wiped his hands on a towel and took a thick package wrapped in silver foil from his pocket. "Vegetarian," he said, lobbing the burrito at Bruce. "Like you asked."

Bruce ripped the foil and tore at the tortilla casing, poking his finger inside the tepid contents. "Shrimp? What the fuck?"

Hector wrenched the top off a cold bottle of Pacifico. "Like I said, vegetarian."

Bruce huffed and set about extracting the shrimp, placing them in a neat line with the tails all facing in the same direction across the coffee table.

"So, how long you gonna be here?" Hector asked, taking a thick throatful of beer. "It's been two weeks and my apartment stinks of you and your shit." He gestured at the pile of clothes stacked neatly at the side of the couch.

Bruce wiped a smear of hot sauce from his lips. "You kicking me out?"

Hector stretched his legs and gestured around the compact living area: one couch, one seat, a flat-screen TV and a rickety kitchen table. "I got one bedroom, you can't stay on my couch forever, man, people might get to thinking we're a couple." He laughed, reaching for a joint he kept in an old tobacco tin above the refrigerator.

"Fuck you," Bruce said, exhaling a foghorn of a burp that seemed to echo off the walls.

Hector pointed at Bruce. "See what you did there? It's not helping your case, amigo."

"What do you recommend? I go back home and wait for the cops to arrest my ass?"

"You make a good point," Hector said, drawing on the joint. "How much product you lose anyway?"

"Enough."

"Like how much enough? Ten, twenty? Thirty grand?"

"About that," Bruce admitted.

Hector made a long whistling sound. "Makes sense, why the boss keeps asking me about you. *'Where the fuck is he hiding? Did he speak to the cops?'* I told him, Bruce, he's solid, man, he ain't no dumb fuck."

"Yeah," Bruce said. "I'm no fuckin' rat. You tell him that?"

"See, that's what I thought," Hector said, leaning forward to emphasize his point. "But then I get thinking, if Bruce is no dumb fuck why was he cutting the boss's product, because that would be a dumb fuck move, right?"

Bruce shrugged. "Don't know shit about that."

"Yeah, I figured, " Hector said. "Because Bruce? He'd be a dead man by now, right, selling some contaminated product to girls like Catalina. You know she was family, right? Her old man, Francisco? Him and me are first cousins."

"Yeah," Bruce said, nodding. "My condolences, man."

"Much appreciated," Hector said. He bunched his fingers

into a tight fist. "When I find the cocksucker who gave Catalina them drugs, I'll cut their balls off, feed them to the rats."

Bruce nodded. "But you kept quiet, right? The boss doesn't know I'm here?"

Hector nodded. "Unless something happens to make me change my mind."

Bruce reached under the couch, slipped out his knife and leapt forward, urging the cold steel against Hector's throat. "Yeah, like what?"

Hector smiled. "I think you got this all wrong, pendejo," he said. "You don't have no leverage in this arrangement. You need me a lot more than I need you stinking up my apartment. The cops got your house under surveillance, your businesses all closed up, cops crawling all over those too."

Bruce drew the blunt edge of the knife up to the soft flesh between Hector's chin and Adam's apple. He pushed on the blade until the skin peaked white, then released the pressure.

"See, that's the action of a reasonable man," Hector said, wiping the palm of his hand over his neck.

Bruce sat, his leg twitching as he contemplated his options ."What now?"

"I give you one week," Hector said, blowing a long trail of smoke to the ceiling. "Then you find alternative accommodation."

"And if I don't?"

"Then I figure you're out of options. Seriously, if I were you, I'd take my chances with the cops. Taking it up the ass in the penitentiary for a few years gotta be better than the alternative, right?"

Bruce ran his hands down his thighs to wipe the seep of sweat that seemed to have permanently settled into his palms, and thought on Hector's proposal.

"Sure the boss would be real appreciative, get you the best

lawyer and everything," Hector continued. "Nice fat bank deposit for when you get out. Boss is real keen on those deals, what's he call them again? IRAs? Insurance Retirement Accounts? Fuckin' funny, right? Like he's offering some legit business deal."

Bruce shook his head. "Not an option."

"Shame, but maybe I got an alternative solution." Hector rummaged in his jacket pocket and took out his cell phone. He swiped through a stream of photographs before stopping at one he'd emailed to himself some weeks ago.

He turned the screen towards Bruce. "Maybe this gringo," he said, stabbing the photograph of Jonas and Catalina kissing. "Maybe he gave her the fucked-up product? You know him, right? Regular customer?"

Bruce nodded. "Yeah, he's a dipshit."

"And maybe he spoke to the cops too? Gave them your name?"

A sudden flash seared through Bruce's mind as he remembered how Jonas kept asking about the night Catalina vanished; how he kept scratching at his hand as if he were nervous about something; real nervous. Then, that time at the lake, when Jonas interrupted his workout and was all hot about talking to the police.

"That's good, very good," Hector said, noticing the anger pooling in Bruce's eyes. "We both got a reason to find his ass and ask him some questions, no?"

Bruce nodded and flipped his knife from hand to hand, sensing where its perfect balance lay.

66

The heat had subsided a degree or two in the past few days, but nothing that would come close to breaking the drought. Blame was passed around like an unwanted Christmas gift. That week, it was the Central Valley almond farmers who were under the glaring spotlight of culpability. According to reports, it took a gallon of water to grow a single almond, and with three million acres of the Central Valley now dedicated to growing the profitable nut, there was growing pressure to ease production until water levels were more robust.

"Such is the plight of these farming communities, locked in an eternal struggle with the elements. This is Laura Sheldon for the California Report."

Jessica was reversing into a parking spot as the local NPR station switched gears into *"donation mode"*. It was the conclusion of the first week of the Summer Fundraiser, when the presenters rallied every ounce of carnival barker salesmanship they could muster and pleaded for donations *"from people like you"* to *"provide the unbiased news you've come to trust."*

"People like you?" — the phrase irked Jessica. The hosts

always sounded so pleased with themselves and the *"essential service"* they provided. Jessica didn't doubt their sincerity, but the constant interruptions to her favorite programs became old quickly, as did the constant repetition of the long list of *"generous gifts"* a listener could choose from for making a donation: *"a FEMA approved four-person earthquake preparedness bucket, a year's subscription to the* New York Times, *all available for a mere, dollar-a-day donation."* She wondered sometimes if the rotating carousel of hosts truly understood what the phrase *"people like you"* implied. If the people she counseled could spare a dollar a day, they sure as hell wouldn't be sending it to their local NPR station.

Jessica was still irritated by the fundraising circus as she traveled the elevators, yet equally annoyed with herself for thinking uncharitable thoughts about decent people who were only doing their jobs. Still, they were experts in laying on the guilt, that was for sure, making her feel like a common thief pocketing their services. She'd promised herself enough times to *"pick up the phone and make the call,"* but never had. Maybe this year she'd break the listening habit of a lifetime and donate, but not today. She was too busy.

Irritation, guilt and procrastination: a holy trinity of emotions and it was barely 9am. Hardly a positive start to the workday. She flashed Alyssa a smile and buzzed herself into the office. Throwing herself in her chair, she shuttered the blinds and was about to poke her computer to life when Jackson Cain bounded in with the enthusiasm of an eager puppy.

Jessica looked up. "See the gout's eased up then?"

"What? Oh, yep, too much uric acid in the system, apparently," he explained, placing a large cardboard box onto her desk. "Stuck a needle the length of a goddamn pencil into my toe, twice. I think the doctor must have missed the first time but was too damned scared to admit it. Young thing, probably didn't know where the hell she was meant to be poking the damned needle."

"You scream like a girl?"

"More like a whimper," he said. "Like an old dog."

Jessica laughed. "So, what? You're all cured now? Gout free?"

Jackson shook his head, his plump cheeks wobbling. "No cure, just pain management. It'll come and go, good days, bad days."

"And this is a good day?"

"For you, it's a very good day," he said, tapping the box. "Remedium. Arrived by courier first thing this morning."

"The antivirus?" she said, examining the box and smiling. "About time."

"No excuses now, Swift, get 'em rounded up. Nab 'em and jab 'em," he said, making a stabbing gesture with his left hand.

"That easy, huh?" Jessica said.

"By the way, there's someone in reception asking for you."

Jessica sensed a tiny whisper of hope in her gut. "Nelson?"

"Damned if I know, just overheard him asking for you as I was passing. Older guy, looks like a lawyer or maybe a doctor."

The whisper of hope fluttered away as quickly as it had arrived.

"Keep up the outstanding work," Jackson said, turning nimbly on his heels. "Remember, nab 'em and jab 'em!"

Several minutes later, Jessica sat with Doctor James Beaufort as he handed over the paperwork. Her heart sank deep into her shoes as she listened. This was not a good day. In fact, it was about as far from a good day as you could get in her job. Her first thought was Sabine, she needed to talk to her; right now. After several attempts at calling and texting, she checked her tracking device. Shit! She ran to her office and grabbed her purse and jacket.

67

Maybe it was a date, maybe it wasn't, Sabine could never be sure. Jonas played fast and loose with the term. "You're not abducting me, are you?" she said, as Jonas drove his convertible jeep onto the Bay Bridge on-ramp. "Because my mom had me install this tracker on my phone, and she'll be here with a SWAT team before you finish tying me up."

Jonas gave her a muted smile, as if it were clicked to the lowest setting of a dimmer switch. "Just delete it."

"You don't know my mom," Sabine said, savoring the rush of wind as they drove over the bridge's smooth tarmac. She could stay here forever, she imagined, a straight-line journey to nowhere in particular, the warm breeze at her face, hair bouncing across her bare shoulders.

Several minutes later, Jonas drove through the exit down to Treasure Island––568 acres of artificial landfill at the mid-point between San Francisco and Oakland––and pulled up at the low wall hemming the shoreline.

Sabine stood and draped herself over the frame of the windshield. "It's beautiful," she said, looking at the glistening San Francisco skyline. "You bring all your dates here?"

"Never said this was a date."

Sabine felt a prick of irritation. *If this wasn't a date, what the hell had she spent the last hour of her life preparing for?*

"Yeah, most people just pass over it on the way to the city."

"They don't know what they're missing," Sabine said, sitting back and waiting for Jonas to make his move. She'd let him kiss her, maybe longer than she'd allowed in the hot tub last week. She knew the shape of his mouth now, how his lips moved over hers. But there was no move, only a tense silence which made Sabine feel uneasy. In a reckless moment, she leant over and kissed his cheek: a peck she hoped he'd take as permission to explore further.

"What was that for?"

"Just thanks, I guess," she said, shrugging.

Jonas kept his gaze to the horizon, as if he were waiting for a more formal invitation.

Sabine turned. "Something up? Is this about the other day in the hot tub?"

"Nope, just enjoying the view."

Sabine decided to change the subject. "You remember the vigil's next week? For Catalina? You're coming, right?"

Jonas shuffled uncomfortably. "You didn't know her, why do you even care?"

Sabine's heart sank a few degrees south. "Of course I care."

"She wasn't your friend or anything, just seems weird that's all, organizing a vigil for some chick you didn't even know."

"There should be a hundred people, at least," Sabine continued, determined to not let Jonas burst her bubble. "But I'm like really nervous too. I've never done anything like this before, except organizing some lame bake sale back in middle school."

"They made all the kids do that."

"Yeah, it was like some big competition."

"Rosemont," Jonas said, shaking his head. "They can turn a bake sale into a freakin' Olympic sport. Can't wait till I go to college, leave all that bullshit behind."

"You're already accepted?"

"Applied to my top five, but my mom's stressing out big time about the whole thing."

"And you're not?"

"Nope. My GPA's 4.1, captain of the lacrosse team. All that privilege they keep talking about, that's me."

Sabine laughed.

"What?" he asked.

"It's just that I didn't expect that level of self-awareness from Jonas Hansen, that's all."

"You thought I was just a jock, right? Like everyone else."

"No, just surprised, that's all. A good surprise," she confirmed, settling her hand gently on his knee. He pushed it away.

"Okay, what's up, Jonas? You're acting like a complete dick."

He looked away and rubbed his hands over his face. His crew-neck sweatshirt with the extra-long sleeves that reached his knuckles, slipped back over his wrists. Sabine's eyes widened as she looked over the welts, like red, raw scars, as if he'd scraped away the top layer of skin.

"Did that get worse, like a lot worse?"

"You ask more questions than my mom," he said, yanking the sweatshirt sleeves back down to his knuckles.

Sabine felt the snap of a breeze from the Bay. "Why ask me out on a date if you're not going to even talk to me?"

Jonas didn't have a suitable answer. He wanted to talk, would have welcomed the relief of unburdening. Sabine would probably freak out, just like his parents would if they found out. He shifted his seat back and stamped his boot on the dashboard as if he were constructing some artificial barrier Sabine couldn't cross.

"Told you, it's not a date, just hanging out."

"Yeah, you like said that already," she snapped, an itch of anger forming in her belly. She was ready to tell Jonas to take her *"the fuck home"* when she heard her name being called. She looked to her right and checked out the brown-colored Camry pulling up next to them, her mother in the driving seat.

Her mouth slacked open. "Mom? What the hell?"

"You need to come home with me, right now," Jessica said, swiping off her tracking app as she climbed from the car.

"Is it Dad?" Sabine asked, a flutter of panic in her voice. "Has something happened to Dad?"

"Not that I'm aware of," Jessica said. "I'll explain later. I'm sure you won't mind, will you?" she added, looking directly at Jonas.

"Oh, hey, Mrs. Swift, what's up?"

As he turned, the light caught the side of his face, highlighting the scar running down his cheek. Jessica's memory was triggered; something Topaz Autumn had said to her and Tanner at the penitentiary.

"Nasty scar, how did you get that, Jonas?"

"Erm, scratched my face on the rosebushes, why?"

"Mom," Sabine said, through clenched teeth. "You're embarrassing me."

"Sure I am. As your mother it's part of my job description."

Sabine clipped her seat belt and folded her arms. "You'll have to drag me out. If that's cool with you, then go ahead."

"Jonas," Jessica pleaded, "you're a smart kid, help me out here."

Jonas shrugged. "If she don't wanna go…"

"I'm very aware of how you got that scar, Jonas," Jessica said, spiking him with a steel-eyed stare. "And this morning I met with Doctor Beaufort. You know him, right?"

Jonas shuffled, unable to look Jessica in the eye. "Em, yeah, kind of."

"Good, then you understand why I'm here." Jessica folded her arms. "I'm waiting."

Jonas's world tilted a step out of focus; the city and the sway of whitecaps rolling across the bay distorting as if reflected in the warp of an amusement-park mirror. He snapped himself back to the moment, leaned over and unclipped Sabine's belt. "Maybe you should go with your mom," he said. "She looks pretty pissed."

"Seriously? Thanks for your support, asshole!" She threw open the door, just missing Jessica's hip.

"Sure, no problem, Lower Rosemont," Jonas said, offering her another low-wattage smile, this one laced with a tinge of resignation.

Sabine pivoted, leaned back into the jeep. "Don't fucking call me that again," she said, stabbing her finger at Jonas. "Not ever!" She flung open the Camry door and threw herself across the back seat in a near-fetal position, kicking against the door with a shrill, frustrated scream.

68

Jonas stayed for a long while afterwards, watching the sun dip low over the Marin Headlands and the slow descending twilight envelop the city. Shit! That was insane! Wasn't the doctor meant to keep his personal information confidential? Maybe he could sue his ass. Beaufort had told him it would clear up with a couple of injections, but he didn't carry the antivirus, he needed to go someplace else; Jonas hadn't even looked at where. He reached in his pocket, pulled out the prescription and instructions. Jonas was to report to Alameda County Health, where Ms. Jessica Swift, Senior Health Examiner, would administer the treatment. Fuck! He slapped his hands hard on the wheel.

As his mind tumbled through his limited options, a large motorcycle rumbled to a stop, parking less than an inch from his door. Behind him, a large truck bumped its wide, menacing grill against the jeep's rear fender.

"Jesus," Jonas said, watching the motorcyclist dismount and walk to the passenger side door. "Dude, what the fuck?" he stammered as the motorcyclist climbed into the jeep, removed his helmet and shook out his long, skunk-like fringe.

"Bruce?" Jonas said, with a twinge of relief—a relief that was painfully short-lived. Bruce extracted his knife from his leather jacket and laid it carefully across his thigh.

Jonas checked his rearview mirror for an escape route. Any exit was blocked by a wiry Latino man who had jumped from the cab of his truck and onto the back seat of the jeep. Before he could process what was happening, the man whipped his arm around, grabbed Jonas's neck in the crook of his elbow, and yanked his head back into the stiff, plastic headrest.

"Don't fucking move," Hector growled, his breath warm and sour in Jonas's ear.

Bruce placed his helmet in the footwell and pressed the cold steel under Jonas's chin.

"You didn't listen, fuckboy," he said, shaking his head. "I told you, be smart, don't go to the cops. I told you that, right, or was that just my imagination?" he added, tapping Jonas's forehead with the thin edge of the knife.

"Yeah, yeah, you told me. I listened, swear to God."

Bruce cocked his head. "Yeah? So why the fuck did two cops turn up at my place with a search warrant? Answer that, dickwad."

"I swear——"

"This motherfucker sure do swear a lot," Hector interrupted, yanking hard on Jonas's neck. "Just like his pops, huh?"

Jonas's head was reeling. *What the fuck did his father have to do with all this?*

"See," Bruce said, leaning close, his mint-tinged breath creeping over Jonas's face. "I remember you came to see me, interrupted my workout, all hot about going to the cops, telling them some shit you had no business telling."

"I didn't," Jonas said. "You told me it was a bad idea, I listened, swear I did, Bruce, straight-up truth."

"You give the cops my name to save your own ass? Maybe you're wired now?" he said, slapping his palms along Jonas's chest and abdomen, lingering a moment too long at the top of his thighs.

"Bruce, you don't need to do this," Jonas said, his throat sand-dry as he spoke.

"Yeah, I fucking do." Bruce pulled back his fist and snapped a bolt of a punch directly into his solar plexus. Jonas exhaled a gruff, muted scream as the air vacated his stomach, leaving a dull, body-numbing pain. For a moment, he imagined he might faint.

Hector pulled tight on Jonas's neck. "You give Catalina those drugs too? The fucked-up ones that killed her?"

"No! Shit! I can't even remember what happened that night. Bruce, you know that, right? Tell him. I was fucked up, man!"

"Maybe you were so fucked up you forgot what you did to my niece," Hector said. "What they call that? Selective memory or something? Maybe I remind you, huh? You gave Catalina some contaminated shit, killed her, threw her in the lake like some piece of trash? Remember now, pendejo?"

Jonas's mind was racing as Hector increased the pressure. Maybe he had done all those things. The night was still a black hole where anything could be inserted to fill the void.

"No, I just do weed, yeah, no H, never, I'm not dumb! Please, Bruce?"

Hector pulled harder at Jonas's neck. "You sure?"

Jonas nodded, the blood pooling in his face and head.

"What you think?" Hector asked. "On the level or bullshit?"

Bruce spat on the floor. "I think we need to teach the dipshit a lesson. Over there," he said, nodding towards the opposite side of the island. "Nice and quiet."

"Works for me," Hector agreed, loosening the gun from his

belt. "And remind your pops, if you ever see him again, he keeps quiet about that shit he saw with Catalina. Understand?"

Jonas barely had time to register the words before Hector's gun came down hard on his skull. His head slumped forward, his world descending quickly into darkness.

69

It was early morning, the sun just visible behind the sleek metal fingers of the cranes sweeping across the Port of Oakland. Jonas woke and turned his head—his neck felt as if it were stuck in a thick brace—and looked around, the scenery gradually falling back into focus. He was still on Treasure Island, on the opposite side to where he'd parked his jeep.

Christ, he was cold. The dawn wind gusting across from the bay seemed to cut through to his bones. He was hungry too; a ravenous, gut-churning hunger that made him dizzy. But most of all he felt rotten, as if everything good inside him was hollowed out like a Halloween pumpkin.

He'd failed his parents, Sabine hated him, Catalina was dead, and he still couldn't remember what he did the night she vanished; *maybe he didn't want to remember.* And he'd been diagnosed with syphilis, which he was sure he caught from that skinny chick with the wild eyes Bruce had brought to one of the Badge Belforts. But he'd failed himself and maybe that was the worst of it; knowing he was better than all this. His mom had always insisted he needed to always be his better self, no matter what, but it wasn't always that easy to stop himself, as if some invisible force compelled him to do the things he did.

He'd heard his father talk about Jonas's grandfather in a similar way; what did he call him, *self-destructive?* He was an alcoholic, had drank himself to an early cremation before Jonas was born. His grandfather had reached the bottom of the barrel, his father had explained. Jonas never really understood that old saying, until now. Was that where he was? Was this what the bottom of the barrel was like? Its smell acrid, its taste sour and bile-churning?

He shuddered, pulled himself to standing and walked over towards the jeep. Was this a warning from Bruce? A trailer teasing the main event? Something that would be worse than a pistol-whipping; much worse? As he fired up the engine and set the heater to maximum, something the Mexican man had said came back to him: *"This motherfucker sure do swear a lot... Just like his pops, huh?"*

70

Sabine hated it when the weather failed to synchronize with her mood. What she wanted were grey skies, a torrential downpour, biting cold, a thunderstorm with flashes of lightning striking down over the Rosemont Rec Center pool. Instead, the heavens had failed to open, and the sky offered only its relentless blueness and searing sunshine that taunted her with its good-natured warmth.

She drew a towel over her thighs and watched one of the seniors she knew from school teaching a group of four-year-old's how to dive. He looked like Jonas, she thought, only less attractive. But maybe all boys were really the same deep down, only after one thing; a blow job, getting jerked off; screwing. She felt a taut wire of anger tug at her shoulder blades; the same as it had done last night when her mom had told her about Jonas. She hadn't taken it well; called her mother a liar, insisted she had him mixed up with some other boy. A small part of her wanted to believe it was all just a misunderstanding, but the more she thought about it she knew her mom was right: the rash on his hands, how he refused to talk. It all made sense; the pieces falling neatly into place and churning in her stomach.

As she applied another slather of sunscreen to her shoulders and arms, she a felt light tap on her ankle. She caught her breath.

"Hey, Frenchie, what's up?"

A momentary and unexpected bolt of disappointment shot through her as she looked down and saw Moonshine. "What are you doing here?" she asked, thinking how out of place he looked here, his John Deere baseball cap pulled low over his eyes, his black "Moonshine Fever" band T-shirt creased and stained. He looked like her foul mood, she thought; the gathering thunderstorm over the horizon she'd been waiting for.

"Looking for your man, Jonas, you seen him?"

"He's not my man."

"Whatever. Haven't seen him since yesterday, he was meant to be staying at my place last night, never showed."

"He's not here, obviously."

"Did he tell you if he was going someplace?"

"No. He didn't tell me anything."

"I'm sensing some hostility here, Frenchie."

"My name's Sabine," she snapped. "Not fucking Frenchie."

Moonshine held up his hands in the mock-surrender manner. "You got it," he said. He looked around the pool. "So, reckon I can take a dip, cool the fuck off in this heat?"

"Members only," she said, gesturing at the unambiguous sign pinned to the fence.

Moonshine looked around at the kids jumping in the pool and their moms lounging in their expensive bikinis, staring into their cell phones. "I figure we're the same, me and you, huh?" he said, tipping up the peak of his cap. "Outsiders, looking in."

Sabine was about to protest when he reached down to untie his laces.

"Only difference is, I ain't waiting for a damned invitation."

"Oh, shit! No!" Sabine shouted.

Moonshine spread his arms wide and let himself fall, face first, into the deep end.

71

Mallory Atkins knocked lightly on Christen's door before entering, her fingers knitting anxiously together as she stood.

"Something wrong?" Christen said, looking up from his screen.

"You should probably see for yourself," she said, stepping back to allow Jonas to enter.

Christen bolted from behind his desk. "Christ! Jonas," he said, as his son shuffled in. His clothes were caked in mud and dust, his hair matted and falling over his eyes. On his neck, Christen noticed a dry speckle of blood.

"I'm hungry," said Jonas, flopping onto the couch at the opposite end of the office.

"I'll get some bagels from the break room," Mallory said, pulling the door behind her.

"What the hell happened?" Christen asked, sitting across from his son. "Are you all right?"

"Yeah, bitch of a headache," Jonas said.

"Tell me what this is all about, son," Christen said, looking at the back of Jonas's head and wincing.

Jonas was about to speak, when Mallory walked back in and handed him a plate of bagels. He smiled weakly and set at the soft dough as if he hadn't eaten for days. Christen gave his son a few minutes. As he watched him eat, for the briefest of moments Jonas was suddenly five years old again; the cheeky smart kid with a mop of dark curly hair sitting at the kitchen island, ravenous after his soccer practice. It took all of Christen's willpower not to grab his son in his arms and tell him everything would be all right, whatever it was, whatever he's done, it would be all right.

Jonas looked up. "Catalina," he said, swallowing hard. "They said you knew Catalina."

Christen's blood ran cold. "They? Who's they?"

"Bruce, and some other dude that was with him, I think he was Mexican or something."

Christen's initial panic rapidly fused into anger. *Hector?*

"Everything. Tell me everything," Christen insisted.

"You won't tell Mom?" Jonas said, rubbing his shirtsleeve across his eyes.

There he was, the young Jonas again. This time he was seven years old, pleading with his father to not tell his mom he was the one who'd set off the firecrackers in the Movies in the Park and scared all the younger children.

"Dad?" Jonas begged.

Christen took a breath. "Just tell me what happened, Jonas."

Jonas talked. He told his father about the night Catalina vanished, about how he couldn't remember anything but he was sure he'd done something bad, how he'd lied to the police about knowing her. Told him how Bruce would supply the drugs and the girls for the Badge Belforts. He told him all of it; even admitting it was him and Moonshine that had stacked up the lawn chairs in the park the night before the Fourth of July.

"Yes, we figured that," Christen had said, with a wry smile.

"I don't understand," Jonas said. "Why did they say you knew Catalina? Why would they say that? Just to scare me?"

Christen had no answer for that; at least not an answer he could tell his son. He rose and stood by the window watching the bustle of morning commuters playing chicken with the traffic crossing Broadway and 13th. Christen felt sick; not the typical nausea, but something different, something malevolent that permeated his entire body. *What kind of man was he?* What kind of father was he that would allow this to happen to his son? What kind of husband cheated on his wife with prostitutes that weren't worth the ground Alexus walked on? Looking down at the road, he knew exactly the kind of man he was. He was the same kind of man his father had been. The man he'd sworn he'd never become.

"Listen, son, you need to know this. Birth is nothing but a woman lifting her skirt up over an open grave. The rest of it, life, is how long it takes your body to hit the dirt."

His father's words, usually uttered at the kitchen table, in the dead-drunk darkness of night, always came back to him at times like this. It wasn't exactly *Chicken Soup for the Soul*, but what else should he have expected from a drunk with severe depression? Christ! He hated how the ghost of his father would attach itself to him, like a boulder on rope strung around his waist. *"Hit the dirt?"*—he imagined he could already smell the fetid earth and taste the dry dirt on his tongue.

"Is that all of it?" Christen asked, turning to face his son.

Jonas nodded.

"Are you sure? Nothing else?"

"No, nothing, for real, Dad," he said, running his hand through his hair.

"Good," Christen said, grabbing his jacket. "We will go to the emergency room."

"Why?" Jonas protested. "I'm fine."

"Why? Because you were pistol-whipped on the back of your head. Now, get your things, and if your mother asks, you fell off one of the gondolas at the lake."

"And the other thing, with Catalina?"

"One fucking crisis at a time, Jonas, please," Christen said, putting his arm tenderly over his son's shoulder as they left the office.

Jonas didn't shrug it off like he usually did––that was some sliver of comfort, Christen thought, but the gesture struck home as to what he had to do. What was that Danish saying his mother was always so fond of? *"Bad is never good until worse happens?"* It was true. You had to pass the bad, get to the worse, then you could move on, make amends, live up to the promises you made to yourself. It was what a man did.

72

"This one right here," Jessica said, gesturing at a bulbous, squat plant resembling an overstuffed pincushion. "Reminds me of my ex-husband."

"Prickly character, was he?" Tanner quipped.

"Still is," Jessica said, examining the name tag sticking up from the warm soil. "Texas Nipple? Figures," she added, moving to the next exhibit down the line.

Tanner followed, his nervousness only slightly less obvious than during the drive to the Dublin Penitentiary. He hoped he'd made the right call. He figured Jessica wasn't one of those women who expected to be wined and dined at some fancy restaurant, or maybe she was exactly that kind of woman: he truly was clueless in these matters. Eventually he'd settled on neutral ground; a Sunday afternoon stroll around the Bonsai Garden at Lake Merritt.

"I always promised Sabine I'd bring her here," Jessica said, resting on a bench under the shade of a wooden pagoda.

"I try to visit twice a month," Tanner said, his knees cracking in their sockets as he sat.

"For the peace and tranquility? Reconnect with your Zen?"

"Just makes me feel like a giant, walking around these little plants," he said, hoping a shot of self-effacing humor might make him appear less anxious than he really was.

"Like Gulliver in Lilliput?"

Tanner laughed. "Haven't thought of that book for years. I think I read it to my children when they were young. My wife, Teresa," he said, "it was like her sanctuary. We... I mean, I just live over there." He gestured to a row of houses just above the lake. "She liked to come here when she had a problem to figure out, or I was bugging the bejesus out of her. I'm guessing she had a frequent visitor's pass or whatnot."

Jessica smiled. "I assume she's passed?" She sensed Tanner stiffen as she spoke and reached out to lay a hand gently over his. "You're still wearing your wedding ring. Divorced men tend to think that's a big red flag to dating."

Tanner twisted the gold band around his finger. The word "passed" had always irked him. Passed? Passed to where? He held no belief in an afterlife or some utopian heaven that would require passing into. Teresa had died, that was the bare bones of it. There were no words to soften the blow or make everything better. If time, as he'd been told, was a healer, it sure was taking its own sweet time in making a house call.

He couldn't hold it against Jessica though. It was one of those phrases you were obliged to say like *"I'm sorry for your loss,"* or *"thank you for your service."* He'd used the former enough times himself when breaking bad news. It was an off-the-shelf phrase that he always expected would be met with a snap of a heated retort like *"Really, how sorry?"* or *"You don't even know me."* But it had never happened, not once in his years of policing. The cliché would always be met with a solemn nod of the head or a whispered thank you. People were typically lost for words when addressing death and reached for what was closest to hand, just like Jessica had done.

"You still with us?" Jessica asked as she watched him twirl the ring around. "Don't worry, I'm not the prying type. You'll talk when you're ready, but just one question, if you don't mind."

"Em, okay," Tanner said, bracing himself.

"How long?"

He nodded and let out a deep exhale. "A year. Exactly a year this month," he said, squinting through the sunlight filtering through the slots in the pagoda's roof.

"That would be a respectable amount of time to grieve."

Tanner smiled. "That's what Teresa always said."

"Obviously a very wise woman." Jessica rose and brushed down the front of her jeans. "Want to go and check out some more little trees, make you feel better about yourself?"

Tanner smiled and heaved his body to standing. "I think I'm ready to move on," he said, hoisting the top of his jeans up over his hips. "Some alcohol, maybe?"

Jessica smiled; the same smile that had seemed to fill the whole car with light the other day; the sort of smile that should come with a government warning attached.

"I think I'd like that very much, Roscoe," she said, slipping her arm through his.

The first spill of twilight settled over the lake in gold and red hues. Not that they'd noticed the shifting light. After three hours of sitting on the patio and making their way diligently through most of the house cocktail list, they were strolling under the glow of yellow lights circling the lake. The afternoon had flowed with the considered cadence of a first date; the slow coaxing open of the surface in preparation of more exploration and discovery somewhere down the line. The conversation had been effortless, stretching well into the early evening, and had chugged along with a lightness that surprised them both.

"It's been a while since I spent my Sunday afternoon drinking," Jessica said, slipping her arm through his as they walked past the gleaming black gondolas slapping gently against the timber stays of the dock. "A woman could get used to it."

Tanner smiled. There was a lightness in his step he hadn't felt for some time. Since at least a year ago; probably longer. The last years tending to Teresa were as painful as her death, if not more so.

Jessica stopped by the pond close to the bird refuge and watched the procession of American coots, belted kingfishers, and a noble-looking white pelican strut around the fenced perimeter. "So are you any closer to solving the case?" she asked.

"According to the chief and the DA, Catalina's just another in a long line of statistics. Teenage drug overdose number whatnot this year. You probably saw on the news that we arrested a young man who admitted selling her drugs. The OPD gets to look good, and the DA gets the conviction she needs without having to apply more police resources to the case. It's what they like to call a win-win situation."

"You not convinced?"

"I'm not buying all the horse hooey the media's been spreading about Catalina, I know that much."

"Then don't give up on it, Roscoe," Jessica said. "Keep at it. If you don't, who will?"

Tanner watched the white pelican spread the full width of its wingspan and take off from the pond with the ease of the wind. Jessica was right. He had to keep digging, not just to secure justice for Catalina, but also to provide her parents with some kind of closure, whatever that meant. There was never closure on death, he knew that much. Closure implied putting a lid on grief, locking it away like it never existed. The best he could offer her parents now was a reason, a motive behind their daughter's death that would help them make some sense of a senseless loss.

As they walked onto the sidewalk hemming the lakeside, the angry revving of a car engine startled them both. A white Mustang barreled down the road and spun in a tight, tire-squealing donut, spewing up clouds of dense white smoke. The passenger door swung open. A young man climbed out and leaned backward from the door, his back inches from the ground. He screamed; a combination of terror and joy as he ghost-rode the spiraling donuts.

"For Mother Francis's sake!" Tanner said, waving the smoke from his eyes, his nostrils thick with the stench of burning rubber. "It's a darned Sunday evening."

The car spun several more donuts, straightened, and tore back down the road in a fury of noise. Jessica thought she recognized the car; the same one she'd seen outside the homeless encampment the morning of July 4th. As the car slowed, the young man hauled himself from the passenger side window and craned his neck to grin at Jessica. It was a cruel grin, laced with youthful innocence. The handgun gesture he made with his thumb and finger, however, contained no ambiguity. Tyler's gesture was as chilling as the first time Jessica had seen it. The half-wink of his eye equally malicious.

"I'll call it in," Tanner said, reaching for his phone, "before this place turns into another Foothill Park. Dang delinquents."

As the car swerved dangerously into the oncoming traffic, Jessica felt a wave of relief. She took a deep breath and composed herself.

"Are you okay?" Tanner asked, slipping his cell phone back into his pocket and putting his arm around Jessica's shoulders.

"Sure," Jessica said, relaxing and leaning herself into Tanner's arms. "You've seen one sideshow, you've seen them all."

For a moment they looked deep into each other's eyes as if searching for some kind of truth and finding something else instead; something more meaningful and absolute.

It was the inevitable conclusion to the evening, and they were both wise enough to know these kinds of moments were fleeting. They savored the first brush of their lips, pulling back momentarily as if to make sure this was really happening, then after confirming it was, pressed their lips tighter. The kiss was long, warm and gentle, but above all else, life-affirming.

73

Jonas had never experienced that degree of anger from his mom before. He expected some nuclear, DEFCON 1 level of fury when she'd found out, but her calmness, like the stillness in the air before a thunderstorm, was more terrifying.

"We always taught you to be careful, didn't we? Protection? Did those lessons sink in, any of them?" Alexus leant her palms on the kitchen island as if she were about to deliver a lecture.

"At least I didn't get anyone pregnant," Jonas mumbled.

"Fantastic," Alexus said, reaching for another glass of wine. "I should be grateful you haven't made me a grandma just yet."

"Let's all calm down," Christen said. "The boy did something stupid and he has learned a tough lesson."

Jonas was slumped across the island, his head on his forearms. It was one thirty in the morning, and he was exhausted. His mom had been taking small chunks out of him, like a piranha fish, for the past three hours and his brain felt like mush.

"My boy," she said, reaching out to stroke his head. "My beautiful boy. Didn't I always tell you people are going to always hold you up to a higher standard because of who you are?"

Jonas shrugged her away. "Not the whole mixed race thing again, why is it always a big deal with you?"

"Because, Jonas, people judge you differently because of the color of your skin, it's just how it is. That's why I've always taught you to be better than this, you've always got to be better than this."

Jonas twisted his hoodie cord around his fingers. "What if I can't be better? What if this is who I am. Did you ever think of that?"

Jonas's words landed with a punch as Christen listened. That could have been him talking, not his son. He swallowed hard. "I think we're getting off point—" Christen said, before Alexus interrupted.

"We always have to be our better angels, there's no excuse not to. So, who was she, this girl you caught this thing from? A girlfriend? Someone you picked up at a party?"

"I don't know who, Mom, honest, I don't."

"It does not matter who," Christen said. "It matters the boy gets treated as soon as possible."

"Well, I hope you're proud of yourself," Alexus said. "If by some miracle we can keep this in the family, no one else needs to know, not even your sister. Understood?"

Jonas shrugged. "Fine by me, can I go now?"

Alexus was about to launch into another lecture, when she heard the familiar stuttering of Dave Maddens-Smith's sprinkler system. She checked the time: 1:40am.

The same bile of anger she'd felt earlier that day when she'd read the itemized bill from her medical insurance company—*"blood test—syphilis, $245"*—welled up like a tidal wave in her belly. As she'd read the bill, her mind had immediately turned to Jonas; Christen would have figured out a way to cover it up, paid out of pocket. Jonas wouldn't have known any better.

As the garden spigots spurted to life, the sound was like a thousand tiny pinpricks poking at her skull. She slammed her wine glass on the counter and marched to the front door.

Christen called out, "Alexus! Where are you going?"

With his wife out of earshot, he leaned in close to Jonas. "You lied to me, son," he said, gritting his teeth. "You told me that was everything, but this?" he said, grabbing the insurance bill in his fist. "This you did not tell me."

Jonas, exhausted, turned to face Christen. "Just like you've told me everything, Dad?"

Christen said nothing, threw down the bill and headed off to stop Alexus doing whatever she'd set her mind on doing.

74

By the time Christen caught up with her, his wife was marching across Dave Maddens-Smith's front garden, dragging the heels of her sneakers over the lush lawn.

"Alexus!"

Alexus wasn't listening.

The spigots shot up like curious gopher heads, spraying in sculptured arcs. Alexus felt the first drops of water shoot at her ankles and shift quickly up to her neck: tiny, irritating pinpricks that fueled her rage. She located her primary target, a large sprinkler spinning furiously in the center of the lawn. She launched the toe of her sneaker into the eye of the storm. The sprinkler jet flew, missile-like, nailing its landing in a nearby rosebush.

Next, she set after the sprinklers buried in the flower beds, kicking each of the spigots until they buckled and water flooded, turning the surrounding soil to mud.

"Christ!" Christen ran towards Alexus, who had now embarked on an all-out assault on the remaining sprinklers, yanking them clean from the ground with her bare hands.

"Alexus!" he shouted, slipping on the sodden grass as he chased his wife. "Stop for a minute, please!"

"It's not right, it's just not right!" she said, sobbing. "He doesn't listen, he never listens!" She fell to her knees at the far-right corner of the garden and got to work liberating the last surviving sprinkler jet. She gathered all her remaining strength and gave it a hail-Mary jerk. The jet relented, spewing a torrent of cold water at her face. She fell backwards just as Christen slid to his knees behind her. He tried as best he could to comfort his wife as her rage subsided into tears; enough to water the damned lawn twice over, he thought.

"He never listens," Alexus sobbed. "He never listens."

Christen's heart seemed lodged somewhere deep in his throat. This was the moment he'd been expecting; the inevitable conclusion. He drew Alexus closer, wrapped his arms around her chest and held her as she cried. There was only one course of action left now; the right course. That was the price for cleansing his sins, confessing and hoping Alexus could find it in her heart to forgive him. It was a steep ask, a negotiation he had no leverage in. A deal that could lose him everything.

As he held Alexus and made himself promises he was so desperate to keep it hurt, he looked up. In the bedroom window a faint light pressed against the glass, and behind the light, Dave Maddens-Smith's face smiling as he brought down his cell phone and stopped recording, just as the blue-and-red police lights turned the corner.

75

For the past twenty-three hours and fifty-nine minutes, Gérard Rosseau had been held in police custody. Detectives Tanner and Shaughnessy had picked him up and hauled him into an interview room in OPD Headquarters. He'd guessed it was Mason who'd given them his name. After the kid's attitude a few days ago, he reckoned Mason was at worst hiding something, and at best scared shitless of someone, or something, that he'd done.

OPD had nothing to pin on him; zilch. Gérard had savored the last thirty minutes of the interrogation when the detectives realized they'd been spun a lie and were running out of time; they either had to charge him or release him.

It was all bullshit. He hadn't seen the girl that night, let alone picked her up like they'd insisted. It wasn't until they got back the forensics from his truck––all negative for any traces of Catalina's DNA––that they'd consented to release him. They didn't even offer him an apology, just told him he was free to leave, no further questions.

But, he had questions, plenty of them, and he was going to get some goddamned answers.

76

"Let me get this straight," Dugdale said, pacing his office. "We held a suspect for twenty-four hours on the testimony of a kid who had his photo taken with Catalina Gomez?"

"On the night she disappeared," Tanner insisted.

"Kids spend their damn lives on those devices. I should know, I've got two teenage girls," Dugdale said. "They're taking selfies every damned second of the day."

"Probably self-esteem issues," Shaughnessy said, avoiding eye contact. "A need for constant reassurance from their peer group they don't get from their parents."

Dugdale slumped back in his chair. "The Catalina Gomez case is dead in the water. You've brought me no evidence that contradicts she died of an overdose, but what we do have are two homicides that you're no closer to solving."

"We're tracing Bruce Ho," Shaughnessy said. "He's probably hiding out someplace, none of his known associates are talking."

"We could use more officers," Tanner said.

Dugdale lifted a slip of paper. "Do you know what this is, Tanner? Overtime approvals for extra patrol officers for that damned vigil tomorrow night. What's your take? We expecting trouble? Unruly factions looking to take advantage of the situation?"

"We didn't hear anything was going down," Shaughnessy said.

"Doesn't mean it couldn't happen," Tanner confirmed.

"Then we go in light. Foot patrols in the vicinity, keep them on the fringes, maybe a few undercovers in the crowd for monitoring."

"Sure, whatever you say," Tanner said, a weariness in his voice as he rose to leave.

"Any developments on that footage I handed you?"

"Yep, making good headway there, Chief, reckon we'll have the perpetrators locked up by the end of the week along with a handful of jaywalkers and a busker from 13th Street BART station," Tanner said, pulling the door hard behind as he left.

Dugdale sat on the edge of his desk. "That stuff about my daughters, didn't mean for that to come out the way it did. You know I'm committed, right?" he said, reaching over and settling his hand on her knee. "It's just that the timing's got to be right."

She brushed his hand away. "Don't make any moves on my account," Shaughnessy said, buttoning her jacket. "I've got no ambitions to be your girlfriend or second wife. Just so we're clear."

Dugdale scrunched his face, as if trying to parse what Shaughnessy had just said; he may as well have had a bright neon sign above his head that said, *"Does Not Compute."*

"Look, this whole babysitting bullshit with Tanner? I'm already a cuckold in one relationship, I don't need to add another to the list."

Dugdale flinched, as if jabbed with a needle. "You agree with him that Catalina's death wasn't an overdose?"

"Jury's still out. But his instincts about Bruce Ho and Tiffiny Grant were right on the money."

"He's a square peg, Shaughnessy, don't get stuck in the same hole," Dugdale said, a sharp edge to his voice.

Shaughnessy offered her almost smile. "Thanks for the career advice. If I'm ever in need of a mentor, I'll let you know."

77

Gérard double-checked he was at the right place. It had taken him the best part of the day to figure out where the kid lived. He'd only found the address after searching through some old invoices he'd sent out to Mason's father some weeks ago.

He checked the time: 5:40pm. He was due to be at the vigil at 7pm, and Sabine had insisted he get there early to hear her speak. He was determined to be on time, and besides, Jessica would be all over his ass if he was a no-show. Thirty minutes at most, put the kid in his place, and ask him two questions. *Why the hell did he set him up with the cops? And what the hell was he so scared of?*

After several unanswered knocks, he slipped into the backyard. Music was coming from what he guessed was the basement; a thick, distorted guitar phased through a flange pedal. He pushed on the door, following the noise towards the end of the hallway. He slow-footed it down the stairs to the open basement door. Mason sat on the couch, his starburst Fender Stratocaster on his lap, his hair falling in greasy strands over his face. The funk of marijuana was thick, with a patina of smoke, like a lace curtain, floating in the room.

Gérard walked across the basement, unnoticed, and yanked the jack plug from the amplifier. It fell to the floor with an angry hum of feedback.

"What the fuck?" Moonshine said, brushing the hair from his eyes and trying to parse the image of Gérard standing in his basement, looking as if he were about to beat the living shit out of him.

"Hey, G-Man, take a seat," he said, wiping a stream of snot from his nose.

Gérard perched his butt on the couch. "Got one question for you, Mason. Why?"

Moonshine laughed—childlike and brittle. "Don't know what you're talking 'bout, bro."

Gérard studied his eyes; the irises like pinpricks, lost somewhere in the fat, bloodshot landscape of his eyeballs, his smile disjointed, as if he wasn't sure why he was even smiling.

"What did you hope to gain? Why do it?"

Moonshine looked at the frets of his guitar, running his fingers along the raised brass as if he were reading Braille and the answer was carved somewhere in the grain. "The big fucking why? You asks the big questions, G-Man," he said, looking up. "I gottta question for you. Why the fuck are any of us here? That's what you should be asking yourself, G-Man. That is the question of the day."

"But, I'm asking you, Mason," Gérard insisted. "Why?"

"Ain't anything anybody does make a gnat's shit of difference," Moonshine said. "You, me, Catalina? We don't matter none to nobody. Whole world's going to shit anyway, may as well enjoy the ride while I'm here, ain't nobody gonna miss me when I'm gone."

Gérard felt a sudden pang of sympathy for the kid. Jesus! Did his own daughter ever feel like this? Was this what it was like to be a teenager these days?

"That's a pretty fucked-up perspective for a young kid."

"Old soul, so my grandma told me," Moonshine said, a distant look in his eyes as if he were searching for something deep in his past. "Wanna get high? Looks like you could use the benefit," Moonshine said, handing over the joint.

Gérard hesitated, then figured he should keep Mason on his side, keep him talking. "Sure," he said, taking the joint.

Moonshine gestured at the small rehearsal area. "You can jam, if you're up for the competition. Choose your weapon."

Gérard hesitated. Mason looked vulnerable, unstable even. Maybe he should stay, God knows what other drugs he'd taken. He'd hang around a while longer and monitor the situation before heading to the vigil.

Gérard selected a black Gibson Les Paul copy.

"Classic choice," Moonshine said, setting his fingers into the shape of an open G chord and running the pick down the strings.

Gérard did the same.

Moonshine nodded as the two guitars were strummed in harmony. It was one of the first songs Gérard had taught him; Lynyrd Skynyrd's "Free Bird". Moonshine sang the first verse, his voice edged with a sweetness and vulnerability Gérard had never noticed before.

78

The searing spotlights had ripped across Lake Merritt, tearing a hole in the night sky, before completing several more expansive circles over the neighborhood. Fifty feet above the water, the chopper had focused its beams directly at the paramedic team as they fought to stabilize the victim's vitals. As the downdraft from the rotor blades pushed the water in thick ripples across the lake, the paramedics had raised the stretcher into the back of the ambulance and sped off in a wail of sirens.

Panic had hemorrhaged through the crowd. A single gunshot echoing through the vigil, the reverent stillness of the minute of silence in Catalina Gomez's honor shattered into a million pieces. Some people had thrown themselves to the ground and covered their heads. Others had scuttled into the side streets and been swallowed into the darkness. The news camera teams that had been on high alert since 6pm had risen from their crouched positions, and when they assessed the coast was clear, had ran towards the spotlight bearing down on the circle of pillars at the north side of the lake.

They captured what footage they could, hustling through the crowd, cornering anyone willing to talk. There was always someone willing to offer their opinion; someone who couldn't resist having their face on the ten o'clock news and would relay with an "OMFG!" breathlessness the events as they'd witnessed them firsthand.

But, that kind of coverage was filler, B-roll to the main event. What the media had craved was a narrative to catapult the incident from another Oakland shooting to a personal story; a story with an innocent victim and a young man with a gun and a grudge to settle.

Or, failing that, there was always the "hero" angle; a good Samaritan who had rushed to the victim, stayed with them until the paramedics arrived. There was talk of an OPD officer who was close by. Someone had seen him show his badge, holler at one of the other officers to call the paramedics, then fall to his knees, plugging the victim's wound with his jacket.

79

An hour before the OPD chopper had shattered the evening air, Jessica slipped her arm through Tanner's as they walked the footpath toward the stage. "Not too shabby for a third date, Roscoe," she said, squeezing his arm. "Not that I wouldn't have been here anyway, but it's nice you cared enough to invite me."

Tanner placed a palm over her hand. "San Quentin State Prison doesn't take reservations," he said. "And besides, I have it on good authority the food's not much to write home about."

"Cute," Jessica said, watching a group of young people launch miniature boats with glowing votives set inside the hulls into the water. Next to a semicircle of pillars, a spread of flowers was rolled out like a carpet, and embedded in the flowers a selection of plush toys with paper hearts pinned into their fur. Photographs of Catalina were glued onto boards with hearts drawn around them and short, simple notes written in bright crayon.

"What do you think? Two hundred people?" Jessica asked, gesturing to the crowd gathering by the stage.

As Tanner looked over the detritus of tributes, the similar

feeling of failure he'd felt that night standing in Catalina's bedroom washed over him. "Probably closer to five hundred."

He checked out the smaller crowds mingling around the edges. These would be the tinderboxes that ignited any trouble. Smaller groups were notoriously harder to monitor, and could easily break off and reform someplace else. "I had no idea your daughter was behind all this," he said, with an edge of concern.

"That's a strange turn of phrase, *'behind all this?'* Like it's some kind of conspiracy."

"No. I didn't mean it in that way."

"How did you mean it, Roscoe?"

Tanner cleared his throat. "All this public grieving? I'm not sure it's good for the family. Sure can't help them move on."

"I'm not sure I'd want to move on," Jessica said. "If something that awful happened to Sabine, I don't know what I'd even move on to. A psych ward maybe?"

Tanner had felt much the same when Teresa had died. There was no place for him to move on to. It was as if his feet were stuck in quicksand. He could maybe move one step in each direction, but that was the extent of it—minor adjustments he hoped would ease the pain.

"It's just a memorial," Jessica said, "but with more people."

Tanner looked over the flanks of police patrolling the lake perimeter. "And supervised by thirty-four OPD officers."

"Worried about the overtime pay?"

"Worried we don't have enough officers if things go the way of those Occupy Oakland protests. Someone put the fox in the henhouse and we're still cleaning up from the fallout."

"You worry too much. Enjoy the evening. It's a peaceful vigil. A few speeches, poetry and music, then we all go home and hug our kids like we'll never let them go."

Tanner turned as a young woman walked over and embraced Jessica.

"Roscoe. This is my daughter, Sabine."

Tanner stopped in his tracks. He hadn't expected an introduction quite so soon.

"Hi," Sabine said, looking at Tanner, then at Jessica with a dramatic eyebrow raise.

He held out his hand. "Roscoe Tanner. Your mom's told me a lot about you... All very good, by the way," he blurted. "Complimentary."

"I'm her only child. She doesn't have a choice."

"I just choose to favor the good over the not so good," Jessica confirmed.

"So, Mom?" she said, drawing out the word "Mom" and eyeing Tanner as if he were a curiosity in a shop window. "Something you want to tell me?"

Jessica waved her arms dismissively. "Later. You've got enough to think on. Remember, back straight, lots of eye contact, and don't forget the pauses, they make you sound smart, like you're taking your time to think things through."

"I know, you told me enough times already."

"Sure is a ton of people," Tanner said. "You're not nervous?"

"Em, I wasn't," Sabine said, glancing at her mother.

"He's a natural worrier," Jessica confirmed. "You go do your thing, I'll be cheering you on."

Sabine rolled her eyes.

"Silently," Jessica quickly said. "Cheering from the inside."

Sabine smiled, kissed her mom on the cheek, and disappeared back into the crowd.

80

Christen recognized the squat, wiry figure of Hector Figuerello from across the pathway. He was leaning against the library wall, smoking a cigarillo. Christen instructed Alexus to take Jonas and Sydney and text him when they'd found a suitable spot. He braced himself and marched over.

Christen glanced at the posters of Catalina taped to the pillars to the left of the stage, along with a hundred or so photographs of other young people whose lives had been cut tragically short. They made Christen queasy, each face appearing to morph into either Jonas or Sydney, their eyes following him, accusing him even, as he walked. He passed a young man sitting on the grass with a guitar, strumming a light Mexican melody to a circle of friends. It was out of step with the mood of the evening, Christen thought, before deciding it was probably perfect. A vigil was a celebration of life. There had been too much sadness lately, and Jonas coming to his office that day had brought that home to him in the worst way possible. It was why he'd insisted the whole family should attend; after all that had happened he hoped the vigil would be a catharsis, a cleansing point from which to move forward.

But there was still one matter to deal with; one final purge.

Christen's mouth felt as if it were packed with dry oatmeal as he strode towards Hector.

"Hey," Hector said. "Que pasa?"

Christen stood an arm's reach away. "Why the fuck are you here, Hector?"

He widened his stance. "Paying my respects, why you here?"

Christen nodded as if he understood things now; had figured out Hector's complicity in all that had happened. "Catalina's parents?" he said. "They know nothing about you, do they?"

Hector poked his finger into Christen's shoulder. "And if you shut your mouth, like I warned, they don't need to know nothin'."

Christen looked at the stream of people passing by. "What if I stand on the stage? Tell your family Catalina was with you that night? Tell them about the Rat House?"

"Then you implicate yourself. No benefit for anyone."

"Maybe I will take my chances," he said. "The word of a successful businessman against a drug dealer and a... I don't really know what you are? A pimp? Gangster? Or maybe you are just a sack of shit."

Hector stepped forward. "Better watch your mouth, amigo."

"Maybe I'll get immunity if I tell the police what I know."

Hector cocked his head, assessing how serious Christen was, and if he was serious, who he'd need to call and what action they'd instruct him to take to silence him. "It's all in your head, amigo. What you saw wasn't what you saw."

"I saw you getting very rough with Catalina."

Hector reached into his pocket and extracted his cell phone. "I already told you that was family. I figure you got bigger problems to attend to," he said, scrolling and stopping at the photograph of Jonas and Catalina.

Christen studied the photograph closely, looking for clues. It seemed they were both traveling in the back of a car or truck, the narrow rear window catching the burst of flash in the glass. Someone in the front seat must have taken the shot; there was the faint outline of a face in the glass, though it was too dark to make out any discernible features. Jonas looked wasted; he had that similar, goofy smile Christen often had when he was drunk, his eyes foggy, his mouth half-open as if he were mid-breath. Catalina's pose was as stiff as Jonas's was loose, as if she were being forced to smile, with an expression that said *"are we done yet?"*

"Cute couple, no?" Hector said, snatching back the phone. "Maybe if things had turned out different we might be family, eh?" He laughed; a wheezy, brittle exhale that made Christen's neck hairs prickle.

"Did you take this?" Christen asked.

Hector flipped the device in his palm. "Nah, I just emailed it to myself."

"From Catalina's phone?"

"See, you're smart," Hector said. "Don't much get past you, huh? I took her phone. Like I said, she was being a little bitch, had stuff on there that could fuck everything up for all of us. So, what you think you saw was not what you saw, *comprendes*?"

"My son has nothing to do with this," Christen insisted. "You touch him again and I swear I will kill you."

"You swear, huh?" Hector said, leaning back on his heels. "You a tough guy all of a sudden? Tough enough to kill someone?" he added, standing back and opening his arms wide.

Christen's gut roiled, but he couldn't put that on display, not to Hector; he'd seize on it, wring the fear out of him until he was bone dry. His instinct was to walk away, fold back into the crowd, but he'd done too much of that lately. Holding Alexus in his arms that night as she sobbed, soaked to the bone on Dave Maddens-Smith's front lawn, had hit him with the force of a sledgehammer. And Jonas too. How could he have not known that about his son? Was he really that absent a father? Like his own father?

He and Alexus had talked long and deep that night, not about everything he wanted to confess. There would be another time for that. In the morning they'd made love; an easy, familiar kind of lovemaking: the sort that shaped the form of a marriage, stoked the fire enough to keep it burning. He'd decided, as he watched Alexus draw herself from bed and walk to the shower, it was time to confront his own weaknesses. It was what a man did.

"The Rat House," Christen finally said. "Close it down."

Hector stamped out his cigarillo with his boot heel. "Fuck, you still don't get it, man. You think it's that easy? Them people only care about themselves. You should do the same. Walk away, forget you were ever there, go look after your family."

"Did they kill Catalina? Whoever this boss is you told me about. Was it him?"

"Catalina died because some greedy fuck laced her heroin. She's another statistic and your son, he gets to live. It's fucked up, right? Maybe it was a fifty-fifty chance your son didn't take the same heroin? Could have been him everyone's crying over tonight?"

As Hector's words sank in, Christen felt the air leave his body. Maybe it was sheer luck that it wasn't Jonas's pictures pinned to the pillar walls and that he and Alexus weren't the parents standing on the stage, their hearts broken beyond repair. His blood pulsed hard somewhere behind his eyes.

"Don't say that, do not fucking say that," he grunted, grabbing a fistful of Hector's T-shirt. As he thrust him against the wall, he was surprised at how easily Hector's body folded, as if he were made of water and flour: a street-taco of a man.

"Close it down, Hector. Close. It. Down."

Hector smiled, pulled back the edge of his jacket to reveal

the nine-millimeter P39 stuffed into his belt. "Maybe you don't get to call the shots, tough guy. Go back to your family. We don't want no one getting hurt tonight. Or worse," he said, tapping the gun barrel.

Christen's nerves were sparking, a dull thumping somewhere deep in his eardrums. "If you'd never brought Catalina to work at the Rat House, she might still be alive. I think her parents would agree with me if I tell them. Seems we both have something to lose."

Hector shoved him. "You don't tell me what to do."

Christen backed off and checked the alert on his cell phone—a text from Alexus. "Someone's going to talk, eventually," he said, looking over towards the stage.

"It better not be you, cabrón," Hector said, making a big deal of hitching up his belt and showcasing his gun once more.

As Christen left, Hector pressed speed dial and lifted his cell phone up to his ear. "Yeah. We got a problem," he said, watching Christen as he joined his family. "Want I should take care of it?"

81

Sabine spotted Jonas leaning against one of the oak trees to the west of the lake. She checked the time. Another fifteen minutes before she had to take the stage and officially start the vigil, plenty of time to say what she'd been preparing in her mind for days.

"So, how's the syphilis?" she asked, approaching Jonas. "Itch much?"

"Jesus," Jonas grunted. "Want to shout that a little louder?"

"I could announce it on stage, over the mic, if you'd prefer."

Jonas shoved his hands into his jacket pockets and avoided her gaze.

"When were you going to tell me? After we'd had sex... maybe?"

He flinched. "It wasn't like that. I wouldn't—"

"Right, so tell me, how was it?"

"I didn't know, all right? Until last week when—"

"When you started not returning my texts or my calls."

Jonas ran a hand through his hair. "Look, it's all shit, I know it's shit, but you have no idea, seriously. My mom? This whole thing? It's like major stress."

"Tell me about it. I've been checking my hands, and wherever, like every five minutes thanks to you."

"Yeah, sorry."

"Really, that's all you've got? Sorry?"

Sabine's anger rose from her feet, rushing through her until it almost picked her up from the shoulder. She could feel her knuckles turn white as her fingernails dug into her palms.

"It's complicated, that's all. It wasn't fair to get you involved."

Sabine shook her head. "But it was fine to date me, ignore me, and not tell me you had a sexually transmitted disease? That was all good?"

Jonas flashed her his thousand-watt smile. "Who said we were dating?"

The words seared like a white-hot poker behind Sabine's eyes. She couldn't help herself. Her hand seemed to have a mind of its own as it swung out and slapped Jonas cold across the cheek.

They both stood there for a moment, frozen, both sensing the sting of the slap on their skins.

"I gotta go," Sabine said, turning and running back to the crowd, wiping her eyes, hoping her tears would dry before she took the stage.

82

Alexus watched Christen walk towards her. "Where have you been? It's about to start."

"I ran into someone from the office," Christen said, taking her hand. He scanned the crowd: he was certain he hadn't seen the last of Hector. "Where is Jonas?"

Alexus gestured at Jonas as he ambled casually towards them, rubbing his hand over his scar, which still stung with the force of Sabine's slap. His shoulders were slumped as if he were bearing the burden of a much older man.

"Think he's going to be all right?" Christen asked, Hector's words still echoing like a portent of something terrible in the back of his mind.

Alexus sighed. "He's had the shots, so long as he takes the antibiotics it should clear up before school starts. I just hope this whole experience has woken him up. Maybe he'll stop all that partying and focus on his schoolwork, it's an important year for him."

"It is a hard way to learn a lesson," Christen said, as he watched his son approach.

"And Sydney?" Alexus asked, looking around.

"With her friends," Christen confirmed, gesturing towards his daughter and her friends sitting in a circle on the grass, faces bathed in the warm illumination of their cell phones.

"At least we got her to come. Small victories."

Christen nodded in agreement. "We need to talk."

"About Jonas? I think I'm wrung dry on that subject."

"No, other things. Stuff we need to talk about."

"Can it wait until later, Christen? It's about to start."

Christen nodded. It could wait. It would give him time to frame exactly what he needed to tell her.

No lies, only truth now. It was what she deserved.

83

Was it him? Jessica looked at the young black man laughing with three other men gathered on the path looping the lake. She looked for Tanner to tell him she'd be right back, but he was deep in conversation with one of the OPD patrol officers.

"Nelson, right?" she said, her smile warm and her body language confident as she approached the young men.

Nelson turned. A flicker of nervousness played across his face, but he quickly salvaged his swagger before his friends noticed anything was amiss.

"You lookin' for an autograph or somethin'?" one of his friends said, puffing a cloud of marijuana smoke into the dry evening air.

"Man, she way too old for you," said the tallest man in the group, giving Jessica the once-over.

"Shut the fuck up," Nelson said. "Ain't none of your business."

"Do I gotta worry about you boning my mom too?" another man said. "'Cause I don't need no bitch stepdad."

"Ain't nobody want to bone your mom, Tig," the taller man

said. "Not even your pop wanted to bone your mom's ass, that's why he gone before you known him."

Tig looked to the ground as the guys laughed and stabbed each other with their elbows.

"Nice," Jessica said, feeling a pinch of pity for the young man. "Now, if you've all finished poking fun at who I assume is a friend of yours, I'd like to speak with Nelson."

"'Bout what?" Nelson said, squaring his shoulders.

Jessica leant in close. "You want to do this here?"

Nelson passed the joint back to Tig. "Be back. Don't go smoking all my shit."

Jessica and Nelson sat at a bus-stop bench and watched the slow procession of passing traffic.

"You got some new shit to tell me?" Nelson asked, his leg twitching nervously.

"The antivirus shipment came in last week. We've been trying to locate you."

"Yeah, so you located me. Now what?"

"Come in tomorrow, we can start the treatment."

Nelson looked down his nose. "How do I know you not lyin'?"

Jessica looked him directly in the eyes with the same steely glare she'd given him that morning at the overpass. "Nelson, you've got to start trusting people who are trying to help you. I don't have a hidden agenda, I just want you to get better."

Nelson's face hardened. "I'm self-made, don't need nobody's help. You take favors, then you got to pay 'em back. The way I see it, if I don't ask people for shit, I don't owe shit."

Nelson scratched at the raw welts across his hand.

"And how's that working out for you so far?" Jessica asked.

"I figured who it was," he said. "The ho who gave me this fucking disease." He leaned close to Jessica and bunched his hands into tight fists. "She's gonna fuckin' pay, I made sure of it."

Jessica's mind immediately jumped back a couple of weeks; Topaz Autumn. Could she have been the patient zero in all this? She'd infected Nelson and Jonas too?

"Tell me you haven't done anything stupid, Nelson," she said, a quiver in her voice.

Nelson's fists tightened. "She's gonna get payback for what she did."

"Don't you think Topaz has paid enough already?" Jessica said.

Nelson's face couldn't betray his surprise at hearing Topaz's name.

"I saw her a couple of weeks ago," Jessica confirmed.

"What the fuck she tell you?"

"Nothing," Jessica confirmed. "I was just there to see if she needed treatment, like you."

Nelson rose, curled his lips. "Thing is, with hos like her it ain't ever enough. You read me?"

"Tomorrow? I'll be in at nine," Jessica called out as Nelson strutted back into the fold of the crowd.

She hesitated for a moment before reaching for her cell phone and searching the number for the Dublin Penitentiary. She was about to hit "call" when she heard Sabine's voice over the PA system. "Shoot," she muttered, shoving the phone back into her purse.

84

Jessica stood close to the stage, the press of the crowd pushing at her back. She imagined her heart might jump from her chest with pride as Sabine spoke in a clear, confident voice. She looked around for Tanner; she'd lost him in the wall of bodies. The crowd tightened as Catalina's parents shuffled nervously onto the stage.

Marta Gomez steadied her palms on the podium and took a deep breath. For now, she'd been winning the battle to fight back the torrent of tears she knew would come flooding if she let them. Francisco lacked his wife's resolve and let his tears flow freely, wiping them with the sleeve of his jacket.

"Good evening, thank you for coming. My name is Marta Gomez, this is my husband, Francisco. Three weeks ago, someone killed our daughter, Catalina. She was seventeen years old."

Marta took a deep breath. It was the first time she'd uttered those words; they lay thick and strange in her mouth, as if they were spoken by someone else but in her voice.

"I have heard people talk about our daughter. They have said hurtful things, many lies. They did not know Catalina like her family knew her. She was full of life, kind, smart, the most beautiful baby..."

Marta paused, placed one hand across her heart and the other firmly in Francisco's palm. "We called her Catalina. In English, it means pure. They say God only takes the ones who are pure, today God has one more angel in heaven, our angel. Maybe one day we can forgive God for taking her away from us, but the person who did this to my daughter? All the lies people have told? That we can never forgive. Parents should not live to bury their children, it is too cruel. It is like we have been given a beautiful gift and then someone takes it away. If we had known Catalina's life would be so short, we would have taken more care of her, loved her more, but we didn't know; nobody ever knows."

Marta's will was fading fast as she struggled to finish her last sentence. "If you have children, hold them tight tonight and tell them how much you love them, because you never know when your beautiful gift will be taken away. You never know."

She composed herself and asked for a minute of silence. The request was moot: the crowd had already fallen into a state of reverent hush since she and Francisco had taken to the stage.

85

Christen felt Alexus's hand wrap tighter around his own as Marta bowed her head and stepped back from the podium. It was at that moment he caught sight of Hector, his eyes full of purpose, an arrogant swagger to his stride. Instinctively, he looked to Hector's belt where the handgun poked from behind the thick brown leather. Was he about to make a grab for the gun? Threaten him? Take a shot at him and his family? The scenarios played like mini-movies in his head, each one more terrifying and lucid than the one before. Hector wouldn't hesitate to hurt him and his family, and he couldn't stand around and let that happen. It wasn't what a man did.

He slipped his hand from Alexus's and barreled towards Hector, confident he could body-slam him to the ground. As he ran, someone stepped into his trajectory. He elbowed the man in the ribs, shoving him to the side.

"Hey, what the fuck?" Nelson shouted, his joint falling as he stumbled from Christen's path.

Closing in, Christen saw Hector's finger curl around the action and down to the trigger. Only a few yards to run, he picked up the pace, dropped his head and plowed his shoulder hard into Hector's chest, sending him reeling to the ground.

As the weapon fell onto the grass, a woman shouted, "A gun! He's got a gun!"

Panic and confusion ignited through the crowd.

Christen fell on Hector, pressing down hard on his shoulders, straddling his knees across his chest; he just needed to keep him pinned until the police arrived.

Hector had other plans.

He scrambled along the grass towards the gun, one side of his face flat to the ground, the other side flushed red as he pushed against Christen. As Hector's fingers scraped the gun barrel, the prize almost in his grasp, the weapon seemed to be spirited away by an invisible force, lifting it several feet above the ground.

Christen and Hector both froze as they watched the young kid gauge the weight of the gun in his hand, stiffen his arms, ease his finger around the trigger and aim the barrel somewhere behind Christen's right shoulder.

Christen snapped his head around, sure his family were directly in the firing line. He was wrong.

Instead, the gun was aimed at a woman he was sure he'd seen once at some school event, but in the chaos couldn't put a name to the face. Before any spark of recognition, the kid pulled back the trigger.

The explosion from the gunshot was deafening and seemed to ricochet through every bone in Christen's body, filling his ears with a dull, thick ringing.

86

Fifteen feet away, Jessica sensed the panic ripple through the crowd. Mutterings had turned to screams as word travelled that someone had a gun and was about to shoot. She tried to move back towards the stage to find Sabine, but the crowd pushed against her, forcing her back with its velocity as people made a run for the side roads and pathways around the lake. As a narrow clearing opened up, revealing a clean path between her and the young boy holding the gun, a death-cold chill shivered down the back of her neck.

The gun that someone had shouted about, which until now was some vague notion, was aimed directly at her, its cruel eye shaking in the young, inexperienced hand. Behind the barrel, the young boy smiled: the same innocent smile, tinged with malice she'd seen that day when he'd stood next to his mother, told her his name was Tyler, and pretended to take aim.

Playtime was over now; this was as real as it got. Tyler eased his finger across the trigger.

"Fuck! No! Tyler. No!"

The shout from behind Jessica's left shoulder made her whip

her head around. Nelson barged in front of her, pleading with his younger brother.

It was all noise to Tyler. He was fulfilling his destiny; a destiny he'd come to believe would define him, deliver the respect he was due. Prove he was no longer a boy but a man.

Steadying his arms, he eased back the trigger, fired at Jessica.

The recoil still vibrating through his hand, Tyler looked on with a dazed expression. The woman he'd shot was still standing. He waited for her to fall, buckle to the ground like the avatars did in video games. There was blood splattered on the ground and on the woman's face and clothes. After a moment, she finally fell to her knees.

Tyler smiled to himself and nodded in satisfaction. Job done. Initiation complete. Destiny fulfilled.

The woman screamed. "He's been shot. Someone call the police!"

For a moment, Tyler's brain failed to make sense of the situation. Then the reality of what he'd done struck him with a force that made his bones quiver. The gun slipped from his hand. His shoulders hunched low like a linebacker, he charged from the lakeside and onto the pathway leading to the BART station.

Confusion and fear arced like electricity through the crowd. Anybody who hadn't made a run for the streets had thrown themselves on the ground, covering their heads with their arms, hoping and praying they'd be spared the next bullet. Children separated from their parents wailed and looked on helplessly. From the fringes of the crowd, the OPD officers drew their weapons and charged to the scene, pushing through the masses, stepping over the people laid out on the grass. On the stage, the PA system was still live, sending a buzz of high-pitched feedback over the area, aggravating the tension.

Roscoe Tanner's instincts kicked in. He sensed where the

shot had come from, ran towards the sound, slipping his gun from its holster as he shoved through the mass of limbs. It took him a few seconds to recognize the woman hunched over Nelson's body, his head cradled in her hands.

"Jessica! What the heck? Are you all right?"

Jessica looked up briefly. "I'm fine. He needs a doctor, Roscoe."

Tanner reached for his radio, but the chorus of sirens were already making their way to the lake. He pulled off his jacket, folded it, and pressed it down hard on Nelson's abdomen.

Jessica put her hands over his, kept on the pressure. "Hang on, Nelson, we've got help coming. Don't go to sleep, stay awake, stay with us."

Twenty feet away, after hearing the gunshot, Christen had released his grip on Hector. Seizing the opportunity, Hector ran, was about to dive down a side street to safety when he noticed Jonas Hansen, dazed, wandering through the crowd.

Hector reached for his knife, the one he always kept strapped to his ankle, and marched towards the kid. "Take it easy, motherfucker." He pressed the knife blade under Jonas's T-shirt and urged it into the small of his back. "Don't turn around and do like I tell you," he said, breathing heavily into Jonas's ear. "Walk with me like we're best buddies and I won't need to cut you up and throw your dead ass in the lake. *Comprendes*?"

Jonas nodded his compliance and walked in lockstep with Hector, the reminder he'd better not veer from the plan pressing cold and sharp into the flesh of his back.

87

Bruce had felt like a caged animal for the past ten days. Unable to run or pump weights, he'd cleared a small space in the apartment and worked out using his own body weight. It helped keep his mind focused on his next move; the only problem being, he didn't have a next move.

His life in the Bay Area was finished. Someone had ratted him out to the police; his first instinct was the Jonas kid, but he figured he was probably too scared, too much of a pussy to make that bold a move. Then there was Hector. Maybe the only reason Hector was letting him stay here was so he could monitor him until the boss decided on what punishment he was planning to inflict for cutting his product.

He ran through a quick mental list of his options. He knew some people running a cocaine cartel down in Culiacán--the capital city of the Mexican state of Sinaloa--there were always men looking to escape their past; no previous employer references and no résumé required. He could do some heavy lifting or menial grunt work, make a little money before deciding his next career move. Not an optimum solution, but the best he had for now.

What Follows

He flopped back on the couch and switched on the TV. Channel 7 was carrying live coverage of the shooting at the vigil. He immediately thought of Hector. The guy had a wild, determined look about him when he left the apartment earlier that evening; an intense anger burning behind his eyes. Bruce recalled it was the same look he'd had the night Wendi Chee was killed, and Tiffiny Grant too.

He sat back and wiped a hand over his face. He could go to the police, tell them everything, but he knew himself too well; he was no martyr, that was for sure.

On the coffee table, his burner phone vibrated twice, then stopped. He waited. One more vibration, then a ping. He understood the code. He clicked on the message.

We're out. Burn it. Tonight.

He read the message three times before deleting it. This wasn't the kind of message you ignored. This was the payback the boss had insisted would come. Bruce just wished it had come later, maybe when he was sunning himself on some beach in Mexico, where he could ignore the demand.

It was a big ask, the biggest, and something the boss wouldn't have sanctioned without good reason and without some kind of backup plan. His blood pumped like the steady pounding of a kettledrum as he sat; it made him antsy. He rose, shoved the coffee table to the side and dropped into a push-up position.

Grinding his teeth, he pushed hard on his palms, made his hands into fists, pressing down harder on his knuckles. He kept pumping, as if the sweat would take his anxiety with it, flood it away in a stream of perspiration. At push-up fifty-eight, he sensed his forearms weakening. Briefly, he turned his head to the left and caught sight of an object attached with duct tape to the underside of the kitchen table. He leapt into a squat, reached under the table and stripped the object from its housing. He held the phone, trying to figure out where he'd seen it before. He flipped it over and recognized the gold case with "Black Lives Matter" embossed onto the back.

A few minutes later, he'd packed up most of his clothes and stuffed the phone into the front zipper compartment of his backpack.

Options, he thought, *it was always good to have options.*

He'd complete the mission the message had demanded, then he was out. He'd find a way to make it across the border. But first, there was his own payback to secure.

Revenge wasn't just sweet, he thought as he left the apartment and slipped the key back under the door, it satisfied every sense and every sensation that made life worth living.

88

Alexus sat in the reception area of the OPD waiting for Christen. She'd already sent Sydney home in an Uber, and Jonas wasn't replying to any of her messages. She'd tried to garner some information as to when her husband would be released, but the surly female officer behind the front desk had surrendered nothing; not a smile nor a word of comfort.

As she sat, a niggling thought had formed at the back of her mind. Why the hell had Christen jumped that man? It wasn't like he'd done anything remotely heroic before, except one time punching out some drunk douchebag outside a bar when he'd stepped over the line and started running his mouth off about *"keeping the purity of the white race, motherfucker."* She must have ran through the events of the evening a hundred times, trying to piece together what had happened. Christen had been acting strangely all night; disappearing when they arrived at the vigil, insisting he had something important to tell her.

She was in the midst of another cycle of questioning when she recognized the female detective marching through the main entrance. "Excuse me," she called out as Shaughnessy signed herself in. "Detective, em, Shaw, right?"

The detective turned, with an impatient scowl. "Shaughnessy. Detective Shaughnessy."

"Sorry, yes—"

"I remember you, the lawyer from Rosemont, you got all pissy when we rained all over your parade."

Alexus let the insult roll over her. "I was wondering if you knew when my husband might be released?"

"I wasn't aware he was under arrest."

"He's not. Just answering questions."

"No idea. I'd sit tight. These things take time. Grab yourself some coffee from the vending machine, it tastes like crap but at least it's warm."

As Shaughnessy buzzed on the door leading to the humming machinery of the station, Alexus called out, "I don't suppose you've had time to look at that footage I sent in? The man is breaking the law, after all."

Shaughnessy ignored her and walked on.

"Great. Very helpful. Thank you, detective," Alexus snipped, threw herself back down on the chair, and tried once again to contact Jonas.

89

Hector shoved Jonas through the door and instructed him to sit on the bed. "Not a fucking sound," he said.

Jonas stammered, "Where? Where am I?"

His eyes scanned the room, which smelled of bleach. The furnishings were sparse; a queen-sized bed, a bowl full of condoms on the nightstand, and a box of tissues. Next to the bed was a brass lamp that seemed salvaged from an estate sale, with a pair of handcuffs padded with pink feathers hanging from the lampshade. On the exposed brick to the left of the bed, bolts had been drilled into the wall, and hanging off the bolts was another set of handcuffs. These were less playful than the others, with a serious steel to them. Several feet below, he noticed another pair. Looking closer, he revised his initial impression. These were shackles, and were bored deep into the wall a few inches above the floor––the optimum position where they could be snapped securely around a man's ankles, should he so desire.

"What is this place?" Jonas asked, his words barely forming, his throat tight and dull.

"Phone," Hector barked.

Jonas hesitated.

Hector whipped the back of his hand against his cheek. "Now."

Jonas didn't require a second prompt.

Hector glanced at the missed calls and alerts. "Someone must be real worried."

He dropped the phone to the floor, and brought the full force of his boot down to bear on the device.

Jonas winced as the glass shattered. Hector urged his heel harder, grinding the electronic innards into the concrete. As he kicked the remainder of the debris under the bed, Hector reached around for his own phone; his pocket was empty, save a single dollar bill that had been through the dark-wash cycle too often.

Shit! His phone must have fallen out when he was tackled by the boy's father. Another sear of anger burned at a membrane close to his frontal lobe; he was familiar enough with the feeling to recognize its purpose. He'd learned to embrace it, not fight it; feed it, not starve it.

"Put it on your wrist and cuff the other one to the bed," he said, gesturing at the handcuffs on the lampshade.

"Are you serious?"

Hector stepped close, spitting in Jonas's face. "Do I look fucking serious to you?"

Jonas understood it was a rhetorical question and slowly reached over for the cuffs, imagining for a moment he could use them as a weapon to crack open Hector's head and make a run for it. But as soon as he held them the notion was stillborn. The cuffs were too light, the kind you bought for a Halloween costume. The cheap, synthetic feathers shed onto the bed as he tried to attach them, his hands trembling.

"Jesus!" Hector reached over and clamped one around

Jonas's wrist and the other around one of the poles of the iron headboard.

Satisfied he was suitably restrained, Hector leaned back on the nightstand. "I got some questions." His voice was thick with menace, his eyes cold. "And if I don't like your answers, then you and me, we're going to have a problem."

Jonas caught the glint of steel in the faint lamplight. It looked like a knife, but longer, wider too; the kind of knife someone might use for gutting fish.

In the dim light, he saw it also had some lettering carved into the steel edge. Before he could make any sense of the string of long, curved words, Hector had skimmed the blade lightly across Jonas's palm, just at the point where his lifeline met his wrist.

It drew just enough blood to clarify his point.

90

"Christ," Shaughnessy said, as she approached Tanner. "You okay?" She gestured at the bloom of damp blood spread across his shirt.

"Better than the kid who caught the dang bullet," he said, loosening his tie a notch.

"So, what can I do?" she asked, noticing several more dried clumps of blood attached to the hairs on Tanner's forearms.

"We've got extra officers drafted in to take the witness statements, but most of the crowd hightailed, so we're left with the crazies and the do-gooders."

Shaughnessy hitched up her belt. "Sounds like my kind of party. Who's in the Deliverance Suite?" she asked, gesturing at the door behind Tanner.

Interview Room #3 was nicknamed the "Deliverance Suite" because it was the room where suspects were more likely to *"squeal like a pig."* The room had a claustrophobic and queasy quality, exaggerated by the ultra-low ceiling, thick, windowless walls, and the stale air which was kept at a constant seventy-seven degrees.

"Christen Hansen," Tanner said, checking his notes.

"Hence the wife pacing reception?"

Tanner showed her a cell phone tagged in an evidence bag. "Found this at the scene. Forensics confirmed it belongs to Hector Figuerello, a petty lowlife with a couple of prior misdemeanors. Can you search through it, and if anything of interest comes up, let me know?"

"Sure thing," she said. "Is Figuerello in custody?"

"I wish," Tanner said. "But apparently Hansen and Figuerello have some history, and according to several witness statements, they saw Hansen drop the guy to the ground like a linebacker."

"Every story's got a damned hero."

Tanner paused. "Do you know the most interesting thing about heroes, Shaughnessy?" he said, shoving his shoulder against the interview room door.

"They don't always get the girl?" she offered.

Tanner shook his head. "The backstory, always the backstory. And I bet this one right here," he said, handing over Hector's phone, "is a real doozy."

91

Francisco and Marta Gomez walked hand in hand down lower International Boulevard, just before it forked into 1st Avenue. A solemn silence hung between them. There was no more to be said. Marta had poured her heart out at the vigil, and now it felt empty, maybe worse than empty, like it would never be full again. The detective had been right. The vigil hadn't eased her grief or her guilt. If anything, with the shooting, it had wrenched the wound wide open until the pain was as raw and searing as the day Detective Tanner had stood in her front room and explained softly her daughter's body had been recovered from Lake Temescal.

For 10pm, International Boulevard was oddly silent, with none of the usual growl of the low-riders cruising the blocks, reggaeton music booming through the over-cranked speakers. Even the glow from the taquerias seemed muted and menacing, as did the thin shards of street lights spilling onto the sidewalk. Maybe that's why she didn't see the man until he was within breathing distance, or maybe she was too lost in her own thoughts to notice. They both sensed him in the periphery of

What Follows

their vision, a shadow sneaking around them, as if searching for an opening.

Instinctively, Marta snapped her purse close to her hip. But the man already had his hands on the opening, wedging it apart. She sensed his hands inside her bag. She was about to scream, when she realized his intentions weren't to steal but to plant.

She turned her head, glimpsing his face for a brief second.

"Ask Hector," the man mumbled, before sprinting down the sidewalk until he was lost in the shadows.

Marta reached in her purse and pulled out the object. She and Francisco stared at it with a mixture of confusion and trepidation, captivated by the screen saver selfie of Catalina.

They both passed their fingertips gently over the cold glass in fear that if they touched too hard, the image would vanish to some place from where it would never be retrieved.

92

"Why would Hector Figuerello want to harm you?" Tanner asked, folding his jacket over the back of the chair as he sat. "Doesn't add up as to why you two would be running in the same social circles. But who the heck knows, maybe you were best buddies?"

"I have never met the man before."

Tanner slid a mugshot across the desk. "Hector has what we like to call, frequent flier miles here at OPD; misdemeanors mostly, but discharging a firearm in a public space, that's quite the career jump."

"Maybe it was mistaken identity," Christen offered.

"Unlikely, Mr. Hansen, you're close to what, six-three on a good day? Easy to spot a tall drink of water like you in a crowd."

Christen's fingers wrapped themselves in knots as Tanner's gaze, which on any other occasion might have appeared warm or kindly, seemed to pierce through him with ice-cold precision. "An accident? Maybe he did not see very well, it was getting dark."

"It sure was, Mr. Hansen. But the thing is, this case, Catalina

Gomez's death? It's been like one dang itch I can't reach to scratch. Ever had one of those?"

Tanner rose, arching his back like a cat waking up from a nap. "I get them all the time, perks of the job. My colleagues call it intuition, a sixth sense or whatnot. Personally, I just call it what it is, an itch; an itch that's gonna bug the tarnation out of me until I haul someone in front of a jury for the murder of that young girl."

"I thought she died of an overdose. That's what the news said."

"If we all had a mind to believe the bull we read in the news, we'd all be throwing ourselves off the nearest tall building, isn't that the danged truth of it?"

"Wait," Christen said, an itch of his own forming in the deep pit of his stomach. "You do not think I had anything—?"

Tanner cut him off mid-sentence. "I probably shouldn't be telling you this, but this old dog isn't buying what the DA's selling. Too many inconsistencies. You and Hector Figuerello for instance, I'd sure like to tie a nice bow around that one and call it an early Christmas gift."

"I saw him take his gun out, I just reacted."

Tanner sat. "Now, I'm not familiar with how they do things where you're from. Remind me again, Sweden was it? Norway?"

"Denmark. I'm Danish."

"Denmark, huh? Always struck me like a civilized country. Not much of this dang gun violence we're dealing with here, I'd guess."

"We are apparently the second happiest nation in the world."

"A silver medal for happiness? Go figure," Tanner said, leaning back. "Anyway, as I was saying, we do things differently over here. This friendly chat? It's like a prologue. I ask you questions, you throw me some horse hooey about never having met Hector Figuerello and it's all loosey-goosey, this way, that way. Then, I show you the evidence that'll shoot down every dang thing you just said and we get real serious, real quick."

Tanner flipped open the laptop on the table and pressed the play bar.

Christen sensed a thick nausea pool in his gut as the video footage played.

"Cameras all around the lake, all live tonight for obvious reasons. This one here is directed at the kiddies' playground, just across from the library. Now, if I'm not mistaken, that's a very tall Danish man talking with a much shorter Latino man. They talk for a few minutes, then the tall man takes a step forward and gets up in the Latino man's face. Now, if you're going to tell me you two were practicing your salsa moves for his daughter's quinceañera, that's going to get me real pissed, real quick."

Christen's head spun, unable to form a coherent thought as Tanner rewound the video.

"So, prologue over," Tanner said, stretching his arms across the table. "What was your connection to Hector Figuerello? And what do you know about an establishment called the Rat House?"

93

Hector had always gotten a kick out of how his vintage Mexican knuckleduster trench knife felt in his hand. It possessed a kind of mystical power, as if the souls of all the men slayed with it were somehow forged into its perfectly balanced steel-and-horn inlays. But what really gave him a hard-on was its dual-purpose efficiency. At one end, a ten-inch blade he kept sharp enough to cut through bone. At the other, a curved steel handle with pitted indentations, like that of a cobra skin, which rose in thick metallic bulges when slipped over his knuckles.

It was this function he used first, slamming the steel down across Jonas's cheek with a force that shook the boy's teeth.

As he wiped a trickle of warm blood off his chin, Hector sat on the bed next to Jonas. "See, I told you, if I didn't like your answers I have to hurt you."

"I swear," Jonas said, spitting a glob of blood on the floor. "I don't remember shit about that night. You've got to believe me. I wouldn't hurt Catalina. I didn't give her any drugs. I swear."

Hector brought the knife close enough for Jonas to read the lettering. "Know what this says?" he asked.

Jonas squinted. He could barely focus let alone translate Spanish.

"Camarón que se duerme, se lo lleva la corriente," Hector said, with a smile that indicated he would never tire of reading the phrase aloud. "The shrimp that sleeps gets carried away by the current. You understand?"

Jonas shook his head; it felt heavy and sodden, as if it were swimming in blood.

"And I thought you Rosemont kids were meant to be smart," Hector said, his mouth a tight smirk. "It means you snooze, you lose. Easy, huh?"

Hector laid the knife on his lap. "See, what with my niece being murdered and looking after my grieving family, I've been preoccupied; snoozing, you know, letting people get away with shit. But I'm done with that, I ain't in the 'letting shit go' mood no more."

Jonas felt his jawbone crack as he spoke. "Bruce..." he stammered. "He, he... always supplied the product."

"Yeah, I ain't dumb, we gonna take care of him. But Bruce, see, he was just the supplier. I know Catalina was clean. Some fucker made her take that dirty heroin."

He ran the dull edge of the knife against Jonas's other cheek. "Was it you, pretty boy? Was it? Did you kill Catalina?"

Jonas's eyes pooled with tears. He could feel them running down his cheeks, their saltiness seeping into the open wound. "I swear, I don't remember seeing her that night."

"I saw her," Hector said. "She was working that night, then she runs off to meet someone in the parking lot. Then, like a ghost, she disappears. With you."

Hector shuffled closer, clamped his hand around the fleshy skin where Jonas's thigh met his knee. "Why did you do it? She wasn't giving out, and you got all rich-boy entitlement shit building up inside you, so you killed her?"

Hector's grip tightened. "I'll tell you this, pendejo, Catalina was no chola. But that don't matter to you, right? She was just another chick you wanted to fuck. Tell me you were with my niece that night and maybe I save your life. Good deal?"

Apart from the wrenching pain deep in his cheekbones, there was another, more insistent ache thundering behind Jonas's brow. The pain of not remembering; the dull, consistent throb of a night forgotten. Hours lost in darkness. A glitch in his system. A memory-bank failure beyond recovery.

"I don't know..." he mumbled. "I don't remember."

"Then maybe you try harder."

Hector whipped back his arm and reacquainted Jonas's face with the knuckleduster.

His scream echoed long and loud off the walls of the room, concealing the other, more urgent sound outside that, if Hector had heard, would have compelled him immediately into action––the growl of a high-powered motorcycle pulling up outside the old warehouse.

By the time Jonas's scream had been absorbed into the brickwork, the motorcycle's engine cut dead, its headlight cooling under the faint moonlight.

94

The overhead fluorescents in the interview room buzzed as if a cloud of houseflies were trapped in the plastic casing. The hard, white light exaggerated every pore on Christen's face and reflected harshly off his scalp, which was slick with perspiration.

"Is he threatening you? Is that why you're scared, Mr. Hansen?"

"No comment," Christen said, the words barely passing his lips.

As Tanner prepared to take another, less subtle angle, Shaughnessy entered the room, and gestured for Tanner to meet her outside.

Alone, Christen settled his forearms on his thighs and bowed his head between his knees. If he told Tanner about the Rat House he was sure Hector would follow through on his threats. Christen had put his own family in danger just to satisfy his own selfish desires; the thought gutted him to his rotten, vile core. He took a breath. The situation was bad, as bad as it got, he thought, as he folded his arms across his cramping belly.

A few minutes later, Tanner and Shaughnessy walked in.

"What brand of car do you drive, Mr. Hansen?" she asked, laying Hector's cell phone on the table.

"A Tesla Model S, why is that important?"

"What color?"

"Silver."

"Is it this one?"

Christen's blood pulsed hard as he looked over the same photographs Hector had shown him at the Rat House. Behind his eyes a hot insistent beat throbbed like a drum. "I want to speak to a lawyer," he mumbled, pinching the bridge of his nose.

"Sure you do," Tanner said, sitting on the edge of the table. "I would in your situation."

He extracted a cotton swab from his DNA sample kit and handed it to Shaughnessy. "But first, it would be very much appreciated by myself, and my partner, if you'd agree to provide a DNA sample; eliminate you from our inquiries."

Christen lifted his head. "And if I don't agree?"

"In case you're unaware of the process, this is how these things play out," Shaughnessy explained. "We can forcibly take a DNA sample after we arrest you for the abduction and murder of Wendi Chee. Should you wish to voluntarily provide a cheek swab, then we can hold off on that arrest, save you the whole tiresome process of mugshots, fingerprinting processing, all of which takes time."

She leaned close to Christen, and spoke in a low but clear voice. "Your choice, Mr. Hansen, but I'd think long and hard before you make it."

Christen looked up at Tanner as if he might offer some guidance or alternative route out of his predicament. Tanner's poker face offered no such comfort.

"Sure would put a nice wrap around the evening's proceedings if you did this voluntarily. Get you and your wife back home before sunrise."

Christen sat back, wiped a palm across his brow. "And I still get my lawyer?" he asked.

"It's your right as an American citizen," Tanner confirmed. "All we're asking is your co-operation, which will become part of our recommendation to the DA. I wager you're as eager to see this Hector Figuerello character taking up space in one of our cells as we are."

Christen exhaled, long and loud, and nodded.

"Wise choice," Shaughnessy said, leaning over Christen. "Now open wide," she added, swirling the cotton swab inside Christen's cheeks, which were bone dry and trembling.

95

Bruce dismounted and removed his crash helmet. From the warehouse, a single light glowed in one of the second-floor rooms. This puzzled him. The boss wouldn't have given him the order if the Rat House was operating tonight; he wasn't the kind of man to needlessly waste lives, that would have been inefficient, a flaw in the business strategy.

He mused on this as he unhinged two full gasoline cans hooked onto the sides of his motorcycle and set them down. There were no cars parked in the shadows, no throbbing bassline coming from the building. He continued regardless, walking towards the side entrance.

The sight of Hector's truck solved the puzzle for Bruce. It was parked on the opposite side of the warehouse where the ink-black water slopped against the dockside. A plan appeared, fully-formed, as he recognized the vehicle––it was a *"fuck me, of course"* moment of clarity. Bruce couldn't resist a smile as he slipped the key into the padlock. Maybe he could salvage a win from this shitshow after all. With Hector out of the picture, the boss would need someone like Bruce. He'd be forced to keep Bruce on, protect him.

The thought gave him a rush as he knotted his bandana across his mouth, unscrewed a cap, and began sloshing the gasoline across the floor and walls, making his way along the hallway and towards the second floor where he was sure Hector was hiding. He'd flush him out. Like a rat from the gutter.

96

An hour or so before Bruce had formulated his plan, Tanner and Shaughnessy had sat impatiently in the observation area of Interview Room #3, waiting for the test results. The new DNA analysis kits OPD was experimenting with—Dugdale had ordered several from an FBI contact of his—guaranteed results in less than two hours. In reality, the FBI kit was far more efficient; seventy-three minutes by Tanner's counting, but it still felt like a long stretch of time staring at Christen Hansen sweating it out. When they were handed the results, they both nodded at each other. They understood their task.

Tanner laid the printed DNA results on the table. "You're an interesting character, Hansen," he said, sitting back in his chair. "A real international man of mystery, huh?"

"Sorry, I don't understand. Is this the DNA result?"

"Sure is," Tanner confirmed.

"Then I want my lawyer."

"Should be here soon," Shaughnessy confirmed.

"Then I have nothing to say until he arrives."

Tanner shrugged. "That's too bad. You want to give him the bad news, Shaughnessy, or should I?"

"I think it's your turn, I did the last one."

"Right you are," Tanner said, laying four photographs face down on the table, before flipping them over as if revealing a winning hand of cards.

"That's your car," he said, pointing at the shot Hector had taken of Wendi Chee leaning into his car window. "Timestamped July 3rd, 10.47pm. The night she was murdered."

"Yes," Christen said, his neck muscles weakening as he spoke, compelling his head to droop forward as if he were about to kneel for confession. "I picked her up. But I dropped her back there later, I swear. She was alive when I left her."

Tanner continued, "These two you might want to brace yourself for."

Christen's stomach cramped as he looked over the photograph of Wendi Chee's body. The other one, a close-up of the bloodied stump of her wrist, made him turn his face away.

"But this one," Tanner said, delaying the reveal on the last picture. "This one, I think you'll be real interested in."

He slowly revealed his Ace.

"The contents of Wendi Chee's purse," Shaughnessy said. "Just like most of us women, bunch of shit in there, lipstick, pepper spray, condoms; a working girl needs her protection. But this here is what intrigued us," she added, pointing at the thin, cylindrical shape in the left side of the purse.

"We had ourselves a heck of a time figuring that out. I mean, a girl carries a partly smoked joint in her bag, but it doesn't have any of her DNA on it? Not a trace," Tanner said. "Doesn't make a whole lot of sense."

A thought, like the snap of a rubber band, formed in the back of Christen's mind.

"Then, there was no match in the DNA database, which got us all hot and bothered."

Another snap of the band as Christen struggled to retrieve the memory.

"But now," Tanner said, stabbing the paper with the DNA results. "Thanks to you, we got that little mystery all cleared up."

"There's a ninety-nine point nine percent probability that's your DNA on the joint we found in Wendi Chee's purse," Shaughnessy said. "Forensics ran some chemical tests. This stuff is pretty strong, not your average THC in this sucker."

The band finally snapped. Christen had an unshakeable grip on the memory. *Hector visiting his office, insisting he take a pull on the joint, then taking it back from him and placing it in a box.* He felt the blood drain from his face, from his body: he was sure if he looked down there'd be a pool of dark red at his feet.

"So, now we have all the cards on the table, Mr. Hansen, and before your lawyer arrives and advises you to stop talking, tell us about the Rat House."

Christen's hands trembled. He shook his head.

"Just an address," Tanner insisted, leaning back. "It's your call as to whose side you align yourself with, and both my partner and I hope you make the right choice. But before you make that decision, ask yourself one question. Would Hector Figuerello protect you if he was sitting right here, in your situation? Would he, Mr. Hansen?"

97

Hector was preparing to pile-drive another five-knuckled, vintage-steel reminder Jonas's way, when he heard a sound in the hallway: like someone urinating loud and long over the floor.

He pressed the flat edge of the blade against Jonas's lips. Jonas got the message and nodded. He had neither the strength nor the will to scream, his throat raw, his mouth swimming in blood, his eyes barely focusing on anything beyond the viscous film of tears.

Hector rose slowly, walked to the door and leant his head against it, listening. Silence. Not that the silence compelled him to drop his guard, in fact it heightened his alertness, tweaked his anxiety up a notch or two.

As he pulled slowly on the door, he caught the first waft of gasoline rising from the hallway. He placed his forearm to his mouth and edged around the door. The hallway was dark, the only illumination provided by a glint of moonlight scraping in through the second-floor window.

That, and the yellow-blue flame of Bruce's lighter, which flickered like a fiery omen at the far end of the hallway.

Hector didn't think twice; there was no time for contemplation, just action. He ran, his knife held directly in front of him, figuring he'd tackle Bruce to the ground before he could throw the lighter onto the slick, glistening floor and set the whole place into a fireball.

The floor where Bruce stood was still dry; he'd calculated he only needed to douse part of the second-floor hallway. Combined with the other can, which he'd already emptied on the first floor, it was plenty to turn the whole place into another Fourth of July.

What he hadn't calculated was Hector's acceleration as he barreled towards him.

Bruce drew back his arm and flung the lighter.

Hector watched as the lighter cartwheeled above him, seeming to fly in slow motion, leaving trails of yellow in its tailwind, before landing and scraping across the wet floor at the opposite end of the hallway.

The floor ignited, sending a flurry of flames up the walls and down the stairwell.

Hector charged on.

Momentarily distracted by the flames, Bruce didn't register the shock of the blade until Hector buried it several inches into his abdomen. By the time his nervous system had messaged his brain, Hector had drawn back the knife, preparing for a second onslaught.

This time Bruce was ready. He snapped his thick, muscular fingers around Hector's wrist, stopping the knife's trajectory in mid-air. He lunged his solid mass forward with the force of a heavyweight fighter's knockout right hook.

It caught Hector clean across the right eye.

Stumbling back against the wall, Hector lost momentary control of his motor functions, the knife slipping from his hand as if its handle were slathered in oil.

Bruce looked down and took his boot to the weapon, sending it spinning across the concrete floor. It came to a grating halt outside the half-open door to where Jonas was yanking hard on the cuffs, trying to free himself.

Bruce and Hector crashed into the room, dragging the knife with them.

At first, noticing the pool of blood across Bruce's T-shirt, Jonas wondered if Hector had the upper hand in the struggle and his own fate was all but sealed. But as Bruce flung Hector to the ground like a sack of potatoes, he felt a faint glimmer of hope.

If Bruce beat Hector, then there had to be some hope for him to get out alive. It was hope, however slim. His choice was ugly; either of the two men would have gladly seen him dead and his options came down to which one he distrusted least. Which of the two men, if the circumstances came to it, would get him out of there alive.

He glanced down at the knife which had landed close to his feet. It was too far to reach with his hand, but easy enough to kick.

He called out. "Bruce!"

Bruce looked up. In that moment, Hector flipped his body, straddled Bruce and pinned his shoulders to the ground, pressing his knee deep into Bruce's open wound. Bruce's scream was guttural and savage; a wild animal cornered and desperate.

Hector wound his fingers around Bruce's neck until Bruce's throat coughed up blood, which came out in halting spurts, landing on his chest.

Now, Jonas thought, it had to be now. He kicked the knife.

Bruce heard the scrape of metal on concrete, looked, shot

out his arm. He grabbed it in his right hand, looked into Hector's eyes, and brought the blade in a perfect uppercut into Hector's chest, carving effortlessly through the bone.

Hector looked down at the blade protruding from his chest and for one moment, before he lost consciousness, savored the sublime irony. Slayed by his own blade. There had to be some poetic justice in that, some nobleness. Not that he had time to ponder on the majesty of it. His eyes quickly drained of life. He fell onto Bruce with a heavy thud.

Jonas breathed a sigh of relief and looked over at Bruce, who was rolling Hector's body off his own.

As Bruce lifted his head and pulled back his hair, which was sodden with sweat and blood, a flash of red lights strobed across the brickwork. In the near distance, a wail of sirens rushing closer.

He staggered, clutching his wound, and hobbled towards the door. The far end of the hallway was an inferno. In minutes it would engulf the entire building. He stumbled into the hallway.

"Wait!" Jonas screamed, a rage of panic in his eyes and voice. "What the fuck! You can't leave me!"

Bruce stopped for a moment, contemplating his options. He dragged himself back inside and extracted the knife from Hector's still warm but now useless heart.

Jonas heard a faint whisper of air leaving the body as he did so.

He stood over Jonas, the knife held high.

"No, please, Bruce, man, don't do this, please."

Bruce offered the faintest of smirks and brought down the knife hard and fast.

As the blade sliced effortlessly through the chain of the cheap handcuffs, Jonas's heart felt as if it might explode through his chest.

"That's the last fuckin' favor I do for you, Hansen," Bruce said. He stuffed the knife in the back of his jeans belt and ran.

Jonas heard the smashing of glass in the hallway. Bruce had made his escape via the second-story window: a twenty-foot drop that was easily survivable with only a lightly bruised ankle if you knew how to nail the landing, which Bruce did. He'd performed it plenty of times swinging off the parallel bars in the gym.

There was barely time for Jonas to register the relief that his life was saved before he realized it was a false assumption.

The smoke from the hallway was billowing through the room in swathes of black, the flames licking their way under the door, hungry to devour everything in their path.

98

Outside the warehouse, Tanner and Shaughnessy ran from their patrol car and stood as close as they dared to the burning building. The flames were raging: a thick wall of heat that stopped them dead in their tracks.

Moments later they were joined by another three cars and six heavily armed officers. Behind them, the sister-wails of the fire trucks and paramedics pulled off the 880 Freeway ramp and onto the surface streets.

The officers exited their vehicles, drew their weapons and crouched in defensive positions behind the car doors. Above, a police helicopter circled, searchlight scrambling anxiously over the debris around Brooklyn Basin.

"*Unknown person fleeing the building, heading north-west,*" the pilot radioed.

"Copy that," Shaughnessy said.

Grabbing her weapon, she turned to two of the more experienced officers she knew. "You're both with me. Keep your weapons drawn at all times."

They nodded, pulling their helmets tight over their brows.

She barked into her radio, "In pursuit of suspect. Give me all the light you've got."

As Shaughnessy fled into the shadows, guided by the searing white beam, Tanner stood back as the warehouse buckled under the intense heat. The wall closest to the dockside collapsed, the wreckage disintegrating into the water, sparks and splinters of wood falling across the surface.

Tanner felt a sickening pit open up in his stomach. All that evidence, literally going up in smoke. Whatever the true function of the Rat House, or if it really even existed, would be near impossible to ascertain now. After all, what did he have other than a hunch and an address? And prosecuting anyone, especially whoever was behind the enterprise, was looking more unlikely with every crumbling beam.

As another section of the warehouse fell into embers, Tanner was sure he saw a shape moving behind one of the windows on the second floor. A faint light passed across the glass, then it was gone. He waited. Maybe it was a code of some sort, a signal to someone. But there was nothing else, just darkness, and the swathe of flames staking claim on their dominion.

99

Dense black smoke billowed through the gaps in the door, filling the room with noxious fumes that settled deep in Jonas's lungs. There was no way out, he understood that now, at least not the way he was brought in. The stairwell Hector had forced him up was probably destroyed, as was most of the hallway.

He scanned the room; there had to be something, anything that would help him get out of there. The brass lamp on the nightstand caught his attention. He wrenched the cable from the socket and grabbed the heavy base, ripping off the shade and throwing it to the floor.

His first lunge at the window cracked the glass. His second shattered it completely, sending a shower of glass down the side of the building.

The shards landed a few feet from Tanner. He looked up as Jonas crouched unsteadily in the narrow frame.

He was hesitating. *Shoot, just jump*, Tanner thought. *Whoever the heck you are, just dang well jump.*

Jonas *was* hesitating. The drop was twenty feet, but it might as well have been a hundred. His brain was refusing to accept that jumping was his only option, and even that option had a slim window of opportunity which was tightening by the second.

He looked behind him, as if the reality of the flames swirling around the doorway and igniting the cheap bedclothes might somehow trigger his brain into doing what was required.

He turned his head back to the shattered window. Below him, the red and blue lights seemed to strobe at the same rhythm as his accelerated heartbeat. Above him the chop of the helicopter rotors thumped with the same dense pulse as the blood throbbing in his ears.

He looked up. The stars were the only constant now, solid and unyielding in their place where everything else around him seemed liquid and transient.

It was at that point, perched on the edge, his head light and woozy with the effects of the smoke, that he saw a girl's face superimposed in the night sky; her eyes two stars in the blackness. Catalina's eyes. It was a hallucination; it had to be, but at the same time it felt more tangible than anything else around him.

In that moment, she reached out her hand, beckoning him to follow her. Jonas stretched out his arm and stepped forward.

He met the ground with a bone-shattering crack which sparkled up through his body with a kinetic energy, the energy coming to a sudden and brutal dead end somewhere deep in his skull.

Before the darkness descended, for a split second, his mind was perfectly clear. The memory of what happened the night Catalina vanished now as present and real as if he were there watching it. The memory offered him some comfort as he passed out.

100

Jessica sat at the edge of Nelson's bed. It was close to midnight, the events of the evening still fresh in her mind. He was attached to a complex network of tubes entering and exiting his body, his torso wrapped in thick bandages and gauzes where the bullet had ruptured his spleen.

Jessica wiped a bead of sweat from his cheek. The humming and beeping of the paraphernalia in the intensive care unit was hypnotic. Her head felt as if it were three times its regular weight, but she'd forced herself to stay awake. She was determined to be there for Nelson when he woke up. If he woke up. The thought ran cold through her. It should have been her lying there, fighting for her life. But fate, or maybe dumb luck, had intervened. She was deep in this grim thought and didn't notice Tanner and Sabine until they were standing next to her.

"How's he doing?" Tanner asked, resting his hand on Jessica's shoulder.

She patted it gently. "They've induced a coma to help with the trauma, but they're preparing for the worst."

"He looks strong. I'm sure he'll pull through."

Jessica smiled, grateful for Tanner's soothing words, but not for one minute believing they were true. "You look beat," she said, gazing at the bloodstains across his shirt and the smudges of soot on his cheeks and hands. "And you smell like you've walked through a fire."

"Long story," he said, a spent weariness to his voice.

Sabine walked to her mother and wrapped her arms around her, nestling her head into her shoulder.

"You gave a pretty good performance," Jessica said. "I'm proud of you, really proud."

Sabine stood back, tears welling. "It was all my fault, wasn't it? I mean, if I hadn't organized the stupid vigil you wouldn't have almost been killed and we wouldn't be here."

She cried as her mother held her. "You did a beautiful thing. Everything else that happened, none of it was your fault, none of it."

"You should listen to your mother, she's a smart woman," Tanner said, stepping back.

"Yeah, she's always telling me that," she said, offering a thin smile as she wiped the tears from her eyes.

"I should probably head back to the bedlam," Tanner said, sensing his presence was surplus to requirements. "Paperwork up the wazoo with everything that went down tonight."

Jessica nodded. "Call me. Tomorrow?"

Tanner smiled. As he pushed on the door, a loud, desperate voice echoed down the hospital corridors.

"Nelson? Where's my boy? You got my boy in there? Nelson?"

As the door was flung open, Jessica immediately recognized Lachelle Welch's frail, shadow-like figure in the doorway as if waiting for permission to enter.

"Nelson. Hell, no! Nelson!" She walked gingerly towards her son and waved her hands as if they had the power to disintegrate the scene, relegate it to another bad dream. When the dream failed to break, she marched towards Jessica. "This ain't your seat to take."

"I was just trying—" Jessica said, gathering up her belongings.

"You don't try nothing more, you understand me?" Lachelle interrupted, settling her handbag on the chair as if she were reclaiming her rightful dominion. "I told you people already, keep your nose out of our shit. Why you even here?"

Tanner spoke, "Nelson stepped in front of the gun that was aimed at Ms. Swift. He saved her life."

Lachelle shook her head, her thin, gold-plated hoop earrings clattering around her lobes like the faint tingle of a distant chime. "No, I ain't buying that. He ain't stupid."

"We have several witness reports…"

Lachelle's eyes hardened as she took stock. "Police?" she scoffed. "What you gonna do? Arrest him for taking a bullet for a white woman? Put another black man away for doin' the right thing?"

"What Nelson did was heroic, Mrs. Welch. You should be very proud of your son," Tanner insisted.

Lachelle stroked her long, manicured nails up the bedclothes towards Nelson's hand. "He ain't gonna be no damned hero," she said, taking her son's hand gently in her palm. "If he don't make it, he won't be nothin' more than a number. Black kids 'round here, they ain't ever be heroes, they just be dead."

Lachelle folded into the chair, which seemed to swallow her as she stroked Nelson's hand.

"Em," Tanner began, softening his voice as best he could. "Your younger son, Tyler?"

Lachelle kept her gaze fixed on Nelson. "One of my sons not enough for you?" she snapped.

"We picked up Tyler around thirty minutes ago in the vicinity of Lake Merritt BART station."

Lachelle turned to face Tanner. "Why? He ain't done shit."

"We have several eyewitnesses that placed him at the scene and saw him fire the gun."

Lachelle sat up straight and pointed at Tanner. "Tyler's a good boy, he wouldn't shoot no one, not Tyler."

"He's been assigned a lawyer and a child counselor. He'll be remanded into care for the time being. I'm sorry, Mrs. Welch."

"You're wrong. Tyler didn't shoot no one, just like Nelson ain't gonna be no hero."

Lachelle grasped her son's hand. "Now get the fuck out of this room, my son needs his momma."

PART IV

AFTERSHOCKS

101

The following morning, Jessica woke late to the sound of her phone alerts pinging like tiny needle stabs in her brain. She checked the number. Dublin Penitentiary. Shit, in the events of the night she'd completely forgotten about Topaz. She was sure it was probably nothing, just Nelson's empty threats. And anyway, he was still fighting for his life, there was not much he could do from his hospital bed. She'd call them back later; she needed some downtime right now. Probably a few months of downtime.

She'd barely put the kettle on the stove when her apartment doorbell buzzed.

"Little late, aren't you?" she said, as Gérard stood expectantly at the doorway. "Even for you, this is a real doozy."

"How's Sabine?" he asked, craning his neck into the apartment hallway.

"Still sleeping, she's had a rough night. You do know you missed her speech, right?"

Gérard wiped a clammy hand behind his neck. "Yeah, something came up." He'd spent the night at Moonshine's, making sure the kid did nothing stupid, then left early in the morning.

Jessica raised her palms in the air. "You know, I really don't care, I haven't cared for a very long time. Your excuses, your bullshit? I was already done with it ten years ago, and I'm in no mood to resurrect that cadaver and give it air this morning."

Gérard took a breath. "Is it true about that young kid? He got shot, saving you?"

"I'm still here, aren't I?"

"Jesus." Gérard took a step forward as if he were going to embrace her in one of his bear hugs.

"Oh, shit no," Jessica said, sidestepping. "That is most definitely the last thing I need."

"What, you gonna leave a brother hanging?" Gérard asked, his arms outstretched and hoping some humor would diffuse the tension. It wasn't working. It hadn't worked for some years with Jessica. He should have known by now, but he's always been a slow learner when it came to women.

"You know the one thing I can't understand?" Jessica said, folding her arms across her chest lest Gérard decided to lunge at her again with another clumsy attempt at intimacy.

"Shoot."

"You say you want to be a part of Sabine's life, but you're never there. It's like this big show you put on for her. You set yourself up to be the cool dad, the outlaw father always promising to make it up, telling her something better's always on the horizon. But there never is, is there, Gérard? There never will be."

Gérard was about to interrupt, but Jessica's laser gaze seemed to have gripped itself around his throat.

"But when you pull that stunt once too often, people stop believing in you, especially kids. They lose faith, Gérard. They build a wall around themselves, it's how they cope, and they don't let you back in because experience has taught them they're just setting themselves up for more hurt if they do. Listen, in two years, Sabine will have gone off to college, and that's going tear me to shreds. Seriously, if you want to have any meaningful relationship with your daughter, you need to do something before it's too late to fix it. Last night was my wake-up call. And, me talking to you now, this is yours. Is that clear enough for you, Gérard?"

Driving home, Jessica's words were still ringing in his ears. Somewhere deep down he knew she was right and more importantly, he knew exactly what to do about it. He'd known it for a long time, he'd just never had the balls to execute. Maybe it was fear; fear that the fantasy of it would always prove richer than the reality. He could talk a good plan, but actually carry it out, that was a whole new ball game.

"Fuck," he muttered. He picked up his cell phone and dialed Natural Foods Market and asked to be put through to his supervisor, Greg Ansel.

"Hey, Greggo, what's up, buddy?"

Greg sounded stressed; his default setting, Gérard guessed.

"Listen, bro, you and Mave still looking for a place to rent when the baby comes? Yeah? I got a proposition I think you're gonna like."

102

Outside the commissary window, Topaz Autumn Coleman bounced anxiously on the tips of her toes as today's volunteer, an older inmate with a cross-hatch of cuts along her forearms that had earned her the moniker, Slash, turned her back and rummaged around the stacks of sanitary pads on the shelves behind her.

"Gotta go round back for those. Don't go nowhere."

"Yeah, like I got someplace I need to be," Topaz said, stuffing her face through the small window. "But hurry your ass up, unless you wanna clean my monthly from the floor."

Topaz leant against the wall and pulled a hand across her belly as another cramp that felt as if her insides were being twisted around barbed wire, made its presence known. "Hey!" she called, exhaling in short, sharp breaths. "Get me some of that Advil shit too. Like today!"

No response.

"Bitch? You hearing me?"

She turned back towards the window. "Hey! You still here?"

Silence.

"Fuck you!" she shouted, shoving her shoulders to the wall.

The corridor was silent, save the fly-buzz hum of the fluorescents above her. It was too quiet. After the lunch rush, the commissary should have had a long line of women hoping to score a sugar rush after the overly salted food. She'd been in enough dangerous situations to trust her senses by now. The air smelled different. She could feel it in the hairs on the back of her neck, taste it on her tongue. It wasn't just paranoia, like her dumbass therapists kept telling her, it was her well-honed survival instinct.

"I'm still here," she said, lifting herself on her toes and leaning on the commissary shelf. "Bitch, where the fuck you go?"

As Topaz stretched her neck, she was slammed hard into the wall until her bones rattled. She felt the solid mass of two bodies wedge either side of her; a vice constructed of muscle and sweat. She struggled as the women pushed harder and jerked back her arms.

A fetid breath that reeked of the day's lunch wafted over her. "Stay quiet, bitch," the woman said, pulling tighter on her wrists.

Topaz turned. She recognized one of the women; a hard-faced inmate who'd worked the same few blocks as her back in Oakland a few years back. Another of Nelson's girls.

"I said, don't you fucking move," she said, pressing the dense mass of her flesh against Topaz's skeletal form.

"What the fuck?" Topaz said, gasping. Her chest felt as if it might cave in and shatter to dust. "What I do to you?"

Topaz saw the flash of a blade in the commissary window.

"Nelson sends his regards," the woman said, smirking.

Topaz felt the blade slice deep and slow into her left cheek, then again across her right cheek in the same controlled action. Before she could scream, a thick, fleshy palm was slapped tight across her mouth. A hot rush of blood flowed down her neck and onto her chest, dripping in steady blotches onto her prison sweats.

"Ain't so pretty now, huh, bitch," the woman said, pulling back the shiv and discarding Topaz, like a used rag, to the floor.

103

Three days later, Tanner stood amidst the rubble of the warehouse. To his left, the slush of inky water slapped against the dockside, and on the water the debris floated like charred driftwood. To his right, the forensics team were combing through the detritus. He looked down, his attention distracted by the glint of something catching the late morning sunshine. He squatted and picked up the metallic object; a shard of a mirror ball he guessed, maybe the same one he'd seen in the photograph of Catalina and Tiffiny. He looked at it for a moment, catching the distorted image of his own face in the glass. As he laid it back down, he saw a small, dark shape in his periphery. A rat, sewer-grey, lifted its head, sniffed the air, then scurried off under one of the collapsed beams.

A deep and familiar sense of weariness washed through him. This work he did? The work they all did. Would it ever end?

After a thirty minute pursuit the night the Rat House had burned to the ground, Shaughnessy and the two officers had apprehended Bruce Ho when he'd passed out on a scrap of wasteland close to the 980 Freeway. Two days later, the doctors at Oakland General had concluded he was well enough to be interviewed; no internal organs were severed, he'd make a full recovery. He'd been *"one lucky son of a bitch"* the surgeon who'd stitched him back up had said.

When Tanner and Shaughnessy had interviewed Bruce, he didn't share his surgeon's sentiments. He was alive, but that was about it. With a long prison sentence ahead of him, there was little good fortune or cause for celebration in that scenario. It wasn't until Tanner and Shaughnessy offered the possibility of a deal that Bruce had talked.

He'd confirmed what Tanner suspected; the Rat House was, in all but name, a brothel; albeit with more exclusive clientele and provided a specialized range of sexual services; whatever the clients desired, so long as they were discreet and had the necessary funds.

Bruce had been responsible for supplying drugs and procuring the girls. Hector was responsible for security and insurance, willing to do the dirty jobs no one else wanted to do. More than willing, he was happy to carry out those kinds of tasks. Severing Wendi and Tiffiny's hands had been Hector's doing; a signature move he'd stolen from the Cártel de Cancún, a Mexican drug gang he'd worked with in Playa Del Carmen some years back.

It had also been Hector's idea to plant Wendi Chee's hand someplace close to Christen's house, *"keep the gringo in his place"* he'd told Bruce. When they'd driven through Rosemont the night before the Fourth of July and seen the stack of chairs directly across from Christen's house, Hector had laughed like a little kid. *"Some fucker's gonna find it,"* he'd said as he'd laid the hand under the stack of chairs. *"Gonna scare the cohones off that mother."*

When they'd questioned Bruce about Catalina, his demeanor changed, as if there was some sliver of regret in his posture. "Catalina had expensive tastes," he'd told them.

"Makeup, clothes; she always wanted to show people she was no chola bitch. She waited tables at the Rat House. Good tips, she could buy all the expensive shit she wanted. She didn't know what she was getting into, thought it was just some lap-dancing club, then one night she finally gets it, figures out why it's called the Rat House."

"The same night she disappeared?" Tanner had asked.

"Hector wouldn't let her go into the rooms, kept her on a short leash; bar service only. But then she got friendly with one of the girls, Tiffiny. Catalina starts helping her out, giving her money, watching her kid. Hector found out, then he sees Catalina taking all these photographs and gets real pissed."

"Angry enough to kill her?"

"No, she was family. But he fired her ass that night. I saw them arguing, I figured it was some family shit, but Hector takes her phone and slaps her. Catalina runs off, I think there was someone waiting for her. I didn't see her after that."

Tanner and Shaughnessy had both sat listening as Bruce spoke. After three hours, his energy waned, his eyes wandering aimlessly around the room.

This had been the right time to drop the big one—save the critical question for when the suspect was at their weakest ebb, when they'd give up their own grandmother to be left alone.

"Who's behind it all, Bruce? Who gives the orders?"

The question sparked some life back into Bruce's features, as if he'd just been shot with a high current of electricity. He clenched his fists and his jaw tight, shook his head.

His eyes had told them everything. Bruce was protecting someone; someone who'd inflict a lot more damage and hurt than a long stretch in a maximum security prison ever would.

Walking through the debris of the burnt warehouse, there was no doubt in Tanner's mind that Bruce Ho and Hector Figuerello were just small cogs in some covert, dark machine that OPD had yet to uncover. Incarcerating the small fry like Bruce Ho was only the first step. Prosecuting those who controlled him, the men who worked in the shadows, the ghosts in the machine? That was the long game, one that would probably continue long after he had retired.

Criminal enterprises were no different to legitimate commercial enterprises. An establishment like the Rat House required a disciplined bureaucracy, an understanding of your position in the pecking order and fealty to a common cause. Evil hid behind a mask of banality; Tanner had always believed that was true. It would take time to bring men like that to justice; if a case ever made it that far. The best he could hope for was to press pause on the operation for a while, hopefully long enough to save another young girl like Catalina from dying at the hands of men who saw women as commodities to be traded and exchanged.

Sometimes, in this dark, grim work they did, that was about as good as it got.

104

Online digital accounts were like treasure troves, Tanner had concluded; portholes into people's lives where their memories lived on forever. And delving into Hector Figuerello's cloud photo storage had yielded a priceless collection of artifacts.

The images looked similar to police surveillance photographs; candid photographs of men in the Rat House, taken without their knowing. It appeared the cameras were hidden deep in the rafters and equipped with telephoto lenses focused on the beds inside the rooms. At some point, the photographs would have been used to blackmail the men, Tanner imagined. You played, you paid; it was the Rat House's insurance policy.

The photographs of interest to Tanner were those of Christen Hansen. Besides the snapshots of Christen picking up Wendi Chee, there were several of him dropping her off at the same place; alive, her limbs intact. There was no reason to hold him after that. Christen had no connection to Catalina's death, and neither it appeared, did his son.

Maybe Tanner had the worst kind of wrong about Catalina.

And maybe Shaughnessy had been right that night at the Jack of Diamonds; he'd gotten too close to Catalina's case, lost the perspective and detachment required to work it professionally. Maybe Catalina had been curious; had injected herself with the heroin and her heart, as big as it was, failed her; just like he'd failed her. The thought left a taste in his mouth that clung to his tongue like a film of sour milk.

Speaking with her parents earlier that morning when they handed in their daughter's cell phone had only made him feel worse. He had no answers as to why Catalina had died. They listened quietly as Tanner explained as best he could the events surrounding her death. Francisco had been anxious during the interview, constantly looking around as if he expected to be jumped at any moment. He couldn't look Tanner in the eyes and seemed evasive, as if he couldn't wait to leave. Tanner sensed it was more than the anxiety of being in a police interview room talking about his daughter's death; as if he were hiding something and the longer he stayed the more likely it was he'd be found out. Tanner pushed a little, but Francisco had clammed up tight like an abalone shell.

Marta and Francisco had walked out as empty-handed as they walked in. Tanner's hands were equally empty. He wished he could have provided them with some sliver of a resolution. Maybe Catalina's phone would surrender some secrets, but he doubted they'd get much more than GPS tracking data for the night she vanished.

It would be at least another hour before Tanner concluded that Catalina's cell phone, her motivation, the lies the media had told about her all meant nothing. The answers he'd been looking for had been directly under his nose the whole time.

He was still feeling as if the whole dang case had run over him like a two-ton truck, then reversed several more times to make sure the job was done, when Shaughnessy turned up and stood over his desk.

"That's some photo album," she said. "Be a lot of worried men if those ever got out."

"Which is why they won't," Tanner said, clicking Hector's cloud storage from the screen.

"Just spoke to Dugdale..."

"Don't tell me, the dang footage," Tanner said, lifting the envelope from his desk and taking out the USB drive.

"That's the spirit," she said. "He figures with your caseload a couple of bad guys lighter, you'll have some time on your hands."

Tanner scratched his head. "How wound up is he?"

"On a level of one to ten, I'd say eleven. He's meeting with the Governor up in Sacramento tomorrow, wants a full report."

Tanner sighed and slipped the USB into the computer.

"Hey, where you heading to?" he asked as Shaughnessy turned to leave. "You might offer to help."

"Shit to do, Tanner, you can handle this."

Tanner shook his head and clicked on the single folder in the drive, which was titled June 3rd to July 2nd––a month's worth of footage. His heart sank.

He clicked on the first file; 9:30pm to 3:30am. Each video was a six-hour window with the same locked-off camera angle looking down on a front lawn. He checked the name in the report––Dave Maddens-Smith.

He scrubbed rapidly through six more files; same footage, different day. 1:40am. Maddens-Smith's sprinklers spritz to life for thirty-five minutes, then stop. Proof, but to what end? The state could do little more than hand out more fines and judging by the size of the neighbor's house––a mock Tudor mansion with ivy crawling up the walls and a front lawn the size of a tennis court—Tanner guessed this character could afford a litany of fines without blinking an eye.

He fast-forwarded through several more days.

Nothing new to see, save the nefarious lawn sprinkler activity and the odd, bleary-eyed neighbor taking their dog for a late-night absolution walk. It wasn't until he opened the file labelled "June 27th" that something clicked; it was the night Catalina had disappeared.

He scrubbed to 10:35pm and rechecked his notes. She had finished her shift at 10pm. The last person to see her was Bruce Ho, who was now in county jail awaiting a trial date, and he'd surrendered as much information as he was willing to part with.

As the timer hit 10:37pm, a large truck pulled up outside the Hansens' house; a white Dodge Ram Mega Cab, Tanner guessed from the badging. He leaned in, his eyes following the figure staggering from the rear passenger door. The young man was either drunk or high, he thought, as he stumbled around the back, gripping the sides of the flatbed as he staggered to the sidewalk. He slapped his palms on the rear cab window and shouted to someone inside.

The cab door swung open, almost shoving the man off his feet. He stepped back, giving the young girl who'd been riding in the back space to exit.

Tanner held his breath—if he exhaled he imagined the whole scene might disintegrate in front of him—as the young girl stepped out onto the truck's running boards. She climbed down to the sidewalk, unsteady in her high heels. Tanner's blood thumped hard under his skin. Her face was unmistakable under the yellow flood of the street lights: Catalina Gomez.

Stepping from the truck, she walked aggressively towards Jonas, shoving him in the shoulders. Jonas fell backwards into the low stone wall at the edge of his front yard. Catalina shouted some more, brushed the hair from her face and clambered back into the cab.

As the truck drove off, Tanner hit the pause button; the perfect angle to scan the license plate. He sat back, a surge of electricity searing through him. Whoever was in that truck was the last person to see Catalina alive.

He ran the number through the OPD's Automatic License Plate Reader. Minutes later, he held the warm printout of the truck's owner and address in his hand. He recognized the surname. He dialed Shaughnessy. The call went to voicemail. He left instructions for her to meet him at the address.

Holstering his gun and slipping on his jacket, Tanner left OPD headquarters, his gait a few ounces lighter than it had been for weeks, though a troubling thought pricked at the back of his mind.

In this whole dang case, answers had never come with any kind of closure, and he wondered if confronting Mason Arnett with the evidence he'd just seen would make a blind bit of difference.

It would. And more than Tanner could have imagined.

105

Moonshine was lounging in the basement when he heard the wail of sirens and noticed the red and blue lights pulse through the narrow window. For a second, he imagined making a run for it, but he had no place to run to. Instead, he flopped back on the couch, wedged the stock of the Sako Finnlight between his thighs and rubbed the tip of the sleek barrel along his temple. It felt cold, but a good cold; like when he rested ice over his wrist after he'd been playing his guitar for too long.

Truth was, ever since the day the two detectives from OPD had approached him at the lake, he'd been expecting a house call. He'd felt bad about dropping G-Man in the shitter with the cops. It had bought him some time, that was all. He'd kept everything from Jonas, everything that had gone down that night. Plausible deniability? Was that the phrase? The less Jonas knew, the less chance there was of him blabbing his mouth to anyone who'd listen. Silence, Moonshine concluded, was fucking golden.

He chuckled to himself as the old song his grandmother loved played somewhere around the periphery of his mind, like the fog of some long-lost memory. Above, he heard the back door opening and the stomp of boots trying to be quiet along the hardwood floors and down the basement stairs.

A shape appeared in the doorway. "Mason Arnett, this is Detective Roscoe Tanner, Oakland PD. If you're armed, I recommend you drop your weapon now."

Moonshine blinked as the scene unfolded like a first-person shooter video game.

Tanner edged slowly around the doorway, weapon drawn.

Moonshine caressed the shotgun trigger, feeling the metal curve flex under pressure. He hummed along to the song that was now stuck in his head; *"Silence Is Golden."*

"Hey, well if it ain't the physics tutor," he said, as Tanner emerged from the shadows.

"Son, you don't want to do this," he said, creeping towards Moonshine with the palm of his unarmed hand wide open in a gesture of friendship and peace.

"You here to talk me out of blowin' my brains out, detective?"

"Just lay down the gun and we'll both walk out of here with our boots on. Sound good?"

Moonshine shrugged, blowing a strand of hair from his cheek.

"Your parents around?" Tanner asked, laying down his own handgun on the couch.

Moonshine cracked a dry laugh. "All by my lonesome," he said. "My pops drew the short straw on the divorce settlement; got to keep me and the truck. My mom got the big-assed mansion in Louisville and the Country Club membership. Happy fuckin' families."

Tanner noticed his eyes trying to lock focus on something in the corner of the basement. "Okay, we're going to talk this out, Mason. Is it all right if I call you Mason?"

"Moonshine's just fine."

"Right you are, Moonshine. Would you be able to lay your weapon down?"

"Suppose I could," he said, smirking, "but I ain't going to."

"Okay," Tanner said, looking into Moonshine's eyes; his pupils were fast-fading pinpricks. "Maybe we'll just talk." He perched himself on the arm of one of the La-Z-Boys.

"Talk 'bout what?"

"About Catalina? The night she died?"

Moonshine exhaled a long, sharp whistle. "You done sweet-talking me already?"

"What happened, Moonshine? After you left Jonas, just you and Catalina in your father's truck?"

Moonshine kept his gaze fixed on the corner of the room. Tanner wasn't expecting a coherent response, especially as the kid seemed high enough to do something stupid. But the longer he kept him talking, the less likely he was to pull the trigger on himself, or Tanner.

Moonshine, however, had borne the burden of that night so heavily and had run through the chain of events so often in his own mind he wondered if it was all just a bad dream. If he spoke it out loud, it would make it real, help him make sense of everything.

"Jonas?" Moonshine said, rubbing the barrel harder against his brow. "Fuck that guy. How come he gets to win the genetic lottery?"

"You were jealous that Catalina and Jonas were together?"

Moonshine tugged down the neck of his T-shirt. "I was always there for her. Hansen did squat, but she still hung round him like some coon dog begging for scraps."

"You liked Catalina?"

Moonshine offered a weak smile. "Girls like Catalina, they need looking after. Ain't good for them to be all alone. Too many bad dudes out there eager to take advantage of a pretty girl like that. You see that, right? With you being a cop 'n' all?"

"Did you look after her, that night, take care of her?"

Moonshine straightened his back, making sure the shotgun was still wedged securely between his thighs. "We'd just finished this gig over in Berkeley. I was going to go home, but Cat texts me, says she needs a ride to this party at some place over in Rosemont."

"But you picked up Catalina from the Paradise Motel, first?"

"Yeah, like I did every Friday night, then she asks me to drive her to the Boba Lounge to start her shift, like I was her personal Uber or some such shit."

"But you still agreed? That was decent of you."

"Yeah, Cat has that effect, pulls you into whatever it is she's doing like some riptide. You can't swim against that shit."

"Hard to say no to a girl like her," Tanner agreed. "So, tell me what happened next."

"I picked her up from her shift at ten and we drove over to this party out in Rosemont." Moonshine clenched his fist. "When we arrive, all she wants to do is find Hansen, like I don't matter shit no more. But Hansen's fucked up in the front yard, lying in the grass, all wasted and shit. Catalina gets real mad at him, but he ain't registering nothing or nobody. I told her, I'll take him home then I'll come back, we can hang out."

"With Jonas out of the picture, Catalina's all yours?"

"I see why you're a detective," Moonshine said. "But Cat's not so agreeable, she wants to blow the joint, asks me to give her and Jonas a ride back to his place."

"And you agreed?"

"Sure I agreed. I drop off Jonas, then me and Cat can spend some quality time together. But in the back of the truck she's giving Jonas two tons of shit about how he's throwing his future away, all that preachy stuff about taking drugs. We get outside

Jonas's place, she jumps out the truck, screams at him some more. I was going to leave her there, but I weren't brought up to leave girls by themselves at night, that didn't sit well with me."

"So where did you take her?"

"Cat figures the night's gone to shit anyway, so she might as well make it worth her while and earn some long green at some private club she knew at this old warehouse in Brooklyn Basin. So I dropped her off, like she asked."

"Okay, sounds like you were being a good friend, Moonshine."

"Yeah, ass deep in the friend zone, that's me. But get this. Thirty minutes after I drop her off, Cat sends me this text, all urgent and shit, asking me to come pick her up again."

"That's a lot of driving."

"Yeah, well my grandma, she always told me to treat women right, be a gentleman."

Moonshine squared his shoulders, pushing them into the back of the couch. "I pick up Cat close to this piece-of-shit warehouse. She's been running in her bare feet, carrying those shoes in her hand like they're the only thing she'd save in a goddamn fire. She jumps in the truck, all agitated and shit. I figure she wants to be dropped off at her place, but she's not for going back to her folks' apartment, wants to take the edge off whatever the fuck was messing with her mind."

"You drove to Lake Temescal?"

"Her idea. When we get there, I reverse the truck so the tailgate's facing the lake. We get on the flatbed. I grab a blanket and we sit looking over the water, counting shooting stars. It was one of those perfect nights, you know?"

"So, what went wrong? What happened between you and Catalina?"

Moonshine's leg jerked, beads of sweat forming over his temple as he ran the gun barrel over his skin. "A man expects some payback, you know, for extending all that courtesy to a girl, but she doesn't want to know. She's like, fuck you, Moonshine, like I'm some piece of dog shit on her shoe."

"Did things get out of hand, Moonshine? You got angry?"

"Not like you're thinking."

"Okay, tell me what did happen."

Moonshine tensed. "I figure if the chick don't want to know, I'll go find my happy place, take a hit. Fuck her and the rest of the world for a few hours."

"A hit of what?"

"H, man. Nothing but the best."

"You and Catalina took the heroin?"

"Nah, you're not listenin'," Moonshine insisted. "I said *I* wanted to take a hit. But Catalina, she watches me take the syringe out and gets right in my face, real hardcore, like she'd done with Hansen. Then she says she's out of here, says she don't want nothing to do with junkies like me."

"That must have hurt."

Moonshine shrugged. "I ain't no stranger to hurt," he said. "But Cat throws the blanket off her, gets ready to leave. I grab her wrist, apologize, tell her I'll do anything, but she's like screaming at me until I don't know what freakin' day it is. All I'm thinking is how she's killing the vibe, like it's all polluted now, like none of that stuff matters anymore because she don't want to be with me."

"Did she fight back, Moonshine, is that what happened?"

"You still ain't listenin'," Moonshine said, shaking his head. "I already said, there weren't no fight, I wouldn't hurt her, not Cat."

A thin trickle of tears ran from the corner of his eyes, trailing down the angry red welts of his acne. "I didn't want her to leave, that's all." He wiped the dregs of snot from under his nose.

"Go on, Moonshine," Tanner said softly.

"I figured if she comes with me for the ride, then she'd understand, you know?"

"You injected the heroin? Into Catalina's leg?"

Moonshine's tears flowed in torrents down his face. "I didn't mean to. She's like kicking at me, trying to get away, trying to put those damn shoes on. I reach out to stop her kicking, but I forgot..."

Moonshine rubbed the weapon harder until welts appeared across his brow.

"Forgot..." he stammered. "Forgot I was holding the syringe. I didn't know until I felt the needle slip in."

"How did she react, Moonshine? What happened?"

Moonshine shook his head, the snot falling from his nose and onto his T-shirt.

"She screams. She's got this look on her face like she hates the bones of me. I just wanted her to stay, looking at the stars, but it's like everything stops, the stars, the wind; like there ain't no one else in the world but me and her. She jumps off the tailgate. I chase after her. She's running towards the water. I figure she's gonna slow down when the H kicks in, but she doesn't. I know something's not right, but I can't do nothing to stop it. She drops in the sand like she's been shot or something. I run over to her, she's not breathing, no pulse, nothing."

Moonshine's face was wet with tears and perspiration, which had dripped onto the polished steel casing of the gun barrel.

"Why didn't you call someone, the police?"

"Yeah, like that's gonna help my situation," he said, his voice cracking. "I see this rowboat, so I drag her over there, put her inside."

"But her shoes, Moonshine? You told me she was barefoot, Catalina was found with her shoes on."

Moonshine smiled, his eyes moist. He wiped a sleeve across them. "She loved those Jimmy friggin' Choos. Bought them used from some chick who needed the money. Didn't seem right to me a girl should die without her shoes on."

Moonshine's eyes seemed a million miles away. Tanner noticed his finger tensing around the trigger. "She didn't make much of a splash when I dropped her in, neither. It was like I just threw a pebble in the water, like she was already gone, you know, there was nothing left of her to make any noise."

Tanner wiped the sweat from his face. His heart felt so heavy it seemed to have shifted to the core of his belly. "Is that when you called Gérard Rosseau?"

"I weren't in no state to drive. Figured he wouldn't ask too many questions."

Moonshine was sobbing, his face wet with tears. "She didn't make hardly no noise, how's that even possible? I didn't get it," he said, shaking his head. "I don't get it."

Tanner took a deep breath. "It's okay, we'll figure this out, Moonshine."

As Moonshine looked down at the trigger and slid his finger along its steely curve, he caught sight of another figure at the basement door.

"Put your weapon down," Detective Shaughnessy barked as she walked into the basement, gun drawn. "Or I will shoot you."

She looked over to Tanner, noticing he was unarmed, his weapon lying on the couch.

"Shaughnessy," Tanner said, raising his palms. "Back off. We're good here, all cool, aren't we, Moonshine?"

Moonshine cocked his head, an idea forming. "Could take one of you with me, huh? I shoot one of you, the other puts the bullet in me. Hell of a way to exit this shithole."

"You will not do that. You will lay your weapon down and surrender, understand?" Shaughnessy said, a bead of sweat forming across her brow as her finger tightened around the trigger.

"He's doing that, Shaughnessy. That right, Moonshine?" Tanner said, an edge of anxiety in his voice. "You're putting the gun down."

Moonshine smiled and slowly lowered the gun, stopping at his hip, the barrel directly aimed at Tanner.

"I told you I had your back, Tanner," Shaughnessy said, her eyes darting back and forth between both of them. "Do you doubt me?"

"No, Shaughnessy, I don't," Tanner said, slowly moving his body within arm's reach of his partner. "But let's not escalate the situation."

"Fucking do it, do it!" Moonshine shouted. "Do it!"

Just as she felt the weight of the Glock 17 trigger give way under pressure, the counterweight of Tanner's left hand slammed down hard on Shaughnessy's forearms.

The 9mm caliber bullet whistled past Moonshine's ear and struck the TV on the wall behind him, shattering the screen

Tanner moved swiftly. He took the weapon from Moonshine and cocked open the barrel; daylight streamed into the empty chamber. He showed it to Shaughnessy. She nodded and lowered her weapon, keeping her finger close to the trigger; a precautionary measure.

"April Fools," Moonshine said, smiling.

Shaughnessy bent over, her hands on her knees, taking deep breaths. "Please arrest that motherfucker, Tanner."

Tanner laid the Finnlight on the couch and wiped a hand across his face. "Shuck, darn it, son, do you know how close you came to getting killed just now?"

Moonshine sat back. "You wanna know the fucked-up thing? I'd have driven her wherever she wanted to go. I guess love's fucked up, right?"

Tanner nodded. "You've got a big heart, Moonshine. Some

big hearts just have bigger targets, that's how it goes," he said, reaching behind him for his cuffs.

Moonshine sniffed. "Yeah, reckon so. But maybe I'll get to see her again real soon."

He tilted his head towards his legs.

Tanner looked down, felt a wave of nausea come over him. "What the heck have you done, son?" he said, his eyes locking focus on the syringe hanging from Moonshine's calf.

"Figured I deserved the same as Catalina, right?" he said, slowly extracting the empty syringe and examining the thin film of liquid clinging to the sides. "What are the odds you reckon, detective? Fifty-fifty that this stuff will kill me the same way it killed Catalina? That'd be divine fuckin' justice, right?"

Moonshine smiled, the life draining from his eyes as his head fell to his shoulder and his body toppled forward.

106

It took ten days for Jonas's discharge from the hospital. The fall had shattered his femur and fractured both his ankles. The oral surgeon had saved the broken teeth, but Jonas's bite would never quite line up in the perfect way it once did.

Alexus was still navigating her own recovery, attempting to heal the pieces of her life that had come crashing down around her. But at least her son was back home, where he belonged. He was hobbling around on crutches, a steel wire attached to his mouth to help reset his jawbone. Alexus had to help feed and dress him; it was like he was a child again. Was it wrong she got such satisfaction from these acts? She didn't care. Jonas was her flesh and blood, her beautiful boy, and she'd go to the ends of the world for him; it's what you did, part of the unwritten contract of parenting.

The unwritten contract of her marriage, though, was a different matter.

After Christen's release, she'd insisted he tell her everything, which he had done so, unreservedly. It had been tough to hear and at the time she wanted to scream, stop him from talking, but she had to know everything, understand what drove him to do what he did. Alexus had barely been able to look at him as he spoke, as if he was a stranger in her home, narrating some story about some other person who wasn't her husband, someone they both vaguely knew. The ball had landed in her court; it was the ultimate injustice of how these matters shook out. Christen had lied and deceived her, yet what happened next would be her call to make.

The burden lay heavy on her shoulders for days after. She could leave him, or she could kick him out. The more she imagined how those two scenarios would play out, the more she realized, that despite everything, she loved him. And there were the children to think of, and the house; her entire life was wrapped within its four walls.

Other marriages had survived this kind of seismic rupture. Other women had stayed after their husbands had cheated on them. Not so long ago, she would have looked down on those women, thought them weak. Her opinion had shifted. She understood now the strength it took to stay with a man like that; to conduct the regular business of marriage would take all the strength she had. Maybe with time, it would become easier, the pain might subside and her anger fade into forgiveness, and if it didn't then she'd reassess the situation, make the necessary adjustments. There were no certainties in life, no guaranteed happy endings.

As Alexus walked from her kitchen and into the backyard, her husband was digging, the warm morning sun beating down on the back of his neck. "I thought we were paving all this over."

Christen stretched out his back with a groan. "Change of plan."

Alexus's sigh was tinged with an edge of irritation. "We

already discussed this. Drought-resistant plants, paving stones, less work."

He stuffed a hand in his pocket and brought out a sheet of paper. "I know, but I think I need this... I think we both need this," he said, showing her his crude, pencil-drawn design.

"Three planter boxes for the tomatoes and other vegetables," he said. "I will make some space for seasonal produce; strawberries, blackberries, whatever berries you like."

Alexus took a sip of her coffee, barely glancing at the paper. "Seems like a lot of hard work," she said. "Tending to all that."

"I'm descended from Vikings, we are hardwired for manual labor. Anyway, I will be home more if I have something to tend to."

"You always had something to tend to, Christen," Alexus said. "You just chose to ignore it."

A flicker crossed Christen's eyes; the kind of subtext between man and wife that required no response or clarification: it was what it was.

"I was thinking we could work on the garden together," he continued. "My therapist says these kinds of things can help with the process, take my mind off the addiction."

"You're still in the guest room, no matter how many tomatoes you plant," Alexus said.

He nodded. The wounds of their conversation still raw to the touch.

Alexus looked towards the kitchen. Sydney was helping Jonas walk across to the refrigerator. If she listened hard enough she could almost hear the past echoes of their laughter traveling over the fresh cut grass, Alexus wrapping their soaking wet bodies in beach towels as they stood shivering in the doorway after an afternoon running through the lawn sprinklers.

"You really want this?" she said, glancing over at Christen.

Christen nodded. "Only if you do."

What Follows

Alexus thought for a moment. "I can live with it," she said firmly, before walking back into the house.

An hour later, as she sat in the home office preparing her notes, the doorbell rang. She hadn't told Christen yet, this was something she needed to do on her own; her plan B.

Last week she'd filed the legal papers with Alameda County and placed the notification in the local paper. As of two days ago, the law offices of Alexus Hansen were a legal entity.

Keeping busy was her coping mechanism; with too much time to dwell on what happened she'd drive herself crazy. Between looking after her son, running for mayor and starting her own practice, she figured she'd have little time for anything else; and for once having little time to think felt like a blessed and welcome relief.

Her first case was pro bono, a hot-button topic she was sure would generate plenty of publicity to get her name out there without spending thousands of dollars on marketing. Christen would have given her the money, if only as a means to aid his redemption, but she needed to do this her own way for no other reason than to prove to herself she could.

She escorted her clients through the hallway, sat them across from her and explained as clearly as she could the difficulties of bringing a case like theirs to trial. Oakland was a sanctuary city, the husband had some leverage there, but he was still an undocumented immigrant in the eyes of the government, and in this political climate, getting his citizenship wouldn't be easy. She asked them if they were prepared for that. Prepared for the fight.

Marta and Francisco Gomez looked at each other. They'd faced worse, hadn't they? Much worse. They held hands. "Yes,"

Marta said. "We are ready. Whatever we have to do to keep my husband with his family."

Alexus smiled, her mind snapping back to that day at the lake when Ben Strauss had called her out on her rowing technique; this was one of those times when the trinity of oar, scull and stroke fused in one fluid motion; the swing—momentarily perfect, eternally elusive.

107

The first rain of the season arrived early that year, in late August. An unexpected late evening shower that barely laid any moisture to ground, but offered a glimmer of hope that a break in the drought would come soon. In her apartment, Moira Shaughnessy watched the drizzle speckle the window. She was sorting through a stack of case files she'd requested from San Jose PD last week and was making slow headway.

Tanner had called her earlier that day with the update on Mason Arnett's case. Each time she thought how close she came to shooting that kid, her stomach roiled. If it wasn't for Tanner's cool head, she would have put a bullet directly in the kid's chest; the fact she wasn't living with that on her conscience was thanks to Tanner.

Mason had survived the heroin injection. They'd got him to the emergency room before the contaminate had solidified enough to cause a blockage. The kid's father had hired an expensive LA lawyer who was negotiating for a suspended sentence in exchange for a long stretch in a $5,000 per day rehab center in Arizona. He'd probably get his demands; his kind always did.

The Alameda County DA had found insufficient evidence to prosecute Shawn Dubose with a crime. Tanner had been right all along, not just concerning Shawn, but also about Catalina's death. If he hadn't pursued it, the case would have been another statistic; a statistic that Chief Martin Dugdale had been eager to move across the balance sheet. It was that realization that had compelled her to sequester the case files she was now working through, scouring for evidence.

Some minutes later, as she was deep in her study, the insistent bark of her apartment buzzer made her jump. She laid down her pen and checked the wall-mounted video monitor.

Dugdale stood under the thin shelter of the entrance, a suitcase at his feet. She stood back from the screen and waited, hoping he'd just vanish, or the rain would wash him away.

What Dugdale had asked her to do, keep tabs on Tanner, babysit him, had made her feel cheap and used. If she wanted that sort of abuse and humiliation, it would be on her own terms, not someone else's.

There was some strength in recognizing that in herself. Dugdale may have been a good cop once, a hotshot even, but she'd witnessed firsthand his attempts to steer the investigation and classify Catalina's death as another drug overdose and it had turned her stomach.

The buzzer barked for a second time. Dugdale was shouting something into the intercom. She couldn't tell what, she had the volume turned down. As she walked back to her desk, he kept his finger on the buzzer, as if he imagined by pressing long enough she'd open up, let him and his damned suitcase in. Dugdale didn't know her at all, not one bit.

She put on her headphones and glanced at the invite to Madeline Ambrose's retirement party propped up against her coffee mug. She wasn't in the mood for a party, not tonight. She flipped through the files. Somewhere in there she was sure there

What Follows

was another Catalina Gomez case; maybe multiples of them. Cases Dugdale had presided over and moved across the balance sheet to make his numbers look good.

She kept reading, making careful notes as she did so, the sound of the buzzer nothing but white noise in the distance until it wasn't sound at all anymore, and she heard Dugdale's car pull away, vanishing like a bad memory into the darkness.

Tanner felt the first drop of rain on his brow as he and Jessica stood on the deck of the Salt Water Restaurant looking over the lush, dark spread of Lake Merritt, the chatter and chink of glasses from Ambrose's retirement party humming in the background.

"So, I guess your case is all wrapped up?" Jessica asked, pulling her shawl tight around her shoulders.

Tanner stretched his back––dancing for the last hour had left its wounds somewhere deep in his lower vertebrae. "Bruce Ho gets sentenced next week, the DA's pressing for twenty to life."

"No less than he deserves," Jessica said, shivering and taking Tanner's hand. "See, you were right. I'm sure Catalina's parents were grateful for what you did, for not giving up on their daughter."

Tanner cast his mind back a few weeks when he'd sat with Francisco and Marta and explained exactly how their daughter had died. A contaminated shot of heroin, and a boy too young to realize the trouble he was getting himself into; a one in a million chance. Tanner wondered if his words had even sunk in, but at least they could move on now, whatever that meant.

He'd always imagined there was no moving on when it came to death. It was a phrase people said to make themselves feel better, a way to forget the past; move beyond it to someplace else. Standing on the deck, watching Jessica tilting her head to look at the quarter slice of moon, the first raindrops falling lightly on her face, he realized how wrong he'd been. Moving on wasn't a betrayal of the past, but an extension of it. It was all connected; loss, death, moving on; it was all one long tail of healing. He reached his arm around Jessica's waist and pulled her close. If this is what moving on looked like, he could live with it; more than live with it.

"You put away the bad guys, Roscoe," Jessica said, snuggling into him. "That's got to count for something."

Tanner had a resigned edge to his voice. "Maybe. We caught the small fry, but I'd give my eye teeth to find the big fish behind that operation, haul their asses into a courtroom."

"Justice all round?" Jessica said.

"Ain't that the truth," he agreed. "So, is your daughter back?"

"Next week," Jessica said; her eyes had a spark of excitement.

"Three weeks in France? Can't be bad."

"Yeah, Gérard's staying on. Apparently he's got a job working the wine harvest. He rented his house out to his ex-boss and his family, so I reckon we won't be seeing him for a while."

"Living the dream," Tanner said.

Jessica turned around and took Tanner's hand, raising it high in the chill evening air. "Care to dance some more, detective?" she said, twirling herself on her toes across the deck.

Tanner's heart seemed to fly from his chest and soar some hundred feet above him as he wondered how the heck he'd got so darned lucky. "I could be persuaded," he said. "I've been reliably informed I possess a natural talent for the Electric Slide."

Jessica twirled around and smiled. "The Electric Slide? I'd pay good money to see that," she said, dropping her arm to her side.

"That could be a little sooner than you expect," Tanner said, removing two tickets from his jacket. "I took the liberty of booking us a cruise. If it's too forward, I can negotiate a refund."

"A cruise? Where to?" Jessica asked.

"Not to Europe or any place fancy. It's more, em, specialized," he said, flipping the tickets nervously against his fingers.

"You're being cagey, Roscoe, what are you not telling me?"

He cleared his throat. "There may be country music involved."

"Okay," Jessica said, hesitantly.

"Maybe a whole lot of country music."

"Right. And am I expected to line dance on this country music cruise you're inviting me on?"

"I could teach you some moves, so you're all prepared."

"Moves? Isn't there just one move, left, right, clap your hands?"

Tanner laughed. "I guess so."

"Then, it shouldn't be too hard," Jessica said, bringing a finger to her cheek where a drop of rain had just fallen.

"Should we head back?" Tanner asked, watching the pinprick of raindrops fall onto the lake, sending tiny ripples across its surface.

"Let's stay here a while longer," Jessica said, scooting closer to Tanner. "It feels good doesn't it? Like all the bad air's about to be washed away."

"Sure does," Tanner said, wrapping his arm around Jessica's shoulder. It did feel good. It felt dang good.

108

Nelson Welch stood on the ninth floor of the gleaming office building which afforded a view across Berkeley Marina and the lazy curve of the Bay Bridge to San Francisco. It was late October, a grey mass of rain clouds hung heavy and low over the downtown skyscrapers. Within the next few hours the clouds would coast silently across the Bay, dumping six inches of rain over the city and inland towards the Sacramento Delta. Later that night, on the higher elevations of Lake Tahoe, the season's first snow would fall in flurries across the mountain peaks.

Nelson walked around the office, glancing at the mahogany bookcases stacked with leather-bound reference books. He extracted one: *Thomson Reuters, Real Estate Law and Practice, Volume One*—and flipped aimlessly through a few pages before slipping it back into place.

He sat on the edge of the desk, a jolt of pain kicking at his left kidney. His scar was healing, but three months after he'd taken the bullet the sting would come back to haunt him when he least expected it; a reminder of how close he'd come to losing his life. And Tyler? He didn't blame his brother. It was an accident, that was all. He reassured his brother every time he visited him in juvie hall. Maybe one day Tyler would end up believing him.

The sound of the door opening startled Nelson. He snapped his head around, his fists bunching tight.

"Little jumpy today, Nelson?"

"Yeah? You keep sneaking up on people like that, you gonna get your ass kicked," Nelson said, relaxing his fingers.

"Appreciate the heads-up," Ben Strauss said, walking to his desk. "Still hurts?" he asked, as Nelson clutched at his side.

"Be all right," Nelson said, dismissively.

Ben dropped into his chair. "Tell me, Nelson, what was it like, being so close to death?" he asked, an expectant glint in his eyes.

"For real? Don't remember much, just woke up with my mom cryin' and my insides shot to shit."

"Nothing? No chorus of angels? A bright light beckoning you home? No burning fires of hell?"

Nelson stuffed his hands in the pockets of his hoodie. "Had some fucked-up dreams I don't remember, that's about it."

"Shame. It's a lucky few who get to face life's greatest fear and live to tell the tale."

"Like what fear?"

"Death, Nelson," Ben said, opening his palms. "The scariest bogeyman of all, the one we're trying to outrun. But you did it, looked the Grim Reaper dead in the eyes and came out the other side. That's a story."

Nelson shrugged. "Ain't got no story, just got my life, I'm grateful for that."

"As is everyone in our organization, Nelson."

Ben pulled open his desk drawer and unrolled a large color print across his desk. "Our new location," he said, gesturing at the roof of an abandoned warehouse in the Fruitvale district.

"Contracts are all squared away, we can take immediate occupation."

"How come you get to know 'bout these places?"

"Amazing the privileged information you have access to when you're the mayor of even a small city like Rosemont," Ben explained.

Nelson huffed. "That's if you get the fuck elected again."

Ben turned his computer to face Nelson and clicked on a video file. "Did you know my father used to be an insurance salesman?" he said. "Door to door. That job sucked the goddamn life out of him. Died at fifty-six, worth more dead than he was alive."

"What's that go to do with anything?" Nelson asked, leaning closer to the screen, and squinting to make out what was going on beyond the shaky camera work and the grainy video footage.

"My point? Benjamin Franklin was incorrect. There are in fact three guarantees in life; death, taxes and..." Ben said, forwarding the footage by thirty seconds, "insurance."

Nelson watched the action unfold on the screen. "Shit, that bitch crazy," he said, laughing as he watched the woman run across a lawn, kicking and wrenching the sprinklers from the grass with her bare hands.

"Alexus Hansen won't be a problem," Ben said, getting up and walking to the window. "There's a lot of work to do, Nelson, people counting on us, are you sure you're well enough?"

Nelson puffed out his chest. "Yeah, I'm cool. Got some new guys I'm checking out."

"Make sure they're loyal."

"You pay 'em, ain't no need to ask for their loyalty."

"This is for the storage facility," Ben said, handing him a key. "I trust you'll find an alternative source of livestock for our game?"

"Got a contact down in Fremont, breeds those fuckers for

feeding snakes or something. His crib smelled like rat shit, so I figure he's legit."

"Like a phoenix rising from the ashes," Ben said, smiling.

"Huh?" Nelson asked.

"Never mind," Ben said, patting him on the shoulder. "You can leave now."

As Nelson shuffled from the room and pulled the door closed behind him, Ben turned his gaze towards the windows and watched the first downpour lash at the glass. The entire Bay looked as if it had been painted a dull, muddied brown, the clouds adding strokes of dark gray across the horizon; a reverse image of itself, drained of detail and nuance.

Within twenty-four hours, the color would return; it always did; the sky incessant in its blueness, the air fresh to the touch as if nothing had ever happened to make it not so.

Ben smiled, his distorted reflection caught ghost-like in the glass. The image didn't resemble him. Like the Bay, his face was captured in negative, exposing a mere trace as to who Ben Strauss really was. The rest, the minutiae and blank spaces, he would let someone else fill in. After all, people always wanted to think the best of their close neighbors and acquaintances, even someone like him.

THE END

ACKNOWLEDGMENTS

I'd like to thank my beta readers Gloria Cerul, Cyn Nooney, Laura Russell-Jones, Justin B. Fawsitt, and Sandra Haven for their patience and vigilance, and most of all for keeping me honest.

A NOTE FROM THE PUBLISHER

Thank you for reading this book. If you enjoyed it please do consider leaving a review on Amazon to help others find it too.

We hate typos. All of our books have been rigorously edited and proofread, but sometimes mistakes do slip through. If you have spotted a typo, please do let us know and we can get it amended within hours.

info@bloodhoundbooks.com